Praise for Mark Abernethy

'*Golden Serpent* is the most accomplished spy-thriller we've seen locally, a discerning read, full of action and a kind of knowing wit.'

The Australian

'Abernethy conjures echoes of Fleming, Ludlum, Clancy and the Jack Reacher novels of Lee Child.'

Weekend Australian

'Abernethy has once again hit the mark. Gripping.'

Herald Sun

'Fast-paced and action-packed, *Second Strike* is one of the better post-9/11 thrillers.'

The Age

'This is a rip-roaring tale of espionage, terrorism and counter-intelligence.'

Sunday Tasmanian

'Abernethy's first novel follows the Tom Clancy model, but with an irreverent, distinctly Australian twist . . . Abernethy writes of a world where Maori mercenaries meet hi-tech shipping and the most inventive ways of killing people . . . For those who like thrillers, this is satisfying fare.'

Sunday Age

'I have had the pleasure in recent years of discovering several Aussie authors – Matthew Reilly, James Phelan and David Rollins – capable of taking on the world's best in the "techno-thriller" stakes. Now add Mark Abernethy to the list.'

Sunshine Coast Daily

Mark Abernethy is a former newspaper reporter and magazine editor whose first novel, *Golden Serpent*, was published in 2007. Its sequel *Second Strike* was published in 2008 and *Double Back* in 2009. Mark lives in New South Wales. Read more at:

www.alanmcqueen.com.au

DOUBLE BACK

MARK ABERNETHY

A R E N A
ALLEN&UNWIN

This edition published in 2010
First published in 2009

Arena Books, an imprint of
Allen & Unwin
83 Alexander Street
Crows Nest NSW 2065
Australia
Phone: (61 2) 8425 0100
Fax: (61 2) 9906 2218
Email: info@allenandunwin.com
Web: www.allenandunwin.com

A Cataloguing-in-Publication entry is available
from the National Library of Australia
www.trove.nla.gov.au

ISBN 978 1 74175 938 9

Typeset in Joanna MT by Midland Typesetters, Australia
Printed in the United States of America

10 9 8 7 6 5 4 3 2 1

DOUBLE BACK

CHAPTER 1

West Papua, August 1999

Forty-seven minutes after flying out of Tembagapura, Alan McQueen looked across at the second military helicopter as they descended through the pre-dawn to the vast Lok Kok copper mine. A blond mercenary to his left unbuckled his seatbelt, stood up and aimed a ceiling-mounted machine-gun out the helo's open door at the lunar despoliation that stretched five kilometres to the rainforest.

Pik Berger's voice crackled in Mac's headset. 'As we planned it, boys,' came his clipped South African accent. 'Red team in the front door – blue team takes the back. I want to be home for breakfast.'

The other five soldiers chuckled and gave the thumbs-up.

'And you, Mr Jeffries,' said the muscular Saffa with a wink. 'You're with me.'

His gut churning, Mac nodded, checked his Steyr for load and safety. His infiltration of the Lok Kok mine was supposed to be a covert assignment on behalf of Australia's SIS, a bit of friendly espionage on a Korean mine that was operating too successfully for the Australian government's liking. The Korean company had been having problems with OPM, the West Papua movement demanding independence from Jakarta. Mac had been 'consulting' to the Koreans under his Don Jeffries cover. However, the mention of Jeffries' military background had piqued the interest of the Korean management and now he was reluctantly accompanying the mine owners' mercenaries in dealing with a hostage drama.

The OPM terrorists had hit during a maintenance furlough for the mine, so only thirty of the usual three thousand employees were involved. During maintenance downtimes, mine security was relaxed, though missing the start-up date on a big mine could cost the company a couple of million dollars a day in lost revenue. So the Koreans were desperate to end the siege, start the maintenance works and get the mine producing again.

Dropping fast to the red clay of the mine's car park, the helos' motors beat like drums in the acoustic bowl. Thirty years ago it had been the peak of a mountain – now the area was a huge open-cut crater.

As the soldiers poured out of the lead helicopter and ran for the cover of a fleet of mine trucks, Mac saw the second Black Hawk thromp over the nearby admin buildings and tilt in a big bank-and-dive manoeuvre.

The lead helo took to the air again in a cloud of red dust, the door-gunner poised in his safety harness like a jumpsuited angel of death. Berger spat his commands over the radio and three soldiers surged forth from their hides behind the trucks, covering one another across the open ground towards the admin block. Readying himself for the 'go' command, instead Mac felt a hand on his shoulder and turned to see Berger motioning for him to follow. The pop and spit of automatic rifle fire issued from the admin block as they moved behind the line of giant yellow CAT 797 trucks, Mac sandwiched between Berger and a soldier called LeClerc.

Reaching the last of the trucks, they edged around the six-metre tyre and watched a row of white demountable living quarters adjacent to the line of trucks. Stopping inches in front of Mac, Berger flicked his eyes upwards in a silent command. Stowing the Steyr across his shoulder blades Mac grabbed the railing of the truck's built-in ladder and climbed the three-storey vehicle onto the spill apron of the dump tray, then stealthed across it until he was looking down into the windows of the men's quarters. The sound of helos thwacked and throbbed in the dawn stillness as Mac took a pair of fold-up Leicas from his breast pocket and focused them on the windows below. The demountables were empty – except the one in the middle. Berger's instincts were correct: the OPM thugs and the hostages were in the living quarters, not the admin block.

'Red Dog, Red Dog,' keyed Mac into the mouthpiece.

'Go ahead, Red Boy,' came the reply.

'Got four tangos in demountable number twelve, repeat number twelve.'

'Roger that. Tools?'

'Looks like M16s, a fifty-cal and three tool boxes – RPGs, my guess,' said Mac, trickles of sweat already rolling down his back as the tropics prepared to switch on the sun.

'Hostages?' asked Berger.

Squinting through the mini Leicas, Mac did a quick count. 'No more than thirty, Red Dog. They're in the common room – they're cuffed and taped.'

A pause opened up as Mac kept vigil with the optics. A long, good-looking Papuan face was looking out at the helos. He wore a white T-shirt printed with the OPM Morning Star flag. To most observers, he was a left-wing troublemaker and terrorist; to Mac he was Kaui – a University of Queensland graduate and one of the best covert operators the Australian government had in this part of the world.

'Fuck,' mumbled Mac under his breath, realising Kaui intended to play out his role, not turn and run like he'd been asked to do.

'What's that?' crackled Berger over the earpiece.

'Nothing,' said Mac. 'Spider bite.'

The radio traffic intensified as Berger corralled his boys, Mac becoming agitated as he realised Berger wasn't going to follow the usual drill. In these situations the terrorists were generally allowed to articulate their political views before releasing the hostages and escaping into the jungle. That was how it worked in West Papua – the terrorists shut down the mines for a few days, gasbagged about capitalism and imperial hegemony, and then everyone went back to work. But clearly Berger hadn't read the script.

'Red Boy, Red Boy,' came Mac's call sign from Berger.

'Copy, Red Dog.'

'How many can you cover from up there?'

This definitely wasn't sounding like a negotiation. 'Negative, Red Dog – no sight lines.'

'What about covering fire?'

'Negative, Red Dog. My sight lines are to the hostages. Repeat, hostages at the front of the common room.'

Calling Mac down from the truck, Berger's voice took on a new tone as he ordered the other soldiers into a gunfight with the OPM terrorists in the admin block. Mac climbed down the outside of the truck, past the eight thousand-litre diesel tank. As he landed in the dirt beside Berger, a soldier came forward with what looked like an aluminium backpack.

'What do they want?' asked Mac, wanting desperately to steer the situation into a negotiation.

'Didn't ask,' mumbled Berger, eyeballing LeClerc.

'Ready, boss,' came the other Saffa's voice, and Mac turned to take it in. LeClerc had put the backpack over his shoulders and was wriggling his fingers into asbestos gloves before wrapping his hands around a handle not unlike that of a herbicide spray gun. Mac had been trained on something similar during his days in the Royal Marines Commandos in England. It wasn't a negotiating tool, unless they planned to set alight the OPM guys before listening to the Marxist rhetoric.

Turning back to Berger, Mac tried to stay calm as the sun came over the jungle canopy. 'Bit early for the barbecue, eh mate? We usually leave that for after the chit-chat.'

Berger's pale eyes chiselled into him for a fraction too long and then the mercenary commander clicked his fingers and LeClerc moved past Mac, his chromed head now covered in an olive-drab protective helmet and mask.

'What about the hostages?' tried Mac.

'You Aussies are so soft,' laughed Berger. 'My job's to restart the mine – nothing else, right?'

'Not in Africa now, mate,' said Mac, as gently as possible.

'A kaffir's a kaffir, bro, and they're all cowards about fire, believe me,' said Berger, inclining his head at LeClerc.

4

Flicking the safety on the handgrip, LeClerc stepped forwards. Before he'd gone two steps, Mac pulled his Heckler & Koch P9s handgun from its hip holster and whipped the butt down on Berger's forehead. Spinning, he dropped the third soldier with a .45 slug to the face.

Turning back, Mac caught the look of surprise on LeClerc's face clearly through the plexiglass faceguard. In slow motion, the flamethrower's nozzle came up level with Mac as he lurched towards it, throwing the nozzle up and to his left as LeClerc hit the juice. Fire squirted ten metres upwards, setting the huge truck tyre alight as the two men hit the dirt, struggling for control of the flamethrower. The heat blasted Mac's left hand as he loosened his grip and he threw a right elbow into LeClerc's faceguard. The plexiglass barely moved and LeClerc let go another squirt of the flamethrower, scorching Mac's eyebrows as the column of ignited gasoline flew just a foot past his face and into the undercarriage of the truck.

LeClerc kicked Mac in the solar plexus and brought the flamethrower around. Deflecting the nozzle with his left forearm, Mac threw a knife-hand into the Saffa's throat and jerked the flamethrower nozzle up under the South African's chin. They struggled like that for ten seconds, Mac trying to get his fingers into the trigger guard, LeClerc attempting to move the flamethrower from his throat as pieces of burning rubber fell off the truck tyre and landed around them.

The Saffa was strong and they clinched in the dirt, until Mac spat in his adversary's faceguard. The Saffa lurched away instinctively, allowing Mac time to dig his finger under the fireproof glove and push his finger down on the trigger. A torrent of fire erupted out of the nozzle, melting LeClerc's face off his skull.

Rolling seven or eight times away from the burning, screaming man, Mac grabbed a handful of dirt and quickly rubbed it through his hair like shampoo – paranoia about invisible fire still strong all these years after his time in the Royal Marines. The skin on the left side of his face pulsed agonisingly, but he was still in one piece and not alight.

Reaching for his Heckler lying on the clay, Mac surveyed the scene, gasping for breath. The radio crackled: one of the soldiers at the admin block giving a sit-rep and asking Berger for orders.

'Hold your positions; hold your fire,' said Mac in his best Saffa accent.

In the silence that followed Mac moved forwards, past Berger prone on the ground, as the giant truck became fully engulfed in flame. At the entrance to the demountable quarters, he paused and knocked. After a few seconds, a torrent of Trotskyite campus-babble flew back at him, containing references to neo-colonialism and the Wall Street oligarchy.

'Yeah, yeah, mate,' panted Mac. 'It's me – let me in.'

The door opened a fraction and Mac pushed through into a dark, air-conditioned boot room.

Kaui's face loosened and he lowered his Kalashnikov. 'Shit, McQueen – who brought the matches?'

Mac leaned away as Kaui winced at the sight of his throbbing left ear. 'Nice effect with the eyebrow too, mate,' he laughed. 'Who needs two of them anyway?'

'It's gone to shit, Kaui,' said Mac, checking the Heckler, a little embarrassed that he'd changed the scenario so dramatically with no Plan B. 'Need a getaway car.'

'What, we don't get to hand over the hostages?'

'These guys don't want to talk,' said Mac.

In the next room a window smashed and the rhythmic slapping sound of a .50-cal machine-gun started up. Moving to the portal window in the door, Mac looked out and saw what OPM's .50-cal was hammering at: Berger's Black Hawk was hovering in from behind the mine trucks, looking for the best vantage point while trying to stay clear of the machine-gun fire.

Moving to the rear window of the boot room, Kaui checked for soldiers in the lane between the living quarters and the rainforest. 'So what happened to the mercs?'

'Dropped a few of them,' Mac mumbled sheepishly.

'A *few*?' said Kaui.

'Two or three.'

'Shit!' the Papuan grinned. 'Alan McQueen joins *la causa*.'

'*Merdeka!*' Mac said – Independence! – as the door-gunner from the helo opened up, turning the demountable into Swiss cheese.

CHAPTER 2

'Got a grenade?' asked Kaui from his crouched position at the back door as the demountable became a blur of splinters.

Handing it over, Mac whispered, 'How many?'

Kaui indicated two with his fingers. He pulled the pin on the small green canister and simply threw it left around the corner of the door without looking. The babble of panicked men sounded from the rear of the demountable and then the explosion tore through the forest and smashed a window in the quarters.

Yelling for the other OPM lads, Kaui leaned through the back door and scoped the area with his rifle. The OPM thugs ran through in a crouch, one of them leaking blood from a wound above his left eye. Kaui yelled a command at the taller one – Albert – who led the other two operators out the back door towards the rainforest.

Dropping to his stomach on the floor as the bullets whistled and slapped, Mac followed Kaui on his elbows into the common room, the walls coming apart in pieces the size of VHS cassettes. Bound and gagged hostages stared at Mac and Kaui from their position near the front windows of the destroyed common room – it had once been the social centre of the mine and was now a mess of smashed glass, ruined TV screens and spilled whisky. Several mine workers were injured where they sat huddled on the floor and Mac could hear moans and tape-muffled screams as the door-gunner stopped shooting.

'They're coming in,' said Kaui, slithering to one of the RPG boxes as both mercenary helos advanced. He handed Mac the rocket-propelled grenade launcher, with its big ugly knob of explosive on the tip of the rocket. As the Papuan crawled to the next RPG box, the door-gunners opened up again, making Mac and Kaui dive flat to the floor.

'Time to ride,' muttered Kaui, giving up on a second RPG.

Crawling back to Mac, he took the RPG, flipped up the back-sights, hit the safety and rose to a classic kneeling marksman stance, the RPG across his right shoulder, its sights lined up with his cocked head. One of the Korean maintenance engineers sobbed with terror as Kaui rose slowly to the level of the windowsill so he could see the helo. After a split second of mutual recognition between himself and the door-gunner, Kaui squeezed the RPG trigger and the rocket whooshed out of the common room and through the truck flames, leaving a wispy trail of vapour for fifty metres before hitting Berger's Hawk just behind the engine bulkhead. The twin sounds of the engine depowering and the expanding fireball filled the mine crater, and then pieces of the helo were raining on the demountable roof.

Mac followed Kaui at a run as a grenade sailed through the air and bounced off the frame of the common-room window onto the claypan outside. They leapt through the back door and kept running into the jungle as the grenade lifted a section of the roof and automatic rifle fire ripped into the building.

Sprinting across a sand and clay track, through a boggy creek bed, they reached one of the mine's outlying service buildings. The massive sliding door was open, revealing a two-storey gas-powered turbine that created the electrical power for the Lok Kok mine. Idling in front of the building was a silver Nissan Patrol 4×4, Albert behind the wheel gunning the engine impatiently.

Kaui jumped into the front passenger seat and they lurched into the rainforest, the Patrol bouncing and screaming for grip on the goat track that passed for a road in West Papua. Beside Mac, the OPM operator with the head wound sagged sideways as he lost consciousness. Kaui fumbled around for the first-aid kit that most mine vehicles carry and found it in the centre console. The fourth Papuan held up his friend and Mac tore open the first-aid pack and went to work on the wound, getting it cleaned out and then patching and bandaging the whole thing. When Mac had finished on the Papuan's injury, Kaui gestured for his friend to work on Mac's scorched face, which was hurting like hell. There was a burns lotion in the kit and it stung as the Papuan applied it, then slowly it dulled the pain.

Taking turns looking out the windows, they tried to find the second helo, unable to hear anything above the scream of the Nissan's engine and the cacophony of birds and monkeys in the rainforest. Mac figured that when the mercs secured the mine site, they'd find the trail of the Patrol and come looking.

'Got a plan?' asked Mac as water bottles were handed out, the humidity of the tropics now filling the cabin.

'Plan was to annoy the mine owners, make them think that OPM was too costly,' smiled Kaui. 'Right, McQueen?'

'Well, it worked with those Brazilians,' shrugged Mac, sipping at the water. 'Trust the Koreans to find a bunch of hard-ons like this lot.'

The four-wheel drive crested a ridge and started into a steep incline down the road connecting the Papuan highlands with the coastal plain. Mac instinctively pulled back into his seat and put his foot on the back of the driver's seat, the sensation like the downhill section of a rollercoaster.

The road went down the side of a large spur for what looked like fifteen or twenty k and Mac knew immediately they'd be spotted from the air. Before he could warn Kaui, the second Black Hawk appeared, about a kilometre across the valley, its '9V' registration marking it as a Singapore-registered aircraft.

'Got company,' muttered Mac, and all heads swivelled to the right side of the Nissan. 'Options, Kaui?'

Keeping his eyes on the Hawk's door-gunner in the opened fuselage, Kaui said something in Papuan to Albert, who replied to his boss then hesitated, glancing at Mac. Mac suspected they'd decided on a plan but were worried about freaking out the Anglo.

Ordering the driver to pull over under the cover of the forest canopy, Kaui looked mischievous. 'Got an idea,' he said, opening his door and sliding off the seat.

'Okay,' snapped Mac. 'But none of that wacky Papuan shit, all right?'

The five of them jogged along the forest floor, the altitude and humidity almost choking Mac's breath out of him as he struggled to keep up with the Papuans. In his days with the Royal Marines Commandos, he'd ended up doing the SBS swimmer-canoeist course which culminated in a survival run in the Brunei jungle. It had almost killed him, and he had a lasting memory of the way a Malaysian candidate had taken the whole thing in his stride, as if eating snakes and scraping leeches in an environment where you could barely breathe was the most natural thing in the world. Mac felt that now – the Papuans loping along in board shorts, talking with one another, while Mac stumbled along in the Saffa fatigues and military boots. In front of him, Albert and the Papuan who'd dressed his burn each carried a piece of the Patrol's back seat, though Mac wasn't totally sure why.

Kaui ran point, slowing every so often to get a sighting of the mercenaries' helo through the high canopy. After ten minutes, Mac saw the Papuans waiting ahead and walked the last fifty metres to them, his legs rubbery, lungs empty.

'Water, fellers,' he gasped as he put a hand on a tree for support. 'Need a drink.'

The OPM boys chuckled and Kaui pointed down to a steeply inclined water race. It consisted of a half-pipe that was at least three metres across, set in concrete braces. Water half-filled the race and it was moving at speed. Climbing one of the concrete braces of the structure, Mac dipped his cupped hand into the manmade rapid and drank greedily. Looking up, he saw that although the forest had been cleared to build the water race, that had been probably ten years ago, and the canopy had almost joined over the half-pipe again.

His thirst sated, Mac turned to find Kaui and the other OPM operators beside him on the large concrete brace, still carrying the Patrol's back seats.

'What are they for?' asked Mac, as Albert laid the foam and fabric back seat on the surface of the rapids, making water rise up and over it.

'Get on,' said Kaui, smiling broadly.

'Get on what?' demanded Mac.

'Your raft,' winked Kaui.

Mac stared at him. He'd first met Kaui at UQ, when Mac was a solid centre for the university rugby club and Kaui was a flashy winger. They'd shared a sense of humour and an understanding of bending the rules as far as they had to be bent in order to win. He liked the man and trusted him, but Kaui also liked to make Anglos uncomfortable when they came into his world.

'This is a wind-up, right?' laughed Mac. 'I'm not getting on that thing!'

Kaui deadpanned him and the sound of the mercs' helo thromped above the screech of birds and the rush of the water race.

'Fuck, mate,' spat Mac, not wanting to lose face. 'What is this?'

'Slurry flume – it's how they get the copper ore from Lok Kok to the loading terminal at the coast.'

'Slurry?' asked Mac, sceptical.

'Yeah, but when the mine's shut down for maintenance, they just run overflow from the reservoir down it,' said Kaui.

'Where does it go? How far does it drop like this?' said Mac.

Shrugging, Kaui said, 'Well, it drops like this to the coastal plain, then it goes through pumping stations to the port at Amamapare.'

'Fuck's sake, Kaui,' said Mac, certain that the other Papuans were finding this highly amusing.

'We need to get off the road,' Kaui pointed out. 'Less you want to run through the jungle all day?'

'You're enjoying this, aren't you?' grumbled Mac as he leaned forward onto the Patrol's foam seat, water immediately rushing up the back of his shirt and through the Steyr. Mac had performed HALO jumps from planes and nocturnal combat-diving missions. But just standing at the top of the big slide at Wet 'n' Wild on the Gold Coast gave him sweaty palms.

'See you down there, Mac,' shouted Kaui, suddenly pushing the foam seat into the rapid. Before Mac could protest, Albert was landing on his back. The makeshift raft took off like a bullet out of a gun and as they accelerated Mac wondered how his youthful visions of being a gentleman spy had turned into tobogganing down a mine slurry pipe in West Papua, being held down by a large local called Albert.

Sensing Mac's fear, Albert whispered into his ear that it was all going to be okay, that it was a cakewalk the whole way down. Then they crested a ridge and the half-pipe turned into a full pipe as it went almost vertical.

Mac's screams echoed for thousands of metres as they free-fell into the darkness.

CHAPTER 3

Mac lay on the floor of the Hino minibus with Kaui as Albert drove through the outskirts of Amamapare, the port on the south coast of West Papua which serviced the major mines in the highlands. The South African mercs would be looking for payback regardless of whether the Korean mining company was still paying them. They'd be staking out the airports in the southern part of West Papua, and if they had connections in Jakarta, the Indonesian military might help them look for Mac and Kaui.

They found a small copying and business centre and Albert went in, opened Mac's mail box and returned with his emergency pack of passports, credit cards and a change of clothes. Driving in silence through Amamapare, the eventual grinding sounds of conveyor belts and ore spreaders indicated they were probably in Portsite, where ships were loaded with what was dug out of the Lok Kok mine.

'Sounds like your stop, Mac,' said Kaui in the darkness.

Still recovering from his terror-ride down the slurry pipe, Mac wanted to be grateful to Kaui but he'd lost his sense of humour. People often misunderstood his special forces background: to succeed in that world was not about reckless risks, it was all about calculated, controlled execution. And free-falling into a slurry pipe was not his idea of control.

The minibus stopped and Mac lifted the tarpaulin he'd been lying under. Through the window he could see the giant gantry and spreader spewing an ore concentrate into a bulker, the whole vision lit up by floodlights which stretched down the wharf and along the decks of the ship.

'Stay cool, brother,' said Kaui as Mac made to go.

Despite his irritation, Mac reluctantly accepted a hug from his old rugby team-mate.

'One hell of a performance in that pipe,' smiled Kaui. 'Was that a scream or a yodel?'

'You'll get a slap one of these days, mate,' said Mac, shaking his head. 'Swear to God.'

After thanking Albert, Mac padded down the steps of the Hino onto the weed-infested wharf apron. Then he walked under the conveyorbelt loader towards the rear of the *Java Princess* in his fresh chinos and shirt. The first officer, a Singaporean Chinese, was expecting him and showed him to a small stateroom.

'We sail at o-one hundred,' said the officer. 'You eaten?'

'Yeah, thanks,' said Mac.

'Need someone to look at that?' said the officer, gesturing towards Mac's facial burn.

'Nah, I'm sweet,' Mac replied. 'But a cold beer might help.'

Smiling and pointing to the fridge, the officer left the room.

Kicking off his shoes, Mac grabbed a can of Tiger, turned down the lights and fiddled with the TV remote as he eased back on the bed. CNN was running footage of chaos in and around Dili – the capital of East Timor – as the Indonesia-backed militias attempted to bully the locals out of voting for independence from Jakarta in the ballot scheduled to start in two weeks. Increasingly, the militias were intimidating the United Nations ballot scrutineers, most of whom were Australians. There was an Australian military operation called Spitfire, which was an emergency extraction of Australian and UN personnel from the troubled island at the southern tip of Indonesia. But commanders in the Australian Defence Force would tell you that they weren't allowed to know the operational planning behind Spitfire – it was being kept a secret in Canberra – so the individual commands were having to plan their own logistics based on rumour.

As sleep crept up on him the chaotic images flashed across the screen and Mac felt for the poor bastard from the firm who was working in East Timor. Then his eyelids dropped and sleep finally took him.

They were steaming north for the Davao Gulf underneath the Philippines when the Australian Royal Navy Seahawk helo came into sight and asked permission to land on the *Java Princess*'s helipad. Finishing his breakfast, Mac thanked the officers in the wardroom and headed down the rear companionways to the stern decks.

Inside the helo Mac was given a flight suit and left alone. They made it to HMAS *Adelaide* in fourteen minutes and Mac spoke with the ship's intelligence officer while the rest of the officers wiped egg yolk off their plates with their toast. They were going to steam north for another two hours and then fly Mac into Zamboanga City in Mindanao.

'And then?' asked Mac, sipping on a mug of coffee.

'Beats me – we're just the delivery boys, right?' shrugged the intel officer, though Mac sensed he knew more than he was saying.

The navy landed Mac at the air base in Zamboanga just before eleven in the morning, where he was met by a local asset known to Western intelligence as Cubby. The friendly thirty-five-year-old shook Mac's hand on the tarmac.

'Got a charter for you, Mr Jeffries,' said Cubby, whose ability to make things happen with minimum fuss was valuable to foreign intelligence services.

'Nice,' said Mac. He didn't like to give too much away to people whose loyalty was based on a cheque.

'Yes, Mr Jeffries,' said the Filipino. 'Two and quarter hour to Jakarta with government charter flight. Everything good for you, sir.'

Jakarta was the wrong direction and Mac mulled on it all the way into Halim air base on the outskirts of the vast capital of Indonesia. For the past eight months he'd been working covertly out of Lombok as Don Jeffries, consultant to foreign logging and mining companies, making sure they were greasing the right palms. One of the big problems with trying to exploit the natural resources of places like

15

Borneo, West Papua and Sulawesi was inadvertently channelling your kickback to the wrong person, the other governor, the chief of police rather than the minister for policing.

Mac's mission had been to infiltrate the companies, the provincial governments and Jakarta's military and political structures, and gather intelligence of the type that could never be gained from cocktail parties and Red Cross receptions. He could only do that from a genuine business position, embedded somewhere away from the Aussie Embassy, and his recall to Jakarta meant a big change of some sort. It might even mean a reassignment, and he fantasised that it was a northern hemisphere posting, perhaps even as a 'declared' SIS officer in a big embassy. Such postings could be thunderously boring and highly PC – especially in contrast to South-East Asia – but they were where you had to go to earn your management credits and move upwards.

As Mac followed the other passengers into the air-con of Halim's military-consular terminal he spotted a woman in her late twenties waiting on the other side of the immigration gate. Using his Alan McQueen passport, Mac eyed the woman while the perfunctory check was made, and concluded she must be there for him: the white blouse, blonde ponytail and blue pencil skirt basically spelled Employee of the Australian Commonwealth.

'G'day,' said Mac to the woman as he walked through.

'Mr McQueen?' she asked, putting her hand out to shake and clutching a clipboard with the other. 'Kate Innes – DFAT.'

They made small talk as she led him to a red Holden Commodore at the rear of the terminal. 'So, what've you got for me?' he smiled, buckling up. 'London? Tokyo?'

'Actually,' she said, pulling out of the park, 'further south, I believe.'

Warming to the mystery, Mac took the envelope she offered and opened it. The Qantas tickets had him flying into Brisbane with a connection to Canberra.

'Must be promotion time, eh Kate?' he joked as they headed for the freeway.

'Umm,' she muttered, and Mac saw a blush under her sunnies.

'Not so good?' said Mac.

'I'm sorry, Mr McQueen – my job was to give you the tickets and drive you to Hatta,' she said, referring to Jakarta's international airport, Soekarno-Hatta. 'I don't really know anything.'

'Be careful with that kind of talk,' said Mac, trying to make the girl feel better. 'They'll make you director-general.'

She started chuckling and then blushed at the career-limiting nature of the humour. 'You trying to get me into trouble?'

'I won't tell a soul,' said Mac, relaxing into the seat with a sigh, yearning for an armchair in the Qantas Club lounge and three or four very cold beers.

CHAPTER 4

Grabbing the cooked breakfast and a glass of orange juice, Mac found a table for two against the wall of the Canberra Hyatt's dining room and ordered coffee from the waitress. The front page of the *Australian* had a story about the Prime Minister rejecting an Australian Republic but also rejecting the Queen opening the Olympic Games in Sydney. Flipping through the pages he kept an eye on the Hyatt's breakfast crowd. Politicians, lawyers, consultants, IT salesmen and all the associated political classes that swarmed around Canberra were mumbling at each other or into mobile phones. It was 7.41 and the daily hunt for taxpayer dollars was about to start.

Mac bought an overcoat from the men's store in the Hyatt concourse, then walked across Commonwealth Avenue and through the stands of trees towards old Parliament House, the clear winter air hurting his lungs; they had become acclimatised to the sooty humidity of South-East Asia. The recall to Canberra played on him – it was obviously something to do with the Lok Kok mine, and folded in his pocket, were two pages of plain A4 paper with a field report he'd typed the previous night at the Hyatt's business centre. Intelligence was a game of information and timing and he wanted his version of events on the record before the 8.30 meeting in the RG Casey building, which housed the Department of Foreign Affairs and Trade, along with the Aussie SIS.

Keeping a brisk pace along National Circuit, Mac glimpsed the lake down the cross streets and smelled the rotting winter leaves on the ground. Crossing the street twice to case a slow-moving Ford Falcon that had doubled back, he walked south to John McEwen Crescent and approached the DFAT building entrance from the side and behind the trees in the forecourt. Showing his passport to the security guard at the entrance, he signed for his DFAT lanyard and wandered across the foyer, lost in thought.

'Nice morning for it,' came a deep male voice.

Turning, Mac saw his boss, the director of operations for the Asia-Pacific, Tony Davidson, reading the *Australian Financial Review* on a leather sofa.

'Tony,' said Mac, walking over and shaking Davidson's hand.

'Macca – thought we'd have a quick chat on the way up, eh?'

Walking through a series of corridors until they reached the secure SIS section, Davidson kept it light as he put his card into the designated elevator.

'Gleeson wants to see us – no biggie,' he said, as the doors opened to reveal two SIS officers locked in terse conversation. They shut their mouths as they saw Davidson looming – it may have been thirty years since he opened the bowling for Western Australia, but at six-five and still built like a country boy, the man had a way of grabbing people's attention.

'So it's hardly related – I mean, shit, Tony, what's the opening of the Olympic Games got to do with our constitution?' said Mac as a verbal veil, but his mind was spinning: John Gleeson was a deputy director-general at the firm – an executive position second only to the DG – which meant Mac was in serious trouble.

The operations floor of SIS was already humming as Mac followed Davidson towards Gleeson's office. The crisis in East Timor and the wider ramifications of the Australia–Indonesia relationship had created a panicked demand for intelligence product from departments such as Prime Minister & Cabinet, Foreign Affairs, Trade, Defence, Treasury, Customs and the Australian Federal Police. East Timor was a tiny province with a Portuguese colonial history, but it occupied an island between Flores and northern Australia, and if its ballot for independence from Indonesia disintegrated into a slaughter of civilians, then Australia had to decide not only how to respond, but whether it would agree with Jakarta's wishes or insist on a universal concept of human rights.

Murphy's Law of intelligence held that the specific intel required by government was never available when they needed it, and the reports that so many officers had worked so hard to create were used to prop up computer monitors. There were forty or fifty people on that floor, many of whom had been going all night, synthesising reports and briefings out of known intel and working the firm's field officers to plug the gaps. And there was still a fortnight until the East Timor ballot. There were times Mac was happy to be a field guy.

Following Davidson into Gleeson's corner office suite, Mac smiled at the secretary as they were shown into an office that looked north so that the jet which fired water out of Lake Burley-Griffin in the distance seemed to be pumping it straight out of old Parliament House's roof.

'Alan,' said John Gleeson, approaching around the hardwood desk.

'Sir,' said Mac, obeying Gleeson's gesture to take a seat on the sofa.

'We're pretty busy up here so I'll come straight to it,' said Gleeson, a trim guy in his early fifties who sat on the edge of his desk with one foot on the ground. 'How did we get ourselves into that fuck-up in West Papua?' He looked pointedly at Davidson, who sat in a chair against the wall.

'It was one of our provocations,' said Davidson in his deep WA drawl.

'The OPM operations? That it?' said Gleeson, annoyed but not losing it.

'That's it, John. It was my call, it's not –'

Raising his hand, Gleeson blinked for two seconds as if managing his stress. 'Spare me the Clarence Darrow act, okay, Tony? What happened? From the top.'

'We have an asset in OPM,' said Davidson. 'We encouraged him to lead a hostage-taking scenario at the Korean-owned Lok Kok mine in the highlands of West Papua while it was in a maintenance cycle.'

'So it was shut down?'

'Correct,' said Davidson. 'About thirty maintenance engineers were staying in the workers' quarters – mostly Korean but also some Americans, Australians and French.'

'And?'

'And the Koreans sent me along with their mercenaries – a company called Shareholder Services – to deal with the crisis,' said Mac, handing his report to Gleeson. 'They worked out that I had a military background, and since I was consulting to the company with local issues –'

'They thought you could sort this for them?'

'Yes, sir,' said Mac, gulping slightly.

'But what happened?'

'When we got to the mine, the mercenary commander didn't want to negotiate – which is the usual way to handle these things in West Papua.'

'Yes?'

'He wanted to use a flamethrower and I argued with him, but he . . . The upshot was that I fought with some of the mercenaries.'

Gleeson's hand went up again as he leaned back on his desk and grabbed a letter. 'This is a diplomatic letter of protest from the Korean legation in Jakarta. They pouched it the day before yesterday, and I had to recall you – which isn't a cheap exercise, right, son?'

'Right, sir.'

'The letter states that Korean economic interests at the Lok Kok mine were sabotaged by a Papua New Guinean national and an Australian national; two security workers in the pay of this mine company were killed – one of whom was set on fire,' said Gleeson, looking up at Davidson and then Mac. 'Several maintenance engineers sustained gunshot wounds but, miraculously, they're alive.'

'Look, it was just one of those things –' started Mac, but Gleeson's eyes shut again and this time he massaged them with his hand.

'No, McQueen, it was not just one of those things. Certainly not the kind of thing that most of us in this building ever get up to.'

'These operations give us invaluable insight into the terror group operating closest to our borders,' said Davidson. 'No other nation – not even Indonesia – has the links we have into the heart of OPM. And we're usually very careful.'

'Oh, really?!' said Gleeson, eyes bloodshot from stress. 'Careful? Then why is there a Korean consular officer sitting in a hospital in Makassar with a cracked skull?'

'A consular –?' said Mac, confused. Then it dawned. 'Oh shit, you mean Pik?'

Holding the letter closer, Gleeson squinted at the name. 'Piet-Marius Berger, a security attaché in the Korean legation to Indonesia.'

Mac laughed, he couldn't help it.

'This is funny?' said Gleeson, shaking the letter and returning to his chair behind the desk.

'No, sir – it's just that Pik Berger might be one of those rare blue-eyed Koreans we've heard so much about,' said Mac.

'Tony,' said Gleeson to Davidson after a pause, 'is your officer laughing at me?'

'No, John – probably just surprised that a South African merc is claiming consular credentials with the Koreans. It got me too, I must admit.'

Sighing at the ceiling, Gleeson slid down in the chair. 'Okay. McQueen, luckily I need everyone on the Timor situation for the next few weeks so I want you around. Tony'll brief you – but promise me something, son?'

'Sure,' said Mac.

'Stay out of trouble, okay?'

'Can do, sir,' said Mac, following Davidson's lead and standing. As he walked through the door, he heard Gleeson's voice again.

'Oh, McQueen?'

Turning, Mac came face to face with the DDG, who waved the field report he'd received five minutes before.

'Rule Number One for young field officers,' said Gleeson, as he tore up the report and passed the pieces to Mac. 'Always wait till after the DDG has kicked the crap out of you before writing your report. Over to you, Tony.'

Having completed the Lok Kok report in Davidson's office – a version that emphasised South African mercenaries and Korean duplicity – they set out shortly before 10 am and were driven into the underground security area of Parliament House, a strange-looking building that sat inside a hill in the middle of Australia's capital.

'I'm not sure about this, mate,' said Mac as they accepted lanyards and were shown into the bowels of the building. They were heading for a meeting of the National Security Committee in Cabinet – the Prime Minister, Deputy Prime Minister, Minister for Foreign Affairs and Minister for Defence. The NSCC was briefed regularly by the peak intelligence body, the Office of National Assessments, and often the ONA briefers held experts in reserve in case the politicians wanted more detail.

'Start getting real sure, real fast,' said Davidson as they swept into an anteroom filled with intelligence analysts from ONA, Defence and Treasury. 'Because I told John you were the best on Indon political economy – you're standing in for Karl Berquist.'

'What?!' said Mac, still wondering what the Gleeson meeting meant for his career. 'I'm standing in for a director?'

'Yeah – and one who listens more than he talks, okay?' said Davidson, turning to leave.

The meeting was held on the other side of the closed doors and Mac found himself sitting in the anteroom, pondering East Timor and Indonesia. In December 1975, the Indonesian military had launched Operation Lotus, which saw elite soldiers and paratroopers invade the tiny remnant of the Portuguese empire after the local commies and non-commies had screwed up Portugal's handover by fighting among themselves. Australia had turned a blind eye to Soeharto's lightning raid on the territory; Catholic East Timor became the twenty-seventh province of the world's most populous Muslim nation and was plunged into almost constant war between the local Falintil guerrillas who had taken to the hills, and the Indonesian Army, which quickly claimed all trade concessions in the province's economy. Now, Soeharto had been gone for eighteen months, full democracy was on the horizon for South-East Asia's largest nation and the new president, BJ Habibie, had acceded to the Australian Prime Minister's request to allow the East Timorese to vote for independence. The Indonesian Army had responded by creating proxy militias which were intimidating and killing pro-independence activists on the island. Looming over the whole scenario was the Asian economic crisis, which had drastically devalued the rupiah, ruined a lot of banks and plunged Indonesia into virtual bankruptcy.

He turned to the man sitting next to him, Colonel Sandy Beech, a military intelligence officer Mac had met in England nine years ago. 'What you up here for, mate?' said Mac.

'Fucking Timor – but they won't ask me in there,' Beech said, flicking his thumb at the heavy wooden door of the meeting room. 'It's a waste of time coming down for this.'

'Why?' said Mac, as both of them checked to see if the Treasury girl typing on a laptop was listening.

'Government's in a holding position on East Timor – doesn't suit them right now to hear about the village clearances and the intimidation of the UN ballot workers.'

'Greater good, right?'

Snorting, Beech shook his head. 'I'm in the UN crew in East Timor, right? And I tell you, Macca, those people are not happy campers.'

'UN's not protected?' said Mac, surprised.

'Lot of AFP women up there, mate, out in the boonies, and they are getting the creeps – these militias are using rape to terrorise the pro-independence villages.'

'And they can't carry arms?' asked Mac.

'Ha!' said Beech. 'I told my command that we needed some support up there, and they gave me a satellite phone.'

'What – to call Mum when you get macheted?' said Mac.

'It's turning to custard, Macca – if we have a ballot, it'll be a miracle.'

It was almost 1 pm when the big door swung back and voices flooded into the anteroom. Feeling the pangs of hunger, Mac assumed they were going to be dismissed for lunch.

'McQueen?' said a smiling bureaucrat, and Mac found himself on his feet, walking into a large meeting room dominated by an oval table with no centre to it. The politicians sat at the head of the table, the ONA analysts at the other end, with a long table behind them staffed by assistants with files and laptops.

Taking the seat offered among the ONA hacks, Mac sat down. The Minister for Defence looked at a silver pen he tapped on the desktop but he was addressing Mac.

'There's some debate about this Wiranto chap,' said the minister, referring to the commander of the Indonesian armed forces and Minister for Defence, General Wiranto. 'We're fairly sure he's coordinating the Timorese militias responsible for all this violence. But you're actually on the ground up there, Mr McQueen – how do Wiranto's political ambitions fit with the Timor situation?'

Leaning forward, Mac kept Davidson's warning in mind. 'Sir, I don't know.'

The room broke into laughter, the Prime Minister finding that particularly funny. But beside him Mac felt the ONA leader bristle.

'Could I ask it another way?' said the Minister for Foreign Affairs, whose jolly round face belied a great intellect. 'How does politics in Jakarta relate to Timor – in your opinion?'

'I don't think you can separate the economy from what's happening in East Timor.'

'You can't?' asked the Minister for Foreign Affairs.

'Well, the Asian economic crisis has uncovered institutional and sociopolitical cracks that were papered over by the trappings of middle class success. The economy meant the end of Soeharto, the economy started the street riots and the capital flight of the Chinese business elite, and the economy is also seeing the rise of Megawati and the interference of the IMF . . .'

'And?' asked the minister.

'Well, General Wiranto runs one of the largest financial institutions in Indonesia – the military – and at a time when the rupiah is fifteen per cent of what it was worth two years ago, export resources such as those on East Timor are not to be relinquished lightly – they represent earnings in US dollars and deposits in Singapore bank accounts.'

'You're saying this is about money?' asked the Minister for Defence.

'I'm saying that Wiranto is stuck between a president who wants the East Timorese to vote on independence, and a general staff that doesn't want to lose income and power. The claim that it's all about Wiranto making a run at the presidency – well, he's had opportunities for a coup, and he hasn't taken them; he was offered the powers of dictatorship by Soeharto. Most Indonesians think he's a constitutionalist.'

'What about Wiranto's role in this violence? In East Timor?' said the Minister for Foreign Affairs, looking out the window.

'Can't comment, sir – all the intel I've seen says the militias are controlled and funded from Jakarta,' said Mac.

'That what the locals are saying?' asked the minister.

'No, sir – the locals are worried about jobs, mortgages and prospects for their children, not a bunch of communists running around in the hills of a province that they couldn't even find on a map.'

The meeting ended forty seconds later and Mac noticed the ONA guys sulking while the politicians smiled at him.

As Mac exited through the anteroom, Sandy Beech was still seated, talking on his mobile phone. The one Australian who was actually on the ground in East Timor was not going to be heard.

CHAPTER 5

Davidson wasn't in his office when Mac arrived slightly late. He was annoyed with himself – Davidson was not only Mac's main mentor in the firm, he also shouted the best lunches of anyone in the RG Casey building.

'Alan?' asked the secretary.

'Guilty,' said Mac, taking the note she passed him.

It was a tasking: back to Jakarta, reporting to Greg Tobin in the Indonesian capital.

Breathing out, he tried to stop himself swearing. Only a few hours ago, the DDG was telling him to stick around, that he was needed during the East Timor crisis. Canberra had always seemed a little tame, but after the chat with Gleeson and the ONA briefing, Mac had glimpsed a fresh start to his career: getting back into the management end of the intel networks, golf at Federal, skiing at Thredbo, a few beers with the lads at Bruce when the Raiders were playing. It was how the office guys worked it and it had seemed within his grasp.

Collapsing on the sofa opposite the secretary's desk, he punched a number into his phone then stared blankly at Davidson's note as he waited for his boss to answer. He was tired and dreaded the thought of another fifteen hours in planes and airport lounges.

'Tony, just got your note,' he said when Davidson picked up.

'I'm in a meeting, mate,' said the West Australian.

'Thought Gleeson wanted me around?' Mac pushed.

Down the line it was obvious that Davidson was excusing himself from his present company.

'Yeah, mate,' said Davidson, slightly breathless, a few seconds later. 'But Gleeson gets a call from McRae at National Assessments – they were at Sydney Uni law school together, right? – and McRae is going off his trolley.'

'About me?' said Mac.

'*Yes* about you!' snapped Davidson. 'What's this shit about Wiranto being a misunderstood genius –'

'I didn't say that.'

'– a *constitutionalist*?! Shit, Macca.'

'I thought they wanted my HUMINT,' said Mac, referring to human intelligence of the type gleaned from interaction with people.

'Yes, Macca – and fucking ONA have been carefully building a picture for the Prime Minister of Wiranto as a man who wants to be president and will inflict any atrocity on Timor to support that. And you walk in there and make him out to be some confused teenager –'

'Actually, I said he was probably responsible for the militias in Timor,' said Mac, not wanting to argue with his biggest supporter. 'But Wiranto believes in constitutional government: he could have taken over when Soeharto was toppled, or launched coups when the riots started in Jakarta or when Habibie announced the East Timor ballot – but he didn't. My point was the economic crisis puts him under pressure from his own generals to hold East Timor, that's all.'

The sound of Tony Davidson sighing hissed out of the phone. 'I happen to agree with you. But that's not where the firm or National Assessments or even the government is headed right now, okay? Gleeson wants you back in the field.'

'Jakarta?' said Mac.

'The section's got something for you,' said Davidson, referring to the intelligence section at the Australian Embassy in Jakarta.

'Pay rise perhaps?' said Mac, but the line was already dead.

***

The driver gave him a sealed envelope as they came into Jakarta in the white Holden Commodore. The note said: *Lunch 1300. Usual place. CR.*

CR was Cedar Rail – the internal code name of ASIS's Jakarta station chief, Greg Tobin, and the usual place was the only place they'd ever met in Jakarta. Mac didn't mind Tobin as much as some spooks did, but he was hoping that his boss didn't want to play cloak-and-dagger. He was too tired for that shit.

Mac got out of the Commodore in the heart of Mega Kunigan – Jakarta's version of The City in London – and walked two blocks north to the JW Marriott. Casing one side of the street, he suddenly crossed at a green signal and stared at the window displays on the other side, checking the reflections. Jakarta was a town of violent surprises – a sort of Australian version of what Vienna had been for British intelligence in the Cold War.

Satisfied there were no tails, he got to the Marriott early and sat in the enormous lobby for ten minutes, reading the *Jakarta Post*. Even when Greg Tobin sailed through the marble-lined area with Anton Garvey in tow, Mac remained seated for a few minutes, looking for signs of surveillance: eyes peering over newspapers, reception staff suddenly picking up a phone, people whispering into their shirt cuffs. Mainly, Mac waited to see if anyone came through the main doors thirty seconds after Tobin, looking too innocent. That was always the giveaway – no one entering the Marriott was entirely innocent.

Seeing nothing suspicious, Mac threw the *Post* on a coffee table and sauntered through to the buffet restaurant, with its open kitchen and talkative cooks. Greg Tobin stood with a smile and shook Mac's hand.

'G'day, Macca,' he said, with all the toothy charm of a politician. 'How are you, old man? Not too serious I hope?' He pointed at Mac's face as he sat, a masculine look of feminine concern.

'No worries, Greg,' said Mac. 'Just a scorch.'

'I missed you, darling,' said Anton Garvey, tanned and bull-like. 'You don't phone, you don't write.'

'Garvs, you old tart!' said Mac, shaking the big paw. Anton Garvey had been in the same graduate intake as Mac, back in the early nineties.

They'd become close friends very quickly, not least because they'd both been boarders at famous St Joseph's schools: Garvey at Joeys in Sydney and Mac at Nudgee in Brisbane.

The three of them small-talked, each of them playing their roles. Tobin, a year older than the other two, saw himself as the going-places leader-of-men. The former crown prince of the St Lucia campus at UQ acted as if he ruled the world and was merely waiting for his business card to reflect it. Garvey was the corporate man – not spectacular enough for a starring role, but a reliable team guy who didn't like too much divergence from authorised behaviour. Mac seemed to have become the ruthless loner, a description he had loved as a younger man but which, at thirty, was starting to isolate him; the events in Canberra had made him feel as if he were cast as a paramilitary rather than a whiteboard warrior.

They got through lunch and Tobin ordered another round of Tigers before leaning into Mac's intimacy zone. 'Got something I need you to do, Macca,' he intoned with a perfect combination of authority and charm. 'Special assignment.'

'One of those management courses in Canberra, eh Greg?' joked Mac.

'Well,' said Tobin, clearing his throat and swapping looks with Garvey, 'not quite, old man.'

Looking around the restaurant, Mac saw foreign business people trying to shake money out of the tree that was Indonesia. 'So what's the gig?'

Stroking his tie, Tobin reached for his beer. 'We'd like to get a better idea of what the Indons might be up to.'

'Up to?'

'Yes, Macca – in Timor.'

Mac could feel Garvs shifting his weight, uncomfortable.

'What about Atkins?' said Mac, assuming that the firm's man in Denpasar, Martin Atkins, was the Timor guy.

'Marty's a controller now, mate,' said Tobin. 'He'll be running you, actually.'

'So we don't have someone in Dili?' said Mac.

'We did,' said Tobin, gulping at his beer, avoiding Mac's eyes.

'And?'

'And we need a good operator to replace him,' said Tobin, now looking at Mac.

'Replace him? What happened to our guy?' said Mac, his gut turning icy.

'Don't know,' rasped Tobin, 'but we'd like to have a chat.'

CHAPTER 6

Garvey came back to the table with two Heinekens and switched the discussion to the rugby league action of the past weeks.

'The problems started with those hits on Martin Lang,' said Garvey before he found his seat. 'Can't run around with your head sticking up like that – did you watch it?'

'Highlights on satellite,' said Mac, his mind elsewhere.

Garvey scoffed. 'Cowboys game was okay, but shit, Macca – losing to the *Roosters*?! That hurt.'

'Why not get us an HR course in Oz for the grand final,' said Mac, sipping at the beer, 'if Tobin's game?'

'Might work – get you retrained on the expenses protocol, mate.'

'Get you an equity officer,' said Mac. 'Rid you of these negative gender-based attitudes.'

'I'll write a memo, get it moving,' said Garvey. 'By the way – see fucking Hugh Jackman's doing the grand final anthem this year? That bloke a poof?'

'Nah,' said Mac. 'It's just the teeth, and he can dance.'

Around them the patrons in the Bavaria Lagerhaus – mainly expats from the embassy precinct of south Jakarta – were getting drunk and yelling at huge TV screens broadcasting sports from around the world. Europeans pointed in disbelief at Steffi Graf playing in a tennis final, North Americans barked at a NASCAR race at Michigan and the Aussies were glued to Aussie Rules footy.

'So, Garvs – what's with Dili?' asked Mac. He was fairly strong on the Jakarta political economy side of it, but the TV reporting showed the island itself in meltdown and he needed some more background before reporting to Martin Atkins in Denpasar.

Looking at the label of his beer, Garvey made a face. 'You heard Tobin. We had someone – a Canadian businessman, actually – keeping an eye on things for us, but he's dropped off the map.'

'Any ideas?'

'It started with a meeting,' Garvey shrugged.

'You asked him to do something?'

'Yeah, we picked up on Indonesian chatter and we wanted him to ask Blackbird about –'

'Blackbird,' interrupted Mac. 'The girl who works for the Indonesian military?'

'That's her,' said Garvey, nodding. 'She's been feeding us for a few months – works in the admin section of the TNI headquarters in Dili.'

TNI stood for Tentara Nasional Indonesia, the armed forces of the Republic and known until recently as ABRI. The military stood to lose the most from East Timor voting on independence from Jakarta, partly due to loss of power and partly because they owned most of the commercial concessions in the province. The logging, the coffee plantations, the oil and gas, and the sandalwood exports were all owned or controlled by military brass or Soeharto cronies. The new president, BJ Habibie, complicated matters: he was a non-military politician removing the army's lucrative Timorese concessions.

'So, Garvs, let's get it straight. Was this Canadian treading on the army's toes? I mean, was he messing with the generals' interests?'

Looking uncomfortable, Garvey tried to avoid the question. 'Look, Macca, let's just say it was our fault, okay? We asked him to make a simple inquiry and he disappeared.'

'Was he alone?'

'Fuck, Macca!' said Garvey.

'What?' said Mac. 'What's the secret?'

'No, Macca, he wasn't alone. Least, I don't think so.'

'So?' said Mac, looking around to make sure no one was listening in; the Lagerhaus was owned by a former Indonesian intelligence agent and you never quite knew who was lurking.

'Look,' said Garvey, 'Tobin wants to keep this simple – find what happened to the Canadian, find Blackbird, debrief and get out of Dodge. That's the gig.'

'Who was with the Canadian?' said Mac, knowing that Garvey would break.

'Shit, Macca. I'm actually not supposed to know that.'

'So who told you?'

'Scotty.'

Mac laughed. Rod Scott was one of the Old School of Australian intelligence, from the Cold War days. After his recruitment and his year with the Royal Marines in Britain, Mac had been rotated into the end of the first Gulf War where Rod Scott had been his mentor and guide. Scotty had showed him where to burrow into a government structure as a war ended, how to get the files and the influence you wanted, how to apply for and get the appointments that would ensure wheat contracts, oil concessions and construction work for Australian interests in the post-war rebuilding. His outrageous stories about Imelda Marcos were legendary and Mac knew that if a rumour came from Rod Scott, it was probably true.

'Who, exactly, was there?' asked Mac.

'Well, Blackbird, for a start,' said Garvey. 'Like Tobin told you.'

'She was there when the Canadian disappeared?'

'Could be like that – or the Canadian never got to the meet.'

They stared at each other, Mac giving his old mate the don't-fuck-with-me look.

'This is why they want it kept simple,' said Garvey. 'The last thing we need is you chasing ghosts all over Timor, doing your superhero thing.'

'Might help, that's all,' said Mac.

'Mate, Marty will take you through that – he's your controller on this, okay?'

'Who else was there?' Mac pushed.

'Tobin will have me shot if I tell you that.'

'I never liked you much anyway.'

'I'm not saying any more,' said Garvey, standing to go. 'Let's just say we're fairly certain he had muscle with him at the time.'

'Who?' asked Mac, getting annoyed.

'Don't make me say it, mate,' said Garvey, grabbing his mobile phone from the table.

Watching Garvey move towards the exit beneath the faux Bavarian tack hanging from imitation hewn wood beams, the picture finally came together, and Mac knew why the firm wasn't admitting to the full scenario.

'Not Bongo?' Mac called to his friend's back.

As Garvey hit the swinging door with his shoulder, he raised his middle finger without looking back.

Mac waited seventeen minutes for the signal from the Lagerhaus security guy that Saba – the bar's owner – was ready to see him.

Bongo Morales was a former Philippines NICA operative who'd been trained in special forces by the Americans for CT work in Mindanao. Because he had a Javanese mother and spoke fluent Bahasa Indonesia, he'd later worked as a freelance hit man in Aceh, hunting the separatist GAM guerrillas for Indonesia's military intelligence. Bongo was smart and dangerous, with a reputation that could easily hurt politically ambitious people like Tobin – hired guns were always the easy way of getting violence off the books, but when things turned bad they could be a liability. Mac suspected that Bongo was being excluded from the official record because the ASIS lunchers didn't want to justify his presence in a ministerial memo, known as a CX. If Bongo was being excluded, it was because something went wrong in Dili and Mac didn't want to land in that disintegrating city with Bongo holding a grudge against Australian intelligence.

They moved down the corridor and the Lagerhaus security guy searched Mac for weapons before leading him into Saba's office, a white-tiled bunker with a desk at one end and a sofa and armchair set-up in the middle. A middle-aged Javanese man walked around the desk and shook Mac's hand, gesturing to the sofa.

'Mr Mac,' smiled Saba, a flash of gold at the bottom of the right front tooth. 'Haven't seen you for a while.'

'Been up in Mindanao,' said Mac.

'Not Irian Jaya?' asked Saba, using the Indonesian term for West Papua. 'That wasn't you at Lok Kok?'

Mac laughed and so did Saba. Spies liked to one-up each other with superior information.

'It's nice up there this time of year – nice and cool,' said Mac, brushing a phantom crumb from his chinos.

'So what can I do for you?'

'Remember a bloke called Bongo?' asked Mac.

'Maybe.'

'I need to talk – and I mean *talk*,' he said.

Saba nodded and Mac pulled an old credit card receipt from his wallet, wrote his mobile number on the back.

'A message?' said Saba, slow and steady like the first sentence of an interrogation.

Mac thought about it. 'Tell him a blackbird sings but I don't know the tune. Can do?'

'Maybe,' shrugged Saba, folding the receipt into an origami bird.

CHAPTER 7

When Mac first spotted him, Martin Atkins was sitting at a small tea stand in a side avenue of the Bird Market, about sixty metres into the sprawling mass of Denpasar's Satrya Markets. On either side of Atkins were lines of birdcages stacked four or five high, their owners walking back and forth with their money pouches, ready with extended hooks should anyone want to inspect a bird.

Ignoring Atkins on the first pass, Mac came back the same way five minutes later having made a few zigzag and double-back manoeuvres to shake whoever was following. Taking a seat in the shade of the tea stand, Mac asked the old lady for a green tea and turned to his controller when she'd left.

'Marty,' said Mac. 'How's it going?'

'Not bad,' said Atkins, sipping his tea. 'You're late.'

'I'm alive – it's a preference of mine.'

Atkins looked away, gave a slight sigh. His hair was a shade darker than Mac's blond, but otherwise they were similar in age, build and background. Where they differed was the emphasis of their professional lives. Mac lived his life as if every day could be the one where he was kidnapped or killed. Atkins wanted to be like Greg Tobin – an office guy with a management instinct rather than any field craft. Waiting for a contact in a market was unnatural for

Atkins; he'd rather be around the corner, in his office, writing a memo that made himself look like the only smart man in a sea of dumb-arses.

'There's a package waiting in your hotel,' said Atkins, looking away. 'You're Richard Davis, going in from Denpasar on the morning flight, a businessman from Arafura Imports. You're based in Sydney and you're looking for sandalwood opportunities, especially Catholic icons – Mother Marys, that shit, okay?'

'Turismo?' asked Mac.

'That's the one – Terri has you in a long-term room, for three weeks to start with and then on a needs basis.'

Terri was the accountant who ran the ASIS front company in Sydney. She took the calls and cleared the mail for Mac's forestry consulting firm, his textbook company – Southern Scholastic – and various other shams, such as Arafura Imports. When people tried to verify Mac's business bona fides they usually got a total going-over as regards their creditworthiness and corporate registrations. Mac always felt comfortable that Terri dealt with the back office.

'So what's the gig?' asked Mac, smiling at the old lady who brought his tea.

'Find Blackbird, establish whether it's viable to start running her again . . .'

'And?'

Looking away at the crowds, Atkins attempted to make himself seem relaxed. 'If you can do so covertly, establish what's meant by "Operasi Boa".'

Mac paused, wondering where that had come from. 'Boa?'

'Like I said.'

'Like a feathery scarf?' said Mac, making sure he had it right.

'That's it, McQueen. Operasi Boa.'

Staring at each other for several seconds, they broke with smiles.

'What's the secret, Marty?' said Mac. 'What is it?'

'That's your job, mate.'

'Oh, come on,' said Mac, too tired for the hokey-pokey.

'All I know is what I've been briefed on,' said Atkins. 'The Canadian was tasked with getting Blackbird to find out about Boa.'

'And?'

'We don't know if he did, or if the meet happened,' said Atkins, gulping his tea. 'It's probably best if you start from scratch rather than guessing at what Boa might be.'

Smiling, Mac decided to let it go, though taking craft advice from a man who did management courses at Melbourne Business School was a little rich. 'You weren't running the Canadian?'

'I was,' said Atkins. 'But a week before we lost him, our higher-ups got a hard-on for this Boa, so I became a conduit. You know how it is.'

Nodding, Mac knew how it was. 'So who is he, this Canadian?'

'Bill Yarrow – wanted by Canadian Customs for import fraud. Owes them millions in unpaid excise. It's in your package.'

'But I'm not looking for him?'

'If he turns up, bring him in,' said Atkins. 'He's of interest, sure, but the priority is Blackbird.'

'Who's my contact?' said Mac.

'Blackbird,' said Atkins, his face grim.

'She still around?' asked Mac.

'We have to establish that one way or the other,' said Atkins.

'How do I get to her?'

'We use a cut-out – but I can't send you to him,' said Atkins. 'He's in a sensitive position and we've guaranteed his anonymity.'

Mac nodded, thinking. A cut-out was an unidentified person who communicated via drop boxes. The theory was that using cut-outs protected the local asset from being compromised, and left the intelligence officer as an unknown person who just left and received notes in a pre-arranged place: the drop box. But while the theory of cut-outs worked well on a whiteboard in Canberra, they were merely a professional challenge to Mac and people like him.

'What's the cycle?' asked Mac.

'Santa Cruz cemetery, twenty one left, seven right, Mondays and Fridays.'

It was currently Wednesday.

'And what's our status with the Indons in Timor?' asked Mac, knowing that although the Indonesia-backed militias were clearing villages in the lead-up to the independence ballot, the Australian government was holding off on sending in a presence.

'Our status is a friendly neighbour, giving moral support at this difficult time,' said Atkins.

They both chuckled. The Australian government had Royal Australian Navy surveillance vessels – declared and covert – steaming the Timor Sea, right across the underbelly of East Timor; there were RAN clearance divers not only in Dili's harbour, but in Atambua and Kupang – the heart of Indonesian Timor. There was nothing friendly about the Timor Gap gas fields off the south coast of East Timor, gas fields that Australia felt it was better placed to control than Indonesia.

'By the way,' said Atkins, 'the phone lines are compromised out of Dili, and that includes cellular. There's a radio for emergencies at Santa Cruz thirty-five right, seven left. Otherwise, you collect the intel and walk it out. To me, okay?'

Accepting Atkins' handshake, Mac stood to go before noticing his colleague's discomfort and pausing.

'Anything else?' said Mac, scoping the crowded market for eyes.

'Look, mate, after the Lok Kok thing, they want me to ensure . . . I mean, it's not my –'

'No firearm – that it?' said Mac, breathing out.

'Wasn't my call,' said Atkins. 'I'd never search you, but just so we're clear.'

Walking up Veteran Street in the heat of late morning, Mac paused by a juice bar near Puputan Square. His hotel, the Natour Bali, was just around the corner in downtown, but he didn't want to head there just yet. He was tired and needed sleep, but he wasn't going to nap until he worked out who his tail was and what he wanted.

After buying a watermelon juice in a flimsy plastic cup he strolled into Puputan Square, glancing sideways behind his sunnies as he put the straw in the hole. His tail was a mid-twenties local in black slacks and white trop shirt pretending to browse at a newsstand thirty metres away. The tail's eyes flicked up momentarily as Mac looked away and kept strolling casually into the square towards the Bali Museum – a sprawling complex of temple-like buildings which doubled as museum pavilions.

Falling in with a party of Dutch and American tourists, Mac wandered across a lawn and through a large temple gate, trying to place the tail. He was a pro, although he didn't have a military build. Mac made some jokes with the Americans in order to give him sight lines on his six o'clock, but he couldn't place the bloke's intention. It wasn't a hit, which was just as well because Mac wasn't armed. If the tail wasn't a shooter, then it remained to be seen if this was about contact or surveillance. Either way, Mac wanted to seize the initiative and panic some answers out of the bloke before he could think too clearly.

Turning to listen to one of the Americans' jokes, Mac saw the tail merge with a guided tour party which was moving towards Mac's group. Mac continued walking with his party into the north pavilion which was cool, thanks to the high, vaulted ceilings of the tropical architecture. They walked through the exhibits of giant Balinese dance puppets, demon masks and shadow puppets. Some of them were centuries old and reflected a culture that the Dutch, Catholics, Javanese and Muslims had been unable to dilute. Keeping the jokes going with the Yank couple behind him, Mac was able to slow his group until the guided party were almost merging with the Dutch and Americans.

Up close he now saw that what had passed for boyish at a distance was more like chiselled early thirties. Sighting a lump on the guy's right hip under his trop shirt, Mac decided to play this carefully.

After half an hour in the Bali theatre pavilion – where Mac heard a commentary from an American about why George Bush's son should be the Republican Party's presidential nominee – they moved out into the midday heat, which Mac put at around thirty-six degrees, ninety-five per cent humidity. Moving across another long lawn to a temple gate, Mac saw his chance and abruptly split from his group, then walked towards a smaller gate on the edge of the lawn to his right. Without looking back, he ducked through the temple gate into a serenity garden. Continuing to walk at pace, Mac bounced out of the heat, up some stairs and into a service pavilion which had a large hardwood-lined hall containing a drinking fountain and seats for mothers, with toilet entrances along the far wall.

There was a fair amount of traffic into the gents, and Mac moved with it, guessing correctly that the toilets would also have an external entrance. Then he scythed through the milling tourists and skipped down the steps outside, jogging across a lawn and through another temple gate, throwing himself against the flat of the far wall.

Gulping for air, the burn on his face now throbbing with his pulse, Mac waited for the tail to follow, wondering what he'd do against a gun. Scanning through the trees along the brick and stone fence, he noticed a guard house set-up on the wall between the temple gate and the next pavilion. It looked ornamental but it might give Mac the advantage of higher ground should he need it.

Moving to his right through banyans and ferns, Mac got under the guard house while staying hidden by the foliage. He clambered up one of the mini-banyans, pushing his right foot against the flat bricks and grabbing onto the ledge of the guard house. Throwing himself across from the tree to the guard house, he scrambled into the small structure just as the tail came through the temple gate. From his hide, Mac saw the tail scout the lawn in front of him and then the trees against the wall on either side of him. Clearly thinking there was no way Mac could have got across the lawn without being seen, the tail started walking casually in Mac's direction, just a relaxed tourist interested in the vegetation.

Controlling his breath and wishing he'd put more analgesic on his burn, Mac ducked down and looked through the filigree masonry of his hide as the tail drew almost level with the guard house. The bloke was about to move on when something caught his eye and he moved closer to the wall in front of Mac, looking at a broken banyan branch.

Shit! thought Mac, as the tail moved closer to the branch. Mac had no choice. Driving upwards with both thighs he jumped clean over the masonry railing of the guard house, between the trees and onto his adversary. The Indonesian didn't see Mac until the last second, but he managed to lift his right forearm as Mac descended onto his chest. The air expelled from the tail as he was catapulted backwards, Mac on top on him as they rolled onto the lawn. Grabbing for the gun at his hip, the tail was fast to react but Mac grabbed his wrist, threw a right elbow into the bloke's teeth and then twisted the tail's right forearm into a wrist-lock before he could recover from the blow. Gasping with the pain, the tail attempted a kick but Mac put more pressure on the wrist-lock and the resistance stopped. It didn't matter how pro you were, no one wanted a broken wrist.

Reaching for the bloke's holster, Mac grabbed the small automatic handgun and threw it into the bushes before using the wrist-lock to get the tail on to his feet and into the cover of the trees. The tail's lips were white with the pain of the wrist-lock as they moved into the shade, and suddenly he went slack. As Mac tried to compensate for the man's slump, the tail reacted, throwing his right knee into Mac's groin and then a knife-hand at his throat. Stumbling from the pain in his groin, and taking the throat-shot on the carotid, Mac ducked and weaved to his left as the tail gave himself enough room to launch a roundhouse kick from his right leg. Mac was waiting for it, and was already weaving to his right, leaving the tail open to a right-leg kick. Mac took the opening and connected perfectly with his own roundhouse to the tail's supporting leg. Taking Mac's kick directly on the anterior cruciate ligament, the tail collapsed with a groan, his knee a misaligned mess. As Mac dived on the man, looking for a carotid choke-point to end it quickly, there was a familiar feeling of steel pushed against his scalp behind the right ear followed by a hammer cocking. Immediately, Mac removed his hands from the tail and let his quarry roll away as a hand grabbed a fist of his hair and the barrel pressed further into his scalp.

Kneeling in the pale brown banyan leaves, hands in the air and panting, Mac wondered where he'd thrown that handgun. And then, suddenly, it felt like time for a prayer – at least if he was going to die, it would be in a Balinese serenity garden.

'So, McQueen,' came an Asian male voice with a faint American accent. 'You called?'

Panting, Mac slowly turned to his right. The gun in his face was a chrome Desert Eagle .45, the forearm was massive and the large round face was as serious as anthrax.

'Hi, Bongo,' Mac rasped. 'How's it going?'

CHAPTER 8

Denpasar's traffic echoed into the silence between Mac and Bongo. Through the opened ranch sliders on the first-floor balcony over-looking Chinatown, Mac was dimly aware of the tail sitting on a lawn chair smoking a cigarette, a bag of ice strapped around his left knee. Inside, Mac and Bongo sat under a ceiling fan, talking over a low coffee table.

'Look, Bongo,' said Mac, gazing down the navel of the Desert Eagle, 'let's start this again, okay?'

Bongo looked from his position on the sofa. 'What, you started for a first time?'

Mac leaned forward from the armchair and grabbed a bottle of Vittel. 'I wanted to talk, Bongo, that's it.'

'McQueen just wants a chat – first time for everything.'

'You know I don't want to kill you, mate,' said Mac, the adrenaline of the fight subsiding.

'Well someone does,' said Bongo, pulling the lapel down on his trop shirt to expose a large surgical dressing taped on his left shoulder.

'Gunshot?' said Mac.

'Wasn't no mosquito, brother. Why don't you start by telling me what's going on? Then we'll have something to talk about.'

'You know I can't tell you what I'm doing. Come on, mate,' said Mac. Bongo understood the rules of their profession.

'Then I can't help you, McQueen,' he said, lighting a smoke.

'You can tell me what happened at the meet, the last one with the Canadian,' said Mac, sensing Bongo had a story he wanted to get off his chest.

'I could tell you lots of things, McQueen, but we should start with what you gonna tell me.'

Sipping on the water, Mac shrugged.

'Like, you tell me why a meet run by the Aussies suddenly turns into an ambush?' Bongo said.

'Mate, I wasn't –'

'Like, how is it that a shooter walks out of a door at this meet and starts putting holes in me?'

'Shooter?' said Mac.

'Three, actually,' said Bongo, smoke streaming out of his nostrils.

Pausing, Mac tried to stay clear about the story. 'Well, Dili's a bit lawless right now, Bongo – maybe they saw the Anglo with a local minder and decided there was some cash?'

'Did I say they was militia?' snarled Bongo.

'Not militia?'

'You think I'd get jumped by some hairy kid with a Castro T-shirt?'

Mac shook his head. Bongo's reputation put him out of the amateur leagues.

'So what happened?' said Mac.

'I was bodyguarding this Canadian dude for the Aussies,' said Bongo, his gun holding steady. 'We go into this mansion in Dili and the Canadian asks a pretty local girl about Bow or Boa – something like that – and the shooting starts.'

'Just like that?'

'Like I said, McQueen – I'm wondering why the Aussies put me in that shit?'

'Okay, Bongo,' said Mac, eyeing the gun. 'I'm going into Dili and I want a heads-up – no one on my side has details of the Canadian or the meet, and I don't like flying blind. I heard that the Canadian had a minder down there and you were the first person I thought of. So I took a punt, put the word out through Saba.'

45

The heavyset Filipino contemplated the floor between his feet and then looked back. 'Maybe we can talk some more, but what's in it for me?' he said.

Having worked with a lot of soldiers over the years, Mac knew they saw their priorities in terms of duty, money and payback, in that order. Bongo's sense of duty might have evaporated when he went freelance, but that left two incentives.

'I can offer you money or payback,' said Mac.

'I'll take both,' said Bongo.

'You'll have to work for it,' Mac countered. 'Maybe I can keep you on the payroll? I'd have to okay it, but –'

'And the payback?'

'Well that'll come down to circumstances, right?'

Bongo didn't look convinced.

'Okay, mate,' said Mac, trying to salvage the deal. 'I'm going to need some protection down there, and if the shooter comes into the open, you take your shot and I look the other way. Fair?'

'Maybe.'

'But only once I've got what I want,' said Mac.

Mac's tension eased as a smirk creased the sides of Bongo's mouth.

'What's funny?' asked Mac, smiling tentatively.

'Nothing, brother,' said Bongo.

'Come on,' said Mac.

'Well, this one won't come into the open,' said Bongo, stubbing his cigarette in the ashtray.

'Why? Who we talking about?'

Bongo grinned. 'The shooter – it's Benni Sudarto.'

Mac's tension returned twofold and his face must have told the story because Bongo slapped his leg with his gun and laughed at the ceiling.

'Still wanna go to Dili, brother?'

The shower pressure was strong by Indonesian standards and Mac savoured it longer than he normally would. He was tired, needed a nap – and the stress of the Sudarto information was playing tricks on his facial muscles, making them twitch and spasm across his forehead and jaws.

Drying off, he grabbed a Bintang beer from the mini-bar, pushed through the bungalow's French doors and looked around the tropical gardens of the Natour Bali Hotel. There was an out-of-sight splash from the pool and, diagonally opposite, two housemaids giggled outside a room. Otherwise, it looked clear.

Pulling back into the room, Mac opened the A4 envelope and shook the contents onto the writing desk. There was a one-page work-up for his cover, both personal and corporate. He already knew his Richard Davis and Arafura Imports details, but he'd never used the sandalwood trader pretext in East Timor, so he memorised the three commercial contacts he would approach and had a quick read of the magazine clippings and LexisNexis printouts about sandalwood prices, the Christian icon trade and the main importer into Sydney.

In a plastic folder were the printed catalogues for Arafura's distribution, with the icons divided into Mexican and Guatemalan imports and their price per hundred. Mac put these pieces of collateral aside – they'd be making the trip with him.

Three code names were mentioned in the operation outline: Blackbird, he was aware of; Centre Stage was the official name for the Canadian; and Mac recognised his own ASIS moniker, Albion. There were also frequency settings for the radio set, should he get that desperate. He didn't need to memorise them; there were only three frequency/bandwidth combinations used by the firm in contact with the Royal Australian Navy, and Mac knew them by heart.

He thought about the mission brief Tobin and then Atkins had outlined for him: find out if Blackbird was still able to be operated by Canberra, and then work on the question of Operasi Boa. What was it? When was it happening? The Canadian was not top of the list, but he was included in the official tasking. His background was also mentioned: YARROW, William Donald, DOB 07/04/1949; graduate of McGill University; accountant from British Columbia. CEO of an import/exporter and distributor, exploring opportunities in Bali and East Timor. Yarrow had apparently cheated millions from Canadian excise over the years, and was wanted by Canada Customs and Revenue Agency for fraud and evasion. Though Canberra didn't consider the

Canadian all that important, Mac decided to make his own decision about him.

Fishing a box of matches from the writing desk drawer, Mac put all the briefing papers in the steel rubbish bin, lit the A4 envelope and threw it in. As the flames consumed the brief, he dug out the Cathay Pacific sewing kit from his toilet bag and ran a cotton line from the French doors to the handle of a coffee cup, which he then looped over the bedpost. There was already a chair under the main door handle. As he crawled under the sheets Mac wondered about the trip to Dili and whether he was doing the right thing by running his own intelligence gathering separate to Atkins and Tobin. It was a bad habit of his, and one that had not made him any friends on the higher rungs. There were always good reasons for staying with the program and going along with the information you were being fed, but Mac had already found an information gap between Atkins and Tobin about Boa and he hadn't been comfortable with Garvey's furtiveness.

Mac was someone who actually worked out the placement of the aircraft's exits every time he flew; he read the fire-escape diagram on hotel room doors. During his time in the Royal Marines, Mac's section leader, Banger Jordan, had drummed into the Commando candidates the credo: there is no mission without an exit. 'If you don't know how to get out, then don't go in!' he would scream at them in his thick Geordie accent.

Lying in bed, he let the scenarios unfold without forcing them too much. Tobin's and Atkins' assertions that they didn't know the fate of the Canadian or of Blackbird seemed genuine because Bongo – who was there – had escaped from the mansion in Dili with a chunk missing from his shoulder and with the Canadian and Blackbird still in the room. Alive.

The complication came with Captain Benni Sudarto. Sudarto's presence in that meet had aroused Bongo's anti-Australian instincts, because Sudarto's training had included time at Duntroon and several rotations in the Australian SAS. So Sudarto had been trained at Australia's elite army academy, mused Mac, but he was also a certified thug, murderer, torturer and filler of mass graves.

Benni Sudarto had moved quickly through officer school and special forces training and then opted for Indonesia's violent special operations regiment, Kopassus. Over the years, Mac had followed Sudarto's career, which could also be plotted by cross-reference to Amnesty International reports. Having made his name in Aceh and Ambon, Sudarto had really become famous in East Timor, hunting Falintil 'terrorists' through the mountains and shutting down villages.

But the part of Sudarto's story Mac was most interested in was the last sighting of him, in that room in the mansion, shooting at Bongo. According to Bongo, Sudarto had been in plainclothes, and so had his two henchies. A Kopassus captain suddenly working without his uniform meant one thing: Group 4, Kopassus intel – and that was a problem for Mac.

Group 4 was a secret unit of Kopassus that performed an amalgam of roles, including military and civil intelligence, SWAT-like operations and a secret police function. As East Timor headed towards their independence ballot, Mac wondered what Group 4 was doing there and why they were ambushing Canadian and Philippines nationals. It seemed like an overreaction, or perhaps a panicked reaction. Sudarto was too smart to start shooting for no reason. He was secreted during the ambush, he was doing surveillance, he obviously had Blackbird made and no one on the Australian side had been aware of it. He had the information superiority which gave him the chance to feed all sorts of rubbish back to ASIS and play Canberra for fools. But, instead, he'd broken cover and started putting holes in the players.

The last thought Mac had before he fell asleep was: why?

CHAPTER 9

The four-year-old Toyota minivan needed a wash and the driver could have done with a haircut, but they were both waiting outside Dili airport terminal when Mac emerged into the sun and dust with the other passengers.

'Turismo?' asked Mac, bringing his black wheelie suitcase to heel as he stopped.

'Sure, boss,' smiled the youthful local, white shirt bleached but frayed at the collar. 'Turismo express! Raoul do it special for you.'

Behind Mac, an American accent asked for the Resende and another voice wondered about transport for the Hotel Dili. Without hesitation, Raoul announced his credentials for those hotels too, while another local man leapt into the group of arrivals and spruiked his own brand of express travel – cheaper, faster and with air-con that worked. Though it might have looked like chaos to an outsider, this was the way people were transported around South-East Asia, and it seemed to work.

Raoul took Mac's bag, then reached for a Malay businessman's suitcase, covered in Malaysia Airlines tags and stickers. The man stood close to Mac in the stifling heat, his Ralph Lauren Polo wafting off him in heady waves.

A group of Indonesian police dressed in tan fatigues wandered along the terminal apron with their German shepherds, keeping a close eye on the visitors and the locals dealing with them. Their flashings were too small to readily identify names, ranks or regiment, but Mac had them as Brimob – the Brigada Mobil – a flying squad of riot and anti-insurgency police who got shifted around the Republic to intimidate troublemakers. Meanwhile, a plainclothes Javanese spook stayed in the shadows, chewing on gum and examining the visitors through a pair of dark Wayfarers.

Sitting in the seat behind the driver, Mac listened to Raoul's running commentary on the tiny Indonesian province. There was plenty of rice, there was work and the dry season was not too bad this year – the crops had come in and there was food.

'So what about this ballot?' came an American voice from directly behind Mac as they moved out of the terminal area onto the notoriously dangerous road into Dili. 'There's a lot of soldiers around, Raoul – we expecting trouble?'

Despite the concentration required to dodge carts and motor-cyclists while trying to go down the Indonesian 'third lane', Raoul nodded. 'My family has food, mister, and no crime, okay?'

'Yeah,' sneered the American, as only the peace-blessed Anglos of the world could sneer. 'But you're gonna vote for independence, right, Raoul? You look like a freedom-loving guy to me.'

Watching the driver's shoulders slump as they slowed behind a 1950s-era truck loaded with large green leaves, Mac turned to face the American.

'Right now it suits me that Raoul's a life-loving guy – with me, sport?' said Mac, smiling at the middle-aged Yank. 'Old Indonesian proverb – driving and politics don't mix.'

Some of the other passengers chuckled with relief and the American's travelling companion dug his elbow into the man's ribs. 'You heard him, Keith. Let the guy drive.'

'Richard Davis – sandalwood,' said Mac, putting out his hand to the American.

'Keith Wilson – telecoms,' said the American, friendly but annoyed.

Turning back to face the windscreen, Mac caught Raoul's eye in the rear-vision mirror for a split second. He'd seen that quietly thankful look in Bosnia, Iraq and Cambodia and, for the second time since the Atkins meeting, Mac longed for a firearm on his right hip.

***

Mac's usual room at the Turismo was small and uncomplicated. He'd stayed in the Turismo several times and room 10 gave him a view over the Esplanada – Dili's main thoroughfare – whereas most of the rooms either looked over the rear beer garden or had no outlook at all. The lack of in-room phone meant one less surveillance tool for unfriendlies, and the placement of the TV on top of the mini-fridge was a nice feature.

Opening a pack of Doublemint, Mac pulled a stick one centimetre out of the packet, and placed it gently in the inside pocket of his wheelie suitcase, at the same time taking a piece of chalk the size of a stock cube from the same pocket. Placing the chalk cube under the hinge end of the door, Mac let himself out and moved down to the lobby.

The manager – Mrs Soares – was friendly but couldn't help Mac with faxing. 'No allowed no more,' she said with a smile and a shrug. 'For the security.'

The Indon military commanders had removed every fax machine from Dili, leaving only one for public use at the Dili Telkom office. Given the way the Indonesian Army operated, thought Mac, word would have gone out and every fax machine in the province would have been ostentatiously sitting on top of the garbage bins the next morning.

Buying a Bintang from the woman, Mac wandered out to the famous tropical beer garden at the rear of the Turismo, nabbing a seat in the shade of a banyan. Chained to the branch of the tree was a macaque, miming something. Mac sat back, slurped on the beer and did his mental work-up for the day. He'd start with the largest of the sandalwood traders – the one owned by the generals – and make a big to-do about new orders, Australian growth markets and suggestions for new products. There were spies who thought their job was to blend into the background and not make too much noise, but businesspeople in South-East Asia who weren't trying to make money attracted attention. Mac wanted the Indonesian spies and soldiers talking about the Australian with the big plan for making money, not the quiet Aussie 'businessman' hiding out at the Turismo asking about fax machines.

'Bad luck about fax, eh?' came a voice from behind him, and Mac spun around slightly too quickly, coming face to face with the bloke from Raoul's bus, the one with the Malaysia Airlines tags all over his bags.

'But, you know, I have fax in my room. Just need to ask, okay?' said the bloke, smiling conspiratorially and extending his hand.

'Rahmid Ali,' he said, the big Malay face creasing at the sides and bursting with the brightness of a lot of white teeth. 'I saw you this morning, yes?'

'Sure,' smiled Mac, standing and accepting the shake. 'Richard Davis.'

'You tell off the American, right?'

'You never really tell off an American, Rahmid,' said Mac. 'You just get ignored rather than bombed.'

Rahmid Ali laughed so heartily that Mac could see his pink tonsils. Gesturing to the spare seat beside him, Mac watched as the Malay sat with a small bottle of Perrier and a glass. He was impeccably dressed in cream linens, glowing with fresh grooming and still smelling of Polo. He was also Indonesian intelligence – BAKIN, probably, decided Mac. Since Anglo visitors had a reputation for thinking all Asians looked alike, Indonesian spooks often posed as Malaysians to get closer to their targets, hence Rahmid Ali's display of Malaysia Air paraphernalia. In KL, the Malaysian spooks pretended to be Thai, in Manila the Filipinos masqueraded as Indonesian and in Phnom Penh the Cambodians acted Thai or Vietnamese.

'You really got a fax in your room?' asked Mac.

'Sure,' winked his new friend. 'I got sat phone, right, and it plugs into mini-fax. If you need to receive fax, just give them my number – I won't tell.'

Nodding, Mac took the Andromeda IT Services business card from Ali, on which the satellite phone and fax numbers had helpfully been underlined.

Above them, on the first-floor interior balcony of the hotel, a man was shouting. Looking up, Mac and Ali saw a short, badly dressed Korean yell into a mobile phone while remonstrating with his cigarette hand.

'I no care – I no care 'bout that!' the bloke yelled, punctuated by awkward and frequent drags on his smoke. 'Why you think I care? That your probrem, okay? I no care.'

Hearing the tone, Mac's hackles went up. All over Asia, Korean businesspeople spoke to their associates and customers as if they were the lowest form of life, and every time Mac had to infiltrate a business and charm people like the one yelling on the balcony, he'd sworn it'd be his last.

Turning back to Rahmid Ali, Mac shared a quick laugh with him. The Koreans were something else.

'I don't know about the fax,' said Mac. 'Where did you say you were from?'

'Kuala Lumpur,' smiled Ali.

'Well, in KL it may be okay to break the law, but you know something?'

'What?'

'The Indonesians have the fairest laws in South-East Asia and I'm happy to support them in their efforts to maintain a civil society.'

Rahmid Ali's face slowly sank from its top-marketing smile to a contemptuous curiosity. 'Yes, Mr Davis,' he finally managed. 'I think I see your point.'

Draining the Bintang, Mac stood to go. 'Nice meeting you, Rahmid,' he said, shaking the spy's hand.

'I'm sure we'll meet again,' said Ali, already recovering his professional demeanour.

Rahmid Ali was going to stand off for a while, thought Mac, but as he walked out of the garden he could feel the other man's eyes burning into his back.

CHAPTER 10

The offices of PT Watu Selatan were two blocks from the Turismo, so Mac decided to walk it. He noticed that the locals shrank back into the darkness of shops and alleys as he moved through the dusty colonial streets, probably scared off by the rising violence from the pro-Indonesian militias. In many of the poorer parts of South-East Asia, visiting Westerners were the ones fearing violence or crime. In Dili, the fear was something endured by the citizens – a dull acceptance of terror, the likes of which Mac had experienced in Phnom Penh at the start of his career.

Mac hadn't been in Dili for a couple of years, but it seemed to be the same old story: locals who talked to a Westerner or laughed with a Westerner were harassed so badly by the cops or spooks that they learned to behave in a purely perfunctory way towards foreigners. There were daily reminders of the ramifications of breaking with this code floating in the harbour or washed up on the city beaches, minus their heads and hands. Even Mac's mobile phone made him feel slightly guilty. There was a Telkom Indonesia cellular network in East Timor, but it was mainly used by Indonesians and visitors. Any local found with a mobile phone had a good chance of enjoying a few nights' stay in the Brimob compound, where calls to their mother might be interpreted as aiding the Falintil guerrillas.

As a blue Land Rover Discovery slipped past, Mac noticed the expensively dressed Westerners behind the tinted glass and the white UN letters on the door. He had them as UNAMET scrutineers, the United Nations team that was going to oversee the independence ballot in two weeks. The UNAMET mission had divided opinion in DFAT. People like Mac couldn't see the point in sending a ballot-scrutiny team into a place as repressed as East Timor where pro-independence figures and their families were already being tortured and killed by the Indonesian Army and its militias. What East Timor needed was an armed UN peacekeeping mission to allow everyone to vote, and Mac's chance meeting with Sandy Beech at Parliament House had simply confirmed his opinion. The other view in DFAT – supported by the Australian government – was that the Indonesian military's harassment of pro-independence Timorese was having a calming effect on the province and it was premature to talk about UN peacekeepers.

The picture was made more complex by the history of Falintil, the Timorese guerrilla army that had been fighting the Indonesian invaders since 1975. As Mac had pointed out to the National Security Committee members, Falintil had Marxist-Leninist roots, and many Indonesians and Australians dismissed them as 'commies', which diluted their credibility.

Turning right into a wide avenue, Mac saw the PT Watu Selatan building right across the road from its real owners, the Indonesian Army. Olive-green jeeps called kijangs and trucks were parked on the street in front of the army headquarters, the large red and white flag of the Republic flying over the modest front steps. Regular soldiers wearing what looked like badges of the 744 Battalion lounged in the shade, leaning on their M16 straps and eyeballing the locals who, like Mac, walked on the other side of the street.

Stopping at the swinging glass doors of the Watu Selatan office, Mac noticed a white recent-model Toyota Camry parked in front of the military headquarters. Three Javanese men sat in the car, a fourth leaning into the front passenger window, his large forearms across the roof of the Toyota. The standing man's head came up and then the other faces turned as one to stare at Mac, their black sunglasses creating a comical look, like a 1960s press photo of the Rat Pack in Vegas. Mac had them as SGI – an intelligence taskforce that was working on the 'East Timor problem'. It was supposed to consist of the various intelligence outfits from the armed forces but in reality it was dominated by Kopassus intel. While Kopassus was the special forces group within the army, its intelligence arm was virtually a secret society: they wore plainclothes and were distrusted by all arms of the military, the police and intelligence agencies.

Attempting a smile but failing, Mac pushed into the air-conditioning of the Watu Selatan office, glad to be out of the tropical heat and away from the glare of the boys from intel.

A middle-aged receptionist with a beehive hairdo asked Mac to take a seat when he introduced himself, then picked up a phone and pushed a button. As she rattled off a reminder, Mac pushed the white gauze curtains back slightly and observed the Kopassus spooks at the Camry. The standing one said his goodbyes and walked into the military building as two of the men in the car opened their doors and got out to stretch on the footpath, their SIG Sauer handguns obvious beneath their trop shirts. The driver leaned out his window and said something, and the two standing on the footpath looked up and started across the street towards the Watu Selatan building.

Releasing the curtain, Mac exhaled in a hiss of tension. This was not how the first contact of an assignment was supposed to go. He had an entire three weeks to be tailed, tricked, trapped and interrogated. They hadn't even got him drunk or sent him the pretty girl, and the Kopassus spooks were already coming at him like a scene from a spaghetti western.

A short Javanese man swept into the reception area, the long sleeves of his batik shirt unusual for Dili. 'Mr Richard!' he gushed as he held out a business card. 'Adam Moerpati – manager – so nice to meet.'

Responding with his own card and gushy greeting, Mac took in the guy's expensive dental work, which was the kind the Jakarta elites had done in Singapore. As they moved down a cool hallway and into Moerpati's office, his new best friend asked about the flight and the hotel.

'Turismo?!' said Moerpati, with a theatrical Javanese shrug, gesturing for Mac to take the sofa. 'For a man of your success, not the Resende?'

Mac loved the way the Javanese wrapped an insult in a compliment.

'Well, you know, Mr Moerpati – they book me where they book me,' said Mac.

'Adam, please,' said Moerpati, offering a box of cheroots and putting one in his own mouth. 'I get you good rate at Resende,' he winked. 'No worries.'

Taking Moerpati through the costs and freight charges with the Panamanian and Mexican icon-makers, Mac explained that his company wanted to dominate the Australasian icon trade and that if they could get better margins from East Timor along with the better shipping rates, he'd like to talk about a deal.

Mac used his basic technique of mixing vagueness with specificity to draw the man closer. Businesspeople felt their souls were appreciated when you could recite a few basic unit volume and margin figures about their trade and allow them to embroider the general comments with their own insights. By the time the receptionist brought the coffee, Mac knew Watu Selatan intended to keep trading after the independence ballot and that the Jakarta elites believed East Timor would not be allowed to entirely secede from the Republic.

Finishing his second cheroot, Moerpati admitted that Mac's visit was well timed. 'We had Canadian here, wanting to deal,' he confided.

'So where is he?' asked Mac. 'Should I be speaking with this guy?'

'No, no,' laughed Moerpati. 'He gone, right? Now you here!'

'So – he's gone,' smiled Mac, keeping it light. 'To Kupang? Denpasar?'

'I not know,' the other man said. 'The peoples come – the peoples go. Who know, right?'

The Kopassus spooks were waiting for Mac outside the building as he emerged into the heat of the afternoon. The larger of the two asked Mac's name, confirmed that he was staying at the Turismo, and asked him to follow.

There was little chance of escape; Mac might have been able to disarm the one to his left, shoot both of his escorts, drop the Camry driver – who was still behind the wheel – and make his getaway in the heisted car. But to where? Timor was an island under military guard, with one soldier for every forty occupants. There were three roads out of Dili and military roadblocks everywhere. So, keeping a smile on his face, Mac decided to bluff it out, even as his gut churned with fear. When Canberra know-it-alls pushed their arguments for appeasing the Indonesian government, they never quite grasped reality. They weren't the bastards getting their feet broken or having quick-lime rubbed in their eyes – the appeasers were never going to physically suffer from their own strategy.

As they got to the entrance of the headquarters across the road, the driver of the Camry got out and followed them into the building. They climbed a set of stairs – one spook in front, two behind – and emerged on the first floor. To Mac's left was an admin section staffed by women and for a split second Mac feared that he was being brought to confront Blackbird in her workplace. This was where ASIS had been gleaning some of its best intelligence on the Indonesian Army's intentions for East Timor.

But they turned right, walked silently down a long hall with several windowed doors and stopped at the one marked MAJ-GEN. ANWAR DAMAJAT. Mac tried to remember Damajat's role from Atkins' work-up. He couldn't be certain, but thought the Kopassus commander was the head of the intelligence taskforce in East Timor.

As Mac was wondering who he had to kill to get a large glass of Pepto-Bismol, the door swung back and his escorts waved him through. Inside the large office a fit-looking military man in his mid-fifties leapt up from behind his desk, listened as a spook whispered in his ear, and then came at Mac with an oily eagerness.

'Mr Richard – Anwar Damajat, at your service, sir. Welcome to Dili and sit please,' he said, smiling and gesturing Mac towards a leather club chair in front of his desk.

Mac's heart beat in his temples as he became aware of a large man sitting on a sofa against the rear wall. He fought with his fear, telling himself to breathe slowly, just like they'd been taught in the Royal Marines all those years ago. It had been drummed into them over and over: if you could control nothing else in your environment, then control your breathing. It could be the difference between life and death.

'Firstly, Mr Richard, let me ask you a question,' said Damajat, sitting behind his desk once more. 'You look like a smart man.'

'Thanks,' smiled Mac, his stomach doing somersaults.

'So why you doing business with those idiots at Watu Selatan?'

There was a pause and Mac focused on Damajat's thumb, which was gesturing back over his shoulder. Then Damajat's face broke into a big smile and he and the spooks started laughing. Heart thumping, Mac managed a smirk as Damajat came around the desk and slapped him on the left bicep. 'Don't tell me, Mr Richard – that old thief offered you free nights at the Resende, right?'

Allowing the tension to wash out of him, Mac played along with the joking. Damajat didn't want to torture him – Damajat represented Watu Selatan's rival, the Anak-Poco Group, which specialised in construction and had such a brutal hold on the local workforce that Anak-Poco guaranteed project completion on time and on budget – an unheard of event in the Indonesian construction game.

'You forget about sandalwood toys, Mr Richard,' said Damajat, handing Mac a glossy Anak-Poco brochure. 'You tell your people in Australia to bring the money up here to Timor, right? This like new Surfer Paradise, okay? Like a Noosa, yeah?'

Mac nodded.

''Cos I tell you, Mr Richard, once ballot is over we gonna finish the troubles and start making the money.'

'The troubles?' asked Mac.

'Yeah, the communist, okay? We got a plan for them, right, and then we open for business.'

Damajat got the man on the sofa, who he introduced as Amir, to pour the whiskies, then waved Mac towards the sofa and a couple of armchairs at the back of the office and started yakking about the West Coast Eagles.

'Mick Malthouse can't leave the Eagles? Surely not,' said Damajat, referring to rumours in the Australian papers that the coach of the Perth-based AFL team was being wooed by other clubs.

'Well maybe he's got a better offer, eh Anwar?' said Mac as he moved towards an empty armchair and watched Amir stretch his big frame into the sofa on the far wall. 'Maybe there's a chance to be owner-coach at the Dili Diehards?'

As Damajat laughed, Mac eased back in his chair and took a glass of Scotch, forcing himself to relax into the meeting. Sipping as Amir made a point, Mac caught a brief look through a gap in the frosted glass around the office. A face in dark Ray-Bans peered through into the office and turned away as Mac looked. Mac had only seen this person in file pictures, but the face and size were unmistakable: Benni Sudarto was lurking outside Damajat's office.

CHAPTER 11

Mac sipped his fifth Bintang as the sun got low in the sky and the mosquitos in the beer garden started their thing. Patting the letter of free passage that Damajat had written for him, Mac was relieved he could now travel anywhere in East Timor and seriously frighten anyone who tried to stop him.

The Damajat meeting had gone well for Mac, and the commercial interests he was developing with the Indonesian military were a perfect cover for moving around what was a garrison-province: a ratio of one soldier for every forty locals was essentially martial law even if Jakarta hadn't declared it yet. There was a defeated, abandoned feel to Dili; a sense of hopelessness pervaded – all the cheekiness and openness of the locals was gone. Despite the ballot taking place in two weeks, the East Timorese wouldn't look Mac in the eye. And there was an energy and arrogance about the Indonesian military that Mac found disconcerting.

In one made-for-media opportunity, the Indonesian generals had announced the withdrawal of its stationed troops, but the troops who'd been paraded in front of the TV cameras had merely been shipped around the headlands and put ashore further up the coast. From what Mac could glean of that episode, the entire sham had been designed for the Australian media. The Australian government knew about the ruse from its signals intelligence, yet said nothing. Meanwhile, in the mountains and farming districts of East Timor, the army-backed militias were killing, razing and raping at will.

In Bosnia and Kosovo, the world had united to end atrocities that paled next to what the Indonesian generals did on a weekly basis in East Timor. The Western world – Australia and the United States in particular – had gone along with Soeharto's Caesaresque dream of a 'Greater Indonesia' in 1975 and the results were obvious in Dili. If you gave bullies the green light to behave any way they wanted, then they'd behave any way they wanted.

Mac had had these arguments with Canberra's pro-Jakarta ideologues, but they'd built their careers on being pro-Jakarta and they couldn't suddenly change their minds now. The last person Mac knew of in DFAT who had the stones to challenge the pro-Jakarta clique was Tony Davidson. He used to say, 'We don't gather the nice product from Indonesia and the bad product from everywhere else – we simply gather product.' But Davidson was also the last senior person in Australia's SIS with an operational background, and when he retired the top ranks of Australia's foreign spy agency would become wall-to-wall theorists, analysts, managers and academics – all of them politically astute enough to be pro-Jakarta.

Checking his watch, Mac decided to grab a meal and then get ready for his next assignment. As he made for the lobby the Korean started yelling into his mobile phone again, this time in his native tongue. The bloke was so loud Mac could hear his voice echoing from upstairs.

'The dining room is open when?' Mac asked Mrs Soares, who told him, 'Ten minutes.'

The chalk under his door hadn't been pushed back to the wall and the Doublemint stick was exactly as Mac had left it. Cranking out twenty push-ups and fifty sit-ups, he had a quick shower with very poor pressure, and dressed in fresh clothes. Then he lay on the bed thinking through what he wanted to do and how hard he was going to push things. He wanted to get an early night and walk out to the cemetery at Santa Cruz before dawn. It wasn't a perfect way to trace Blackbird, but it was a start: get eyes on the cut-out, follow him and get him talking. For now it was the only approach he had.

What he knew for certain was that finding the Canadian was going to have to be dropped from his unofficial task list. The entire feeling in Dili was extremely dangerous and if the priority tasking was Blackbird and Operasi Boa, then he'd have to leave the Canadian to someone else.

Was he scared? Damned right he was.

The dining room was small and only three tables had been set. Mac took the table at the far wall, wanting a better observation point over Rahmid Ali. He expected Ali to have recovered from the morning's conversation, and be ready to try another tack.

The specials blackboard said that 'Baucau Chicken' with rice was the chef's recommendation for the evening. Chicken in East Timor was prepared in the spicy Portuguese style and was usually – for some reason – served cold. There'd be plenty of chances for cold chicken at the roadside *warung* that infested East Timor so Mac chose the fish of the day and asked for a beer.

The Korean announced his presence even before entering the dining room, yelling into his phone as he walked in and looking around with studied contempt. Putting the phone to his chest, the Korean faced Mac with his bottom lip slack, eyes yellowed with hard liquor.

'That it?' he asked, pointing at the specials board with his cigarette.

Giving him a wink and a nod, Mac decided not to engage the Korean in actual conversation. Snorting at Mac and then shaking his head in disbelief, the Korean swaggered out of the dining room leaving a fug of smoke and BO.

Relaxing into his chair, Mac mentally prepared his next twenty-four hours, trying to forget Benni Sudarto peering through that window at the Damajat meeting. Mac reckoned there was a fifty per cent chance he'd been made and it remained to be seen what Sudarto was going to do about it. Would he assign a tail, let Mac run? Would he shut Mac down and start pulling teeth? Feed him up with bullshit and send him back to Atkins with tall tales designed to confound Canberra? Or was he just keeping an eye on who Damajat was entertaining?

Slugging at the beer, Mac wondered how long he could keep his nerves at bay with alcohol. Catching a movement from his right Mac put his beer down. Expecting Ali, Mac found himself looking at a woman instead – early twenties, blonde and very attractive.

'Is this the dining room?' she asked in a North American accent, the set to her face making the question into a joke.

'Actually, it's the broom closet but we hide them away when we hear there's an American coming to stay.'

'Special treatment for special guests, huh?' she smiled, open and natural.

'Nah,' drawled Mac. 'Just means we can charge more for the room.'

'Oh, thanks,' she said, rolling her eyes.

'What can I say?' said Mac, standing. 'You guys'll pay anything.'

The woman laughed and Mac took a step forward, offering his hand. 'Richard – how do you do?'

'Jessica.' Her handshake was firm. 'Don't tell me – went sunbathing, fell asleep on one side?'

Touching the scorch mark on his cheek, Mac retorted. 'Cheeky Yanks!'

Sitting, he gestured for her to join him. 'No sunbathing on this trip, I'm afraid – here to buy sandalwood, of all things. And you?'

'I'm Canadian, actually,' said Jessica, turning serious as she sat, 'and I'm looking for my father.'

CHAPTER 12

Slipping through the tropical darkness, Mac stayed in the shadows of the trees that lined most of the avenues in Dili. It was 3.58 am according to his G-Shock and he was making good time, slipping along one of the minor streets behind the Dili Stadium, heading inland from the harbour.

Dressed in a black sweatshirt, dark baseball cap and Levis, he blended with the background and the moonless night as he alternated between running across open ground and waiting behind cover, heading quietly southwards.

A light flashed down the street from two blocks away, and Mac ducked behind a frangipani tree. Waiting, all his senses on high alert, he watched the Brimob SWAT van turn into the deserted street and move slowly towards him. A Brimob officer's head and shoulders stuck out the top of the roof and swivelled a searchlight through the darkness as it approached. Ducking for cover, Mac used the lee of the frangipani to crawl into a stormwater culvert that ran the length of the avenue. Lying in the dog shit and rotting leaves he held his breath as the diesel growl of the Brimob truck came alongside his position. He exhaled, relieved, as it kept moving, 'I Will Always Love You' echoing out of the vehicle's radio, sung rather painfully by an Indonesian male. One of the eternal wonders of the universe was why Indonesian men felt the need to record songs associated with Whitney Houston, Mariah Carey and Olivia Newton-John.

Dusting himself off, Mac got in behind the frangipani tree and watched the Brimob truck fade into the distance and then turn right – probably scouting for kids around the stadium.

Feeling naked without his gun, Mac kept a steady pace from one hide to another as he continued on. Heading left into a larger avenue, he became exposed to streetlights and crossing the dusty street to the sanctuary of the darkness on the other side, his panting and footfalls seemed to echo down the empty avenue. Suddenly a light went on in a mansion somewhere behind the trees he was hiding in. Mac froze as an Indonesian woman in a housecoat stepped out onto her veranda, not six metres away, and made a high-pitched musical call. Two cats darted out of the shrubbery and shot past the woman's calves into the house like a couple of lightning bolts.

Pulling back into the house and shutting the door, the woman killed the lights. Mac gulped down the stress and moved on.

Using a small banyan to get himself to the top of the cemetery wall, Mac lay along the top of it for ten minutes, assessing the ground. There was no movement, no whispers and he couldn't smell cigarettes or aftershave. Sliding down the opposite side of the wall, he found one of the walkways and moved swiftly to the main road of the cemetery. Staying twenty metres off the main track, he dodged and weaved through the tombstones and fenced plots until he located the twenty-first path. Finding it, he counted seven gravesites until he was looking at the drop: a modest plot, squashed between two larger ones.

Holding back for a few minutes, Mac waited for movement, wishing he hadn't drunk so much beer the night before. Pretty girls with a ton of charm sure did make the world go around, but they didn't help with work the next day.

Satisfied that he wasn't walking into an ambush, Mac found a decent-sized tree and created a hide with a sight line to the drop box and also a view of the cemetery's main road. Placing the water bottle on his 'chair', Mac left the hide and moved at a crouched jog to the main road, scuttled across it, wanting to check on how observable the water bottle was to those approaching it.

Moving to the other side of the cemetery, he numbered off the side paths until he was on the thirty-fifth on the right, and then numbered the plots back to the seventh on the left. Breathing deeply, he stayed still, waiting for movement or sound. The only action came from the trees where a bat was feuding with a bird. Fumbling in the dark, he ran his hands over a white marble gravesite and headstone. It was immaculately maintained, just like all the plots at Santa Cruz. The crypts were whitewashed, headstones were scrubbed and polished, there were no weeds and the edges were all trimmed. Mac marvelled at how the world's poorest and most oppressed people so often had the most beautiful graveyards. He'd seen the same in Phnom Penh and Rangoon. Was it stupidity or defiance?

There were no moving parts on the grave cover or the headstone, and for a second Mac wondered if he was at the wrong site. Counting it back again, he confirmed he was at the right grave; then he lay down and got his face closer. Behind the headstone was a steel box with a lid and as Mac moved closer in the dark he saw the lid was padlocked.

'Fuck!' he mumbled.

Hitting it with his fist in frustration, he was about to move on when he realised the whole box had rocked. Pulling the box back on its hinge, Mac saw a dark canvas bag and, opening it, he found the radio and the plastic-covered frequencies. He rummaged under the machine until his fingers wrapped around a solid object. Pulling it out, and holding it in front of his face, Mac smiled at his find: a Beretta 9mm handgun with a replacement mag secured to the grip with a rubber band.

The drop box proved simpler. The marble casement slid sideways, revealing a cavity about the size of a shoe box. Mac dropped his note in it and slid the casement back to its original position. Then he grabbed one of the red flowers from a neighbouring grave and put it into the stainless-steel cup that was bolted into the headstone just above the engraving of SALAZAR, EUGENIO CLAUDIO.

Back at his hide, Mac took a seat, lay back and wondered where the assignment was going. He'd kept the note in the drop box quite vague; he didn't like drop boxes at the best of times. The note asked for a Blackbird meet, and was signed 'Albion'.

It made him feel vulnerable so he was going to even things up a little. How long he could wait was another thing entirely.

His mind was on other things, too. Jessica Yarrow had walked into that hotel like a flash flood. It had totally floored him – he'd been so ready to sidestep the whole Canadian issue that he'd simply reduced Bill Yarrow to *the Canadian*, trying to convince himself that the man didn't matter. But he did. You couldn't use someone like Yarrow as a local asset, have them risk their life for intelligence, and then walk away because he'd been caught by the bad guys. It wasn't the Australian way.

Now the sun was fully up and the searing heat of South-East Asia was gathering intensity. Mac finished his water and was happy for some shade, although he could've done without the centipede crisis. They were everywhere in the undergrowth and he had to shift his hide twice to escape the little bastards.

Visitors came and went from the cemetery as the morning progressed. They painted, they cleaned and they socialised; they brought flowers, they strummed guitars and sang songs. Meanwhile, Mac hid among the trees, sweating profusely as the humidity raced to keep up with the temperature. At 10.03 am Mac took a quick pee-break and turned back to see a Timorese man moving towards the drop box. His heart rate rising, Mac got down into a crouch, slipping the Beretta into his waistband at the small of his back. The man – white baseball cap, tallish and middle-aged – walked past the drop and continued for another ten plots. Then, looking around, seemingly casual but doing a full sweep, he moved back the way he'd come and stopped at the Salazar grave.

His pulse pounding in his temples, Mac tried to stay composed. Dropping to his knees, the man looked around again, moved the casement lid sideways, trying to hide the manoeuvre with his body. His hand came back, went into the right pocket of his chinos, pulled something out and then the lid was back in place and the man was on his feet.

Panting with nerves, Mac watched as the man took the red flower out of the cup and left the grave, wandering along as if he had all the time in the world. As the cut-out retraced his steps onto the main road, four Brimob cops in tan fatigues strolled into the cemetery, one of them with a German shepherd straining on a leash. Gulping, Mac watched the cut-out check the threat and keep walking. Smart guy, thought Mac as the cops totally ignored him, lost in some joke they were carrying on.

The morning was almost blown. Mac couldn't check the drop box with Brimob in the graveyard and he was faced with either following the cut-out or waiting half an hour until the Brimob cops moved on and then grabbing the note from the drop box.

If Mac wanted to make contact with the cut-out, he'd have to stay in the cemetery until he could clear the box.

There were several pressures on Mac's time, not all of them official. Jessica had talked deep into the night. He'd heard about growing up in Canada and student life at UCLA, but one thing had stuck in his mind and he winced at the memory. She'd held his hands and wept with appreciation when he'd said one of the dumbest things he'd said for a long time: 'I'll help you find your father.'

CHAPTER 13

Mrs Soares had a message for Mac when he got back to the Turismo. It said, *Luzon Inc. samples arrive at 2 pm.*

Looking at his watch, Mac groaned. He had two hours to hydrate himself and get a kip before Bongo turned up. He was exhausted.

Folding the message and putting it in his pocket, he asked Mrs Soares for two large bottles of water and a lunch menu, then headed for the beer garden. Relaxing at his table in the shade of the banyan, Mac cased the hotel's internal balcony that wrapped around two sides of the garden like a dress circle. The upstairs areas seemed abandoned, but that didn't mean no one was up there.

There was a garden tap with a green hose looped over it. Mac knelt and washed his face and neck and then let the cool water run through his hair. The cemetery drop had been a washout. Brimob patrolled the place on regular loops and Mac hadn't been game to break cover and clear the box. It would have to wait for the evening, and now he'd lost the cut-out too. Mac liked to have information and he liked to have more of it than the other guy.

Mrs Soares appeared with two big bottles of Vittel and Mac ripped the top off the first and started drinking. After gulping at the refrigerated water for ten seconds, he realised Mrs Soares was still standing there waiting for his order.

'The chicken, thanks, Mrs Soares,' he said, pushing the menu back across the table.

'Make that two,' came a woman's voice.

Jessica Yarrow, looking flushed, took the seat opposite without being asked and poured from the second bottle of Vittel into the glass. After gulping at the liquid, she kicked off her yachting moccasins.

'I can't believe how hot it is,' she gasped. 'How do you cope?'

'Just gotta keep drinking water,' said Mac.

Dropping her sunglasses to the table, Jessica drank some more and then rubbed a handful of water over her face and into her hair.

'Try Dili later in the year,' said Mac, 'when we're building for the monsoon.'

'What's the deal?'

'Deal is forty degrees in the shade – what you guys call one hundred and five. Add to that the ninety-eight per cent humidity and lots of whitefellas just pack it in. They go mad.'

'You'd probably find me in that bunch,' she said.

'Out at the airport at three in the morning, wandering around in your nightie, screaming for a plane?' said Mac, and chuckled.

'That's what happens?' she asked, wide-eyed.

'Sure,' winked Mac. 'Especially if they have to share a bed with a snorer like me.'

The Nokia glowed in the dimness of Mac's room as it rang. Reaching over, his face set badly from sleep, Mac saw the display *Luzon inc* on the screen.

'Hey, mate,' he croaked as he answered.

'Mr Davis, it's Mr Alvarez here from Luzon Incorporated. About our appointment?'

'Right down,' he said, throwing the phone on the bed and heading for the bathroom. Because he knew the cellular system was so easy to intercept, Mac had asked Bongo to stick with a protocol.

Walking into the blistering heat of the garden, Mac saw Jessica readying to leave a table. Saying his farewells to her was Bongo, now a blond-haired man with an earring and big Italian sunnies.

'Have fun,' said Mac as Jessica brushed past him.

'My shout for dinner tonight,' she said over her shoulder, not slowing. 'Okay, Richard?'

She was gone before Mac could tell her it was fine with him.

'Feeling better, sweetheart?' asked Bongo as Mac sat.

'Like the hair, Bongo,' said Mac, nodding at the Filipino's adventures with peroxide. 'And the earring too. What's your cover – Homo from Manila?'

'Lady man from Angeles City,' smiled Bongo, extending his big paw.

Shaking, Mac sat and eased back in the chair as Mrs Soares came into the beer garden. Over Bongo's shoulder, Rahmid Ali was reading a newspaper two tables away.

'Tell you what, Mr Alvarez,' said Mac. 'Man's not a camel.'

As Mrs Soares walked away with their order for beers, Mac became aware of Rahmid Ali at his right shoulder.

'Ali!' said Mac. 'Care to join us?'

Standing, Bongo put out his hand.

'This is Manny Alvarez, another sandalwood trader . . .'

'And coffee,' chimed in Bongo.

'From Manila. We're just wondering if we're the luckiest guys for having no competition around, or if we just don't know the bad news?'

'I think many businesses not letting people come to Timor for a while,' said Ali, a hint of anxiety about him. 'I won't join you. Just wanted to apologise for offering you my fax number. I wasn't trying to get you in trouble, Mr Davis.'

Laughing it off, Mac and Bongo watched Ali go as the Bintangs arrived.

'So, Mr Davis,' said Bongo, lighting a Marlboro and exhaling into the banyan. 'What we got?'

Going over his first day and night in Dili, Mac told Bongo about the competing military-commercial interests in Dili – one of which seemed to be run by Kopassus and the other by the mainstream army. Then he admitted to his failed attempt to follow the cut-out, the meeting with Damajat and the Sudarto sighting.

'If you met Amir, then you met Benni's younger brother,' said Bongo. 'He spent a lot of time in Aceh with Kopassus, but I saw him around Dili when I was bodyguarding the Canadian.'

'Well, shit,' said Mac, sipping at the cold beer. 'He's bigger than Benni.'

'Amir's scholarship at Northwestern?' said Bongo. 'That was for wrestling, brother. These people don't fuck around.'

'Nice family,' said Mac.

They talked it through and Mac admitted he needed to see the note in the drop box and then collar the cut-out. The rest of the gig would follow from that.

'Okay,' nodded Bongo. 'I got an idea. But if Benni's in Dili, then he's still my priority, right?'

'Sure, mate. Got a car?' asked Mac.

When Bongo gave him a *what the fuck do you think?* look, Mac got to his feet and stretched. But Bongo didn't move.

'Had a chat with the girl,' the Filipino mumbled, peeling the Bintang label.

Mac sat down again. 'Oh, yeah?' he said, sensing trouble.

'Yeah, Mr Davis, and she's a nice girl.'

Nodding, Mac waited for it.

'She's Canadian and she's looking for her father,' said Bongo, slugging at the beer but not taking his eyes off Mac.

'Look, mate . . .'

'It's a sad story, and she's gutsy for coming down here,' said Bongo. 'But let's not promise this girl something that might get all of us killed.'

'Shit, mate, I –'

'I don't understand you Anglos,' interrupted Bongo as he rose from the table and flicked his cigarette butt. 'You think you are the only ones who get horny?'

CHAPTER 14

Bongo came out of the Chinese general store with a pack of smokes and a small paper bag. Flicking his rupiah change to the kids in the shade of the awning, he got into the Camry. They drove south-east for a few blocks before Mac looked into the paper bag and found several strings of large red firecrackers, the ones called 'Thunder Bangers' when Mac was a kid.

'Diversion, huh?' said Mac, nervous.

'Keep it simple, McQueen – what I tell the Yankees.'

Passing the Dili Stadium, they turned left into the boulevard fronting the main gates to the Santa Cruz cemetery. Forty metres on, Bongo stopped the car and left it running to keep the air-con blasting.

'Meet you at the north wall,' said Bongo, lighting a Marlboro and checking the rear-view mirror. 'Reckon got five minutes, seven at the outside. And remember, brother – wait for my signal.'

Nodding, Mac slipped out of the car and onto the footpath, then Bongo did a U-turn, and headed back to downtown. Mac tried to cross the road casually, resisting the urge to run. There were slow-moving locals in the shade, a few mini-horses pulling their little carts and a handful of Timorese on pushbikes. Making it to the trees against the cemetery wall, Mac hid in the shade, feeling ragged from nerves and the intense heat. He'd dehydrated and exhausted himself in West Papua, and he should have taken a week off to recharge. But here he was again, talking to himself and losing track of time while he tried to work.

Two minutes later, Mac heard shouts and saw smoke rising over the houses from two blocks away. He waited, and waited, and then they started: a few bangs at the start, and then multiple noises, like a gunfight. One minute later a Brimob troop of four ran out the main gates, babbling excitedly as they cocked their M16s. Mac wanted to get running, find the gravesite and retrieve the message but the call didn't come. As he made to key his phone and call Bongo, the phone rang.

'Give it thirty seconds, brother,' said Bongo.

'Really?' panted Mac.

'Yep . . .'

As Mac waited, another troop of four Brimob stormed out of the cemetery.

'Didn't want to run into them, right, Mr Davis?'

'See you in five,' answered Mac, and set off.

Scaling the wall he landed in the shelter of the trees. The locals in the graveyard – mostly women, children and grandparents – mobbed together like sheep waiting for the wolf to show itself. In the massacre at the Santa Cruz cemetery in 1991, more than two hundred Timorese mourners had died after Indonesian soldiers and their irregular 'teams' had opened fire.

So the locals didn't feel safe in the cemetery anymore, and Mac was with them on that. He watched as they flocked towards the south of the cemetery, which put them further from the site Mac was focused on. When the ground in front of him looked clear, he broke his cover and stealthed through the plots. Making good time, he reached the twentieth path and paused behind a white crypt with a gold-painted crucifix over the door. Panting, he cased the area while the firecracker bangs continued.

Crossing the path Mac walked in a crouch between the plots, irritated that the cemetery was so spotless that there wasn't even any long grass or wild shrubs to hide in. The twenty-first path looked different by day, but Mac was alone and the locals had moved a hundred metres away. Mac crept towards the Salazar grave, trying to stay lower than the surrounding headstones.

Crawling the last few metres, he got into the lee of the casement and lay flat on the brown grass around the plot, listening for vehicles or footfalls. Raising his head slightly, he realised the bangs had stopped but the smoke was now high in the sky. Taking a deep breath, he pushed himself to his elbows and slid the casement sideways, opening it easily to reveal the cavity.

Which was empty.

Mac paused for a second, the ramifications pounding in his head.

'It says,' came a voice very close by as Mac started in surprise, '*She's not here. In case you're wondering.*'

Very slowly, Mac turned his head away towards the neighbouring gravestone, and found himself facing a small Colt handgun that was gripped firmly in a beautifully manicured hand. Rahmid Ali's other hand screwed up a small piece of paper and threw it at Mac. It bounced off his damp forehead as he lifted his hands in surrender.

'This is a little dramatic for me, Mr McQueen,' said his captor. 'Can we talk now?'

Staying as still as he could, Mac let Ali talk. Since being let loose on his first work-alone assignment six years earlier, Mac had dreaded the moment a Chinese or Indonesian agent got hold of him and demanded answers. He'd trained for it, thought about it and done all the mock exercises, and for good measure, he'd never tried to establish the identity of other field guys. He'd cultivated his own ignorance so if someone really wanted to pull his teeth and get intimate with the crocodile clips, they'd get a few corporate front addresses and nothing more. Now, sitting in Santa Cruz cemetery, a bit zonked from dehydration and the heat, he wasn't sure he had the fortitude for an interrogation.

'Things aren't what they seem,' smiled Ali, gesturing Mac up with the Colt.

Standing slowly, Mac let Ali expertly frisk him, taking the Beretta from his waistband and the Nokia from his breast pocket. Then, feeling a small push, he moved out onto the path and waited for instructions.

'Get your hands down,' said Ali. 'Go right.'

Mac did as he was told, his brain racing for the options. Either Ali was going to torture him and get one or two basic answers, or he was going to take him into the trees by the wall and execute him. Either way, Ali was heading to the wall where Mac was meeting Bongo. Would Bongo come looking for him? Probably not, mused Mac. Having created the diversion, Bongo would want to be heading away from the fire. He wouldn't even get out of the car.

Entering the shade of the trees, Ali kept his distance and gestured for Mac to sit down against the wall.

'Please listen,' said Ali, voice controlled. 'You must hear something.'

Pulling a folded sheaf of white A4 paper from his back pocket, Ali tossed it at Mac and shook a cigarette from a soft pack.

'Read it,' he said, as he lit up and inhaled.

There were three pieces of paper, stapled at the top left corner. The first page bore the Indonesian Army crest of a large eagle, wingtips touching over its head, a red and white shield on its chest. At the head of the document was the heading OPERATION EXTERMINATION, with the injunction in large bold type: GENERAL STAFF – EYES ONLY.

Scanning it, Mac picked up the gist from the intro and the headings. It seemed the Indonesian military intended to intimidate the Timorese population out of voting for independence; they were going to kill, imprison and deport pro-independence figures and their families, and if the ballot still favoured independence rather than integration into the Republic, the military and its militias were going to destroy public infrastructure, destroy crops and livestock, burn villages and . . .

Mac had to shake his head, get his eyes focused. The heat and fear were killing him.

Having wasted the villages and their farms, the military would engage in mass deportations of East Timorese to West Timor – the Indonesian side of the island – and Irian Jaya. The document was chilling; East Timor was a subsistence economy. If you wiped out the villages, the livestock and the crops, you'd be looking at a famine. The Indonesians had already killed a third of the East Timorese population since their invasion in 1975. Adding famine and mass deportations was a blueprint for genocide.

Throwing the paper on the soil beside him, Mac shrugged.

'Proud of yourselves?'

'Not me, McQueen,' said Ali. 'The generals.'

Mac wasn't sure what that meant. 'Is this new?' he asked, nodding at the papers on the ground.

'You read it before?' asked Ali, still steady.

'Well, I think we've come to conclusions about –'

'Have you seen that document?' Ali insisted, his eyes on Mac's.

'No,' said Mac, 'but the generals releasing their documents in English is a nice touch, Ali. On a silver platter for the Australians to go running off on a wild-goose chase.'

'We translate them,' said Ali. 'And get them to your guys at the section in Jakarta.'

'Really?' said Mac, surprised.

'Really.'

'This one?' asked Mac.

Ali paused, exhaled his smoke and finally broke his stare with Mac. 'No, McQueen – not this one.'

'Why not?'

'Because your people aren't interested,' said Ali.

Mac blinked hard to maintain concentration. 'You said *we* – who are *you*, Ali?'

'I'm working for the President.'

'Oh really?' scoffed Mac. 'Don't tell me, *personally* working for Habibie, that it?'

Ali stared back, no comment.

'Okay,' said Mac, slightly intimidated by a direct approach from the President's office. 'What do you want?'

'We need enough people in your DFAT and ASIS, and your armed forces, to see this. It's genuine.'

'Why not go direct to the Prime Minister's office?' asked Mac, confused now. Presidents dealt with prime ministers, not with spies crawling around in cemeteries, pretending to be sandalwood merchants.

'No use,' said Ali and shook his head. 'The Australian government has been swayed by the generals' propaganda, and the President is in no situation to stop this Operation Extermination. He wants a genuine ballot and a peaceful transition to independence if that's what East Timor wants.'

'He told our Prime Minister that?'

'Sure,' smiled Ali. 'The ballot is being held at your government's urging, remember?'

Mac nodded. 'So the generals undermine the President, and –'

'And your government sides with the generals, tells the world that the militias are not connected to the military, that it must be *rogue elements*, right?' Ali said. 'The President can't do this alone from Jakarta – he needs Australian government help. If the Aussies will change, the Americans will also change their East Timor posture.'

'Shit,' said Mac, sensing a trick. 'You're good, mate. You're very good.'

'I can't do anything more, except ask you to get this to the right people – people with open minds, if they still exist.'

'So, you BAKIN?' asked Mac, meaning Indonesia's version of the CIA.

'No,' said Ali, lighting a new cigarette. 'I was Kopassus intel –'

'Oh, great,' said Mac. 'Now I'm feeling comfortable.'

'But I became a military attaché and then diplomat under Soeharto, and I spent a decade in France in private business.'

'So?'

'So, I was asked to come back by my president – he needed an untainted intelligence operation that answered only to him. An inner circle.'

'Secret too, right?' smiled Mac.

'I'm still alive aren't I?'

Mac mulled on how quickly Ali would be assassinated if the generals knew he was doing secret intel work for Habibie.

'So why me?'

Ali laughed, and looked down at the handgun that was still steady at Mac's heart. 'There is a Javanese saying that you need a pure heart to be a pure warrior.'

Now Mac laughed. 'Mate, I'm no warrior – you know exactly what I am, so spare me the Asian proverbs.' His head swam with the possibilities: did Indonesia have a person in Canberra or at the Aussie Embassy in Jakarta? Who had fingered Mac as a man not with the pro-Jakarta program?

'You have the papers, they are genuine,' said Ali, looking around for an exit. 'I wasn't going to tell you this, but you may as well hear it. I believe, from sources on the general staff, that the document I gave you is a false flag for another campaign.'

'False flag? Inside the general staff?' said Mac.

'Maybe. They get the order signed off, so they're legal and they cover themselves,' said Ali. 'But there's either sections of the orders that most of the general staff haven't seen, or there's ambiguous clauses that let the rogues do what they want – you know how it works, McQueen.'

'Sure, so what operation is being hidden by this false flag?' he said, nodding at the document.

'Have you heard of Operasi Boa?'

Mac's head snapped up at that. 'Well, ah, maybe. What is that?'

Ali looked around, distracted for a split second. 'Something happening in the Bobonaro region. From what we can gather, it's –'

Ali's focus changed, his gun aimed upwards and a crack sounded half a second before a piece of Rahmid Ali's head disappeared, his immaculate linen chinos folding at the knees as he collapsed in the bushes. Trying to get to his feet, Mac was almost collected by Bongo as he landed in the leaves.

'I was going to jump him,' said Bongo, breathing heavily as he holstered his Desert Eagle, 'but then he was aiming at me. You okay?'

Mac was going to say something like *no worries*, but his head swam, his balance deserted him and as he reached out to Bongo he swooned like he had a really bad case of jetlag.

And then he was falling into darkness.

CHAPTER 15

The cacophony of bird and monkey cries roared into the room as Dili's late afternoon turned into evening. The fragrance of blossoms mixed with the smells of the Turismo's kitchen in the warm breeze. Slowly opening his eyes, Mac winced at the pain in his head then took in his surroundings. He was back in room 10 at the Turismo, tubes in his forearm, a dark-skinned man craning over his bed, and blond-haired Bongo leaning on the doorjamb.

'Mr Davis,' said the Tamil man, leaning down into Mac's face.

'Yeah,' said Mac, realising the Tamil was a doctor.

The doctor shone a pen-light into each of Mac's eyes, holding up his eyelids. A stainless-steel stand stood nearby, with two clear water bags hanging from it.

'My name is Dr Puri,' the man said, forcing Mac's mouth open and poking around on the back of his tongue. 'You fainted.'

'I did not!' snapped Mac, trying to sit up.

'Aah, doc, it was more like he collapsed, okay?' said Bongo, smothering a chuckle.

'Okay, so you collapse,' smiled Puri. 'But it same anyhow – you have a bad heat exhaustion, and you must rest.'

'I'm fine, doc,' said Mac, dizziness swirling in his brain as he eased himself upright. 'Just need some water and she'll be right.'

The headache intensified, causing Mac to sag back into a lying position, gasping from the pain.

Turning away from the bed, Dr Puri addressed Bongo. 'The drips must stay in until they're finished – should be about four hours. I'll come by, see how we doing tomorrow morning. Okay?'

'Okay, boss,' said Bongo.

'And, Mr Alvarez, don't let him walk around – he'll stagger like he drunk.'

'Situation normal, doc,' said Bongo as Dr Puri turned and left with his medical bag.

After making sure the door was locked, Bongo came back into the room and pulled a chair to the bedside.

'Thanks back there,' said Mac, pissed off that Ali was dead but thankful that Bongo had his Six. 'Ali wasn't going to shoot, but thanks.'

'I remembered him – no good,' said Bongo, shaking his head, lighting a Marlboro.

'Ali?'

'Yeah. Kopassus – remember him from the NICA days, and Ali's not his name.'

'And . . .'

'And I took care of it, okay, brother?'

Mac nodded. 'Looked in his room?'

'Affirmative.'

'Well?' asked Mac.

'Shipping dockets, requisitions, invoices for – I dunno – chemicals? And some other stuff.'

'Other stuff?'

'I'll show you later,' said Bongo. 'But I got something else.'

'Something else?'

'By the way, the Canadian girl is after you.'

'Coulda told you that,' smiled Mac.

'I'm serious – she's trying to find you,' said Bongo.

'Send her up – and what's this something else?'

'Well, actually,' said Bongo inspecting his thumbnail. 'It's more like someone else, but I didn't have a choice, okay?'

***

83

The visitors car park behind the Turismo was shrouded in darkness except for one weak floodlight. Mac felt the still-warm dirt on his bare feet as Bongo opened the boot of the Camry. A pair of panicked brown eyes looked back out of a man's face, his mouth gagged with shiny grey duct tape, dried blood caked around his ears and eyebrows.

Looking around again for Brimob or soldiers through the vine-covered wire fence, Mac looked back at the man. 'So this is the cut-out? You sure, mate?'

'He admitted it.'

'If you bashed me for long enough, mate, I'd admit to having a thing for Elton John, okay?'

Raising his eyebrows, Bongo nodded towards the man's face. 'That wasn't for his identity,' said Bongo. 'That was for Blackbird and Sudarto.'

Mac had almost forgotten that Bongo's main plan was to drop Benni Sudarto, but for obvious reasons he didn't want to do it in the Kopassus headquarters in Dili.

'And?'

'And he don't know where Sudarto's living, but he says the rumour is that Blackbird is alive and in the mountains somewhere.'

'A prisoner?'

Shrugging, Bongo pulled out his cigarettes, shaking one straight into his mouth.

The cut-out squirmed and Mac saw he'd wet his pants.

'Let him out,' said Mac, standing back.

'You kidding? Why don't we just walk into Damajat's office, ask him to start breaking our fingers? You're still not right,' said Bongo, twirling his index finger around his temple in the international gesture for insanity.

'He's not going to Damajat, and he's not going to Brimob,' said Mac, looking back into the boot. 'He's told us too much, which means he'd die too if he ratted us out, and his family with him.'

The cut-out's throat bobbed at the mention of his family and Mac reached down, tore the duct tape off the bloke's face, bringing some black hairs with it. Gasping and spluttering, it took the cut-out a few minutes to regain his composure. Gesturing for Bongo's pocket knife, Mac cut the wrist and ankle ties and helped the man out of the boot.

Leading him towards the shadows, Mac grabbed the cut-out by the elbow. 'I'm not going to hurt you, okay?'

The bloke nodded, fear still etched into his face.

'I don't want to know your name, and believe me, mate, you don't want to know mine,' said Mac. 'What I need is everything you have on Blackbird, okay?'

The bloke, early forties and intelligent-looking, started with dignity but quickly fell into a sobbing mess. 'She's beautiful young girl, from good family, just trying to help her people,' he cried, tears streaming down his face. 'Why do these *Malai* take her? What right have they?'

'What's her name?'

'Maria. Maria Gersao.'

'You think she's still alive?'

'I have heard,' sniffed the cut-out, pulling himself together.

'Heard what?'

'That she in the mountains, being interrogated.'

'Lots of mountains round here, mate,' said Mac. 'Can we narrow it down?'

'People say Maliana, in Bobonaro, which is –'

'Yeah, I know. You said interrogated – about what?' asked Mac, trying to test the rumours. 'What would she know?'

'I don't know – I just organise the meetings,' he stuttered. 'I was never there. But she worked for the army in Dili and someone tell me she working on the intelligence floor – maybe she seeing things, hearing things, yes?'

Envisioning the first-floor admin section he'd seen on his trip to Damajat's office, Mac realised Blackbird would probably see all sorts of documents and security pouches in the course of a week. If she was young and cute, the Indonesian officers might have assumed she was stupid and gradually treated her as if she wasn't there.

'Was she hearing things about Bobonaro?' pushed Mac.

'I don't know, I –'

'Did you hear things about Maliana?'

'Yes, yes I did,' he sparked up. 'They say Sudarto is now based up there, and Damajat take a trip there three weeks ago.'

'What about the Canadian?' said Mac.

'I didn't know he was Canadian till he was beating me,' said the cut-out, pointing briefly at Bongo. 'He had a code name, I was the cut-out – you know?'

'The code name?'

'I'm not supposed to say that,' said the cut-out, flinching as Bongo shifted his weight.

'Starts with "centre",' said Mac.

'Okay – "stage". It's Centre Stage.'

'So you heard nothing about the Canadian?' asked Mac.

'Nothing.'

'I told you – I won't hurt you, mate,' said Mac, increasing his grip on the bloke's elbow. 'But this is important. So think – a successful white man disappears in Dili, and no one knows anything?'

'Nothing,' said the cut-out, looking at the ground.

Mac was momentarily overcome by dizziness and he shook it off before continuing. 'What do you do? For a living?'

'I don't know, that's not part –' he started, before Bongo fronted him, looked him in the eyes.

'Well? Not a state secret is it?' asked Mac.

'I'm a lawyer.'

'Really?' asked Mac. 'Anything we should know about?'

'That's a breech of my security,' said the cut-out, trying to look at Mac instead of Bongo's menacing face. 'I'm not to be indentified!'

'Then I guess you won't be needing that retainer from us any longer?' Mac needled.

'That's not fair – I did my job!'

'You doing any legal work for the generals?' asked Mac.

The cut-out kicked at the dirt, his face changing from defiance to shame. 'These people have made us slaves and whores, Mr Skippy. And like everyone else around here, I have to act like one of those things to make a living. What would you know about having to live like that, huh?'

Mac was about to say something clever about life in Rockhampton but then he saw tears in the man's eyes.

'You ask the Brimob and army,' said the lawyer, crying now. 'They say I make the paperwork – I make it legally clean – for their courts;

you ask the Falintil, and they call me a whore who sleeps in the murderer's bed.'

'Okay –' said Mac.

'You ask my children, Mr Skippy, and they say their father alive and can buy them shoes.'

'Look –' said Mac.

'So do not come into my world and be the judge of me!' yelled the cut-out, whipping his elbow out of Mac's hand.

'Okay then,' soothed Mac, shaking his head slightly at Bongo, whose hand was going for his Desert Eagle. 'On your way.'

Rubbing his wrists, the cut-out sniffed back tears, wiped his eyes with his forearm and looked from Mac to Bongo and back again, sensing a trick.

'I mean it,' said Mac. 'On your bike.'

As the cut-out exited the car park, Bongo turned to Mac. 'That stuff about the Canadian – he was lying.'

'I know,' said Mac, 'but now he's a liar who might feel he owes me something.'

CHAPTER 16

Finishing his breakfast mango, Mac reached for the coffee pot and refilled his cup.

'So where's Jessica?' he asked Bongo, who was eating toast opposite him in the Turismo dining room.

'Don't know,' said Bongo, making a show of checking his G-Shock. 'Told me she was starting early – thought we were meeting here.'

'Meeting?' said Mac, suspicious.

'Told her we could give her a lift somewhere, help her out, you know?'

'Bongo!' said Mac with a growl.

'I know what I said yesterday,' conceded Bongo. 'But she's serious about her father, so now I think it would be best if we keep her close and stop her getting into trouble. She has no idea, brother.'

'She having any luck with her old man?'

Bongo stopped his chewing. 'Her luck is not being arrested, not being killed. She's been in all the wrong places.'

'Fuck,' muttered Mac.

'Yeah, I been trying to keep an eye on her, but she's got the strong head.'

Checking for messages on his Nokia, Mac pondered the day ahead. He and Bongo were heading into the mountains, up to Ainaro and then down to the coastal plain on the south side of East Timor. That's where the sandalwood growers operated, and if he wanted to stay sweet with the military-commercial oligarchy that ran East Timor, it would help if he appeared to be doing business. On their way back to Dili, they were going to follow up on the papers Bongo had retrieved from Rahmid Ali's room. There was an Indonesian Army corporate front that Ali had been interested in, operating in the highland border region of Bobonaro, where it looked as if Blackbird was being kept.

But first Mac wanted to make sure Jessica wasn't doing anything stupid. She was smart and funny, but she had that North American assumption that the world was going to accommodate her assertiveness. That was fine in a bar in Santa Monica, but you only had to make one mistake in South-East Asia and you could find yourself in prison, or a lime pit. Mac felt protective about the girl, and Bongo looked uneasy about her no-show too.

Mrs Soares brought a new pot of dark Timorese coffee and Mac asked her if Miss Jessica was about.

'She gone,' said Mrs Soares.

'When?' asked Mac.

'Hour ago,' shrugged Mrs Soares. 'Two hour?'

Mac hissed as he looked at his G-Shock, which said 8.06 am.

The road south wasn't as bad as Mac remembered it, but as Bongo aimed the Camry at the mountain road it fast turned into a classic South-East Asian jungle track – ruts, one-lane corners, trucks and tractors trying to share the road with horse carts and women carrying baskets on their heads. They climbed steadily, the steep road bumpy and washed out in parts, smooth and winding in others. Monkey and birdcalls filled the air, the thick foliage that loomed over the road seemingly alive with animals.

'You still think this Ali was the real thing?' asked Bongo.

'Well, there was something about what he was saying – it fits with some of the problems I'm having with my government.'

Bongo sniggered, and Mac gave him a look. What Mac wasn't going to tell Bongo was that the defection two months earlier of

Tomas Goncalves had vindicated Ali's suspicions about Australian foreign affairs and intelligence. Goncalves was a long-time Soeharto confrere who'd established his own militia in the Emera region of East Timor in 1998. But after the generals had ordered the killing of pro-independence organisers, and then delivered three pick-up trucks filled with automatic weapons to the Emera militia, Goncalves defected. He was taken by ASIS to Macao, and was debriefed at ASIS's Hong Kong station. The Goncalves case was assigned away from Jakarta, which meant Goncalves could not be run as an agent and his subsequent debriefings were discredited in Canberra. It was a wasted opportunity, and illustrated a certain amount of policy blow-back in Canberra, where intelligence assessments are crafted to please the government of the day. That's what Rahmid Ali had been hinting at in wanting to speak directly with Mac.

'Okay, so you think Ali was telling the truth – why?' said Bongo, lighting a smoke.

'First, Rudi Habibie is a reforming president and that means the generals are against him. He's also from Sulawesi – he's not Javanese – which is a problem in Golkar. So it makes sense for Habibie to have his own intel operation.'

'He'll get killed for it,' smiled Bongo. 'But a new president, isolated from the military, would probably need his own spies?'

'Precisely,' said Mac. 'Secondly, BAKIN wouldn't try a provocation like that – sending Ali out to bait me – it's not their style. And the miliary intelligence guys? Why would they go dropping a document like that on me? What would that achieve?'

'Running in the wrong direction, McQueen – you know how that works.'

'Sure,' said Mac. 'But Ali said Operation Extermination might be an internal false flag, a cover for something worse.'

'Like the CIA leaks an eyes-only dossier on one thing, to keep the desk guys happy,' said Bongo, leaning on the horn behind a horse and cart, 'but the hard-ons are using it as cover for the real bad stuff? The black bag shit?'

'Yeah,' said Mac, aware that the Agency used that trick primarily as a funding mechanism. 'Ali wasn't trying to cover that – he *alerted* me to it. That's a bit too deep to be a simple deception.'

'So what's with the paperwork?' said Bongo, peering over at Mac's lap. 'What was he holding back?'

Shuffling the eight pages of A4 that Bongo had retrieved from Ali's luggage – all of them photocopied and initialled on the top right-hand corner – Mac thought about it.

'Well, Ali was collecting invoices and dockets from two companies which, judging by his notes, he believed were owned by the generals.'

'What do they do?' said Bongo. 'The companies?'

'Sumba Scientific calls itself a biochemical research company,' said Mac, flipping to a new page, 'and Lombok AgriCorp – Ali has a note that they claim to be coffee exporters and also developing agricultural technologies.'

'So why's Ali so interested?'

Mac looked back at the papers: Lombok AgriCorp had a Maliana address, but seemed to be out of town. Maliana was near the border with West Timor, in the militia-dominated Bobonaro region – a wild-west part of the world in which US spy satellites kept finding mass graves and NGOs no longer allowed their operatives to enter. Mac knew that the Red Cross had made Bobonaro a no-go area after the Indonesian Army was accused of chasing Falintil guerrillas using assault helicopters painted white and boasting a large red cross.

'What's that one?' asked Bongo, one eye on the road and the other on the papers.

Mac read the Bahasa Indonesia aloud with Bongo translating. The single-page, one-paragraph document was headed DEVELOPMENT REFORM CABINET – EYES ONLY: TIMOR TIMUR TRANSMIGRATION SOLUTION.

As they climbed higher into the mountains, Bongo translated a memo from early April which recorded a new policy being pushed by military elements in Habibie's cabinet. It advocated a new transmigration of families from Sulawesi and Java to East Timor, known as 'Tim-Tim' in Jakarta. The cabinet members wanted the government to support the migration policy with land, bonuses and an infrastructure build-out in the poorest of Indonesia's provinces. The Indonesian Army would supply logistics support.

'Sounds serious,' said Bongo.

'There's a final sentence,' said Mac, reading it aloud.

'What it says,' Bongo explained after a pause, 'is that the policy should aim to have one million migrants from Java and Sulawesi settled in Tim-Tim by 2009.'

There were just over seven hundred thousand East Timorese in the province, which was essentially a subsistence economy subsidised by Jakarta. The one million settlers would not be additional – they would have to be a replacement population.

'Shit, Bongo – what do they do with the Timorese?'

Before Bongo could respond, they rounded a tight corner and almost ran into the rear of a blue Land Rover Discovery belonging to the UN. Pulling over into the weeds, they waited as two UNAMET police in sky-blue shirts and UN baseball caps approached and motioned for Bongo to wind down the window.

'There's been a militia attack a hundred metres up the road,' said the Aussie officer. 'We're just clearing it for safe passage – if you could give us five minutes?'

Nodding, Mac could see a group of UNAMET police – civilian cops from Australia and Japan – walking back to the convoy. As Bongo pulled his Desert Eagle from beneath his seat and Mac touched his own Beretta for luck, the group reached their vehicles but one of them kept walking to the Camry.

'Any Australians in here?' asked a flushed ocker as he leaned in Bongo's window.

Mac opened the door and followed his fellow intel operator, Grant Deavers, around the back of a truck.

'Fuck's sake, McQueen!' snapped Deavers as they stopped. 'What the fuck are you doing up here?'

'Nice to see you too, Devo.'

'And please tell me, please assure me – that is not Bongo Morales with the hairdo?' said Deavers, fumbling for a smoke from his UN shirt pocket.

'Well, you know, Devo –'

'He still working the airlines?' asked Deavers, referring to Bongo's cover as a peroxide-haired first-class steward on Singapore Airlines, entrapping adulterers, homosexuals and paedophiles, then black-mailing them on behalf of Philippines intelligence.

'He's helping out,' said Mac sheepishly.

'He's with *us*?!' screeched Deavers, exhaling the smoke through his ginger moustache. 'Bongo's working for Aussie intel?'

'Mate!' said Mac, looking around. 'Do you mind? And by the way, it's Davis – Richard Davis, okay?'

Sucking on his smoke, Deavers shook his head. 'Sorry, mate, but this is getting on top of me. Dead set, Macca – *Richard* – this whole place is out of control.'

Grant Deavers headed the civilian police component of the UNAMET scrutineers but the cops had been denied the use of firearms during their mission in East Timor. He was from the intelligence arm of the Australian Federal Police and he had a military background. So the Indonesian generals played chicken with Canberra: your spook can run UNAMET's police, but there'll be no firearms. Before Deavers and his lieutenants knew what was happening, they were going to the new Killing Fields without so much as a six-shooter on their belts – not a happy scenario when the militias were using M16s.

'He was at the meet where some of our assets were snatched,' said Mac. 'Bongo lost a piece of his shoulder in the ambush.'

'Okay, Macca, but keep him away from the militias, okay? Last thing I need up here is that whole macho Filipino thing.'

Nodding, Mac asked what was happening beyond the convoy.

'Shooting,' said Deavers. 'Bunch of women walking to market.'

'Militias?' asked Mac.

'Yep,' snarled Deavers. 'The ones that don't exist, according to Canberra.'

'So, can we go through?' said Mac, pointing beyond the UN vehicles.

'Waiting for the soldiers to clean it up, secure the area,' said Deavers, his cigarette hand shaking slightly. 'Where you off to?'

'Maliana, Balibo – all the quieter spots,' said Mac.

'Do me a favour, Macca, and don't? Please?'

'That bad?'

'Bobonaro is wall-to-wall shit,' spat Deavers. 'It's a joke.'

'I'll think about it – we're looking for a local girl who may be up there.'

Deavers shrugged

'Her name's Maria Gersao, probably being held by Kopassus intel.'

Raising his eyebrows, Deavers shook his head. 'Kopassus has a depot in Maliana but it's a bloodhouse, mate, I'm warning you.'

'Where?' said Mac.

'The Ginasio – big place in the middle of town.'

Swapping phone numbers, Mac shook with Deavers. Then, looking up, he saw an army troop truck rumbling downhill. Through the canvas sides Mac could see the soldiers sitting on the bench seats. Among the regulars were young men in T-shirts and jeans.

The second troop truck stopped and while Deavers had a quick chat with the driver, Mac got a clear look through the canvas sides.

Stunned, he stared at the departing trucks as he staggered to the Camry, sagged into his seat, almost disbelieving his own eyes.

'Everything okay?' asked Bongo.

'No, mate,' said Mac, reaching for his water. 'There were militia in the back of those trucks.'

'That surprise you?'

'They were wearing army boots.'

'So?' asked Bongo.

'Aussie army boots!'

CHAPTER 17

They found Jessica entertaining a couple of Aussie UNAMET officials in a coffee shack on the outskirts of Aileu when they stopped for lunch.

'It's not safe out here, Jessica,' murmured Mac, stopping at her table. 'Thought I told you that.'

'I'm okay – got Dan and Lance helping me out,' she said, smiling towards her drivers. 'Have a seat.'

'Boys,' said Mac, nodding at the blokes as Bongo came to the table, glaring at Jessica and then the Aussies.

'Richard is a sandalwood merchant,' Jessica told her new buddies, blue eyes flashing beneath a blonde fringe. 'I thought he was going to help with my father, but –'

'But I can't help you with anything if you go off hitchhiking into militia country,' said Mac, trying not to sound annoyed with her. 'There are people out here who'd be happy to put you in a grave with twenty other women.'

'I didn't hitchhike. The boys picked me up outside the Turismo this morning,' she said, ignoring Bongo, who was clearly seething.

Mac and Bongo's order arrived – cold spiced chicken on warm rice.

'You boys armed?' asked Mac, starting his meal.

'Nah,' said the blood-nut called Dan. 'Not allowed, mate.'

'So how were you going to defend her?' asked Bongo, eyeballing Lance. 'Don't you think a pretty white girl would get some attention out here?'

The blokes shrugged, embarrassed.

'Let's get it straight, Jessica,' said Mac. 'The Bobonaro regency is thirty k that way,' he said, pointing west. 'It's militia country – death squad country. It's the most dangerous eighty square kilometres in the world right now, and you're walking around with your arse hanging out of your shorts?'

Looking down at her exposed midriff and short shorts, Jessica dropped her smile. 'I'm sorry,' she said, looking up at Mac.

'No wukkers,' said Mac. 'Let's eat up and we'll give you a lift back to Dili.'

The tailing vehicle followed at a professional distance as Bongo, Mac and Jessica sped down the river valley road to Ainaro. Mac assumed the black Toyota LandCruiser with game-fishing aerials was Indonesian intel. If it was soldiers or militia, they'd be in a ditch by now.

'He's standing off,' mumbled Bongo, who rejected Mac's offer to take the wheel. Like many Asian drivers he didn't feel comfortable with the way Anglos handled a car.

'Who is?' asked Jessica, who had been demanding to know what Mac and Bongo would do to help her find her father, if she wasn't allowed to do it herself.

'Other driver,' shrugged Bongo. 'Thought I might let him go through.'

'Nah,' said Mac, looking out at the brown-grass grazing areas interspersed with stands of bush.

'No?' asked Bongo.

'Nope,' said Mac, who wasn't happy with the ground. The Royal Marines had taught him that if you had the opportunity – if it was your call – you should always make the choice about the battleground. Mac didn't want to stop out in the bush, on the side of the road, and allow some trigger-happy Kopassus intel hoon to approach from behind and do what he wanted. Sometimes it was easier to keep the balance by continuing to move.

Throwing his arm over the back of his seat, Mac turned and spoke with Jessica, though his eyes stayed on the LandCruiser.

'So, what was the disappearing act all about?' he asked, sipping from a bottle of water.

'Had a tip-off. Someone said Dad was in the mountains, near the border,' said Jessica.

'Tip-off, huh?' said Mac. 'From who?'

'Well, a rumour more likely.'

'From a little bird?' said Bongo, looking into the rear-view mirror.

'A local man followed me into a cafe, in Dili. He told me it was better not to hear his name.'

Mac frowned. In South-East Asia, being followed wasn't good for the health.

'Should have waited for us, Jessica,' said Bongo.

'I thought the UN option was safer, all things considered,' she replied.

Mac and Bongo swapped looks.

'All things considered?' smiled Mac.

'I don't know how you do business in this part of the world,' she said, levelling her gaze. 'But what I saw in the car park last night didn't look like a negotiation.'

Sighing, Mac turned back to face the road. 'Sometimes, Jessica, the way business works in South-East Asia –' Mac caught himself as he sensed Bongo hissing at him to stop. 'Um, I didn't mean your dad,' said Mac, turning to look at Jessica. 'I'm sure he's fine.'

But the moment had gone and Jessica looked mournfully out the window, putting on a brave face.

Turning back, Mac copped a withering glare from the Filipino.

'We okay for gas?' said Mac.

'Getting low,' said Bongo.

'Ainaro?' asked Mac.

'Ainaro,' said Bongo.

The three Pertalima pumps sat on the street outside the general store on the Ainaro main street. As they pulled up, Mac and Bongo reached under their seats for their handguns.

'My watch has fallen under my seat, Jessica,' said Mac. 'Could you grab it, please?'

As Jessica leaned over and searched under Mac's seat, the Land-Cruiser pulled alongside the Camry on Mac's side. Heart pounding up into his throat, the pistol grip slid in Mac's palm as the driver of the LandCruiser lowered his tinted window. Holding the Beretta just below the windowsill, Mac felt a surge of adrenaline and then a flood of relief as a familiar, well-groomed Indonesian face wrapped in dark sunnies appeared. Slowly, Mac lowered the concealed Beretta as the Indon's face lit up with a smile.

'Mr Richard,' said Amir, the spook he'd met with Damajat two days' earlier. 'Major-General Damajat extends his warm greetings and asks you to join him for lunch tomorrow.'

'Lunch,' rasped Mac, having dropped the Beretta into the door's map pocket. Bongo had backed off too.

'Yes,' said Amir. 'Major-General Damajat wishes to show you the facilities, sir. In Maliana, Mr Richard.'

'Okay, Amir,' said Mac, and listened to the directions.

As the LandCruiser sped away, Mac slumped in the seat.

'Okay,' said Jessica, chastened. 'Now I see what you mean about doing business down here.'

'Damajat runs an army-owned company on Timor,' said Mac. 'So if he wants to see me, I guess he'll see me.'

'Nice way of introducing themselves,' said Jessica.

'Yeah, well, I'm about ready for a few beers and an early turn-in,' said Mac.

'Amen to that, brother,' said Bongo.

The Republica guest house was behind Suai's main market area, on a small hill covered in lush greenery, beyond the wall with the graffiti reading I Love you Military. Faces peered out of shacks and tumbledown houses. Some houses had been reduced to charred stumps, others were peppered with bullet-acne. What looked like a makeshift refugee camp dominated the church grounds. It was a shanty town of blue and green tarps with scared white eyeballs staring out of the darkness beneath them. Suai's history in the last three months had been similar to the rest of East Timor's south coast: young men executed, women raped, houses and crops burned, markets ransacked. As if to underline the terror, someone had written *Lak Saur* on the churchyard fence, referring to a violent militia group operating from across the border in Indonesian West Timor.

Sitting in a lawn chair in front of the colonial-era guest house, Mac sipped on a Tiger beer courtesy of Mickey Costa, the owner. Mickey's establishment had seen better days, with its sagging iron roof and wave in the floor. Old garden furniture was dotted around the overgrown garden and by the deep red of the setting sun Mac could make out a few posts and some chicken wire that had once surrounded a tennis court.

Mickey appeared, brooding as usual despite his pixie face and spritely movements.

'No dessert, okay?' said Mickey, picking up plates that had contained leftover Portuguese chicken and the B-grade rice reserved for non-family diners. 'Keeping the fruit for breakfast, right?'

'Sure, Mick,' said Mac, smiling.

'Breakfast till eight, then no more. And in rooms by ten, okay?' snapped Mickey. 'Don't want soldier thinking free beers for him, right?'

'Good night,' called Bongo as Mickey walked away.

'Yeah, yeah,' came Mickey's muffled response.

Jessica grabbed more beers from the cooler and Bongo gave her his pocket knife to open them. After a couple of laughs, Jessica paused. 'Suppose I owe you two an apology, right? About this morning.'

'You'd be really sorry if the militias had got hold of you,' said Bongo. 'I've seen some bad places in my time, but this one . . .'

'I just got so frustrated, you know?' said Jessica, shaking her head. 'The Canadian Embassy in Jakarta had no idea what was happening in Dili and didn't even want to send anyone to find Dad – said they were taking people out of East Timor, not sending them in.'

'Smart guys, the Canadians,' said Bongo.

'Well, you two are here,' countered Jessica. 'It can't be *that* bad.'

'It's that bad,' said Bongo, expressionless. 'We went through Ainaro today. Remember?'

'Sure,' said Jessica. 'How could I forget that lunch invitation?'

'A few weeks ago a whole bunch of foreign aid workers and UN people were evacuated from Ainaro because the Australians uncovered a plot,' said Bongo.

'What kind of plot?' said Jessica, sipping her beer.

'The local militia group was going to tell them that the road to Dili was closed, and send them up to Dadina instead.'

'What's at Dadina?' asked Jessica, eyes wide.

'The Kara Ulu river – the militia planned to drown the lot of them because the locals had been telling too many stories of atrocities.'

After that Mac tried to keep the talk away from the violence in East Timor. Jessica had some guts and determination about her and as much as he wanted her back in Dili and out of the way, it seemed unfair to frighten her into abandoning her search.

They'd almost finished the Republica's beer supply when Jessica got enough momentum to hold forth on why the Indonesian military might be justified in its violence.

'It's all the postcolonial oppression,' she said. 'You know – doing unto the son what was done to the . . . I mean, well you know, passing on the brutality . . .'

'They teach you this at UCLA?' asked Bongo.

'It's just the facts – it's a cultural renaissance after being oppressed by the European hegemony.'

'Indonesia became a republic fifty years ago,' said Bongo, amused. 'And they invaded East Timor twenty-four years ago.'

'Well, yeah –' started Jessica.

'So I suppose now it's the turn of Falintil guerrillas to massacre people? 'Cos that's been handed down, right?'

'You know what I mean, Manny – it *started* with the Europeans,' Jessica retorted.

'No, Jessica, it started with the Malay archipelago being a sought-after resource, fought over by maritime traders, Malay dynasties and pirate-kings. *Asian* ones!'

'Yeah, but Europeans subjugated their culture!'

'Really?' laughed Bongo. 'Ask someone from Ambon or Aceh if the Javanese culture is *subjugated*.'

Annoyed, Jessica turned to Mac. 'What about you, Richard? You agree with me?'

'Nuh.'

Bongo laughed, slapped his leg and picked a cigarette from his soft pack.

Grabbing three more beers from the towel-covered case, Jessica levered the caps and sat down. 'You've been very quiet – you must have an opinion.'

'About Indonesia?' asked Mac.

'What else?' she said.

'I agree with Manny – this region was always important because of the maritime trading routes which brought power and money. It has nothing to do with the Dutch or Americans.'

'And now? I mean, Indonesia has been through decolonisation, and Soekarno and Soeharto and the development into a modern nation –'

'Yes,' said Mac, 'and it still represents maritime power. The United States, Japan and China fear an Indonesia that can't hold at the centre and so they usually back the military, to stop the country disintegrating.'

'Why don't they want Indonesia disintegrating?' asked Jessica, puzzled. 'I thought everyone was out to destroy Indonesia?'

'Well, that's a nice theory in a leftie classroom,' said Mac, swapping a smile with Bongo. 'But Indonesia sits across sea lanes that bring LNG, iron ore and coal to Japan and China, and crude through the Madura Straits for the California refineries. If Indonesia fell apart it would hurt the super-economies – the Chinese wouldn't let it happen. And that's before we get to the Yanks.'

'That bad?'

'One theory says that if East Timor and Aceh separated, then Mindanao would follow and so might southern Thailand and Ambon. Pakistan and Iran would aid the Muslim separatists, and there'd be pressure on nations like the Philippines and Australia to help the Christians in the South Moluccas. As far as trade is concerned, it would be a mess.'

When Jessica left for the ladies, Bongo cleared his throat. 'Something you should know, McQueen.'

'Yeah?' said Mac.

'Yeah – I agreed to do some basic bodyguarding of our princess here,' said Bongo, gesturing with his thumb. 'She shouldn't be here, but since she is, she needs protection.'

Mac looked Bongo in the eye. Locals protecting foreigners was not unusual in South-East Asia. 'So long as it doesn't get in the way of our arrangement, that's okay,' he said.

Bongo stood and messed Mac's hair. 'Don't need you in my room tonight, sweetheart – you snore too loud.'

'Nah, mate,' said Mac, blushing a little. 'It's not like that.'

'Try telling *her* that,' said Bongo, winking and making for his room. 'Oh, and by the way –' He stopped as something occurred to him.

'Yeah?' said Mac.

'Be careful of Damajat tomorrow, but pay extra attention to your new friend, okay?'

'Who, Amir?' said Mac.

'He's out to prove himself to his big brother,' said Bongo. 'So stay cool and none of the smart mouth, okay, brother?'

With Bongo gone, Mac repeated his concerns to Jessica about a pretty white girl wandering around East Timor asking questions about her missing father. 'But if you really have to be here,' he said, 'I'm glad Manny's looking out for you.'

'I'm trying to be careful,' she said. 'And I don't want to create any trouble. But, you know, he is my father. I can't just sit back in LA and wait for a phone call.'

Mac nodded his understanding.

Then, with a flash of her blue eyes, Jessica asked unexpectedly, 'So are you gay?'

'What made you ask me *that*?' asked Mac, laughing.

'Well . . .' she said, indicating a pair of shapely tanned legs sticking out of her shorts.

'Yeah?' said Mac. 'So?'

'You spend two days with me and don't even flirt?'

'What was that first night, in the dining room? That didn't count?'

'Nice warm-up,' teased Jessica, sipping her beer, 'but no follow through.'

'Jesus Christ!' said Mac to the night sky. 'I've been busy, okay? We're not in high school here.'

'I wasn't that interested anyway,' said Jessica.

They looked at each other for a moment and then beer spurt out of Jessica's mouth as she laughed along with Mac, an emotional release from an unhappy, stressed woman.

'Now look what you've made me do!' she accused, looking down at the beer on her blouse.

'That'll teach you to keep your shirt on when you drink beer with me.'

As their laughter subsided, Jessica tucked her feet under her bum and fixed Mac with a look. She was so beautiful, thought Mac: high cheekbones, large blue eyes and thick blonde hair falling to her shoulders. Her political views were not as irritating as he pretended – they were similar to the opinions held by many Australians who worked in Canberra and dabbled in Indonesian politics.

'Manny gone to bed?' she asked.

'Yep,' said Mac.

'Shame to wake him.'

'What I thought,' said Mac, holding her stare.

'There's something I want to tell you,' said Jessica, putting the empty Tiger bottle on the ground. 'Yesterday, when I was asking around, showing pictures of Dad, I ended up at a hotel called the Resende – heard of it?'

'Sure,' nodded Mac.

'The manager wasn't around and I went down this hallway, looking for him.'

'Okay,' said Mac, trying to sound neutral but not liking the idea of Jessica interrogating people in a hotel owned by the Indonesian Army.

'I got talking with this Timorese woman – I think she was a housemaid or cleaner.'

'Yep,' said Mac.

'I showed her the picture of Dad, and she recognised him instantly, even said *Canadian* when she pointed at the photo.'

'So she knew something?' asked Mac, alert.

'She said Dad used to have lunch twice a week with the military, at the hotel,' said Jessica, clearly confused. 'What do you think that's about?'

Mac shook his head and said he'd have a think about it. 'Could mean his import-export work was with the army's companies. You know they own most of the trade concessions in East Timor? That's one of the reasons they don't want to let this place go.'

Silence fell between them for a while until Jessica yawned, rose from her chair, then stretched and bent over Mac, putting her hands on the top of the lawn chair on either side of his head. The kiss lingered and Mac didn't lay a glove on her – he was tired and let himself enjoy the kiss and the smell of her hair.

'I'm off to bed, Mr Richard,' she said as she surfaced. 'Wanna tuck me in?'

'Sure,' said Mac. 'Be with you in a minute.'

Sitting back, Mac thought about how Jessica's conversation at the Resende fitted in with the last page of the papers recovered from Rahmid Ali's room. It was a memo saying the bills of loading and the freight contracts were written through a freight forwarder in Surabaya called Millennium Freight Inc. The last sentence of the short memo had read: *Millennium has offices in Fremantle, Surabaya, Manila, Hong Kong and Osaka. Its head office is in Vancouver.*

Mac exhaled and wondered how he could have missed it. Bill Yarrow wasn't some random fool selected by the firm to risk his neck in Dili. He was more than likely the import-export arm of Damajat's business interests. If you were a Dili-based import-export guy like Yarrow, you were doing business with the generals, and Mac should have seen that from the beginning – it should have formed part of Atkins' work-up on the Canadian.

Jessica's dad hadn't wandered innocently into something he didn't understand, thought Mac. The Canadian had known too much.

CHAPTER 18

They set off before dawn and drove north, Bongo regaling Mac and Jessica with tales of the impact his rather difficult Javanese mother had on his childhood in Manila.

'The whole neighbourhood was scared of my mum,' said Bongo, lighting his first cigarette for the day. 'They wondered what kind of Catholic tells off the priest for his Easter service.'

'Sounds like my mum,' said Mac, laughing. 'At least, what she sounded like in the car on the way home.'

'No, brother – my mum is telling him off when we're filing out. Everyone called her "Java", and Java was never wrong about anything.'

Approaching the crossroad at Zumalai, Bongo turned left and drove straight into the first roadblock of the day – a white wooden boom lowered across the dirt track with a hut on the side of the road surrounded by sloppy sandbags.

Waiting in the Camry, the engine humming, the tension built in Mac's stomach as the soldiers failed to show. Finally, a guard in the flashings of the 745 Battalion emerged, squinting at the car, his gait unsteady.

Bongo lowered his window as the soldier pointed his M16 and looked in at the occupants of the car. The reek of stale booze floated into the Toyota as another soldier skulked out of the hut, squinting like a vampire.

As Bongo chatted with the first soldier, Mac picked up enough Bahasa Indonesia to sense a shakedown in progress: a car full of foreigners was going to attract a toll. But when Bongo produced Damajat's letter, the soldier's bleary eyes widened, then he staggered backwards and passed the letter to his colleague.

Keeping his cheery demeanour, Bongo continued his patter. Mac's fear made the morning coffee rise in the back of his throat and he felt the Beretta with his fingertips, under his seat.

The two soldiers suddenly shouldered their rifles and pointed at Bongo, who put his hands in the air. Then, just as quickly, the two men laughed, Bongo laughing along with them.

'Fuck's sake, mate,' muttered Mac as they accelerated away from the post, carefully folding the Damajat letter. 'The sense of humour isn't working for me.'

As they rounded the first corner they encountered a scene on the side of the road.

'Don't stop,' said Mac, as they approached and saw a small crowd of women and kids huddled in front of a bunch of militias who were throwing baskets in the back of a Toyota pick-up. One old woman was struggling with a youth, not letting him take two chickens she was holding in a bamboo cage.

'What are they doing?' asked Jessica as Bongo drove past with a brief wave to the armed youths.

Twisting to look behind, her voice rose. 'They're *robbing* those women!'

Mac and Bongo exchanged a look and breathed out.

'Look to the front, Jess,' said Mac firmly.

'I'll look where I want, thank you,' she said, leaning over the front seats. 'Why don't you two do something?'

'Like what?' asked Mac, happy that Bongo was keeping his foot on the gas. 'And don't look back – it might be misconstrued.'

'You!' said Jessica, hitting Bongo on the arm. 'You're my body-guard – I want you to go back and stop that!'

'Are they following?' Mac murmured to Bongo.

'Not yet,' breathed Bongo. 'Just standing and looking.'

As they rounded the corner, Mac turned to face Jessica. 'You gotta watch how you look at armed men in this part of the world,' he said quietly. 'Those women will be lucky if they just get robbed. If we stop it could easily turn into a massacre, and we'd be part of it, understand?'

'I can't sit in a car and watch an old woman be robbed!' said Jessica, furious.

'Better to be ashamed and alive,' said Mac.

'That old woman back there didn't agree,' said Jessica. 'At least she's standing up to those thugs.'

'She could be lying down too,' retorted Bongo. 'With a bullet in her.'

As Bongo checked his side mirror, Mac watched Jessica's middle finger rise and point at Bongo.

'Saw that,' smiled Bongo.

'But didn't see that back there?' snapped Jessica.

Mac let the argument go and settled back in his seat for the ride up to Bobonaro, his breakfast churning with worry.

The second roadblock was placed on the major spur out of Lepo, before the descent into the town of Bobonaro. This time the roadblock was deserted.

Getting out of the Camry, Mac and Bongo checked in the guard house and found it abandoned, a portable CD player with Glen Campbell's *Greatest Hits* playing at half-volume. Looking more closely, Mac saw that the player was on 'loop', giving him no idea of how long the soldiers might have been gone. Fifty metres along the road was a yellow Toyota pick-up, with no sign of passengers.

Shrugging, Mac lifted the boom gate and they were heading back to the car when they heard whimpering noises coming from behind the guard house. Mac nodded at Bongo and they both retrieved their handguns from the Camry as quietly as they could.

'Stay here, Jessica,' said Mac, then closed the door softly.

Following Bongo into the bush, Mac swung the Beretta in arcs, looking for soldiers or militiamen. Several metres into the jungle, Mac ran into the back of Bongo. Sitting in front of him, against a tree, were five local children aged roughly four to nine, huddled together and scared.

Bongo started talking gently and once one of the kids was at least nodding or shaking her head, he squatted in front of them. Hearing his calm voice, and watching the kids respond with more expression at every question, Mac realised Bongo must have worked with distressed kids before.

As the kids pointed further into the jungle, some wide-eyed and crying, Bongo stood and turned around, fury in his eyes.

'Their mothers and sisters are down there, in the creek bed,' he hissed. 'The soldiers and militia too.'

Gulping, Mac wondered how he could deter Bongo from a take-down. Mac's identity was a cover and he didn't want a shoot-out ruining it.

'How many?' he asked, hoping Bongo would be prepared to walk away from the bad odds: *be alive and ashamed*.

'Five militia, three soldiers,' muttered Bongo, clearly fighting the inner argument between being realistic about the odds and wanting to engage with the enemy.

'Let's get to Bobonaro, mate,' said Mac, hating the words even as they came out of his mouth, but knowing it was the right choice. 'It's not our fight.'

'Timor your fight, McQueen? Jessica your fight?'

'Come on, Bongo,' said Mac.

'I heard about that village in Mindanao – you didn't have to do it that way, brother, 'cos it wasn't your fight, right?'

Shrugging, Mac kicked at a leaf. The Mindanao job was a lapse in judgment, a risk he'd taken to help some women and their kids.

'In the army, we had a rule,' said Bongo. 'We all matter or none of us do.'

'About time,' came a female voice from behind Mac, and he spun around to face Jessica.

'Shit, Jess!' said Mac, annoyed at the danger she was putting herself in and embarrassed at his role in the conversation with Bongo. 'What the fuck are you doing down here?!'

'What are those?' asked Bongo. Jessica carried an M16 in each hand.

'They were in that pick-up,' she shrugged. 'Thought maybe we could use them?'

'There's no *we*, Jessica,' said Mac, reaching for the weapons. 'You stay here with the kids – we'll go have a look, okay?'

Checking the M16s, Mac ejected the mags and weighed them in his hand; they were thirty-rounders and felt almost full. The kids cuddled into one another as Bongo handed Jessica his Desert Eagle and gave her basic directions on how to use it. Then Bongo and Mac stealthed in the direction the kids had indicated, making good time through the thin-undergrowth/high-canopy jungle.

They heard the soldiers before they saw them. Shouts, drunken laughter, aggressive lewdness, and wafts of Tuaka – an incredibly powerful Timorese palm wine.

'We do this,' whispered Mac as they crept forward, 'and we'll be fighting these pricks for the next two weeks.'

'Then we'll make it clean,' whispered Bongo.

Feeling the mission sliding out of control, Mac tried one last time. 'This isn't the gig, mate. We should be back in the car.'

'Tell that to the kids,' said Bongo, turning to look Mac in the eye.

It was a while before Mac broke Bongo's stare. 'Guess we're not talking about prisoners?'

'Who's talking?' said Bongo.

Gesturing Mac to stay behind a tree and move in one minute, Bongo shouldered his rifle and arced away to the left. Mac checked his G-Shock and shouldered his own weapon, steeled himself and prepared to count down the rounds from the twenty-five he suspected were left in the thirty-rounder mag.

His G-Shock showed thirty seconds till 'go' and Mac set the firing mechanism to 'single', cocked the M16's slide and started moving forwards through the light scrub, downhill towards the creek bed. Coming over a small spur, he walked up behind a hide created by a low bush and ducked down in kneeling-marksman pose as the scene opened before him: militiamen and soldiers, wandering around drinking, women's clothing across the ground, a set of knickers dangling from a tree branch and men standing around a naked girl – no more than fifteen – egging on another soldier who was having sex with her. Several women's bodies lay about the place with what looked like shots to the head. Obviously the brave ones who fought back, thought Mac.

Beading up on the nearest rapist, Mac took a quick look at his G-Shock as his heartbeat amplified. It was 'go' and he waited for the first shot, which came almost instantaneously from across the copse, taking out a soldier's head as he leaned back to swig from a bottle. Mac drilled his first target in the back, his second in the side of the ribs and then the head. The third target was a young militia member in a khaki T-shirt. Mac missed with his first two shots but then shot him twice in the upper chest as he bent for his rifle. The opening round was over in ten seconds. As the cordite cleared, the rapist lying on the girl was caught alone in the copse, unsure whether to go for his pants or his rifle. As his victim rolled away across the leaves, then looked for something to cover herself with, Bongo walked out of his hide, M16 shouldered, and executed the youth with two shots to the face.

Stalking out, adrenaline pumping, Mac saw seven or eight women moving in the undergrowth, looking for clothes, dazed, split lips, broken noses and black eyes. As Bongo murmured to them, Mac vomited, the rape and the blood too much for him. Surfacing from his retching, he was about to call Deavers at UNAMET and get him up to the scene, when the sound of Jessica's voice rang out through the jungle, followed by the Desert Eagle's distinctive boom.

'Shit,' muttered Mac, then ran across the creek bed and up the slope from where they'd come. He'd not gone ten strides before the boom of the Desert Eagle was responded to with the clatter of M16s and the crack of branches.

His heart pounding in his chest, Mac sprinted back to where they'd left Jessica and the kids, but as they got closer, Bongo came up from behind and grabbed Mac by the arm, gesturing for him to stop and look around. Militia members were now obvious through the trees to their right, distinctive in their khaki T-shirts. They were not close enough to have overrun Jessica's position, although they were now heading that way.

Opening fire with a few rounds, Bongo and Mac picked off some of the youths who were surprised by the flanking barrage. Hoping he could get to Jessica and the kids before the militia, Mac set off again to his left. Bongo's voice roared in his ears as he sprinted, but it wasn't until he almost stood on the still-rolling grenade that Mac realised Bongo had yelled, *No!*

Swerving two steps to the left, Mac dived over a large fallen tree thinking that if he got in close behind the trunk he'd survive the grenade. But as he sailed over the tree, his shoe caught a twig and pulled him head-first into a rocky outcrop. Not able to get his hands up in time, Mac watched the ground rush towards him and took the entire impact on his left temple.

CHAPTER 19

Mac slowly opened his left eye but the pain was so great that he immediately shut it again. Pulling himself into a sitting position as he opened his eyes again, he saw his M16 through the bushes and waited for footfalls or voices. None came and he staggered to his feet, wincing at the pain in his head. His temple wasn't bleeding but a golf ball had started under his hair. Moving to where he could see over the tree, he looked around. The area looked clear: there were no voices to be heard and the normal sounds of monkeys and birds had returned to the jungle.

His G-Shock said it was 10.49 am which meant he'd been unconscious for about twenty minutes. Finding his feet, Mac retrieved the M16 and scanned the spooky terrain. It was high-canopy jungle which gave fairly good vision but played tricks on the eyes, the slanting sunlight creating phantom humans where there was only trees and wildlife. His heart hammering, Mac moved carefully through the bush, wanting to call out for Bongo and Jessica but not game to identify his position and trigger more violence.

Doubling back to the tree where Jessica had stayed with the children, Mac found a number of bodies in the jungle, their khaki T-shirts with 'Hali Lintar' stamped in black, advertising them as local militiamen. But no Jessica – no kids.

Leaning on the tree, he checked and re-checked the rifle as he struggled with his guilt. If he'd followed Bongo's instincts, gone straight down to the river and dealt with the rapists – rather than arguing about it – then they would have been back in time to look after those kids. His desire for self-preservation had got in the way and he felt terrible. People in his position were supposed to look after the vulnerable and it reminded him of the night his father, Frank – chief of detectives in Rockhampton – had attended a scene where a violent drunk had been trying to scare his wife with a gun by shooting the wall around her. One of the bullets had killed the man's nine-year-old daughter in her bed. Mac's Mum, and many women around Rockie, had wanted that wife-basher dealt with years earlier and Frank had taken the episode very hard. He'd blamed himself, which was how Mac felt now.

Deciding to expand his search, Mac headed back down the slope to the river. The rapists and their victims were lying where Mac had last seen them, but there was no sign of the children or his travelling companions.

Trying to pull himself together, he realised there was still time to make Maliana and the meeting with Damajat. Stopping to deal with the rapists had been a disastrous move but if he played it right, he'd still have a shot at locating Blackbird and perhaps salvaging something out of the situation was the best he could expect.

At the road Mac stuck his head out slowly and noticed Bongo's Camry was no longer parked outside the guard house. Looking left and right down the road he realised the yellow pick-up truck was no longer around and the guard house still looked empty.

The road echoed with the sounds of vehicles approaching and Mac instinctively ducked behind a tree. Checking the M16 for load and safety, his breathing already fast and shallow, he realised he had no plan. What was he going to do? Ambush an army patrol? Hold up a militia convoy? At the same time, he couldn't wander around in the countryside; he'd already drawn too much attention.

Trying to calm himself, Mac watched as three dark blue Land Rovers pulled up to the guard house and a thickset Anglo man in sky-blues leapt out and walked in the door. Re-emerging, the man put his hands on his hips and looked up the road to where Mac was now standing in the open, waving.

**

Grant Deavers was not happy at Mac's appearance and was openly irritated by his story of being jumped by the Lintar militia.

'I thought we had a chat about the Bobonaro district, Davis? Those Lintars are the worst, mate.'

'Yeah, mate, I know,' said Mac, jammed between two Japanese cops on the back seat. 'But I had this meeting with Damajat –'

'Major-General Damajat?' asked Deavers, swivelling around to look at Mac.

'Well, yeah,' shrugged Mac. 'He wanted me to see his set-up. You know how it is. He's got no sandalwood but he wants me to see his operation.'

Deavers turned, staring at the terrain ahead. As a former intelligence officer in the AFP he wasn't about to ruin Mac's salesman cover, not in front of the Japanese cops. The problem with the UN was that the world's governments saw it as an easy way to get spies into a territory that might interest them, and the fact that Deavers was referring to Mac as 'Davis' hinted that he thought the Japs worked for Tokyo's intel apparatus.

'Yep, I know how it is – the country's going into meltdown and you blokes are running around trying to do business.'

'I had no idea how bad it was till I got into the mountains,' said Mac.

The Jap cop to his right was staring at him with hard eyes.

'*Konichi wa*,' said Mac, and held out his hand. 'Richard Davis – sorry about all this.'

'*Konichi wa*, Richard-san,' said the Jap, who bowed and introduced himself as Yoshi, but without taking his eyes off Mac's, contrary to the Asian custom.

They chatted for half an hour as they made for Bobonaro, Mac letting the Jap subtly test his salesman cover. As the town of Bobonaro came into view, Mac decided it was time to turn it back on Yoshi.

'So, champion, *Keischicho*, huh?' said Mac, using the nickname of Tokyo's metro police department. 'You know Shinzo Aso?'

Yoshi's face was blank.

'He was in your *Keibibu*,' said Mac cheerfully. 'A captain in section three?'

Yoshi feigned understanding, but he didn't have a clue. Which was fine, because neither did Mac.

Deavers dropped Mac at the market area in the centre of Maliana. To his left was a three-storey house that looked as if it doubled as a hotel, and across the road locals milled in the shade of an old banyan tree. This was the capital of the Bobonaro region, the border with Indonesian Timor just a mile or two away, and one of the nastiest parts of the world. The Hali Lintar militia – known as a *milsa* in Indonesian – had been implicated in public beheadings and the cutting out of tongues and eyes. There was no law in Bobonaro, except as laid down by the military – the same military which ran the Hali Lintar militia.

A yellow Toyota pick-up across the road caught Mac's eye as he walked north. Young thugs in Lintar T-shirts lounged around a stack of M16s on a tarpaulin, staring evenly at Mac as he walked past. Most of the shops were closed and three black water buffalo were wandering along further down the main street. The market area – a thriving hub in most parts of South-East Asia – featured a few blankets on the ground selling seven taros or one chicken. Women in brightly coloured woven skirts drifted about with items on their heads and kids either in slings or running behind. It was an eerie place that lacked the raised voices or kids' laughter of most markets, and Mac double-checked for his Damajat letter.

Not long after, he arrived outside the Ginasio Municipal Maliana, a large Portuguese-built structure with an indoor basketball-volleyball stadium. Vehicles were lined up on the grass in front of the white concrete veranda at the building's entrance and Mac's breath shortened as he noticed Bongo's silver Camry among the intel LandCruisers and troop trucks. The temperature had risen to a dryish thirty-nine and the midday sun beat down on Mac's latest injury. Bongo and Jessica were adults who had taken their chances in a volatile part of the world, he reasoned. Mac wasn't their keeper any more than they were his. Still, the sight of the empty Camry among the Indonesian military vehicles filled him with sadness. You never quite knew what to make of the intelligence that came out of East Timor, but if half of what Mac had heard about the Ginasio was true, it was the Kopassus interrogation centre for the western part of East Timor. The questions had probably just begun for Bongo and Jessica and it would be a very long day for both of them.

'Mr Richard,' came a voice and, looking up, Mac realised Amir and the other Kopassus spooks from Damajat's office were standing in the shade of the veranda.

'Boys,' said Mac warmly, still slightly surprised at Amir's size – it wasn't everyday that an Indonesian looked down on Mac. 'Sorry about the delay – I got bushwhacked on the way up.'

Moving into the veranda, Mac shook with Amir as the doors flew open and Major-General Damajat emerged, perfectly groomed, short-sleeved military shirt, gold paratrooper wings clipped to his breast and as chirpy as a boxer about to get in the ring.

'Mr Richard! Perfect timing,' he said, slapping Mac on the bicep.

Gulping, Mac turned to follow Damajat, determined to stay ashamed and alive. *It's not your fight*, he told himself as he slid into the black LandCruiser. *Not your fight.*

The lunch was fancy Javanese seafood rather than Timorese peasant cooking. The table looked out over the collection of large white buildings in the middle of the Maliana bush that were known collectively as Lombok AgriCorp.

'So you see, Mr Richard, these communist are dangerous,' said Damajat, with a theatrical Javanese look of concern. 'I tell the foreign journalist, but they not listen!'

The Kopassus spooks and a couple of scientists who shared the table laughed at Damajat's insistence that the Lintar militias who Mac had blamed for the lump on his head were in fact Falintil guerrillas. Mac had included Bongo and Jessica in his story, based on the theory that the best lies are built on truth. Where he diverged from fact was in telling Damajat that he had met them at the Turismo and hitched a ride to the south coast to meet with sandalwood growers. When they had left the car to check on something, Mac had stayed in the car and only left when he heard gunfire. He told them that when he'd entered the jungle to investigate, he was immediately hit with a rifle butt.

'You saying that the Falintil communists wear Lintar shirts,' asked Mac, pretending to be aghast, 'so that the militias get the blame?'

'For sure!' said Damajat, opening his eyes wide in a liar's tell. 'That what I'm trying to say!'

It sounded like the reverse of the story where the militias burned houses while wearing Fidel Castro T-shirts, hoping that the locals would think that Falintil was attacking them. But Mac decided to keep that one to himself.

'Well, I guess the army will have to take control at some point, eh Major-General?' mumbled Mac, not knowing what else to say.

'So true,' said Damajat, his face darkening. 'I tell politician, we have tried the soft talk – time now for the hard hand.'

The tour through the Lombok facility was a waste of Mac's time. The massive coffee bean roasters smelled great and the bulk packing room looked clean and busy as the beans were consigned to Melbourne, Athens and Dubai – all the places where coffee was consumed dark and strong. Though the villages and crops were burning, the Indonesian generals were still making their cut on East Timor's biggest cash crop. It had nothing to do with sandalwood statues of Mother Mary and it didn't look like the kind of facility where the Indonesian military would keep a traitor like Blackbird. If anything, the presence of a coffee-packing facility might be a front for criminal activity. The world's crime lords had used bulk coffee shipments to mask a variety of contraband over the years: drugs, diamonds, firearms and children, depending on whether the beans originated in Africa, South America or Asia. Mac's real agenda was to stay close to Damajat, get his trust, keep him talking and find a way to Blackbird. He doubted that Lombok AgriCorp was it.

Standing back at the LandCruiser, Mac started getting edgy. He wanted a ride back to the Turismo, to a hot shower and a cold beer, without being stopped at roadblocks or shot at by militias. He was going to reconnect with the cut-out – the lawyer he'd cut loose – and find another way to get to Blackbird. There was always another way, and in the process he might be able to do something for Bongo and Jessica. But for now, he was more concerned about his own safety. The Bobonaro district was malevolent, and Mac wanted a firearm.

Damajat walked towards Mac, deep in conversation with Amir Sudarto. Stopping, they looked at Mac, then Amir peeled away so that he and his henchman stood at his nine and three o'clock as Damajat walked straight at Mac. Keeping his shoulders soft and his breathing deep, Mac waited for it, but being unarmed he did not like his chances.

'Perhaps we should drop the pretence, Mr Davis,' smiled Damajat, smarmy but dangerous.

'Pretence?' said Mac, his heart pounding in his tonsils as he saw Amir push up his trop shirt to expose the SIG Sauer on his right hip.

'Yeah – see, we know who you are, Mr Davis,' said Damajat, putting an arm over Mac's shoulders and steering him towards another, larger building. 'And I think it's time we talked about some real business, okay?'

CHAPTER 20

The cool of the warehouse calmed Mac's heart rate slightly as they strolled through stockpiles of chemicals, alkaloids, peptides and enzyme reagents from all parts of the world.

'You see, Mr Davis,' smiled Damajat. 'I know about your procurement work at Surabaya in '97, right?'

Joking along, Mac tried to keep tabs on the spooks behind him – if he could get them at the correct angles, he might be able to kick one and grab a gun. He wasn't game to meet Amir in a fist-fight.

'After you come to the office in Dili, I run the checks, right?' said Damajat.

'Well, Major-General, I suppose I do have some abilities beyond sandalwood –'

'And contacts,' snapped Damajat, squeezing on Mac's arm.

'Well, those too. Sure,' said Mac. As Richard Davis, Mac had made a successful infiltration in Surabaya, where Canberra thought there might be an illegal drug facility being developed. It turned out to be a bunch of Thais trying to counterfeit paracetamol. Mac had inveigled himself into a role as the go-to guy on the feedstock procurement side – a man with the ability to source chemicals from all parts of the world, camouflaging them in paperwork so confusing that no one would ever be able to put the jigsaw together.

Stopping to let a forklift go past, Damajat guided Mac further down the stockpiles of supplies.

'You see, we are on the verge of a big breakthrough in terms of – how you say it? – life sciences, biotech. You know this term?'

'Yeah, I've heard about it,' said Mac, thinking of it as messing with genetics to get a rice crop that grows faster; or messing with a prospectus and get a stock that mutates on the NASDAQ. 'So, Major-General, where's all this come from if you need a procurement program?' Mac added, pointing at the barrels and canisters.

Signalling for Amir and his sidekick to move on, Damajat strengthened his grip on Mac's arm and said in a conspiratorial tone, 'We had somebody looking after it for us – but he no longer with us.'

'Really,' said Mac, now understanding who the Canadian had been working for while spying for ASIS. 'Looks like he knew what he was doing.'

Pausing, Damajat looked deep into Mac's face. 'Time to show you something, yeah?'

'Okay,' shrugged Mac, knowing that Damajat had revealed knowledge of his criminality in Surabaya as a threat of exposure.

'But from this point, no talk about this place, this people, okay?'

'Sure,' said Mac, feeling the man's gaze.

'I must trust you on this, Mr Davis, for your own safety, right?'

'Sure, Major-General.'

'Because you start talking and some people not like it, right?' whispered Damajat. 'They think you a spy.'

They looked at each other until Damajat winked. 'Call me Anwar,' said the Indonesian, before turning and gesturing for Mac to follow him out of the warehouse.

'I'm impressed,' said Mac, looking out from Damajat's mezzanine office through triple-glazed glass. Below them was a white-tiled laboratory where people in biohazard suits moved about like actors in a 1950s space movie.

'Twelve million US!' said Damajat as the secretary put the coffee tray on the desk and poured. 'German engineer, Israel scientist – it a bio-safety level-three facility, the best outside of Singapore.'

'And built by Anak-Poco Group, right?' said Mac.

'Of course,' said Damajat. 'On time, on the budget – the Timors not try the lazy native with us!'

Sipping at his coffee, Mac tried to make sense of it. The place was filled with centrifuges, computers, glass-sided sealed boxes, banks of switches and lights. He'd just been offered a retainer of $30,000 a month to procure the supplies, with a $200,000 bonus when the job was completed. The whole thing reeked of a 'black books' program, using foreign nationals as procurement agents to hide an Indonesian military project. The question was, why?

'So, what are we making here?' Mac asked casually, intent on not seeming too curious.

'Let's say it a medical breakthrough,' said Damajat, putting three spoons of brown sugar in his coffee.

'What's the disease?' asked Mac.

'You don't need to know that, Mr Davis,' said Damajat, hardening. 'Let's say that there's a virus that is fatal, but if you have good scientist, you can re-engineer virus so it don't kill no more.'

'Sounds brilliant,' said Mac, losing interest. His real focus was how to use Damajat to find Blackbird.

The intercom buzzer sounded suddenly and Damajat spoke into it. Rising from his seat he whisked a file off his desk. 'I'm back in five minutes. Look at this, tell me what you think, right?' he said, handing Mac two pieces of paper. 'Let's talk about what is easy and what is not, okay?'

As Damajat's shouts echoed along the corridor, Mac looked down at the procurement lists on the A4 pages and saw the kinds of words he'd memorised in high school chemistry. There were huge volumes of the stuff – this wasn't a small operation.

Standing, he walked to the glass and had another look down on the facility. The people in biohazard suits walked about slowly and one person seemed to be running the show. Mac had no interest or expertise in what he was looking at – he wanted to find Blackbird, establish the meaning of Boa and then get out of East Timor before the place imploded. The scene with the militia rapists was not Mac's idea of a job well done. His job was to collect inform-ation covertly and pass it on, and stopping to deal with a bunch of drunken militiamen on the side of the road had been a total screw-up.

Moving to the door, he listened but heard no voices. He started with a quick search of the ceiling for a security camera and, not finding one, moved to the walls; there was a large day-planner with letters in red texta marked on some of the days, and a portrait of Rudi Habibie, President of the Republic – but no safe behind either.

Doubling back to check the day-planner, Mac scanned the dates. They were mostly acronyms but he fixed on the box for 7 September: he couldn't think of any date it corresponded to except it was the day after the results of the independence ballot would be announced by the UN. The box contained a simple diagonal cross in red texta.

Pausing beside the day-planner for a moment, Mac scanned the rest of the wall, which featured regimental bunting and photos of Damajat in his Kopassus beret, one with Norman Schwarzkopf and another with a big group that included Damajat and an Australian Minister for Defence, which looked like it was taken at the Jakarta Golf Club, and definitely after lunch.

Under the golf photo was a bronze bust of Soeharto – smiling for once – sitting on a steel security cabinet.

Moving to the dark wooden desk, there was a diary-blotter, several yellow post-its with messages and numbers scrawled in cursive. Of most interest to Mac was a fifty-centimetre security monitor with six boxes of black and white imagery moving on it. One of the boxes was a lengthwise shot of the corridor outside Damajat's office, which was empty. Keeping one eye on the corridor camera, Mac checked the three drawers down each side of the foot well. The top two drawers were locked so he pulled at the unlocked ones; there were files in Bahasa Indonesia, old tennis balls that look like they'd been chewed by a dog, personal Visa card statements and a Nokia phone. Turning off the phone, Mac trousered it. Then, checking the last drawer, he saw a small ring of keys. Picking them up, he checked the security monitor again and, moving swiftly to the steel security cabinet, fumbled with the keys, his fingers getting sweaty with panic.

Voices sounded outside the door and Mac leapt back to the desk, threw the keys in the drawer, shut it with a swinging foot and stood at the window, blood pumping.

The voices moved on and Mac collected himself, checked the security monitor and grabbed the keys again. The doors opened first time and as they swung open Mac found himself disappointed. What he hoped might have been card-file boxes of agents, assets and suspects – the typical fare for a chief of intelligence – was instead several trays filled with protective foam and tiny plastic vials pushed into slots in a grid pattern. Wondering if anything in that cabinet would interest Canberra, Mac looked over at the security monitor which showed Damajat approaching down the corridor with his cocky walk. Grabbing one of the vials, Mac fumbled with the lock and returned the keys as the major-general burst into the office. Turning from the window with his cup of coffee, Mac smiled, the vial tucked snugly in the tube where his laces wrapped around the heel of his boat shoes.

'So, Mr Davis, that list okay?' asked Damajat, joining him at the window.

'Right as rain, Anwar,' said Mac. 'I can have this freighted out of sixteen different countries. There'll be no customs intel on this one, if that's how you want it?'

'That's how I want it,' said Damajat. 'And I need you to start now.'

'Now?' asked Mac.

'Yes, of course. It's most urgent.'

Damajat gave Mac a work-up that contained various billing details, bank accounts and corporate fronts that had to be used and then Damajat grabbed a manila folder and they walked out of the building and into the car park.

Mac wanted to push for a Blackbird connection before leaving.

'You know, Anwar,' said Mac, trying for a tone that was at once authoritative and obsequious. 'This is not going to be a problem from my end, but maybe we should talk about the security of your organisation.'

'Security?' said Damajat.

'Yes. I prefer not to know what the development program is up here,' said Mac, 'but all it takes is one set of loose lips in your operation, and then we have customs sniffing around our containers and the whole thing goes pear-shaped.'

'I see what you're saying,' said Damajat, motioning for Amir's driver to escort Mac to the car for a lift back to the Turismo as arranged. 'But you should not be concerned, Mr Davis.'

'No?'

'No,' said the major-general, slightly raising the manila folder in his hand. 'We have friends where it counts.'

CHAPTER 21

Mac turned the corner of the warehouse to find Amir Sudarto leaning against the waiting LandCruiser, his black SIG Sauer aimed at Mac's chest. As Mac slowly raised his hands, the driver pushed him in the back, making him stumble forwards.

'Well,' said Mac, seeing there were two soldiers beside Amir. 'This'll certainly be a secure ride.'

As the two soldiers closed in from his sides, Mac lurched to his right, grabbed the driver by the wrist and swung him into the other thug. Caught by surprise, the soldier pulled up his gun as Mac leapt over the driver and lunged at the soldier's throat, grabbing it with his right hand as he got his left hand on the gun wrist.

Falling to the dirt, Mac twisted so he landed on the soldier then headbutted the bloke's teeth. Using his momentum, he ripped his right hand away from the throat and got both hands on the soldier's gun hand. Pulling up, Mac aimed the captured gun – hand and all – at Amir and pulled back on the soldier's trigger finger as his assailants advanced.

Nothing. Not even a click.

Sudarto walked up and trod on Mac's left wrist, preventing Mac from rolling away. Then Amir Sudarto's gun came down between his eyes.

'So,' said Amir, smiling. 'They say you were in army, but don't know what safety is, right?'

The driver laughed, but the other soldier on the ground touched his bloody bottom lip and spat at Mac.

Amir's smile suddenly hardened. 'Time for chat, right, McQueen?'

They dragged Mac through the shower block of the Ginasio, into a dank room with a concrete floor and high frosted windows with wire through the glass. The Kopassus thugs made him kneel at one end of the room, hands and ankles wired behind him and wire flex around his neck. Then they walked away, leaving Mac with his fears.

Mac's old footballer's knees started to seize on the wet concrete as the blood dried in his nose. Forcing himself to keep his breathing regular, he worked it through: Amir Sudarto knew his name, which meant they'd levered the truth out of Bongo or got a surveillance shot of Mac and run it past some corrupt friendlies, most likely CIA or NICA. Or perhaps Amir was sent to do the dirty work by his big brother, Benni. There was a chance that Benni Sudarto was running a separate operation with a different agenda to that of Damajat and his commercial masters. Mac had no idea what it was, but the fact that Amir had grabbed Mac in the car park – not in the Lombok AgriCorp building – suggested a side venture.

Mac tried to think quickly about what Amir wanted and how far he'd go to get it. The Indonesians had already retrieved his phones and the materials that Damajat had given him, but the leaked documents from Rahmid Ali were hidden in Bongo's Camry.

Sounds of beatings and pleading echoed throughout the vast building. People cried, men yelled; women screamed, voices threatened and hard objects hit soft flesh. Mac didn't expect to walk out of the Ginasio.

Voices came closer and then there were footfalls in the shower block and Amir Sudarto was standing in front of Mac. One of the soldiers from the car park – the driver – put a shallow box on the wooden slat seat. Mac could see his own phone, Damajat's Nokia and the list of items to be procured.

Sitting down on the slatted seat in front of Mac, Sudarto stretched his thick legs in front of him, taking his weight with his arms, muscles flexing under his green trop shirt.

'Tell me what I need, McQueen, and I'll make it fast and . . . *relatively* painless, okay?'

'Can we define *relatively*?' said Mac, the wire flex digging into his larynx.

'Don't be funny,' said Sudarto, the trace of an American accent a reminder of his stint at Northwestern. 'We're in this situation, right? But we're both soldiers, and I'll give you the fast way if you cooperate.'

'Thanks for the offer, but it sounds too much like suicide, maybe euthanasia. And I'm Catholic – see what I mean?'

Sudarto's nostrils flared and he looked away.

'What brought you up here?' asked Sudarto.

'Major-General asked me for lunch, remember?'

'What were you looking for in his office?'

'I wasn't.'

'So what's this?' said Sudarto, reaching over and picking up Damajat's Nokia.

'It rang,' said Mac, shrugging and stalling for time.

Sudarto bounced his thumb across the keypad of the phone. 'No it didn't. Last received call 11.39 this morning.'

Looking down at Sudarto's black Hi-Tec boots, Mac concentrated on his breathing and remained silent, stony-faced.

'Major-General Damajat keeps his phone in his desk, so what were you looking for?'

Mac shrugged it off again, trying to find a part of himself that wasn't swamped with fear.

'What about Dili?' asked Sudarto, pulling a cigarette packet from his breast pocket and fishing one out with his teeth. 'What's happening in Dili?'

'Looking for sandalwood opportunities, and –'

'Come on, McQueen,' snapped Sudarto. 'We're past all that.'

The accepted style of interrogation in the intelligence community was to ask a number of narrative and factual questions over and over, find the inconsistencies and work at them. While working at the inconsistencies you suddenly dropped a clanger into the dialogue to surprise and confuse the interviewee. Mac expected a clanger in the next few minutes to try and knock him off his game.

'Do you know a man called Alphonse Morales?'

'No,' said Mac.

'Known to most people as Bongo?'

'I may have met him, I don't –'

Sudarto gestured to his sidekick and a black-and-white eight-by-five print was suddenly thrust in front of Mac's face. It was a telephoto shot of Bongo at the wheel of the Camry, with Mac shutting the passenger door. Mac's mind completed the picture – it had been taken just before he'd crossed the road to the wall of the Santa Cruz cemetery.

'Oh, you're talking about Manny? Manny Alvarez?' said Mac, using Bongo's NICA cover at the Jakarta Shangri-La.

'Don't be clever, McQueen,' snapped Sudarto, lunging forwards and backhanding Mac across the face so hard that it sent him sprawling sideways.

The sidekick picked him up, put him back in the kneeling position, blood again pouring from Mac's nose onto the concrete.

'I met Manny when he was a concierge at the Lar,' continued Mac, 'and he agreed to do some driving for me in Timor.'

Lunging forwards again, Sudarto hit Mac with a backhand-forehand combo, spraying blood across the room. Although he stayed upright this time, Mac wondered how many of the heavy strikes he could take.

He was in big trouble: the Bongo connection put the conversation right back in the meet that had gone wrong, where the older Sudarto brother had shot Bongo. It meant the Sudartos had connected all the dots – the Canadian, Blackbird and Operasi Boa – which had led him to Mac. But was there anything else? What else did he know? What more could Amir Sudarto want from him that he didn't know already?

'Let's talk about the cemetery,' said Sudarto, sucking on his smoke.

'The cemetery?'

'Yeah, McQueen. Santa Cruz.'

'It's a nice place.'

'Nice?' said Sudarto.

'Yeah – it's a pretty place,' said Mac.

'Sure, it's pretty, McQueen,' said Sudarto, looking straight through him. 'But maybe you meet someone there?'

Oh fuck! thought Mac, since Amir could only be referring to Rahmid Ali and his approach in the cemetery.

Trying to control the adrenaline that hammered in his temples, Mac realised his position was much worse than he had first thought. Benni and Amir Sudarto, and Kopassus intelligence, had discovered Mac in Dili because they'd been tailing Ali. They'd been tailing Ali because he represented the new President Habibie, whom the military wanted to hobble before democracy could break out.

Mac's pain and fear deepened as he suddenly saw his predicament: he'd gone and put himself in the middle of a turf war between the Indonesian military and their president.

CHAPTER 22

The beating continued until blood ran from Mac's face and his left inner ear throbbed.

'I told you,' shouted Mac through mashed lips. 'He collared me in the cemetery while I was checking on the radio transmitter. You don't have a telephoto of this?'

'Tell me again, McQueen,' said Sudarto. 'Start from the beginning.'

'He called himself Rahmid Ali, he walked me at gunpoint into the trees against the wall of the graveyard and interrogated me about being in Dili.'

'Say where he from?'

'No – I assumed BAKIN,' lied Mac. 'He kept on about a company called Ocean Light in Dubai and what he called the "Singapore transactions". I told you this!'

'Singapore transactions?' sneered Sudarto, losing control and not happy about it. Good interrogators had their theories confirmed; they weren't necessarily wanting new information.

'Yeah, Amir – that's what he kept pushing me on. I had a SIG in my face, and it was all about these Singapore transactions and Ocean Light, and –'

'What else, McQueen?'

'That's it. He was angry, kept demanding why Canberra would send a Treasury investigator to Dili.'

'You Treasury?'

'No, mate – and I have nothing to do with this IMF shit, okay?' said Mac, referring to the International Monetary Fund consultants helping Indonesia with the *Monekris*, who'd been making unpopular demands about corruption and collusion under the cover of IMF policies.

'So?'

'So, I didn't get to hear the end of his story because Bongo sorted it,' said Mac.

'Bongo?'

'Yeah, he, you know . . .'

'Yeah, I know,' said Sudarto.

There were sounds from outside and Amir and his sidekick exchanged glances.

'We'll get to the bottom of that one when Benni gets here, right?' said Amir, glancing at his watch.

'Benni?' said Mac, trying to keep his neck straight so the wire didn't dig into his Adam's apple.

'Yeah, McQueen, he wants to talk to you.'

Lighting a cigarette, Sudarto cocked his head to another sound outside the building and shot a look at the other spook, who left the room to investigate.

'There's a blonde girl, McQueen,' said Sudarto. 'Pretty. She your girlfriend?'

Mac smiled, his back now in spasm from his awkward kneeling position. 'No, she's looking for her father.'

'Father?' said Sudarto, facetious. 'Can't go losing your father.'

'She suspects foul play – she's in Timor to find him.'

'She registered at the Turismo as Yarrow,' said Sudarto, narrowing his eyes at Mac. 'Her passport's Canadian, address in Los Angeles.'

'She's at UCLA,' said Mac.

'Good cover, eh McQueen?'

'Look, Amir,' said Mac, trying to sound forceful, 'she's not in our world, okay?'

'No?'

'She's a girl scout, a civvie whose father dropped off the map a few weeks ago and she can't get answers from the Canadian or Indonesian governments.'

'Why doesn't she ask the Aussies?' said Sudarto, smiling now, enjoying himself.

'Mate, whack me for the Canadian, okay? It's over, you win the back nine – *whatever*. But, shit!'

'So she just good friend with Bongo, too?'

'Bongo's with me, bodyguarding – he's freelance these days, right?' said Mac, trying to breathe out his pain.

'Really?' said Sudarto, picking up the envelope with the photos. 'So all these people, from Australia, United States and Philippines – they just meet at Turismo and all these coincidence happen, right?'

'Amir, I've asked that girl three or four times to leave the island, swear to God, and I told her not to go into the mountains. I found her at a cafe in Aileu – she'd hitched a ride with the UN for fuck's sake!'

'She got mind of her own?'

'Knows everything there is to know,' said Mac.

Pulling another eight-by-five black-and-white from the envelope, Sudarto glanced at it and then held it in front of Mac's bleeding face.

'Taken four days ago – Denpasar,' said Sudarto, exhaling smoke.

Mac's heart sank as he looked at it: a telephoto shot of Jessica Yarrow, dark sunglasses and a white polo shirt, talking with a man under a Bintang umbrella at an outdoor cafe. Mac knew how to cover his feelings and use a poker face, but his mouth must have gaped.

'Looks like it'll be a fun night with Benni, eh McQueen?' chuckled Sudarto, sliding the photo back in the envelope. 'So much to catch up on.'

Mac tried to make the pieces fit. Mac knew the man in the photo as 'Jim', and although he didn't know his surname he certainly knew his employer: Defense Intelligence Agency, the Western world's most powerful spy network.

Sudarto was right. This would be an all-nighter.

The explosion came at what Mac reckoned was 6.30 pm. The blast shook the walls and a flash of brightness came through the high windows. As Mac tried to get his head around to see what was happening, Sudarto lashed out with his foot and caught Mac on the corner of his left jaw, increasing his agony.

'You move when I tell you to move,' snapped the big Indonesian, a new tone in his voice. The sidekick hadn't returned from his errand and Mac had noticed Sudarto taking a couple of furtive glances at his wristwatch.

A dull glow filled the room and they heard panicked voices from outside as tendrils of smoke started coming in under the fanlights. Standing, Sudarto whipped a Nokia from his pocket and hit a speed dial before snarling at the machine. Wherever he was, the sidekick wasn't answering his phone.

'Guess we pick this up later, okay, McQueen?' said Sudarto.

'What?' said Mac. 'And leave me to burn?'

'Said you didn't want the fast way, yeah?' said the Indonesian, the orange of the flames reflecting on his slab-sided face. 'But Catholics make you a saint if you burn, right?'

'Fuck you, Amir,' said Mac, struggling as more smoke trickled into the room. 'And that's a martyr, not a saint.'

As Sudarto picked up the tray with the phones and photos, there was a new sound of automatic gunfire. Freezing, Sudarto dropped the tray and, pulling his SIG Sauer from his hip rig, ran out of the room.

Mac struggled with the flex holding his wrists down onto his ankles, but couldn't budge it. They'd crossed his wrists and tied them down to his ankles by lashing the cross-brace created by his hands. It was a professional job, and with the flex also holding his head back by the throat, he couldn't make any headway.

Mac attempted to calm himself, knowing it was easier to get out of a bound position if you were relaxed. But he just couldn't do it: the gunfire continued, occasionally splattering across the concrete of the Ginasio and shattering the glass at the top of the wall. Not even able to duck as the glass showered around him, Mac struggled to keep breathing, the smoke growing thicker and the roar of flame now audible over the sounds of gunfire. He suspected Falintil guerrillas on a raiding party had torched either a couple of trucks or a fuel depot, and then opened fire when the soldiers came out of their chow tent to fight the fire.

The fire got louder and brighter and the smoke became oily, choking Mac as the room filled with floating gasoline soot.

Coughing, tears pouring down his face, Mac resigned himself to death and found himself thinking about the events that had brought him to this point: the decision years ago to take a UQ campus interview with what he thought was DFAT; the way they'd whisked him into the Royal Marines to undergo Commando training, which he'd pushed so far that he'd ended up doing the SBS survival course in Brunei; the stress of his job, the lying and pretending, the cajoling of people into betraying their employers and their governments; the lack of real relationships and the loneliness that went with it. He thought about the night at the Republica guest house in Suai and a beautiful girl who was so sad for her father. Mac knew Jessica had slept with him because he cheered her up, not because he was in her league.

And he thought about turning around in the car to face a girl who wanted to help some victimised women, and telling her to be ashamed and alive, realising in his heart how totally inadequate that philosophy was.

As the smoke entered his lungs, Mac sagged forward, tightening the flex on his throat. It was over, he was sliding into black. If he could do it all again, he'd tell Bongo to stop the car, put a gun in that militiaman's mouth and let Jessica poke the bully in the chest, let her tell that cocksucker to hand the dammed chicken back to the old woman. Now! Drop his professional hardness for thirty seconds, and let the good guys win one back. For once . . .

And then Mac was turning, pleading . . . *Sorry, Bongo. Shit, I'm sorry.* Mac felt himself crying. *Tell her I'm sorry, Bongo, fuck I'm sorry* . . .

He must have slipped into pre-death unconsciousness before a large hand slapped at him, and he awoke in the heat of the dark room, spluttering and disoriented.

'You okay to move, brother?' came a voice as his wrist and ankle flexes were snipped. Then there was the feel of steel against his neck and a snipping sound and the flex came loose and, next thing, Mac was on his side on the wet concrete, coughing and vomiting, his stomach and lungs heaving.

Strong arms helped him up and then a voice he knew well was in his ear as he staggered forward on creaky knees, groping for something to hold.

'It's Bongo, okay, brother? Can you hear me?'

'Yep,' rasped Mac, clinging to Bongo in the dark.

'We're outa here, brother,' said the Filipino. 'You okay to walk?'

'Yep,' nodded Mac, his stomach convulsing, his eyes feeling like they were on fire.

'Okay to run?' asked Bongo, as they moved out of the room and into the blackness.

'Yep,' said Mac.

'Sure?' asked Bongo as they entered the Ginasio's main stadium and headed right for the exit.

'Good as gold,' Mac replied, clinging to Bongo's shirt like he was holding on to life itself.

CHAPTER 23

They gave him five minutes' rest in a small copse overlooking Maliana. Retching until he thought his jaw was going to seize, Mac allowed Bongo and a guerrilla named Joao to wash his eyes with bottles of water from the creek.

'Don't rub, Mr Richard,' said Joao, a straight-haired mestizo local who was built like a middleweight. 'Just let water do the work, okay?'

As they got the petroleum soot out of his eyes, Mac saw that Bongo had re-dyed his hair to black. His eyes slowly stopped running with tears and he became aware of three other men crouched around him, dressed in various combinations of jungle fatigues and armed with automatic rifles.

'Ready, brother?' asked Bongo, looking at his watch.

'Well, I can see. Does that count?' said Mac, throat like sandpaper.

They stood to go and Bongo did the introductions, at which point Joao took over, saying, 'We travel all night, okay, Mr Richard?'

It was one of those South-East Asian statements made as a question in order that everyone save face.

'That would be fine, Joao,' said Mac, still croaky. 'Thank you. *Obrigado.*'

'And, not the offence to you, sir, but please – no question about where we going?'

'That's fine, mate,' smiled Mac as he tested his knees again. 'Anywhere out of Bobonaro is good with me.'

Joao packed water bottles into a small rucksack and they got into formation, one of the guerrillas at point with Joao in behind, and Mac sandwiched between Joao and Bongo. Turning to Bongo, Mac remembered something: 'Mate, we need to get back to the Camry –'

Bongo smiled and held out Mac's Beretta and Rahmid Ali's papers. 'Thought you might want these, brother.'

'Better watch it, Morales,' said Mac, jamming the papers in his chinos pocket. 'Someone might think you're a professional. What happened to you guys, by the way?'

'We lost you after we dealt with the rapists, then we picked up with these guys.' He pointed a thumb over his shoulder. 'That's what the gunfight was about – these guys and the Lintar militia. They weren't after us, we just got caught in it.'

Taking a deep breath, and preparing for the worst, Mac got a question off his chest. 'Mate, the kids – did they make it?'

'They made it,' said Bongo.

'Are you sure?' said Mac, wanting to be absolved. 'I mean –'

'Yeah, I'm sure,' said Bongo, laughing. 'That girlfriend of yours made sure of that – she's a real tigress, that one.'

'So where's Jessica?' asked Mac as they started walking under a half-moon.

'She's safe,' said Bongo, who had his own rifle – a Heckler & Koch G3 by the look of it. It was old now but still a good weapon, and the best you could buy in the 1970s.

'Where?' asked Mac, checking his Beretta for load and safety.

There was a loud throat-clearing sound and the guerrilla leader was suddenly in Mac's face. 'Simple rule when you travel with Falintil,' said Joao, 'don't ask where you going, don't say where you been. Okay?'

True to his word, Joao made them walk through the night. Mac had it as westward, which worried him. He'd hoped to be tabbing east, away from the paranoia and malevolence of Bobonaro.

They spent two hours climbing into the mountains, Joao handing Mac a heavy drill shirt as it got cold and damp. Then they were descending, into a landscape that was punctuated with greenery but with rolling alpine grasslands and outcrops of rock between the stands of bush.

Finding a river bed in the lowlands, they drank and rested under a stand of trees for fifteen minutes, speaking in low tones.

'Probably wondering why we going west, right?' asked Joao, opening a parcel of waxed paper and sharing out a carcass of cold chicken.

'Sure,' said Mac, chomping on the spicey wing but tasting only gasoline soot. 'Thought you guys liked to travel through jungle?'

'Got something to do first,' said Joao. 'Mr Manny asked if we could get you on our way, okay?'

Mac nodded then checked the vial in the laces loop of his boat shoe. It was still there. 'So, Joao, what's your story?'

'Just doing my part,' said Joao, his eyes not leaving Mac's.

'You military?'

Smiling, Joao turned to the other guerrillas and rattled off something in Tetum, and they all laughed.

'What's funny?' asked Mac.

'He's a teacher,' said Bongo quietly, 'but trained in the seminary. Joao's ordained, okay, brother?'

They reached their destination and lay behind a bushy spur while Joao and Bongo moved to the ridge and took turns with the binos. Mac's G-Shock said 4.41 am. He yawned and shivered, a little unsettled at being out of the loop.

Returning to the main group, Joao did not look happy.

'It looks abandoned,' said Joao. 'Gates hanging open, and, um . . .' he cleared his throat and looked away.

Mac got a look from Bongo and decided to stay quiet.

'What Joao's saying is there seems to be bodies in there,' said Bongo softly.

'Bodies?' asked Mac.

'Yes!' said Joao, chest heaving. 'Lots of them.'

The camp was deserted but the barracks and the offices had been left, with all of the furniture and beds removed. The ablutions block

– built for at least thirty men – was cleared of everything, including the taps and shower heads.

'Left nothing but the bill,' muttered Mac as they followed Joao's torch outside.

'The Java way,' snorted Bongo, lighting a cigarette. 'Why give when you can take? My mum told me that, and she should know.'

The six of them stood on the veranda of the main office and looked over the camp's outdoor area. There was a large open-sided shelter to the right – iron roofing held aloft on telegraph poles – and a cyclone fence around an open grassed area of about six hectares. To the left, the cyclone gates hung open, a dirt approach road shimmering in the gloom of pre-dawn.

As they walked down the slight slope, bush rats fled across the ground like a dark carpet. The first bodies were two women and three children – all naked. Mac crouched, inspected the younger of the two adult corpses, looking for a cause of death. On the other side of the group of corpses, Bongo was doing the same thing.

'No bullets,' said Bongo. 'No strangulation. No struggle, no violence. No obvious lesions or punctures.'

Waving for Joao's torch, Bongo had a closer look at the female corpse's face. The lips were swollen.

'Poison?' asked Mac.

'Probably, but let's look, okay?' said Bongo, moving off.

'Guess you're not a salesman either, right, Mr Richard?' asked Joao, but not challenging.

'Like the wise man says,' said Mac, moving behind Bongo, 'don't ask, don't tell.'

As the light increased, the scale of the deaths became apparent. As many as a hundred and thirty naked bodies lay across the grassed area.

'It's like Jonestown,' said Mac, panting slightly as they got to where the bodies were most numerous, under the shelter.

'All Maubere,' said Joao, meaning they were Melanesian Timorese locals, as opposed to the Portuguese and Indonesians.

Two shoes lay on the ground just outside the shelter, worn and mismatched. Looking around at all the barefoot bodies, Bongo spat. 'Java thieves – even took their *shoes*.'

They stood staring, overwhelmed by the combination of evil and pettiness.

'What is this place?' asked Mac finally. 'Concentration camp?'

But Joao didn't respond because he was on his knees, vomiting.

They sat around the communal water pipe, drinking water and eating the last of Joao's chicken from the waxed paper lying on the dirt. From the east, Mac saw the line of pale blue and red pushing at the horizon.

'This wasn't what you expected?' Mac asked Joao, trying to work it out.

'No. We'd been hearing about this refugee camp since early this year,' he answered in a faraway voice. 'The militias and soldiers have been clearing the villages and moving displaced people up here for months, but no one ever came back – it was all rumour.'

'Refugees? From where?' asked Mac.

'From the south coast, Mr Richard,' said Joao, slightly sarcastically. 'You know, Cassa, Betano, Same, Suai? Anywhere they burn the house, steal the animals, kill our people.'

Mac nodded. 'So the rumours? What were they?'

'Our people in FPDK,' said Joao, referring to the pro-integration movement that opposed independence, 'they tell us that the military is up to something in Bobonaro, something that they not telling.'

'Jakarta's keeping it secret from the local pro-integrationists?' asked Mac, surprised that FPDK wasn't more involved with plans to keep East Timor in Indonesia.

'Yeah, and maybe a secret inside of military too,' said Joao. 'We have people inside army and they didn't know. Then we get some defections, right? From the 1635 Regiment.'

Mac nodded; the Indonesian Army's biggest locally raised regiment in East Timor was the 1635.

'This defector – Antonio – he really upset when he gets to us, tells about the camp south of Memo where he drove a truck,' said Joao.

'That where we are? Memo?' asked Bongo.

'Yep, about twelve kilometres south.'

'What did this defector see?' Bongo continued, lighting a cigarette.

'Antonio said they always delivering people, but the population never seemed to rise,' said Joao. 'That's how the rumours started of the death camp in Memo. This place.'

A diesel engine revved somewhere over the horizon, and they all stood, following Joao in a jog towards the gates. Turning left, they climbed to higher ground and Mac crouched in the scrub as the diesel revved through a gear change.

Short of the scrub, Bongo stopped. 'What's that?' he demanded, pointing at the shelter in the camp yard.

Ducking back behind the scrub, Mac couldn't see anything except bodies in the dim light of pre-dawn.

'What?' asked Joao, going to Bongo's shoulder.

'There! *There!*' said Bongo, bringing his rifle across his body.

But Mac didn't look where Bongo was pointing, because five hundred metres to their south a black LandCruiser was cresting the rise, followed by an army transport truck with a D6 bulldozer on its trailer.

'Guys,' hissed Mac from his hide, still feeling vulnerable after the beating at the Ginasio. 'We've got company!'

Ignoring Mac and the two vehicles, Bongo and Joao stood in the open looking over the camp yard.

'*Guys!*' said Mac, desperate to stay concealed. 'Get down – the Indonesians are here!'

Joao handed the binos to Bongo and, putting his hand on the Filipino's big back, pointed. Bongo's head went up and down twice and Mac heard him mutter, '*Yep, yep.*'

Mac groaned inwardly, realising his day was about to fall apart: he wanted to get to a phone, and to Blackbird – and he wanted to get to the bottom of Operasi Boa. And then he wanted to get as far away from Bobonaro regency as he possibly could. A tall order, but one he could keep juggling and resolving if he could just keep his momentum and stay away from whatever Bongo and Joao were dreaming up.

Bongo slid in beside Mac in the hide, checking the mag on his rifle.

'There's a girl down there in the camp, still alive,' he said, excitement in his dark eyes.

'Pity about the timing,' said Mac, wanting Bongo to drop the whole thing.

'Timing's perfect,' smiled Bongo, slapping the mag into the G3.

'For what?' screeched Mac.

'Save her,' said Bongo as Joao crouched behind him. 'We'll just make it if we move now.'

'We?' asked Mac, but Bongo and Joao had already gone, leaving the three guerrillas to cover the camp yard.

Every fibre in his body wanted to turn the other way, run back into the hills and get back to the gig. But when Mac started running, it was in a crouch, behind Joao.

CHAPTER 24

Landing almost on top of Joao on the other side of the fence, Mac tried to get a grip on the situation.

'So, we got a plan?' he asked.

'Save the girl,' said Bongo. 'How's your Beretta?'

'Full load,' Mac replied, looking at Joao. 'You really want to pick a fight with the Indonesian Army? In the middle of Bobonaro?'

Slamming a new mag into his G3 and then letting the mag fall out of his Browning into his hand, Joao shrugged. 'Did it last night to help an Aussie out of the Ginasio – now we do it to save a girl.'

'I'm not saying it like that,' said Mac, blushing, aware that Australians could easily sound racist to Asians.

'No?' asked Joao.

'No, mate, it's just that it would be nice to report this place to the UN or the Australians without tipping off the Indonesians, right?'

Bongo and Joao exchanged words in Bahasa Indonesia.

'What's up?' asked Mac.

'Just saying, *Yeah, first we tell UN, then we tell our teacher*,' said Joao, then set off.

As he readied himself to follow, Mac caught Bongo's eye.

'Don't say it again, mate,' said Mac. 'Don't even start.'

'Wasn't gonna,' said Bongo, close behind Mac as they followed Joao to the corner of the building they were hiding behind.

'Besides,' said Mac, feeling guilty about his reluctance. 'That phrase? That thing you said before we shot those rapists? We used to say that in the marines too, but it referred to the whole troop – not to every damsel who needs saving.'

'Must have got it wrong then,' whispered Bongo.

'She's crawling,' said Joao, pointing at the shelter. 'Cover me.'

Moving out from behind the camp building, still in the remainder of pre-dawn darkness, they crouched as they watched the LandCruiser and dozer transport about three hundred metres away and in no hurry.

Crouching in the kneeling-marksman position, Bongo and Mac beaded up on the approaching vehicles as Joao crawled through the bodies, his rifle across his shoulder blades. Mac could now see the girl, about eight years old, dark shoulder-length hair, in a white cotton dress, obviously dazed and trying to crawl away from the bodies. He watched as Joao got to the girl and gently levered her down, stopped her moving around.

'I don't know about this,' snapped Mac, a bad feeling about the whole venture. 'How many spooks in the LandCruiser?'

'We'll be fine – and Benni's mine, if he's here. Okay?' said Bongo.

'That what this is?' hissed Mac, not believing what he was hearing. 'This is still payback on Sudarto?!'

'That's our deal, remember, McQueen?' said Bongo, squinting down the G3's barrel.

Shaking his head, Mac focused on the approaching vehicles, two hundred metres away. 'Don't be disappointed if you can only find Amir – you were right about Benni, he's not coming into the open.'

Glancing back towards the girl, Mac saw her nodding at Joao, then both were crawling back, staying low. Joao and the girl were now no more than ten metres away and making good time. They might make it, thought Mac. If they worked it properly, they could stealth back behind the camp building, get the girl over the wall and just hope the spooks didn't want to have a look around.

Suddenly, the girl looked up, saw Mac and Bongo, and shook her head. As Joao reached up to pull her back down, she whipped her arm away and started running out into the camp yard.

'No!' yelled Bongo, before running after the girl.

As Mac rose from his crouch, Joao dashed after Bongo and the LandCruiser slid to a halt in the dirt as the transporter slid past it on the far side, crushing corpses as it went.

Everything unfolded like a nightmare as Mac stood transfixed: the spook who he'd headbutted the day before leapt from the driver's door of the Cruiser with his SIG Sauer and, unsure who to shoot first, shot at the girl as she ran through the spill of the 4×4's headlights. Missing with the first shot, he lined up for another but his head disintegrated as Bongo's G3 shuddered and spat a casing.

As the spook with the fat lip fell to the dirt, Joao opened up on full auto into the open door of the Cruiser, knocking the passenger out the other side of the vehicle, shattering the glass and tearing up the interior.

Jogging into the open, Mac saw Bongo drop the G3 and draw the SIG from under his trop shirt. Then Bongo took three running strides past the girl and leapt up onto the running board of the Mercedes-Benz transporter cab, where he tore the door open and looked in. All Mac saw was four puffs of powder and the spent casings glinting in the pre-dawn as they tumbled to the dirt.

Swinging the Beretta in panicked arcs, Mac got to the middle of the yard and saw that Joao had secured the girl. Running around the other side of the LandCruiser, he closed on the spook who'd been in the passenger seat, the same one who'd assisted Amir Sudarto in Mac's interrogation. Mac threw himself to his right and rolled across the dirt as the injured spook got off a shot. Coming up in a cup-and-saucer stance, Mac squeezed the trigger and hit the bloke in the right shoulder, knocking him onto his back and throwing the gun five metres.

Standing, Mac advanced as the spook held on to his shoulder wound. Shutting down the Benz transporter, Bongo jumped from the cab and came to Mac as Joao picked up the girl, put her on his hip and walked her to the shelter.

Standing over the injured spook, Mac gestured with his Beretta. 'Phone?'

The bloke nodded.

Waving his gun, Mac said, 'Just show me, don't touch it – you know the drill.'

Grimacing with pain, the spook pointed with his left hand.

'In the Cruiser?' asked Mac.

The spook nodded before passing out.

'Fuck!' muttered Mac, moving to the 4×4.

'What's up?' asked Bongo.

'I wanted a chat,' said Mac, looking into the interior of the LandCruiser, which was now plastered with blood and hair. 'But a bloke in shock might not be very talkative.'

Reaching over to the centre console, Mac pulled out half a Motorola phone.

'Won't be getting much out of that, brother,' said Bongo, kicking the spook's face.

Climbing into the cab, Mac took a closer look in the console and glove box, but there was nothing of interest. The dozer made it obvious why they were up here but there were no written orders to confirm it.

The other three Falintil guerrillas jogged through the gates, wide-eyed and breathless. Seeing Mac and Bongo, they peeled away to Joao and the girl under the shelter.

Gulping down the adrenaline and the stress, Mac's face pulsed where he'd been hit by Amir Sudarto. His left jaw still ached. Checking his Beretta, he spoke softly to Bongo.

'I was cool to go along with this, but now I have to get back to Denpasar, okay, mate?'

Nodding, Bongo looked around forlornly as the sun strengthened behind the horizon. 'Guess cross-country with Falintil is going to be too slow, right?'

'Yeah, and after this,' said Mac, gesturing around him with the gun, 'it may be too dangerous.'

'What about the UN?' asked Bongo. 'They got a helo in Maliana.'

'I'm not going back to Maliana, and I'm not trusting my life to the UN,' said Mac.

'Okay,' nodded Bongo. 'So, the Cruiser or the truck?'

'The Cruiser's an intel vehicle – draw too much attention,' said Mac. 'Have to be the truck.'

'Okay, McQueen,' smiled Bongo. 'I got an idea, but we gotta move fast, okay?'

Joao and his guerrillas had surrounded the spook and were lashing out at the man with kicks as Bongo and Mac moved for the truck.

'Don't interrupt,' whispered Bongo, as Mac slowed.

'I need to ask him something,' whispered Mac as they got to the cab of the truck and Bongo unbuttoned his shirt.

'We need to get going before the sun comes up,' said Bongo.

'Can we take him with us?' asked Mac.

'No, brother – this is Falintil's kill, not ours.'

Mac decided not to argue. The spook might know every last secret about Blackbird, but he wouldn't tell Mac in a hurry.

'So what are they saying?' asked Mac, unnerved by the ferocity of Joao's anger.

'He's saying, *Who are you to betray your fellow human?*' said Bongo, a little reticent as he pulled off his slacks and folded them. Mac noticed a Conquistador crucifix tattooed on his left shoulder blade, the legend INRI inscribed inside the cross piece.

Spittle flew off Joao's lips as he reached down, picked up one of the stolen shoes and threw it at the spook's face.

'What's he saying now?' asked Mac.

'Now he's saying, *You kill hundreds of my people, and then you steal their shoes? What kind of man are you?*' said Bongo, pulling on the truck driver's fatigue pants and buttoning the army shirt.

Walking over to the Falintil leader, Mac offered his hand.

'Thanks, Joao,' said Mac. 'If you can get any intel on what was happening here, please let me know?' He handed over his Arafura business card with his mobile phone number on it.

'When I know, you'll know, okay?' said Joao, tears welling in his eyes. 'Your friend has my phone number.'

'I won't forget what you guys did for me, okay?' said Mac.

'You better not,' said Joao, 'because you gotta tell Australia what you saw up here.'

Striding in, Bongo gave the lot of them hugs, then turned for the truck and pushed at Mac's shoulder.

'Time to get you out of here, McQueen,' he said, lighting a smoke and reaching for the cab door.

Climbing in the other side, Mac looked back at the spook with the Falintil guerrillas.

'What happens now?' asked Mac, as the truck went into first and Bongo released the handbrake.

'That intel guy – he gonna die the local way.'

'The local way?' asked Mac, confused.

'See those machetes?'

Mac nodded. Most rural Timorese carried machetes that they sharpened fastidiously.

'They gonna take his skin off and hang it on the fence, brother, and his scalp gonna hang above it, like a halo,' said Bongo, continuing the truck's long arc around the Falintil group and then reaching for third gear as they accelerated through the camp gates.

'Pretty heavy punishment for a guy just doing his job,' said Mac, finding a full bottle of water in the console.

Snorting, Bongo reached forward to the radio dial.

'What!' demanded Mac.

'Well, I left out something that Joao was saying.'

'Like?' asked Mac.

'Like, he's saying to the intel guy, *How were you going to make us vote against independence, by having sex with our children?*'

'I see,' said Mac, feeling sick.

'Not like Australia, brother,' said Bongo. 'This the local way.'

CHAPTER 25

They made fast time north in the transporter before the sun came up. Indonesia may have possessed one of the world's largest standing armies but it wasn't one that rose with the day.

Sitting in the half-cab behind Bongo, Mac stayed out of sight and allowed Bongo to play the cheery army truck driver, delivering a bulldozer to another part of the island. Heading north from Memo, then taking the triangle road that would allow them to avoid Maliana, they hit the main road to Balibo at 5.41 am and had it to themselves.

'Won't be like this in ninety minutes,' said Bongo, lighting a smoke. 'Be Timor rush hour.'

'What does that look like?' asked Mac from his rear perch.

'Horses, buffalo and women walking,' said Bongo. 'Some militia too,' he added, more serious.

'Speaking of militia,' said Mac, 'is Jessica safe?'

'Hope so, brother. The Falintil women gonna walk her down to Zumalai, get her into a UN convoy.'

'You think she'll go?' asked Mac.

'Well, you know her, right?' grimaced Bongo. 'I told her she had to go now – being raped and killed is not a good way to find her father.'

'What did she say?'

Bongo took his time answering. 'She said, *I worry about my father —
you worry about Richard.*'

'She said that?' asked Mac, a smile breaking out involuntarily.

'Yeah. She like you, that one. Like you a lot.'

Bongo kept the big rig at an even sixty kilometres per hour, not
getting past fourth gear. Even the main thoroughfares of East Timor
were unsealed and winding, and frequently punctuated by washouts
from beneath or landslides from above.

Slowing for a washout that had been filled in and paved over in
a big uneven dip, Mac had to get out of the cab and signal Bongo
through the gap to avoid falling in the gorge while not bogging in
the roadside ditch.

'How long have the roads been like this?' asked Mac, getting back
into the half-cab.

'Twenty, thirty years,' shrugged Bongo, getting the transporter
moving again. 'The locals just fix it themselves. Some rocks, some trees.'

'Jesus, Bongo,' said Mac. 'We're in a forty-tonne vehicle, driving
over washouts that have a few rocks laid over the top of them?'

'Now you mention it,' said Bongo.

After half an hour of driving, Bongo broke the silence. 'So, we're
getting you to an airport, but we got a plan?'

'I have a plan, mate,' said Mac. 'You've done all I've asked. Get me
near to Dili or Baucau and I'll cut you loose.'

'What's the plan?' asked Bongo, looking for Mac in the rear-vision
mirror.

There wasn't much to tell. Mac needed to get back to Denpasar,
regroup and perhaps rethink the assignment. He'd been blown
by Kopassus intelligence, which was all-powerful in the hills of
Bobonaro, and if Blackbird was up there, it was not sensible for Mac
to be operating covertly. If Aussie intelligence really needed to debrief
Blackbird, they'd have to send in some poor bastards from special
forces to get her.

'Plan is to get out of Dodge,' said Mac. 'I was hoping to have more
information before I left — a nice secret document that fell off the
back of a truck, or a phone.'

'Damajat's?' asked Bongo.

'I thought Damajat's phone logs would lead me to Blackbird, maybe even tell me more about Lombok AgriCorp.'

'What about Rahmid's sat phone?'

'I'd like to have a look at that too – see who he's been speaking to.'

'So where's the phone?' asked Bongo.

'It's either in his room –'

'No it ain't,' said Bongo.

'– or it's in his car.'

'Rahmid had a car?' asked Bongo.

'Yeah.'

'Didn't find no keys in his room,' said Bongo.

'Then . . .' said Mac, hoping Bongo would offer.

The Mercedes-Benz engine wasn't enough to drown the Tagalog cursing. Then Bongo caught Mac's eye in the mirror and held it.

'Okay,' snarled Bongo, his dark Ray-Bans barely able to contain the malice in his eyes. 'But I'm not touching him, right?'

'Okay,' said Mac, breathing out.

'I'll show you the place, but I don't rat a man once he's buried, okay?'

As the sun came over the hills, they slowed and stopped for their first military checkpoint. Ducking down into the bench seat of the Mercedes' half-cab, Mac listened to Bongo bullshit his way through it like a seasoned pro. Even without enough Bahasa Indonesia to follow all the conversation, it was clear to Mac that Bongo was regaling the guards with tales of a colonel's halitosis or the crap food the 744 had to endure while those lazy 745 bastards in Dili got to eat anything they stole.

Handing out the cigarettes he'd found in the truck cab, Bongo got the rig moving again.

'Don't know what you said, but it sounded masterful,' said Mac, coming out of hiding.

'Pretending to be soldier is not hard in South-East Asia,' said Bongo. 'Just talk about how the brass don't know what they doing, how politician are thieves and every base has a cook who can't cook.'

Relieved, Mac mused on how fate had brought him together with one of the legends of spying in this part of the world. Bongo was allegedly so smooth in his covers that he sometimes found himself in tricky situations. Although known for his lisping blond concierge and his campy first-class steward covers, there was a rumour he'd once flown a Garuda 747 from Jakarta to Nagoya after his work-up had slightly oversold his experience.

'Is that jumbo jet rumour true?' asked Mac. 'You know, the one about you flying to Japan?'

'You kidding me?' laughed Bongo. 'You think they'd let *me* fly a 747?'

'Guess not,' said Mac.

'Nah, brother. It was a 737 and it was only to Denpasar. The Indonesians are crazy, but they're not stupid.'

The radio crackled to life as they crested a hill and Bongo keyed the handpiece. The conversation went back and forth, with Bongo maintaining the same sort of patter he'd managed with the checkpoint guards.

Hanging up, Bongo sighed as he fished for his cigarettes. 'Time to find a new ride.'

'What's up?' asked Mac.

'Colonel in the engineers corps, reminding me that we have to be nice for our visitor and make it look like we busy and disciplined,' smiled Bongo.

'So what's the problem?' asked Mac.

'They're expecting the visitor at the camp at 0900 hours,' said Bongo, lighting the smoke.

Mac looked at his G-Shock: 6.16 am.

'And his name's Captain Sudarto,' added Bongo.

The next checkpoint was on a natural rise, and as the Mercedes-Benz slowed to a halt with a hiss of air brakes, Mac and Bongo still had the road to themselves.

Peeking from behind the driver's seat, Mac saw a guard house with a green *kijang* parked beside it. A couple of bleary-eyed guards followed a more erect, more awake soldier out of the hut.

'Why is there never a suppressor when you need one?' muttered Bongo as the guard with the sergeant chevrons came around the front of the truck, ostentatiously noting the army rego plate on his clipboard as he passed.

His heartbeat ramping up, Mac waited behind the driver's seat, his Beretta swimming in his hand as he waited for the imminent outburst of violence. Bongo wanted to dump the truck and he wanted to do it fast and clean. But having to drop someone created anxiety for Mac in the build-up and the aftermath; with his military training he could sleepwalk the actual assassination but controlling his fear and his guilt were the parts he had to work at.

The sergeant tried the officious tone and Bongo kept joshing. Then the tone changed and the sergeant squawked a second before a gun fired. Mac sprang from his hide in the half-cab and crawled across the centre console into the passenger seat which faced the guard house.

Running around the front of the Benz, Bongo shot the two sleepy guards before they could even present arms, while Mac jumped to the ground and rushed into the guard house. Kicking at the door on the side wall of the office, Mac surged through, his Beretta in cup-and-saucer which he swung in short arcs. In front of him, a soldier in white underwear reached for his rifle and Mac dropped him with two shots to the chest.

Swinging back, Mac beaded on two shapes sitting on a lower bunk bed. They were young women, holding sheets over them, wide-eyed with fear.

'Hands,' said Mac, gulping for air as the soldier gurgled on the wooden floor.

Whimpering, the girls stared back but kept their hands under the sheets.

'I said hands!' screamed Mac. 'Tangan! Show me your hands!'

Behind him, Bongo stormed into the bunk house and immediately the girls lifted their hands from the sheets and stood up, covering their naked bodies.

Talking gently, Bongo moved the girls to a table and got them sitting in the chairs, though they shook with fear.

'You okay?' asked Bongo, when he realised Mac wasn't moving.

'I don't know, mate,' said Mac, breathing rapidly. 'I don't think I can do this anymore.'

'No kidding?'

Turning back to the girls, Bongo asked a few questions and then when one of them nodded and attempted a smile, he turned to Mac.

'Can you hold things together for two minutes?' he asked.

'Yep, sure,' said Mac, making his feet move. 'Just tired, I think.'

'Good,' said Bongo, collecting the guns from the room and saying something to the girls as he and Mac headed outside.

After they'd loaded the dead soldiers into the cab of the truck, Bongo got behind the wheel and drove it into the widest point of the road, pointing towards the trees. Then Bongo forced the dead sergeant's foot onto the accelerator as he pushed back off the step. Revving to the red line, the Mercedes pushed into the bushes and hauled its trailer and bulldozer with it. They stood on the side of the road and watched the rig launch down the ravine, crashing through trees as it made its way to the bottom.

To the passing motorist, there would be no sign that a forty-tonne transporter and its bulldozer had just driven off the edge, which cheered Mac slightly. What wasn't pleasing was the way he'd jammed up in the bunk house. His instructor in the Royal Marines, Banger Jordan, would have described his behaviour as *about as useful as a cunt full of cold water*.

'So far, so good, yeah?' asked Bongo, dangling the keys to the *kijang* as they walked back to the guard house.

'Sorry about that – you know, before?' said Mac, still not breathing easily.

'It's okay, McQueen.'

'Really?'

'First you got the heat exhaustion, then you got interrogated and beaten, and you haven't slept for two days. You get brain-fade – happens to everyone.'

The sun finally came up as they walked to the *kijang*, and Mac wanted to be in that vehicle, making fast time for Dili.

'Where you going?' asked Bongo.

'We're outa here, aren't we?' said Mac, his hand reaching for the vehicle's door.

'Forgot to tell you, McQueen,' he smiled. 'That girl you nearly shot?'

'Which one?'

'The pretty one with big smile?'

'Yep?' said Mac.

'That's Florita Gersao.'

Mac didn't get it.

'You know, McQueen,' said Bongo. 'Sister of Maria Gersao – Blackbird.'

CHAPTER 26

Bongo dressed the girl called Marta in a soldier's outfit, pulled her hair up and put an army cap on her head. Marta wasn't happy with the arrangement but she wanted to be out of Bobonaro so she sat up front with Bongo while Mac sat under the canvas cover in the back of the pick-up truck, talking with Florita.

'Maria alive?' asked Mac.

'Maybe, yes,' said the girl, who Mac guessed was about sixteen.

'You know where she is?' asked Mac.

'No, mister,' said Florita, big sad eyes.

'Rumours?' asked Mac, knowing that East Timor had a jungle drum that was better than most newspapers for speed and accuracy.

'Army got her, in Bobonaro. Maybe in Nusa Tenggara.'

'Where's your family?'

'Maria taken by army, then Mum and Dad,' she sniffled. 'Then soldiers come . . .'

'It's okay,' said Mac. 'You don't need to tell me.'

'Thank you,' she said, pushing her palms into her eyes as she started to cry.

'Your parents, Florita – they CNRT?' asked Mac, referring to the grouping of Timorese organisations endorsing an independence vote in the ballot. 'They politically active?'

'Don't think so,' said Florita, shutting down. Even the kids knew not to talk politics with strangers in East Timor.

'Were they doing anything that would make the soldiers take them away?'

The kijang's horn sounded and Bongo yelled at someone. Leaning back, Mac got a sight line through the flapping canvas canopy. They were going past Balibo's soccer ground and a bunch of youths in Hali Lintar militia T-shirts were waving and holding their M16s aloft as the army kijang went past.

'You from Jakarta?' asked Florita.

'No, I'm from New Zealand,' he said.

'Must not say you see Marta with soldier,' said Florita, regaining composure and wiping tears with her fingertips. 'Okay?'

'Okay, sure,' said Mac. 'Why not?'

'Her father very strict – so, you not saying, right?'

'Agreed,' said Mac, holding his hand out and shaking.

'My parent do nothing,' she continued.

'Never in trouble?'

'No, mister.'

'What about Maria? She political? In trouble?'

'No, mister. She work at army office – they check her out.'

Mac's brain swam with fear and fatigue, making it hard to concentrate. Since she couldn't tell him where Blackbird was being held, there was nothing else to ask.

'Well, that's it then,' smiled Mac. 'We'll have you back in Dili soon.'

'You know, my sister a good person, mister.'

'I'm sure she is,' said Mac, distracted and wondering what Bongo's promised alternative route into Dili might be.

'Army trust her, and intel too.'

'Intel?' asked Mac, not quite on the pace.

'Yeah, she had meeting with intel – she say she don't,' said Florita, her expression conspiratorial. 'But we see her in car with the intel man.'

'The intel man?' asked Mac, very slowly.

'Yep.'

'How did you know he was intel?'

157

'Everyone know the captain,' she said.

'Captain?'

'Yep, mister,' said Florita. 'The big *malai* – Captain Sudarto.'

After a couple of hours Bongo stopped the *kijang* and opened the canvas canopy.

'Where are we, mate?' asked Mac, squinting in the intense light and reaching for the sunnies hanging on his polo shirt collar. About one kilometre down a gentle, scrubby rise was the sparkling tropical sea that separated East Timor from Alor to the north. Shacks were interspersed with stands of trees and sand dunes, and a small grouping of houses and fishing boats was visible at a wharf on the rocky point.

Getting back in the *kijang*, Bongo drove it deep into a thick stand of bush and downwards into a creek bed.

'You girls,' Bongo said to Marta and Florita, and then continued in Bahasa Indonesia, pointing back to the road and the jungle above it, and then swinging around to point to the fishing village.

After he'd finished, he turned back to Mac. 'They'll take their chances through the bush. Perhaps you'd like to give them a little something?'

'Something?'

'Yeah – US dollars would be best,' said Bongo, hands on hips like he didn't have all day.

Mac fished in his once-khaki chinos and came out with the wad of dollars he'd last used in Suai, when he'd asked Mickey to open up the ice carton and liberate a carton of Bintangs.

'Ten okay?' asked Mac, handing a tenner to each girl.

Bongo reached over, pulled another two ten dollar notes from Mac's pile and handed them to the girls as he said something in Bahasa Indonesia.

Turning, Florita looked at Mac. 'Thank you, mister, and remember what we agree, okay?'

'Okay,' said Mac, smiling at her.

The girls walked up the sand and gravel road before darting into the bush.

'So where are we?' asked Mac as he followed Bongo down to the creek bed where he'd dumped the kijang.

'Batugade's eight kilometres that way,' said Bongo, pointing to his left. 'And Dili is thirty-five kilometres that way.'

After stripping out of his soldier's gear, Bongo dressed in his slacks and trop shirt. Then he leaned into the covered back of the kijang and pulled out two of the M16s confiscated from the guard post, throwing one to Mac.

As they moved away from the vehicle, the military radio sprang to life and a torrent of hysterical Indonesian poured out of the speaker.

'Found the checkpoint,' said Bongo as they moved out for the fishing village. 'Let's hope they don't find us.'

The walk to the fishing village took twenty minutes, and when they arrived at the wharf Bongo gave Mac his gun and told him to sit on a stack of fish crates and not move.

'I'll need those greenbacks, McQueen,' said Bongo, holding out his hand.

'Don't suppose I can get a receipt?' said Mac, handing over most of his stash.

'Just show 'em you alive – that's the receipt,' said Bongo disappearing.

Down the main pier, three sail-powered fishing boats strained on hawsers. Two deckhands walked towards Mac, young men with fish crates on one shoulder and carrying each end of a large net between them, so that the middle dragged on the decking. One wore the Indonesian fisherman's dress of singlet, sarung and plastic sandals while the other one – a Timorese – wore Lakers basketball shorts and old canvas sneakers.

They barely acknowledged Mac as they walked past, their faces the mask of constant exertion worn by their profession.

When Bongo appeared five minutes later, it was with a middle-aged Timorese man who shook Mac's hand and introduced his workers: the two young men Mac had watched before.

'We got a ride, brother,' said Bongo.

'Are we, I mean, this is okay?' said Mac, unsure of the deal.

'Yeah, it's cool,' said Bongo, gesturing for his M16. 'Fishermen don't care about politics – they're too busy or too tired.'

They made their way into the back of the vessel and Mac found a good position on a pile of canvas bags, hoping he could grab some sleep. As they sailed around the point at Carimbala, Bongo lit a cigarette.

'Get anything from Florita, McQueen?'

'She said that Maria had been meeting with Sudarto, in his car. Know anything about that?'

'No, I would have told you,' said Bongo.

'Well, it's made everything more complex. What do you make of it?'

'Can't say, brother,' said Bongo, shrugging. 'The Canadian never really spoke to me, and I wasn't in the room when he met with Blackbird.'

'What about the last time?'

'Well, yeah – I was checking the windows and balcony when he started into conversation with Blackbird. Normally, I'd secure the room and wait outside. I think he was stressed, like he wanted it over. It was a strange afternoon.'

'You never saw Blackbird with Sudarto?'

'No,' said Bongo, 'but it wouldn't be unusual.'

'No?'

'Benni Sudarto is Kopassus intel, so maybe he's not answering to SGI.'

'Okay,' said Mac.

'This SGI is a taskforce, right?' said Bongo. 'You ever been on an intel taskforce?'

'Yep,' said Mac, thinking of the intelligence empires that are so vigorously defended every time one agency is expected to cooperate with another.

'So maybe Benni gets his own suspicions about locals working in the taskforce, and he questions them – puts some pressure on, see who cracks. You know how that works, McQueen.'

Mac sure knew how that worked, but Florita's tone of voice suggested a closer relationship between Blackbird and Sudarto, unless that was just a sixteen-year-old getting it all wrong.

'And you know something, McQueen?'

'What?'

'Benni got it right – he made Blackbird. By the way, what did you agree to with Florita?'

'I said I wouldn't tell anyone about those girls being with the soldiers, in case Marta's father found out.'

'Okay,' nodded Bongo, looking away.

'Florita said he's strict – I guess he'd blame her, right?' asked Mac.

'No, probably not,' said Bongo, condescending. 'They don't tell the father in case he go shoot some Indonesian soldiers, and that's no good for anyone.'

'Really?' asked Mac.

'The father will kill anyone who messes with his daughter,' said Bongo, chuckling at Mac's expression. 'That what strict means in East Timor.'

The point south of Dili's main wharf area came into view shortly after 2 pm, just as they were finishing a meal of rice and fish served in a banana leaf. Pulling out his Nokia, Bongo dialled a number and spoke Bahasa Indonesia in a friendly tone.

The vessel slid into a small fishing wharf and, jumping onto the pier, Bongo and Mac waved their farewells, Bongo saying something and pointing at the M16s in the back of the boat.

Making their way down the pier, Mac felt paranoid, seeing a hundred chances for one of the locals to pick up a phone and inform. At the chandlery store, Bongo paused in the shadows and lit a cigarette.

'So, we walk into Dili?' asked Mac.

'Thought we'd get a cab, like normal people,' said Bongo, winking.

From a distance, a deep whining sound vibrated and got louder as Mac pushed further into the shadows of the chandler's, his overwhelming fatigue now making him anxious.

'UN,' said Bongo, pointing to the pale blue sky. A white C-130 transporter plane with *United Nations* painted in black down the tail section of the fuselage flew over their position, lining up for a run at Dili's Comoro Airport.

'Democracy – we deliver,' said Mac.

'That thing?' asked Bongo.

'Probably the voter kits,' said Mac. 'From Darwin.'

Mac watched a Toyota minivan approaching down the white gravel road through the palms and the fishermen's shacks. It pulled up with a crunch and the driver leapt out and came around to open the sliding door.

'Greetings, Mr Manny,' said the smiling driver.

'Hi, Raoul,' said Mac as he followed Bongo into the van.

'Hello, mister,' said Raoul, slamming the door.

They drove for twenty-five minutes and when Raoul pulled up it was two blocks away from the eastern wall of the Santa Cruz cemetery – the same wall that Bongo had been perching on when he shot Rahmid Ali.

Grabbing the bottles of water supplied by Raoul, Bongo and Mac walked the streets to Santa Cruz cemetery. It was the steaming hot middle of the day and many Timorese were having a post-prandial sleep. Dogs slept, a horse-drawn cart clopped past and two old women gossiped under a Bintang umbrella half a block away. No one showed any interest in them and they got into the shadows of the trees along the eastern cemetery wall and stealthed north until they found the tree that gave easy access over the wall.

Waiting for five minutes on the top of the wall, they cased the cemetery for Brimob cops and, when the ground looked clear, they dropped down in the cover of trees on the other side.

'So where's this body?' asked Mac as they regrouped, now regretting that he'd insisted on searching Rahmid's corpse for the car keys.

'There,' said Bongo, kicking a branch out of the way and sitting down with the two big bottles of water.

Following Bongo's finger, Mac saw a fresh grave with a pile of reddish earth piled on top, the casement and tombstone not yet in place.

'Fuck's sake,' Mac muttered, as he found his own patch of dry leaves and lay down in the merciful shade.

'What?' demanded Bongo, his voice sounding half-asleep. 'It was the best I could do, brother.'

'Is there a prayer for this?' said Mac, his brain now floating on a lilo. 'I mean, that's consecrated ground, right?'

'What about, *Sorry, boss — I'll make this fast?*' whispered Bongo.

Laughing with his entire body, Mac let himself go into sleep. 'You're a lunatic, Morales.'

'Man's gotta do, McQueen,' mumbled the big Filipino. 'Man's gotta do.'

CHAPTER 27

His beeping G-Shock stirred Mac at 8 pm. Shaking himself awake, he turned to Bongo.

'Keep your fluids up,' said Bongo, passing a water bottle. 'You okay?'

'Yep,' said Mac, the act of sitting up causing a sensation in his brain like motion sickness. 'How we looking?'

'Half-moon, no Brimob – we're clear.'

'Guess we should find a shovel,' said Mac, cricking his neck.

'Got it,' said Bongo, pointing to a gravedigger's shovel in the leaves in front of him. 'Cheap locks.'

Rahmid Ali's shattered, bloody face looked out at Mac after clearing just a metre of soil, but he kept digging around the body to get good access to his pockets. Something squeaked in a tree, causing Mac to drop his shovel and reach for his Beretta.

'Just a bat, McQueen.'

'Yeah,' said Mac, resuming his digging. Now that he'd had some sleep, the memory of the death camp in Memo was affecting Mac big time. He was feeling drained and morose.

Lowering himself carefully into Rahmid's shallow grave, so he didn't touch the body buried beneath, Mac started with the dead man's breast pocket and then frisked down his torso to his chinos.

Checking in the pockets of the dirt-covered pants, Mac again came up with nothing. He wasn't certain what he'd been expecting: spies made a habit of not carrying too much with them, certainly nothing that could illuminate their identity. That's why Bongo had only briefly ratted Rahmid before burying him, concentrating instead on a search of his room.

'Nothing,' muttered Mac, checking Rahmid's rigid legs before trying to turn over the body. 'Can I get a hand?' he groaned as he tried to shift the deadweight.

Mac checked the back pockets and then frisked the backs of Rahmid's legs.

'Maybe the shoes,' said Bongo, looking around the cemetery, SIG Sauer held behind his back.

Sliding his hands down Rahmid's ankles, Mac felt something just above the left shoe.

'Here we go,' he muttered and pulled up the trouser cuff. There was a bulge on the outside ankle under a dark sock. Pushing his hand inside, Mac felt a Velcro flap.

'Sock-pock, yeah?' asked Bongo.

Mac pulled out a wad of US dollars, which he handed up to Bongo.

'Thousand-dollar notes,' sighed Bongo as Mac reached for the other ankle. 'Six of them.'

'Toyota key,' said Mac, smiling as he held up his find. 'One of them.'

Waiting on the cemetery wall for the 9 pm rendezvous with Raoul, Mac played with the Toyota key in his pocket. Short of discovering a cache of secret documents, or a well-used cell phone in that car, Mac would be leaving for Denpasar with nothing concrete. He'd sighted Rahmid Ali's documents, allegedly a cry for help from a beleaguered Indonesian president. And he had the documents that Bongo had found in Rahmid's room at the Turismo. He'd let the analysts at the section in Jakarta pick over whatever he could bring them, but it felt incomplete. He'd been sent to find Blackbird and establish the meaning of Operasi Boa; he'd done neither.

'Don't be hard on yourself, McQueen,' said Bongo, picking up on Mac's contemplation. 'You've done the best you could – you were never going to walk in here and work it out in two days. Dili's very complicated.'

'Yeah, I know,' said Mac, tired and hungry. 'But I've been thinking that the key to it was really the Canadian – that's where I should have started.'

'Yeah, well you have a few things to take with you.'

'Not much, mate,' said Mac.

'Not much, sure,' said Bongo. 'But forget these boys in the office, right, brother? They think secrets are just thrown in our face. What do they –'

'What?' said Mac.

'You know, McQueen, they think –'

'You said *face*,' replied Mac. '*Secrets thrown in our face.*'

Bongo looked confused but Mac was already down the inside of the wall and casing the cemetery for Brimob.

'Where you going?' hissed Bongo. 'Raoul's here any second.'

'Hold that cab,' said Mac, setting off.

Creeping among the white crypts of Santa Cruz, Mac got within twenty metres of the Salazar grave and crouched as he cased the immediate area for ambushes. When Bongo had spoken about things being thrown in his face, Mac remembered the note Rahmid Ali had retrieved from the drop box at the Salazar grave. He'd read something from it, then balled it in his fist and thrown it at Mac's face. What had Rahmid said? Something like, *She's not here.*

Moving slowly towards the Salazar grave, Mac reckoned the note from the drop box might still be around the gravesite. It had only been two days, and it hadn't shown up in Rahmid's clothes.

Mac had no doubt the note said more than Rahmid had voiced – especially if the drop box was the main avenue for communication between the Canadian and the firm. Besides, spies were experts at lying about what their documents contained. Mac once read aloud a steamy love letter to a female agent he was managing in Malaysia. The woman's reaction confirmed she was a double agent; the letter was actually a supplies requisition variation from one part of Energy Australia to another.

Jogging the last few metres, Mac dropped to his knees and searched the grassy area for the note in the light of the half-moon. It was one of the less-immaculate plots in the famously tidy cemetery and Mac had to pull apart stands of long grass. Crawling around the back of the casement, he found the balled-up white paper sitting between the grass and tombstone, and shoved it in his pocket.

About two hundred metres to the south, Mac noticed movement and flashlights, suggesting a Brimob patrol. Crawling away from them, he found a line of crypts which gave him cover as he moved back to the cemetery wall.

'About time,' mumbled Bongo as he offered his hand and dragged Mac up to the top of the wall. Parked on the street was a minivan, engine running and lights on.

Raoul asked no questions as they slid into the rear seats and drove for the Turismo using the route that avoided the main roads. Mac had him as a seasoned conduit for visiting spies, diplomats and journalists.

Hitting the overhead light, Mac flattened the note from the drop box and had a look. It was a piece of A4 with one line of black print in 12-point Times New Roman, and another line handwritten in blue ballpoint. The handwritten line read: *She's not here.* The printed line started with an asterisk and read: *Nothing on 'Tupelo' or 'Deetupelo' – please supply more.*

Thinking back, Mac tried to work out what he was reading. In his note, he had asked if he could meet Blackbird. He'd watched the cut-out arrive, open the box, pull something out of his pocket and then the drop was over and Mac had watched him leave the cemetery as the Brimob made a pass.

The only way it could have happened was that the cut-out carried a note from the firm in Denpasar or Jakarta to be dropped at the Salazar grave. So the printed reference to Tupelo was from Australian SIS, and when the cut-out saw Mac's note, he didn't even bother to transmit it to the firm – he simply wrote on the note.

So who or what was Tupelo? wondered Mac as Raoul took them through the back passages of Dili, around the military checkpoints. He would follow it up in Denpasar but for now it meant nothing. The Canadian had made a query and ASIS didn't know.

'Mate, can I borrow your phone?' he asked Bongo.

Keying the numbers, Mac waited eight rings before an Aussie male voice picked up.

'Devo,' said Mac. 'Davis, here. Richard Davis?'

After hesitating slightly, Grant Deavers picked up on it. 'Sure, Richard – how's things, mate?'

'Good, thanks,' said Mac. 'The contracts are all signed and I was going to send some of the product home – when does the next flight leave?'

'Top of the dial,' sighed Deavers, 'into Darwin.'

'Room for product?'

Deavers paused and Mac was sure he heard the words *fuck's sake* in the silence.

'Should be room, but don't be late, okay? Thanks, Richard, gotta go,' said Deavers before hanging up.

Raoul made a slow pass in front of the Turismo and then along the side entrance where the fenced car park was accessed, before stopping one block east in the darkness of a banyan. Thanking their driver, Mac and Bongo walked into the darkness and moved along the leafy street, past rubbish bins and stray cats. The warm night was not attracting people into the Dili streets; the Aitarak militia, headquartered at the Hotel Tropical, had made a night out a dangerous prospect.

Slipping over the cyclone fence of the Turismo's car park, Mac and Bongo edged around the borders of the dirt compound until they were squatting in a dark corner, away from the floodlight, looking at nine cars in a line.

'Eight Toyotas,' said Bongo above the din of crickets. 'Lucky dip?'

Shrugging, Mac pressed the 'unlock' button on Rahmid's key and the silver Camry closest to the hotel gate blinked its indicator lights once.

After a quick glance around, Bongo opened the passenger door, then reached in and shut off the interior light. Joining him in the Camry from the rear driver's side, Mac searched the back seat while Bongo did the front.

There was nothing left in the car – not even a chewing gum wrapper in the rubbish bag hanging from the glove box.

'Let's do the boot,' Mac whispered as he pushed his hand under the driver's seat.

'Hello, mister,' came a woman's voice, very close. 'You want the bag?'

'Shit,' hissed Bongo, hitting his head on the inside of the windscreen as Mac threw himself flat on the back seat, grabbing at the Beretta in his waistband.

Looking out from where he lay on his back, Mac saw the shape of a large head on narrow shoulders peering down on him.

'Mrs Soares,' he said, trying to sit up and get his Beretta under his leg, his pulse whacking against his temples. 'Nice to see you again.'

'Mr Davis,' she bowed, already in her silk housecoat, her hair in a net. 'And Mr Alvarez. You must want Mr Rahmid's bag, yeah?'

'Bag?' said Bongo, getting out of the car and pouring on the charm.

'He left a bag with me, in the safe,' said Mrs Soares. 'You with him, right?'

'A bag?' smiled Bongo. 'Gee, he confused us, right, Richard?'

'Yeah,' said Mrs Soares. 'He not come back, I think, but you all friend, right?'

'Sure,' said Bongo. 'Shall we take a look?'

The safe was an old black German two-key hotel lock-box, about a metre high and covered in brass plates and filigree. Opening the heavy door, Mrs Soares pulled out a black leather overnight bag with a shoulder strap and side pockets and handed it to Bongo.

Taking the bag, Bongo sniffed the air and spoke rapidly in Bahasa Indonesia. When Mrs Soares showed no interest in his sniffing, Bongo produced a US twenty-dollar note and Mrs Soares led them into the dining room, which had obviously been closed for the night.

'I don't like this,' said Mac, his heart still going crazy from the fright in the car compound. 'Intel will have eyes.'

'They won't think we'll come back to Dili, let alone the Turismo,' said Bongo, just as Mrs Soares appeared with two Tiger beers. 'Besides, we gotta eat brother.'

Going through the bag, Bongo turned up a manila dossier that had probably once contained the papers found in Rahmid's room, and a copy of the orders that Rahmid had translated and given to Mac at Santa Cruz.

After giving the documents to Mac, Bongo continued searching while Mac had a quick look at the dossier. It was in Bahasa

Indonesia but all of the papers carried official Indonesian military and government letterheads. He'd get it translated at the section in Jakarta.

Pulling out a manila envelope, Bongo handed that over too and they both covered up as Mrs Soares delivered the evening meal. As she walked away, Mac pulled out a thin stash of eight-by-five black-and-white photos.

'Jesus,' he breathed as he saw the shots: Mac wandering through the Bali Museum in Denpasar; Mac being walked into an entrance way of an apartment building in Denpasar, Bongo close behind with his hand on something in his waistband; Mac standing in front of the sliding glass doors of Bali International Airport, looking around with a black wheelie bag in tow.

Each of the pics had a thin white tape along the bottom with date and location printed in black.

Shuffling through them, Mac stopped at the last two, checking back and forth, making sure he was seeing what he was seeing. One showed an Asian man in sunglasses at an outdoor table under a Vittel umbrella – a man Mac knew as the Korean, a guest at the Turismo. The tape along the bottom gave the date as a month earlier, the location was HCMC – Ho Chi Minh City, or Saigon.

The first photo showed the Korean remonstrating with some-one, his cigarette hand pointing at a person obscured by a waiter. The second photo showed another man, a middle-aged Anglo with thinning hair and sunnies, shrugging at the Korean with a smile.

Mac had never met the man, but he'd been chasing his ghost. It was Bill Yarrow, the Canadian.

'This is that Korean bloke,' said Mac, too tired for this. 'Did you meet him?'

'Sure,' said Bongo. 'Jessica had some words with him when you had the heat exhaustion.'

'Jessica?' asked Mac.

'Yeah, this guy thinks she a prostitute – asks her how much,' said Bongo.

'And?' smiled Mac.

'Jessica said, *At least seven inches, buddy – sorry 'bout that.*'

***

Bongo killed the lights and brought Rahmid Ali's Camry to a quiet halt on the west side of Comoro, opposite the military annexe where they could see the white United Nations C-130 being loaded under floodlights.

'That's your ride, McQueen,' said Bongo. 'Better get moving – I don't want to be here all night.'

'You not coming?' asked Mac, confused.

'Nope – heading north, I reckon,' said Bongo, exhaling cigarette smoke.

Suddenly feeling emotional, Mac opened his door.

'Got enough?' asked Bongo, pointing at Rahmid's bag. It wasn't a ton of stuff, but along with the Operation Extermination papers and the work-ups on the Lombok and Sumba companies, it might put some pieces together for someone in Canberra, especially on the eve of the independence ballot. It might even persuade some of the politicians that East Timor needed peacekeepers.

'It'll do for now,' said Mac, though he felt piss-weak. 'Thanks, mate,' he said, and they shook.

'Oh, I almost forgot,' grinned the Filipino, plunging his hand into his breast pocket. 'Half is yours,' he said, fanning the thousand-dollar bills.

'You keep it,' said Mac, getting out of the car.

'What?' said Bongo, leaping out into the balmy night air. 'Finders keepers, brother – you gotta take yours!'

'What were they paying you? To bodyguard the Canadian?' asked Mac.

'Three hundred Aussie a week,' said Bongo, flicking his ash.

'You took a bullet for that, Bongo. What about this gig? The same?'

'Sure,' shrugged Bongo.

'You saved me from the interrogation, mate, and then you got me out of Bobonaro with my nuts still attached,' said Mac, wanting to be serious but chuckling. 'That's the bonus, okay?'

Shrugging, Bongo walked Mac to the hole in the security fence.

'What will you do with the car?' asked Mac.

'Dump it on the north side,' said Bongo. 'But you know what?' he asked, turning back to the Camry.

'What?'

'You could do with a change of clothes,' said Bongo. 'You look like shit. Rahmid's about your size – perhaps a little skinny. Could be some clothes in the trunk?'

Walking to the back of the Camry, Bongo looked over his shoulder. 'By the way, McQueen, no one can handle that stuff we saw this morning, okay?'

'The –?'

'That camp, okay?' said Bongo, putting the key in the lock. 'Too much death hurts a man here,' he said, tapping his chest.

Bongo lifted the boot lid open and they both jumped back.

'Fuck!' said Bongo as they looked down at the illuminated interior. It was the Korean with two bullet holes in his forehead.

CHAPTER 28

The Camry's engine pinged as it cooled in the night air, punctuating their ragged breathing as they stared at the corpse.

'Bloke from the hotel,' mumbled Mac finally. 'Ali did this, right?'

'Sure,' said Bongo, reaching across the corpse and grabbing the handles of a black Adidas sports bag.

The Korean's pockets yielded a Motorola mobile phone, a money clip containing US dollars and a small leather fold with a DBS Visa card and an American Express card, both in the name of Lee Wa Dae. Reaching into the pockets under the card slots, Mac pulled out a stash of paper and unfolded it.

'Bloke's name is Lee Wa Dae,' said Mac, 'and judging by his love of the Hotel Maliana, he's based in Kupang, or spends weeks there at a time.'

Bongo gave a low whistle as he pulled a transparent plastic Ziploc bag from the Adidas bag and handed it to Mac before grabbing another. The size of a small cushion, the bag was filled with wrapped stacks of used US dollars, mostly hundred-dollar bills from what Mac could see.

'Must be fifty, sixty thousand in here,' said Bongo, checking the extremities of the sports bag and coming up with a stainless-steel Colt Defender   a compact automatic pistol favoured by women because it fits in a purse.

'What's this?' asked Mac, holding the plastic bag in front of Bongo and pointing at the Thai or Cambodian script stamped in blue ink on the bag. 'That say Palace or something?'

Nodding, Bongo traced his finger under the lettering. 'Yeah, brother – I think it say *Vacation Palace Hotel and Casino, Poi Pet, Cambodia*.'

'Isn't that . . .?' asked Mac, his voice trailing off as he saw lights moving through the trees at the other end of Comoro's runway. They had company, probably military security.

Heart thumping, Mac shut the trunk, plunging them into complete darkness. About a mile south a Toyota 4×4 with the military police light-bar on the top motored across the base of the runway. It slowed, then turned left towards Mac and Bongo.

'Gotta go, brother,' said Bongo.

'Want some?' said Mac, pointing at the Korean's money as he picked up Rahmid Ali's overnight bag.

'Only if you take some too,' said Bongo.

'Not for me personally, mate, but take a bag for yourself.'

Grabbing a cushion of money, Bongo hustled into the Camry. 'I'll put some into that safe-deposit box of yours. Remind me – Pantai in Makassar, right?' he said, referring to a hotel in Sulawesi where Mac kept money, guns and alternative identity documents.

'Don't get cheeky,' said Mac as Bongo started the car. 'Get out of here, and call me in a couple of days, huh? Let me know you made it.'

'Sure, brother,' said Bongo, then floored the Camry onto the ring road, keeping the lights off.

Grabbing both bags, Mac ran in a crouch to a small hole in the fence, where the cyclone wire had peeled back from a concrete post. The military police vehicle revved louder, its headlights splashing around the scrub as Mac pushed the Adidas bag and Rahmid Ali's leather hold-all through the gap and made to go through himself.

Putting one foot through the hole and then ducking down to push himself through sideways, Mac had his back to the concrete post as the MP 4×4 slowed, its tyres crunching on the gravel. Lurching away from the hole, Mac aimed for the drainage ditch where he'd already thrown the bags, but came up short.

'Fuck!' he muttered to himself as his belt caught on the concrete post.

As he struggled to free himself, the military police vehicle came to a stop, pretty much where Bongo had parked the Camry. Mac lay down as flat as he could, hoping the grass around the fence line would cover his body. The vehicle's engine whirred and Mac listened to the voices of the soldiers chattering as a hand-operated searchlight strobed back and forth along the fence, illuminating Mac as he hovered above the ground, held by his belt.

Gulping, his heart going crazy, Mac slowly reached behind to the Beretta in the small of his back as the military police radio crackled close by. Getting his fingers around the grip, Mac eased the handgun out of his chinos and brought it around under his face, so he could smell the gun oil. Then, without moving his head, he looked back at the 4×4 and was instantly blinded by the searchlight as it penetrated his grass cover.

Trying to control his nervous panting, Mac stretched his right thumb over the cocking hammer of the Beretta and drew it down as slowly as he could, the clicking sounding louder than a drum solo to his ears. He assumed there were two MPs, perhaps a dog. He brought his handgun down level with the headlights, ready to take out at least one of the soldiers if he heard a rifle being cocked or footsteps getting too close.

The adrenaline pumped inexorably, and then came relief as one door slammed, muffling the military radio, and then another, before the 4×4 was put into gear. Finally, Mac exhaled as the engine tone changed and they were accelerating away.

Mac waited until he could no longer hear the 4×4 before sticking his head up over the grass. The night had returned to tropical stillness, a faint breeze from the Banda Sea gently touching the trees and scrub.

Working himself into a kneeling position, he unhooked his belt from the bolt that had a large washer on the end of it, and crawled into the drainage ditch. Standing straight, he tried to breathe deeply and calm his nerves – he wanted to have his shaking hands under control before he presented at the UN's airport depot.

Mac made his way to a canvas hammock seat inside the C-130 and put the two bags between his feet. Trying to sleep, he sat back and let the events of the past four days roll over him while the Dutch aircrew loaded the cargo plane. There was a story somewhere in all that information, he thought, but he had to sleep before he could put it all together.

Voices sounded at the rear of the plane, and a tall Anglo man and a Timorese woman holding a baby in her arms approached the seating area.

'G'day,' said Mac, taking his hand off the Beretta. 'How's it going?'

'Not bad, if we get out of here before the Aitarak arrives,' said the man. 'Ansell – Ansell Torvin,' he said, offering his hand.

'Richard Davis,' replied Mac, shaking Torvin's hand as he tried to place the familiar name.

'What's your story?' asked Torvin, helping the woman belt herself into the opposite hammock seat.

'Businessman in Dili, threatened by the militias,' said Mac. 'And you?'

'I run an NGO – Rural Rehabilitation International – in Lospalos.'

'Dangerous part of the world.' said Mac. 'What's happening out there?'

'The militias lure poor young men with money that comes from Jakarta,' said Torvin wearily. 'They hold big rallies in the soccer stadiums where they indoctrinate these youngsters against independence and give them automatic rifles and cash – it's disgusting.'

'You reported this?' said Mac.

'Yes, we've told DFAT about it,' said Torvin.

'And what do they say?' asked Mac.

'Ha!' said Torvin, looking down at the woman, who smiled back. 'They tell me I'm too close to the East Timorese.'

'Discredited you?' asked Mac, sleep coming on him.

Ansell Torvin laughed. 'They're such cowards, those Foreign Affairs bastards. They know the Prime Minister won't hear a word against a Catholic NGO like ours, so they smear me politically.'

'How?' asked Mac, a little embarrassed.

'They said I'm a mouthpiece for Falintil,' said Torvin. 'Can you believe these people? They called me a commie!'

CHAPTER 29

Waking to the smell of bacon, eggs and coffee, Mac stretched and glanced at the Timor Sea through the window of his apartment. Breakfast usually finished at 9 am at Larrakeyah Army Base in Darwin, so he showered and shaved quickly, trying not to dwell on his battered face when he looked in the mirror.

Registering at the mess, Mac waited to be assigned a table as an athletic woman in civvies was leaving.

'Macca,' she said softly, as she came alongside.

'Badders,' said Mac, disappointed he'd missed the opportunity to have breakfast with Gillian Baddely, one of the few female officers in Australian military intelligence. 'My timing sucks.'

'As usual,' said the cute brunette, giving him a look as she walked away.

Perusing the *Australian* while he ate toast and nursed a plunger of coffee, Mac pondered on how his life could have taken a different course. Gillian Baddely was the woman who'd told the Australian Army to go screw itself after it agreed to an Iraqi demand that the International Atomic Energy Agency inspectors should all be male. Gillian had dug her heels in and won the appointment, which had not made her many friends among the diggers.

Mac liked her and thought the whole feminist thing was quite funny. They'd got very drunk one night in Amman after her IAEA rotation, and the poor timing she referred to was his falling asleep before anything could be consummated.

Looking up from his paper, Mac saw the steward approaching.

'Phone call for you, sir.'

Looking to see if any of the stragglers in the mess were taking too much interest, Mac wiped his mouth with the napkin and went to the wall-mounted phone beside the steward's station.

'Davis,' he said.

'Catnip, please confirm,' said a woman's voice. 'Repeat, Catnip, please confirm.'

'Catnip, this is Albion,' said Mac, looking away from the other diners.

'Albion – status,' said the voice.

'Status Masquerade,' said Mac, referring to the name given to the operation to find Blackbird. If he was in danger or under duress, he would've given his status as 'Limelight'.

A click followed and a powerful voice boomed down the line. 'McQueen – Davidson,' said Tony Davidson.

'Hi, Tony,' said Mac.

'Can't speak for long, mate – walking for a plane.'

'Where are you?' asked Mac.

'En route – I'll be there about midday, okay?'

'Okay,' said Mac quietly.

'Meet you at the office, right?' said Davidson. 'Bring everything you've got – and let's keep this between us, okay, Macca? The section can wait.'

As he finished his breakfast, Mac thought about the call and Davidson's rush to Darwin. It was probably an attempt to intercept Mac before he was recalled to Denpasar to debrief with Atkins and maybe Tobin.

There was an ongoing power play between Davidson and Carl Berquist, the ASIS director of analysis, over the key messages contained in the weekly ASIS reports that went to the Office of National Assessments before being synthesised into the intelligence advice the Prime Minister's security committee received. Technically, Davidson controlled the field officers who collected raw intelligence, while Berquist controlled how the intelligence was interpreted. Both had the power to skew an argument, but Davidson only retained his edge with timing: controlling the reports from officers like Mac before they were written. Once a report got to Tobin in Jakarta and Davidson in Canberra, Berquist's analysts could pull what they wanted from it and develop their own narratives.

Needing a wake-up for his battered body, Mac bought some swimming trunks and goggles from the base store and made for the swimming pool. Starting slow, he numbered off thirty laps of the twenty-five-metre outdoor pool, feeling his back and shoulders stretch out, letting his face relax and his lungs fill up.

Once he'd hit his rhythm, Mac thought about how he was going to play Davidson: straight down the line, probably. When Davidson said he liked clean product, he meant it. He thought an intelligence outfit should simply do its job as best it could, and he'd long hated the lie that there was no credible link between Indonesia's army and the East Timorese militias.

Walking to the poolside seating, Mac grabbed a towel and dried off, wondering where Lee Wa Dae came into the equation and why Rahmid Ali had whacked him. Mac wanted to be sure of what he told Davidson. If he wavered, an office guy would be assigned to help him write the report – a scenario Mac had always avoided.

Throwing the towel around his neck, Mac noticed a blonde woman sitting with a group of officers.

And then Jessica Yarrow looked straight back at him and she was on her feet.

'Oh my god!' she shrieked and ran towards him, throwing her arms around Mac's neck and giving him a kiss. 'You're alive!'

Shrugging, Mac looked over her shoulder and gave the confused army officers a smile.

'Where have you been?!' she demanded, grabbing him by the biceps. 'We thought you were dead, Richard! Manny went back for you. Is he here?' she asked, looking around.

'No, but he found me,' said Mac, smiling.

'Jesus, Richard,' she said, hand going up to Mac's cheekbone. 'What happened to your face? Who did this?'

'Walked into a door,' said Mac, breaking into a chuckle.

'What's so funny?' asked Jessica. 'Is something funny?'

'No,' said Mac, feeling an emotional release. 'I'm just glad you made it.'

Mac and Jessica walked along the grass of Bicentennial Park, the enormous public area on the waterfront of Darwin, lined with red poincianas and rain trees. Mac told her about being caught by Kopassus, without going into details, and the story of Bongo bailing him out, leaving out the bodies in trunks, disinterment and death camps. When women said they wanted to hear everything, they never meant it.

'After Manny rescued me, it wasn't safe to leave through the commercial airport, so the UN flew me out – just like you,' said Mac.

'I'm still waiting for a new passport,' said Jessica as they walked under the clear skies. 'But army food isn't too bad.'

Buying a couple of ice blocks from a vendor in the park, they wandered along the military displays that lined the foreshore, reading the plaques about which US warships had been sunk and how many Japanese planes made up the raiding party. Darwin had a fragrant, tropical ease to it, not unlike Honolulu. And like Honolulu, Darwin had a strong military and strategic significance.

They eventually strolled down to the semicircular lookout that surrounded a World War II naval gun. Gazing out over the Timor Sea they were silent for a few moments, before Jessica tucked herself into Mac's arms.

'I was so scared, Richard,' she said, tears running down her cheeks. 'After we found those kids, I've never been so terrified in my life. I'm still shaking.'

'But what's this about you and those kids?'

'Did Manny tell you?' said Jessica, embarrassed.

'He said you'd made sure they were safe – what was that about?'

'The militia was coming, they were shooting at the guerrillas and being driven back into us.'

'Yeah, so?' asked Mac.

'So, I got the kids behind that tree and then I – well, you know, I had Manny's gun.'

Her voice had lost all its former cockiness and Mac felt her fingers digging into his arms.

'You did the right thing, Jessica.'

'I killed two human beings, Richard,' she sniffled. 'Shit – they were just teenagers.'

'Teenage rapists with assault rifles,' said Mac, looking into her eyes. 'Look, you got through, mate, and you looked after those kids – it balances, believe me.'

'Don't mention kids – please,' she said, pushing away slightly.

'What?' said Mac.

'I can't sleep anymore,' she said, and then took a deep breath. 'Did Manny tell you that after the gunfight we went with the guerrillas to their camp in the hill?'

'No' said Mac.

'There were women and kids and grandparents in this camp, Richard. It wasn't a bunch of boozed freedom fighters. They weren't preaching Marxism.'

'For some East Timorese, Falintil means safety and food,' said Mac.

'I saw something terrible,' she said, nestling into Mac's chest so he could feel her warm tears through his shirt. 'We arrived in the evening and there were all these children who looked strange – something was wrong with them but I couldn't work it out. There was only the firelight.'

'Yes,' said Mac.

'One of the mothers saw me staring, and she told me why they looked different,' she said, bottom lip quivering.

'She told me the militias had cut their ears off, Richard. Their fucking *ears*! The army offered a bounty payment for Timorese ears! I can't get it out of my head!'

Mac held her while she sobbed and it took some time before she had recovered enough to speak.

'My father's not alive, is he?' she said, her beauty and sadness a heart-rending combination. 'I mean . . . that place, I . . .' She tried to go on, before breaking off, tears in her eyes.

Mac was tempted to say something gallant, but it was a luxury he couldn't permit himself.

'I didn't find Dad,' said Jessica, almost talking to herself. 'And if I was missing, Dad would find me, I know he would.'

They held a stare for too long.

'Look, Jessica, East Timor is a disgrace,' said Mac quietly. 'You're braver than ten men to go in there and demand answers about your father. Most people would spend one afternoon in that hotel and be on the next flight out – scared witless. You did what you could.'

'You've probably heard the rumours about my father, and maybe they're true,' she said, flicking hair out of her eyes. 'Dad's not perfect, but he's my father and I can't just walk away.'

Silence fell between them. Mac had been in this situation before, as a young intelligence officer in Cambodia. He'd promised more than he could deliver and had vowed never to do it again. But Mac knew from his own family that you didn't walk away from kin.

'Manny's still on the island,' said Mac. 'But I beg you – don't go back there, okay?'

'I don't know if I can go back,' she admitted. 'But I don't know if I can just do nothing. Manny's still there?'

'Yes, but he knows what he's doing,' said Mac quickly. 'Leave it to him – I'm sure he'll keep an eye on it.'

'I hope so,' said Jessica. 'The Americans didn't pay him to take a holiday.'

Stiffening, Mac pushed her away slightly. 'The Americans?'

Jessica admitted that Bongo's protection services were not contracted between them at the Hotel Turismo, as they'd led Mac to believe. An officer from the US consulate in Denpasar had helpfully insisted that she go to Dili with Bongo, who would keep an eye on her.

Thinking back on the pictures of Jessica and Jim at the Denpasar cafe, Mac realised the consulate guy was 'Jim' from DIA. He was relieved that at least Jessica's involvement seemed to be purely civilian.

But he wasn't happy with Bongo. Working for DIA was something Bongo should have shared with Mac. Not because Bongo was compromised, but because it showed that the Pentagon was interested in Bill Yarrow.

CHAPTER 30

Mac ran up the front steps of Arafura Imports in central Darwin, and entered the reception area, pushing up his sunglasses.

'Just in time for your new phone, Mr Davis,' said Sally the receptionist, pushing a brown box across the counter. The Arafura Imports office on Cavanagh Street was a corporate front for Australian SIS, and Sally sometimes found herself working as a stewardess in Qantas first class or as a concierge in the Marriott group.

'Suppose a nine-mill is out of the question?' joked Mac, as he signed the receipt docket.

Sally found a spare mug, poured Mac a coffee and escorted him through two PIN-enabled security doors and into one of the meeting rooms, where Tony Davidson sat at a conference table, phone to his ear.

Putting his coffee and bags down, Mac took a seat on the other side of the table and listened to his boss make placatory sounds to a desk-jockey. As the phone hit its cradle, Davidson stood to his bearish six foot five and extended a paw.

'Macca,' he said with a smile. 'Didn't your mother tell you to stay out of fights?'

Shaking his boss's hand, Mac smiled back and said his hellos. His face was still a mess: two black eyes, a fat lip and a big lumpy shiner on his left cheekbone. Whatever disagreements Mac had with Bongo's operating style, he now had total empathy with the Filipino's need for payback – Bongo could have Benni Sudarto, Mac would take Amir.

'Larrakeyah okay?' asked Davidson, taking off his suit jacket and hanging it on the back of the door. 'No one playing at nosey-buggers?'

'No, it seems fine – but if you want me staying five-star, I'm game,' said Mac. 'Sheraton will do.'

Starting with a brief story of the East Timor mission and its dual goals – Blackbird and Boa – Mac included Bongo's role as subtly as he could, although it still elicited a wince from Davidson.

'Shit, Macca – Morales is a hit man, isn't he?'

'He was also at the meet where we lost the Canadian and Blackbird,' said Mac. 'I wanted him to brief me, and, well we came to an arrangement and he rode security for me.'

'Okay,' said Davidson, a little annoyed.

Answering some basic questions about the operation, Mac went over the meetings in Dili, describing how the Indonesian military-commercial establishment was still operating as if they expected no political change in East Timor. Then Mac told of being invited to the Lombok facility in Bobonaro district and being asked to do some procuring for Major-General Damajat, the man who appeared to be running the show. Putting the vial from Damajat's office on the desk, Mac disclosed where he'd stolen it from.

'It might be nothing,' said Mac, nodding at the vial. 'He says it's about re-engineering a disease in order to cure it. But their procurement is covert and I'm fairly certain the Canadian was doing this job before me.'

'Sydney'll take too long – be faster to get it analysed by the Americans in Denpasar,' said Davidson, poking at the clear vial which contained a tobacco-coloured liquid. 'So, you're in his office and Damajat thinks you're the Canadian's replacement – but then the Sudartos make you?'

'Yeah – I'm Damajat's best buddy, and then I get jumped by Amir Sudarto and a couple of Kopassus intel goons.'

'So, a possible schism in the Indonesian military?' said Davidson, making a small note in his ever-present detective's pad. 'Sudartos and Damajat not working to the same agenda?'

'Perhaps,' said Mac.

'What about this death camp?'

'Between a hundred and a hundred and thirty bodies, all ages and genders, all dead,' said Mac, pausing as he remembered the sight. 'Actually, one girl was still alive – Falintil rescued her.'

'Were they shot?' asked Davidson.

'Poison, probably.'

'Official?' asked Davidson. 'A military operation?'

'Kopassus, for sure,' said Mac. 'I had an eyewitness account, third party. Joao – the Falintil leader – told me that a bloke called Antonio who had defected from the 1635 Regiment, was –'

'That's the locals' regiment?'

'That's them,' said Mac. 'This Antonio drove an army truck in Bobonaro district and he said that he'd delivered supplies to this secret camp up in the hills behind Memo.'

'On the border.'

'Correct.'

'I agree – Memo sounds like a death camp of some sort,' said Davidson, mulling on it. 'But what sort of supplies do you take to a death camp?'

'Don't know,' admitted Mac. 'But probably not food.'

For the next hour, Mac worked with Davidson to integrate some of the stranger revelations of the operation into a cohesive narrative.

'The first problem came with Rahmid Ali.'

'The guy from the President's office?' asked Davidson.

'Yeah,' said Mac, wondering how much credence to give the Indonesian spy who had ambushed him at Santa Cruz cemetery.

'You believe he was there on the President's authority?' said Davidson.

'He seemed genuine, and I got his sat phone to see who he's been calling,' said Mac, pointing to the pile of evidence he'd brought back from Dili.

Leaning forward, Davidson pushed a button on the desk phone and asked Sally to come through.

'So what do you think he wanted?' asked Davidson.

'He wanted me to take that,' he said, pointing at the English translation of Operation Extermination that Davidson held in his hands, 'and he wanted it to be taken up by Aussie intel and military.'

'Why?'

'Because Habibie's isolated and he needs Canberra to be kicking up a fuss about the Indonesian Army in East Timor, not going along with the generals.'

There was a knock at the door and Sally entered.

'Get me the full logs on this phone, okay, Sal?' said Davidson.

'Sure, boss,' she said, smiling at Mac as she took the phone.

'And I need it asap.'

After she closed the door, Mac continued. 'Revealing something like Operation Extermination could weaken the generals, but only if there's international outrage.'

'And if Habibie sticks his neck out too far in Jakarta, he gets it chopped, right?' asked Davidson.

'Yep,' said Mac. 'He's trying to take the Republic into a democratic era but he doesn't have a military power base. The military is also worried about the DPI gaining too much popularity post-Soeharto,' said Mac, referring to the left-wing political party headed by Megawati Sukarnoputri.

'Okay,' said Davidson, weighing the documents and staring at Mac over the top of his reading glasses. 'Let's say Operation Extermination is real and there's a deportation project planned for East Timor – what's this false-flag thing that Ali was talking about? What do you make of that?'

'Ali said the real campaign that was hidden behind Operation Extermination was called Operasi Boa,' said Mac.

'We know about that, right?' said Davidson, flipping back through his notebook.

'It was one of my targets in Masquerade,' said Mac. 'The meaning of Operasi Boa was what the Canadian was supposed to establish at his final meeting with Blackbird.'

'Of course,' said Davidson. 'And?'

'Well, then Bongo took him out – he thought I was being threatened.'

'So let's get it straight,' said Davidson, leaning back in his chair and clasping his hands behind his head. 'The President's office signs off on orders from the general staff. Those orders are Operation Extermination, a depopulation program for post-ballot East Timor. But the President's office has a spy among the generals who reveals there's something much worse hidden behind Extermination – it's called Operasi Boa and we have no idea what it might be?'

'That's where we're up to,' said Mac.

'I suppose it comes back to Ali's credibility, and he's not totally the good guy,' said Davidson, reaching for his coffee, 'because you found a corpse in his car, right?'

'The Korean – Lee Wa Dae,' said Mac, spelling the name.

'Who is?' asked Davidson, jotting a note.

'I thought he was just a rude Korean businessman – he was staying at the Turismo. But in Ali's bag there was a bunch of telephotos, two of them featuring Lee Wa Dae meeting with Bill Yarrow,' said Mac as he handed over the manila envelope.

'Yarrow's our Canadian, right?' said Davidson, pulling the eight-by-fives out of the envelope and going through them.

'That's him,' said Mac, craving another coffee.

Pausing and looking back and forth between two of the telephotos, Davidson's forehead creased.

'Saigon?!' he said. 'What the fuck is our Canadian doing in Saigon with this Korean prick?'

'That's what I wanted to talk about, Tony,' said Mac, pushing the black Adidas bag across the table. Pulling out one of the cash-cushions, Davidson held the US dollars in front of him and looked down at the logo on the bag. 'We know what this says?'

'Vacation Palace Hotel and Casino, Poi Pet.'

'Oh really?' spat Davidson, throwing the cash on the conference table and looking at the ceiling. 'Poi Pet! That's great, that really is.'

The Vacation Palace was a Cambodian money-laundering operation run by the North Korean generals. Their heroin money came back from the United States, Canada, Australia and France and was exchanged for chips in their own casinos. Having been laundered, the subsequent US dollars paid out by the cashiers were used to buy real estate, gold and businesses all over the world.

'Fuck's sake,' whispered Davidson, reaching for the phone and dialling.

'Judy,' he said into the phone, 'I need a priority work-up on Lee Wa Dae – Korean or North Korean – and I need it yesterday, okay?'

As he spelled the name Mac could imagine Judy Hyams scrawling on her notebook, putting her ego aside to deal with Davidson's demands. A part-time lecturer at the Australian National University and a full-time head of research at ASIS, Judy suffered Davidson's demands in a way that women weren't supposed to in the 1990s. Still, she always got the leave she wanted and Davidson religiously remembered her birthday.

'Thanks, Jude . . .' he barked, but didn't put the phone down.

'We do?' said Davidson, addressing the phone with a new tone in his voice. 'Let's have it.'

He listened and then, putting the phone down, took off his glasses and massaged his eyeballs with his left hand.

'Lee Wa Dae is known to us, apparently,' he said, peering out from now-bleary eyes.

'Who is he?' asked Mac, troubled by Davidson's demeanour.

'He's a bag man for the North Korean Army's drug business.'

CHAPTER 31

The doors to the gents flapped and Davidson was back in the public bar of the Victoria Hotel. Outside, tourists meandered along Smith Street mall in the tropical heat.

'So I guess I don't need to say this, Macca,' said Davidson, checking his watch. 'But when you debrief with Atkins, why don't we leave out the Rahmid Ali involvement? For the time being, eh?'

'You mean that the President's office tried to speak to me direct?'

'Yes, that,' said Davidson, looking around the pub. 'I'm thinking there might be another way to move on this. I'll tell him about it later, when we've explored it.'

'Another way?' said Mac.

'Trust me – do your meeting with Atkins in Denpasar.'

'What if he takes it, tries to write it himself?' said Mac.

'Do nothing, Macca, just call me,' growled Davidson. 'If Atkins really wants to step up a weight division, then it'll be *me* writing the CX, okay?'

'Okay, Tony. But . . .' started Mac, before trailing off.

'Get your phone charged and call me as soon as you've looked at Rahmid's phone logs,' said Davidson. And then he was out of the air-conditioning and into a cab parked at the kerb.

Sipping on the remains of his beer, Mac thought about his

evening flight to Denpasar and what awaited him there. Martin Atkins would be uncomfortable with too much intelligence that slandered the Indonesian military and possibly messed with his own corporate advancement plan. Mac would have to be particularly careful about the Canadian: Bill Yarrow was connected with Atkins and any bad news about the Canadian's true loyalties would have the potential to hurt Atkins' career. If that looked likely, Atkins would do what all good office guys did: blame the field guy.

The tail didn't stay hidden and didn't make any of the standard gestures that would blend him into the streetscape: no magazines or newspapers, no caps pulled down over dark glasses, no ostentatious tourist maps. Judging by the chinos, polo shirt and Annapolis ring, he was American, and as Mac left the Victoria the tail simply rose from the park bench and followed.

Keeping a normal pace, Mac walked through the afternoon sunshine of Darwin, down Smith Street towards the Civic Centre and then around in a loop past Parliament until he was walking north-west down Mitchell Street through all the tourists and backpackers. The crowds gave him a chance to think about what was going on. Was the tail a remnant of the East Timor operation – had Jessica debriefed with the Defense Intelligence Agency and inadvertently made Mac more interesting than he wanted to be? Or was this tail the CIA, tailing an Aussie in Darwin?

Whatever species of Yank it was, it was a tad fucking cheeky.

It was also inconvenient. Sally had him on the 11 pm flight into Denpasar, and he'd wanted to catch a bite to eat with Jessica before heading for the airport. Cloak-and-dagger didn't fit into the schedule.

Mac dived into a backpacker's hostel built around an arcade and sped up, shooting through the cool alley lined with shops and tour-booking agencies, coming out the other end. Walking across the car park behind the arcade, Mac checked the tail in a van window's reflection – he was still coming.

Crossing the Esplanade, Mac scoped plenty of joggers, mothers pushing prams and tourists strolling under the trees at Bicentennial

Park. Lacking a firearm, he wanted some kind of disincentive to someone pulling a gun.

All of the park benches faced away from the street, over the Timor Sea, which was starting to chop up with the afternoon breeze. So Mac walked to the wall around the naval gun, leaned against it facing the Esplanade and waited, his hand tucked down in the small of his back to intimate that he was armed.

The American slowed but kept coming. Mac had him as six-one, late thirties, former athlete, probably tennis.

His heart beating up in his throat, Mac stiffened as the tail got to twenty metres away, stopped and put his open palms out sideways. It was the first time he'd seen the bloke without a black baseball cap.

Exhaling, Mac brought his hand out and showed his own empty palm.

'Wouldn't usually do this, McQueen,' came the educated American voice.

'Man's gotta do,' replied Mac. 'How you been, Jim?'

They strolled south along the pathways of the park, then walked around Parliament and the Supreme Court building. Mac was always on edge with another intelligence outfit, even with Australia's other intelligence agencies. When they first trained intelligence officers, the firm gave lessons on cellular information sharing, conducting exercises showing how easily those cells could be broken, secrets compromised and human lives with them. But Mac's relationship with the Pentagon's DIA had always been cordial.

'Notwithstanding my charismatic personality and good looks, Jim,' said Mac as they stopped and sat down at a park bench overlooking Frances Bay, 'what the fuck do you want?'

Laughing, Jim pulled a soft pack from his chinos and lit a smoke. 'Thought we might do an old-fashioned swap.'

'Intel?' asked Mac.

'Sure,' shrugged Jim, ''less you got the Aussie version of Cameron Diaz.'

'Okay, wise guy,' said Mac. 'Shoot.'

'Someone told me you'd infiltrated Lombok AgriCorp, had eyes in Damajat's office?'

'Nice story, Jim.'

'Interesting place they got up there,' said Jim, sucking on the smoke. 'Lots to think about.'

'I said to a colleague of mine that if McQueen actually got in there – if he managed to get into Damajat's office – then I'd bet twenty to one that he came out with a little souvenir.'

'Jim – I need you as my PR man,' said Mac. 'What do you want, mate?'

Pausing, Jim flicked the cigarette. 'If you got a sample from Lombok – anything, man – then we need to take a look. It's important – maybe urgent.'

'And I get?'

'You name it. I'm assuming we have the same interests in East Timor.'

'Okay,' said Mac, looking at his watch – he wasn't going to miss his date with Jessica. 'Tell me – what's Lee Wa Dae doing in Timor? He's from the North Korean general staff, isn't he?'

Running his hands down his thighs, Jim looked away. 'Well, that's fairly advanced, McQueen.'

'What did you think I was doing in Timor?'

'Looking for your Canadian friend and getting to know Bongo Morales a little better.'

'Well?'

'Shit, McQueen – I thought you'd want to know about Yarrow.'

'And Maria Gersao.'

'We've heard that Bill Yarrow was at the Kota Baru barracks in Baucau,' said Jim.

'That's a Kopassus base, isn't it?' said Mac, his hope of finding the Canadian fading fast.

'Sure is, McQueen – so don't go getting that girl's hopes up, I don't care how pretty she is.'

'Me?!' spat Mac. 'I'm not the one giving her a bodyguard, encouraging her to go wandering around the hills of East Timor!'

'Yeah, well, you know how it is, McQueen,' shrugged Jim. 'It wasn't planned that way.'

'And Maria?' asked Mac.

'The local girl you're running?'

'Worked at army HQ,' said Mac.

'I'll let you know if I know, okay?'

'Okay, Jim.'

Mac thought about throwing the Canadian's 'Tupelo' query into the mix, but decided to clear it with Atkins first.

'So – the samples?' asked Jim.

'In a consular pouch to Denpasar.'

'To us?'

'Yep – the Defense Department lab will do 'em faster than Sydney.'

'Great,' said Jim, relaxing visibly. 'I won't cut you out, by the way.'

'From your reaction to my mention of Lee Wa Dae, I'm assuming there's more to discuss,' said Mac.

'What do you know about him?' asked Jim, looking out to sea.

'Right now, probably a lot more than your mob,' countered Mac. 'But officially, he handles the finance side of the North Korean heroin rackets.'

Jim chewed his lip. 'You around? Not running off?'

'I'm around, mate,' lied Mac.

'Good,' said Jim, slapping Mac on the shoulder as he stood. 'Then maybe we'll talk again, huh?'

Opting for an outdoor table at a modern Japanese restaurant, Mac and Jessica watched the crowds go by on Mitchell Street. Busying himself with the wine list, Mac let Jessica run the food side of the equation.

'I'm sorry I dragged you into this, Richard,' said Jessica after the waiter had poured her glass. 'I had no idea what I was doing.'

'Seem to be doing okay,' said Mac. 'Sounds like you can handle a gun.'

'I'm a farm girl – trucks and tractors are no problem, either,' she said. 'I was just annoyed with my government for letting my dad disappear without making any attempt to find him.'

'Maybe they were?' asked Mac, unobtrusively clocking every set of eyes in the pedestrian traffic.

'Well, maybe,' she shrugged. 'But if that American – Jim – hadn't hooked me up with Manny, I wouldn't have lasted long.'

'What about your mother? Brothers or sisters?' asked Mac. 'They pitching in?'

'Only child . . . and Mum hates Dad,' she said, in a matter-of-fact tone. 'They divorced when I was fourteen, and even though our comfortable life ran on his money, she made it hard to know him.'

'Handy dad for a place like UCLA,' said Mac. 'It's not cheap.'

'Actually,' she said, fixing him with a stare, 'Dad pays my fees and accommodation – I work for everything else.'

'Really?' asked Mac. 'You work?'

Sighing at him, she crossed her tanned arms. 'Wednesdays, Thursdays, Fridays at a campus bookstore, and I do telemarketing for a company in Century City. And there's no end in sight now I'm in the School of Law.'

'Okay,' said Mac, surrendering.

'Oh, and you might have noticed – I buy my own drinks.'

'Amen to that,' said Mac, raising his glass.

'Dinner doesn't count,' said Jessica, clinking glasses and giggling. 'I'm independent, but I don't go Dutch.'

Jessica made a production of ordering the dishes, but without losing her sense of humour. And as she handed the menu to the bowing waitress, she fixed Mac with a grin.

'So, Richard – how does a man trying to find sandalwood opportunities end up driving around with someone like Manny Alvarez?'

'Same as you,' said Mac, as light as he could. 'You stay in hotels like the Turismo often enough, then you meet people like Manny. If you find them useful to travel with, you make a friendship, come to an arrangement.'

Sipping at the excellent New Zealand sauvignon blanc, Mac wished Jessica would get off the occupational line. He lived his work and there were times when he just wanted to enjoy the wine, appreciate the company and not have to do the dance of the seven veils.

'You know, Jessica, I've been wondering about you.'

'That's a good start,' she said.

'Well, actually – you're probably sick of talking about you,' said Mac, smiling.

'Oh, you *bastard*!' she shrieked, but finding it funny. 'That's not fair.'

'I was wondering why you don't have a boyfriend? I mean, you're –'

'You mean, am I a psycho?'

'It had occurred to me,' said Mac.

'Ha!' she laughed, looking around. 'I had a boyfriend. *Wayne.*'

'Can he still chew food?' asked Mac.

'Very funny, Mr Richard!'

'Social issue?' Mac asked.

'Like?'

'Like at fifty-seven, why's Wayne living with Mum?'

Jessica chuckled and then lowered her voice. 'Actually, when men say they like a smart girl, they don't always mean it.'

'What happened?'

'Undergraduate was fine – making law school was a bridge too far for a man just starting his career as a junior marketing manager.'

'So?' asked Mac.

'We were dating. I got accepted. We broke up. The end,' she said, shrugging but sad.

Sipping in silence, they avoided one another's eyes until Jessica put her hand across the table and grasped Mac's forearm.

Opening her mouth to speak, nothing came out.

'Yes?' said Mac.

'Umm – nothing,' said Jessica, releasing her grip and sitting back. 'Where's the bathroom?'

Standing beside the taxi as it idled outside the officer apartments, Mac was torn. He could get in the cab, do the Harold Holt and go to Darwin airport, or he could try to make amends with Jessica. Perhaps say a proper goodbye. The past few days had been emotional for both of them, worsened by his reticence about starting a relationship with a girl who didn't even know his real name. If they'd met while he was visiting his folks in Rockhampton, he'd have been plain old Alan McQueen. But, short of marrying her – not on the cards at this stage of his career – Mac was not going to reveal his true identity. There was no statute of limitations on the kind of anger he'd engendered in his professional life. His only protection was hiding his identity, an advantage ruined once you revealed it to a civilian woman.

But there was one conversation he could have with her, if he could convince himself that it wouldn't ruin his other objectives.

'Shit!' he said to himself finally, and asked the driver to hold for a minute.

Knocking on Jessica's door, he was edgy, even if he hadn't worked out what he was going to say.

'Go away,' came Jessica's muffled voice from behind the door.

'Look, Jessica,' he whispered, not wanting half the base to come out and ask him what was up. 'I'm sorry about the flight, okay?'

'Oh piss off!' came the response.

'It was the only flight to Denpasar, and my company booked me on it – I'm sorry,' said Mac, trying not to yell.

'Sorry?!' she said, the door opening with a flourish. 'You take me to dinner, and take me to bed, and then as an afterthought you tell me you're flying out tonight?'

'Can we keep it down?' asked Mac, looking around. 'People are trying to sleep.'

'It's ten past nine,' said Jessica, and Mac could see her eyes were puffy. 'I wanted to spend time with you, Richard – I can't do this on my own.'

'I know,' said Mac, putting his arms around her.

'I'm scared,' she sobbed into his neck. '*Really* scared.'

Over Jessica's shoulder, Mac saw Gillian Baddely emerge from an apartment, give him a nasty look and shake her head.

'I have a plane to catch,' mumbled Mac, and pushing himself away he headed for the cab, trying to put Jessica's sobs out of his mind.

The one thing he could have told her was that her father was last seen in the Kota Baru barracks in Baucau. But Mac had decided not to, and he didn't want Jessica looking into his eyes.

CHAPTER 32

Mac's new Nokia buzzed while he was standing with other travellers at Bali International Airport, waiting for the stragglers to assemble in front of the minivan driver with the *Natour Bali* sign. Looking at the phone, Mac dialled into the secure voicemail servers in Canberra and got a message from Marty Atkins: the late-night debrief meeting was postponed, new time eleven o'clock the following morning.

After running some basic security checks on his bungalow at the Natour, Mac jammed a chair under the door handle, stripped and made for the bathroom. The shower felt good and Mac sensed his energy making a comeback as he padded through the spacious bungalow at the Natour, keeping the lights down and checking the windows from the side of the curtains. Grabbing a cold Bintang from the mini-bar, he sat at the writing desk and opened his wheelie bag, taking the seven pages of logs from Rahmid Ali's phone.

The account had only been opened three weeks earlier and Mac ran his eyes down the list of dialled numbers, looking for the patterns. There was one number that recurred – Mac noticed it because it had a '61' prefix, followed by a variety of mobile numbers, meaning Australia.

Another cluster of numbers showed eighteen calls to a number with a '6221' prefix on the day Mac flew into Dili. The times for the calls went from the morning of Mac's arrival to the morning of the next day. So Rahmid Ali had been feverishly calling someone in Jakarta, even as he watched Mac at Dili's airport.

The numbers, dates and durations started from the left side of the pages, and on the right were the work-ups on each number. They were notated as if in stylised speech bubbles for a cartoon. Most of them were to the Presidential Building in Jakarta, where Ali probably had his office, or at least someone to answer to. There were calls to the Dominion Bank of Singapore in Singapore – not surprising, since most educated elites in Indonesia had their doctors, banks and dentists on the island republic, even as they spruiked Indonesia's place in the world.

These weren't what Mac was looking for. He wanted something that looked like a front or a cut-out – a number either unlisted or burdened with a nondescript name. As Mac leaned back, rubbing his eyes, he suddenly remembered the business card Rahmid Ali had given him in the garden of the Turismo.

Mac rummaged through the side pockets of his wheelie bag and pulled out the card. In dark blue printing were the words *Andromeda IT Services* and then the sat-phone number which Ali had underlined in fine black ballpoint. It also listed a corporate address in KL, a landline and a fax number. Comparing the numbers with the phone logs, Mac ran his finger down the list but didn't come up with a match. The Andromeda numbers were fronts, and when Rahmid Ali really wanted to speak with his organisation, he probably did it direct with Jakarta.

Keying his Nokia, Mac waited for the pick-up and the challenge. He gave his code and the operation name, and even though it was one o'clock in the morning in Canberra, he still had a research assistant on the end of the line. The Telstra mobile service he used wasn't the kind you could buy retail – it ran on the government-consular security network, and when he worked in South-East Asia it was diverted through Singapore's security cellular system.

'What's your name?' he asked the woman, who had a faint subcontinent accent.

'Leena, sir,' she said.

'Okay, Leena, I need a reverse-listing on a Kuala Lumpur number, and then we're going extension hunting, okay?'

Leena was fast and good – in twenty seconds she had the physical address for the KL numbers which Mac wrote down on the Natour Bali letterhead.

'Okay, Leena, can you get the phone book for the Presidential Building in Jakarta, please?'

Leena said she'd call back when she had the book, and Mac rang off.

Grabbing another beer, Mac thought about his debrief with Atkins. Operation Masquerade was still active as far as Mac was concerned. Blackbird remained missing and Boa unexplained. Mac's problems with Atkins would come with the revelations about the death camp in Memo and the increasingly out-of-control environment in Bobonaro. Mac would argue that matters were sufficiently serious in East Timor that Masquerade continue, without getting so carried away that Atkins would worry that the operation was going to result in a damning report about the behaviour of the Indonesian Army.

Operasi Boa was worth investigating, thought Mac. It was serious enough that the Indonesian President's spies were trying to contact ASIS directly. And besides, a false flag was not as outlandish as it sounded. Military intelligence operatives routinely swapped operations, created 'ghost' documents, inserted false information in the more openly available files and held deliberately inaccurate briefings, all in order to misinform the spies, the media and their own leaders – many of whom couldn't be trusted with sensitive military information. When Mac first rotated into Iraq at the end of the Gulf War, Rod Scott's abiding lesson in intel gathering was to treat everything as a lie – especially the 'hidden' documents covered in EYES ONLY stamps, the ones in the military files that pointed a finger at the politicians, the ones in the intel files that blamed everything on Saddam's secret police, and the coincidental files 'found' by the fleeing Sunni elites that fingered their Shia underlings for every criminal decision. So the idea of Operation Extermination veiling something more serious wasn't troubling Mac; the puzzle was Operasi Boa itself.

Remembering himself back at Santa Cruz that day, Mac recreated the scene and tried to evoke Ali's voice in his mind. As he played the scene over and over, Mac was sure that when he'd looked up from reading Operation Extermination, he'd summed it up as a 'deportation' project. Ali had agreed with Mac's interpretation but had later re-phrased deportation as 'depopulation'.

Was there a difference? One meant shipping people out of a territory, the other translated as?

Mac's mobile rang and he grabbed at it.

'Leena,' he said, sitting back at the desk. 'Got it?'

'Yes, sir,' she trilled in that uniquely musical Indian way. 'And we're in luck; its last update was ten days ago.'

They worked through the numbers in the Presidential Building and one by one Mac put a cross beside them. There was a number in accounts, a number for the main switchboard and two for the chief of staff's office.

Mac was looking for more, something a little out of the ordinary, something that connected Rahmid Ali to another name. Before he stomped into a potential diplomatic snafu in Jakarta, he needed to know exactly who Ali was aligned with. Jotting the notes down as he went, he flipped through the pages again and picked up a mobile number with a Singapore prefix – the notes to this number had a user ID of Penang Trading Co. with a postal box address in Singapore.

'Leena, can you get me our person in SingTel, get me a street address for a Singapore mobile number? I'll hold.'

Waiting for Leena to complete the inquiry, Mac wondered about Operasi Boa, the mere mention of which had resulted in Blackbird and Bill Yarrow being snatched and Bongo shot. Weren't the Indonesian military now beyond embarrassment? This was an organisation that had systematically terrorised and repressed East Timor for twenty-four years, in which time they'd already wiped out a quarter of the province's local population.

'SingTel confirms a physical address at that mobile number,' came Leena's voice over the phone.

Writing the address on his pad, Mac wasn't overly hopeful about what it would yield. Commercial front organisations were set up the same way all over the world and the goal was to avoid being surprised.

As he went to sign off, a small column of letters grabbed Mac's attention. Looking down the column of the logs, most of the spaces in the column had a dash, which was why he hadn't noticed it, but at the end of the document a few lines of the column held a simple letter 'S'.

'Leena, what does the S mean on these sat-phone logs?' asked Mac.

'Which bill is it?' she asked.

Looking around the header, Mac found the TI logo. 'It's Telkom Indonesi, and underneath it says *Powered by InMarSat*.'

'Okay,' said Leena, the sound of a pencil clicking against her teeth as she flipped through her telecom manuals. 'The S on the TI sat phone means *setempat*.'

'Remind me . . .' mumbled Mac, embarrassed that he had such basic Bahasa Indonesia after working for so long in South-East Asia.

'Setempat means local – a local call.'

'Okay,' said Mac, his adrenaline pumping in his temples. Running his finger down the last page to Rahmid Ali's final activity on the sat phone, he found a cluster of calls made to an 'S' number during the two days that Ali had been in Dili. Maybe Rahmid's connections weren't in Jakarta or KL. Perhaps they were in Dili the whole time.

Reading out the number, Mac asked for a reverse-listing. He wanted a street address.

'Nothing on that one, Albion,' said Leena.

Looking back at it, Mac saw the last numerals were 4216.

'Leena, try it again, but the last digits are four, two, zero, zero.'

Tapping rang out from a cheap keyboard. 'No luck there.'

'Okay, try four, zero, zero, zero, as the last four digits,' said Mac, massaging the side of his face.

The keyboard rattled again and Leena – warming to the chase – chuckled. 'That's pretty good, Albion.'

As he listened to Leena read the street address, it immediately registered and Mac could see it as if he was standing there. He didn't need her to give the listing's name; it was PT Watu Selatan.

'Thanks, Leena,' he said, signing off and walking around the room. Watu Selatan was a large organisation, and the next challenge was to find out who sat behind the extension that Rahmid Ali had called. Mac had been in there, sat with Adam Moerpati, and Moerpati had tried to butter him up, get him into the Resende.

Staring at the phone logs from the other side of the room, Mac told himself it couldn't be – Habibie's personal intel operators surely wouldn't be that brazen . . . would they?

Sitting at the desk again, Mac picked up Adam Moerpati's business card and looked down the list of phone numbers. The first was for the switchboard, the second was his direct number: it ended in 4216.

'Well, fuck me,' whispered Mac in the gloom. The President's men weren't simply brazen, they were near suicidal: they had a spy across the road from army headquarters.

CHAPTER 33

After walking each side of the street for six minutes, Mac moved to the entrance of a three-storey building tucked between Denpasar city centre and the suburbs. Having been identified by the receptionist, who pushed a button on her desk to unlock the glass entrance door, Mac walked into the nondescript offices of Triangle Associates, a once-thriving Perth construction consulting firm. Aussie SIS had bought out Triangle's partners in 1991 and slowly let the best people go. Now it was operating in Denpasar and headed by Martin Atkins, which – Mac used to joke – was where you landed when you got rid of your best people.

'Macca!' said Atkins, reaching out a hand of greeting in the lobby. 'Sorry about the change of plans, but someone flew in overnight.'

Leading Mac through to the meeting room, Atkins chirped on about the weather and Indonesian politics. Mac's heart sank as a fifty-something Anglo male with a bullfrog neck stood and held his tie to his stomach.

'G'day, Alan, how's it going?' said the bloke, trying an overhand shake.

'Not bad, Carl,' said Mac, looking into the wonky eye of Davidson's long-time rival, Carl Berquist. 'Didn't expect you to be here.'

'Oh, you know, mate,' said Berquist, trying to be chummy. 'Just keeping an eye on what we're up to.'

Mac managed not to snigger at the optical reference – Berquist's punter's eyes could be disconcerting if you hadn't been around them for a while.

'And I guess Tony's in Canberra, keeping an eye on your analysts, right?' said Mac, trying to make it light but failing.

Atkins gave Mac a death stare.

'Alan's been in the field for a while – tough time in East Timor,' said Atkins, then held up a finger to Berquist. 'One minute, Carl?'

Turning to Mac, Atkins was white-lipped as he led Mac out of the room by the elbow.

'What the fuck do you think you're doing, McQueen?!' he hissed as they reached the water cooler in reception.

'Me?!' said Mac, furious. 'What the fuck are *you* doing, Marty?'

'I'm debriefing you on fucking Masquerade, McQueen. It's what we *do*, mate!'

The receptionist, a young Anglo woman, cleared her throat and disappeared through a door behind the desk.

'See what you've done now?' said Mac, aware that a couple of former footy players arguing might seem intimidating.

'Grow up, Macca!' said Atkins, as he straightened his tie.

'I don't need to be lectured on how debriefs work, Marty,' said Mac, pointing at the meeting room door. 'But we don't debrief to the analysis and assessment people.'

'Gee, sorry, Macca. Didn't know you were making the rules for Aussie intelligence now.'

'We do it the way we do it so I can say things to you informally that might not go into the CX.'

'You think Carl can't tell the difference?' demanded Atkins, as furious as Mac. 'He's a director, Macca! He was spooking when you were in primary school.'

'So they say, but Tony's the relevant director,' said Mac.

'*Relevant?!*' growled Atkins. 'Try some relevant manners.'

'*Me?!*' snorted Mac, breathing shallow. 'That's rich.'

'Yes, manners! You're not going to come into my office and speak to the director of analysis like that, mate. Not how it works,' said Atkins, his face red.

Taking a breather, Mac and Atkins put their hands on their hips.

'You could have told me, mate,' said Mac, taking the edge off his voice. 'Frankly, I would have liked some warning that I was going to be discussing Masquerade in front of someone like Carl Berquist.'

'What do you mean by that?' asked Atkins.

'Come on,' said Mac, trying to push Atkins back to the meeting room.

'No,' said Atkins, shrugging off the hand. 'What did you mean by that comment?'

'Come on, Marty – Berquist is pure Jakarta Lobby.'

'*What* lobby?' snapped Atkins.

'You know, the ones who say there are no militias in East Timor, and if there are, they're not connected to the military, and even if they are connected it's a rogue element, but even if they're not, they're a calming influence on the violence, et cetera, et cetera . . .'

'Oh, *that* lobby! You mean the people who want some kind of evidence of homicidal militias controlled and funded from Jakarta before we write reports that the Prime Minister is supposed to rely on? Is that the conspiracy we're talking about?'

'Marty – it's a mess over there, mate. I wanted to debrief, just a couple of field guys talking it through.'

'Fuck's sake, McQueen! Berquist *was* a field guy.'

'Oh, really?' Mac goaded. 'He had a few lunches in Beijing or Tokyo?'

Sighing, Atkins shook his head. 'I know you get stressed, okay? You get the worst gigs and it must be mentally tiring . . .'

Mac nodded, needing air. Atkins was playing the stress leave card.

'But not everyone's out to get you, Macca,' said Atkins. 'So let's go and do the debrief and show me what you've got.'

Nodding again, Mac bit his bottom lip and turned towards the meeting room.

'And Macca?' said Atkins, lowering his voice. 'Just so you know – he's here on authority of the DG, okay?'

'The DG?' asked Mac, confused. 'What, our DG?'

'Yeah, mate – I think they want to retrieve you.'

As he turned away, Mac managed a snigger at the intel-speak. But it didn't matter what pseudo-American terminology they used, Atkins was saying the Director-General of the firm wanted him back in Canberra.

CHAPTER 34

By the time Mac was five minutes into his run-through, the meeting had become Berquist's debrief, and every point Mac tried to make became an exercise in Canberra's scepticism.

'No, Carl, I have no evidence linking the death camp to Jakarta, except the bulldozer on the army truck,' sighed Mac for the umpteenth time and sick of the questions framed for the listening posts. 'It's corroborated by third-party intel from a Falintil commander.'

'The terrorists?' said Berquist, his wandering eye starting to annoy Mac. 'You had good reason to trust these terrorists? Their bona fides check out?'

'Let's just call them Falintil, okay, Carl?' said Mac, refusing to be baited. 'They got word of a refugee camp for the villagers moved out of the south coast – a camp that no one seemed to return from.'

'We confirmed this?'

'They took me to the camp,' said Mac. 'I sighted as many as a hundred and thirty bodies.'

'But we didn't confirm that this was the camp?'

'Falintil identified it.'

'What about the identity of this Antoine, Ant –'

'Antonio? No, I didn't confirm his ID but I sighted the camp and the bodies and the bulldozer was on an army truck and the intel spooks escorting it were –'

'We know who ran the camp?' interrupted Berquist.

'Antonio was a soldier in the local regiment, the 1635, and he was ordered –'

'But we didn't confirm who Antonio was, or if he even exists?' asked Berquist.

Mac felt physically exhausted and overwhelmed by Berquist's relentless style. Worst of all, Berquist may have been right: all Mac had was a visit to what he thought was a death camp, a run-in with some Kopassus spooks and a bulldozer driver. The only evidence for Antonio's identity was the say-so of a guerrilla commander.

'You're right, Carl,' said Mac, beaten.

'You obviously saw a lot of corpses at that camp,' said Berquist. 'And it's affected you. But that doesn't mean foul play, does it? Perhaps they were sick?' He turned to Atkins, who nodded.

'Here's another scenario,' said Berquist. 'The militias clear some villages on the south coast, the refugees are walking west and they catch, say, typhoid, and the Indonesians try to quarantine them in a remote camp.'

Remembering Davidson's warning to do the debrief in a friendly manner, Mac shifted the focus of the conversation.

'I've told you about the Lombok AgriCorp facility, Carl. What do you make of that?' said Mac.

'Could be legitimate, yet confidential,' said the director of analysis. 'Most armies have R&D programs. The Australian Army spent years trying to develop counter-malaria medicines, all of it hush-hush.'

'So why is Lombok such a secret?' asked Mac, genuinely interested.

'Maybe they don't want nosey Aussie spies finding out what they're doing. Our own CSIRO is all security-vetted now,' said Berquist, referring to Australia's scientific research agency. 'You have to go through ASIO to work there.'

'Something's going on up there,' said Mac. 'Yarrow was procuring for Lombok AgriCorp and he was associated with the bag-man for the North Korean Army's heroin business.'

'But you didn't bring the procurement list?' asked Berquist, already aware that Mac had lost it when he was caught.

'No, Carl,' said Mac.

'No Blackbird? No Canadian?' asked Berquist, his voice clear and neutral.

'No, Carl – and no fingerprints, no confessions, no smoking gun,' said Mac, before a sudden insight made him sit up straight. Mac remembered the vial he'd grabbed from Damajat's office. It had gone in a consular pouch from Darwin to the US Defense Department's lab contractors in Denpasar, and the return address was the building they were sitting in.

'The vial,' said Mac, clicking his fingers. 'I grabbed a vial from Lombok AgriCorp – from Damajat's office. It should be here.'

'It is,' said Atkins, producing a bubble-wrapped courier bag and sliding the vial onto the table.

'Well?' asked Mac.

'Trial vaccine,' said Atkins, pulling a letter from the bag and flipping pages over. 'The lab says it's a vaccine for something like a, what's it called? Here it is – a community-acquired MRSA. A powerful pneumonia, apparently.'

'Vaccine?' said Mac, reaching for the letter.

'It gets better,' said Atkins, pointing at the pages in Mac's hands. 'All of these vaccine programs – if they're legitimate – have their own ID number, a sort of registration with the World Health Organization. It's all on a database, mate, and Lombok AgriCorp has one.'

'Shit, Marty,' said Mac, heart not in it. 'We've got North Korean drug dealers and people like the Sudarto brothers connected with this, and we're supposed to believe it's a *vaccine*?'

'We?' asked Atkins, deadpan.

Mac glared at Atkins for a solid seven seconds, then broke it and looked down at the letter and spectral analysis from the American lab. Berquist and Atkins had played him perfectly. He was so tired, so upset by what he'd seen in East Timor, that he wasn't entirely sure where the facts stopped and supposition took over.

'I guess I should tell you why I'm here,' said Berquist. 'DG sent me up to retrieve you, Alan.'

'Really?'

'Yes, there was a formal complaint lodged by the Republic of Indonesia,' he said, pulling a black-covered dossier from his briefcase and opening it. 'They cited a theft from their vaccine program, an attack on an army garrison at Maliana resulting in seven Indonesian deaths. They've implicated you in the bombing of a fuel store in which two buildings were razed and three army staff cars written off.'

'I see,' said Mac.

'There was also the assassination of two Indonesian army officers and two army personnel at an unspecified location outside of Memo, and the execution of four Indonesian soldiers at a checkpoint between Balibo and Batugade.'

'The streets aren't safe anymore,' quipped Mac.

'This isn't a joke, McQueen!' snapped Berquist. 'East Timor is sovereign territory – it's Indonesia! Our friends and neighbours, mate!'

'I know,' sighed Mac.

'This job isn't a licence to go playing Rambo, okay?' said Berquist. 'I thought that had been spelled out after the Lok Kok debrief.'

Mac looked at his hands.

'The frigging diplomats were running round Canberra all day yesterday trying to pin this on us, and they've succeeded,' said Berquist, referring to the fact that Australia's SIS shared the same corporate stable with the diplomatic corps from Foreign Affairs.

'It's what they do,' said Mac.

'And our thoughtful Javanese neighbours included a bill,' said Berquist, holding up a page of figures to Mac. 'Three hundred and eighty-seven thousand dollars – US – for one military heavy road transporter and one D6 bulldozer that they found at the bottom of a gorge on the road to Balibo.'

'Okay.'

'There's a bill for the fuel and cars, a draft note to the UN, given that we're so involved in the promotion of free and fair elections in East Timor. Oh, and you might like to see these,' he added, pushing several black-and-whites across the conference table.

Mac saw a still of himself bending over the tray in Damajat's locked cabinet and a time-series of Bongo, walking across an open area with a G3 in his hands, fire spewing from the barrel.

Mac shrugged. 'Busy night.'

'The Indonesians have identified one Alphonse Morales as the man in those pictures,' said Berquist. 'They say he was working with an Australian claiming to be Richard Davis, but who is known to their intelligence as an undeclared ASIS officer, previously associated with embassies in Jakarta, Manila and Singapore.'

'I see,' said Mac.

A knock sounded at the door and the receptionist stuck her head in, looked at Atkins and mouthed the words, *Tony Davidson*.

'I'll call him back,' said Atkins.

'He's at the front desk,' whispered the girl, with a sense of drama, before slipping back out and closing the door.

Face darkening, Atkins stood, not sure who to look at. 'I'll be back soon,' he said, smiling without conviction.

'Whatever happens here today, mate, there's a way back, okay?' said Berquist suddenly.

'Really?' said Mac.

'And by the way, it wasn't Beijing – it was Shanghai.'

Embarrassed at being overheard, Mac nodded. 'Look, I –'

'And it wasn't lunch, 'less you count a few nights with the MSS as eating.'

'I'm sorry,' sighed Mac, feeling stupid. The MSS – China's CIA – had a fearsome reputation for their interrogations.

'It's a funny distinction we make between the office guys and the field guys – I used to make that distinction too.'

'What happened?' asked Mac.

'The Chinese took my eye,' he smiled, pointing at his tricky peeper. 'And I couldn't do it anymore – nerves went, mate.'

'I'm sorry,' said Mac.

'Talking about office guys, can you guess who my controller was for that gig?' asked Berquist with a big smile.

'Who?' asked Mac.

'Same bloke who's out there trying to extract you from this long-drop,' chuckled Berquist. 'It's just business, okay?'

Taking the offered hand, Mac sat back, humbled.

The door opened and Atkins strolled in slowly, reading a letter. Behind him, Tony Davidson filled the door, all smiles.

'Carl!' he said, advancing and shaking Berquist's hand. 'Nice to see you here.'

'Nice to see you too, Tony,' said Berquist. 'What's up?'

'McQueen's been seconded to the Yanks – hush-hush,' said Davidson.

'Nice idea but bad timing, Tony,' said Berquist, friendly. 'I'm here to retrieve McQueen.'

'Oh yes?' asked Davidson. 'Whose authority?'

'DG's, I'm afraid,' said Berquist, pulling a letter from his briefcase and slapping it on the table.

'Better look at this, Carl,' said Atkins, sliding his own letter across to Berquist, who had the grace to smile as he read it.

'Congratulations, Alan,' said Berquist, forcing a grin as he looked up. 'You've been bailed out by the Minister for Foreign Affairs.'

CHAPTER 35

Mac ordered the Golden Lantern's famous duck and a couple of beers, then sat back.

'You okay?' asked Davidson, examining Mac's face.

'I'm tired,' said Mac, sipping at a cold beer while the throng of Denpasar passed on the street. 'But I'm okay.'

'You'd tell me, wouldn't you?'

'Sure, Tony,' said Mac, well aware that, in the intelligence game, emotional or psychological problems were an express lane to a desk job.

'Okay,' said Davidson, casing the restaurant, 'get some rest and you'll be contacted by your new controller tomorrow.'

'We know who?'

'Yep. Jim, from DIA,' said Davidson.

'Why the Yanks?' asked Mac, thinking back to his chat with Jim in Darwin.

'They've been on Bill Yarrow for a while, as I understand,' said Davidson. 'They don't like the company he keeps. Now they hear an Aussie officer's been in this, um, facility . . .'

'Lombok AgriCorp?'

'That's the one – it's of interest to the Pentagon.'

'Why?'

Davidson took a swig of his beer. 'When was the last time anyone from DIA spoke to you in a full sentence?'

'Probably the last time I saw rocking-horse manure,' said Mac.

'Done any work on our presidential problem?' asked Davidson, lowering his voice.

'I haven't been able to find Rahmid's controller,' said Mac. 'Although I think he was working out of a front in KL.'

Unfolding his hotel stationery, Mac gave Davidson the phone numbers and addresses of Penang Trading and Andromeda IT, which Davidson jotted on his detective's pad.

'The controller is going to be difficult,' said Mac, 'but I think we've found who Rahmid was running as an agent in Dili.'

As Davidson went to write the name and address on his pad, he stopped and looked up at Mac. 'That's PT Watu Selatan,' he said, looking around the restaurant. 'That's a company set up by Soeharto's generals!'

'Yeah, I know,' said Mac.

'Good work, mate,' said Davidson. 'But it's still hush-hush, okay?'

'Sure, Tony. Are we going to approach this guy?'

'We have to,' said Davidson.

'Be careful who you send,' warned Mac.

'Careful doesn't come close,' said Davidson.

Watching the All-Star baseball game on the big screen, Mac washed down shots of Bundaberg rum with cold Bintangs at the Bar Barong, a few blocks from Puputan Square. American commentators screamed about what Mark McGwire was doing wrong and what Sammy Sosa wasn't doing at all as Mac lounged on his stool.

On the bar in front of him sat a small white envelope that Jessica had slipped into his wheelie bag at Larrakeyah. It said *Richard* on the front, in blue ballpoint, and had a small heart beside it. He'd avoided opening it, not wanting to get mired in distractions. The letter would either profess a love he couldn't return or it would make him feel bad about her father, as if he and Bongo hadn't done enough. And maybe they hadn't. Mac had withheld information about Bill Yarrow's whereabouts and, as much as he could justify it, he didn't feel good about it.

'Another, mister?' asked the barman.

Mac nodded, dropping the rupiah on the wooden counter as the commentators turned their hysteria to Ken Griffey's ability to hit the advertising hoardings at the back of Fenway Park.

Bundy burning in his stomach, Mac slugged at the Bintang, deciding that the last thing he needed in his fatigued state was a female complication. Jessica Yarrow was beautiful and fun but she was way out of his price-range. Jessica was going to graduate from law school, join a big law firm and move to the suburbs with the perfect husband. By contrast, Mac had a detective father and his mother was a nursing sister at Rockie Base Hospital – he was a rugby league player who went to Nudgee College on scholarship to play rugby union. Thanks to Nudgee, Mac had gained the education and the self-belief to go to UQ and apply to the Department of Foreign Affairs and Trade. But in his heart he was still a footy player from Rockhampton who was never going to chase the kind of money that the Jessica Yarrows expected as their due.

'Rubbish, mister?' asked the barman, pointing to the letter on the counter after he'd picked up Mac's empties.

'No,' said Mac, trying to think. 'But it can go in the can.'

Watching the barman toss the letter in the trash, Mac felt something move inside him. It wasn't relief.

The mango and rockmelon went down nicely with strong coffee for Mac, who was nursing a medium-sized hangover in his corner of the Natour Bali's dining room. A *Jakarta Post* lay unopened at the empty table setting opposite and Mac picked it up to use as a prop to look around the breakfast crowd: corporate and government types, mostly, he surmised, and no eyes. The Natour was not the hotel you stayed in for a beach holiday. It was in the centre of Denpasar and Mac liked it because it was hard to hide behind a loud shirt or a silly holiday hat.

Jim appeared at the maitre d's dais just before 9 am. Mac raised his hand unobtrusively and Jim made his way across the room, seeming casual but seeing everything.

'Jim,' said Mac, shaking hands. 'Want to order something?'

'No thanks,' said the American, sitting. 'Already ate.'

'Hope you don't mind,' said Mac, buttering his toast.

'No, go ahead. Nice place you've got here,' said Jim, ostentatiously looking behind him, along the skirting board and up the walls to the ceilings.

'Pretty sure we're clean,' said Mac, who'd already scouted for listening devices and cameras.

'You're in, I hear?' said Jim.

'Sure,' said Mac, spreading honey.

'Good. Welcome to Operation Totem.' Jim leaned across and speared a piece of Mac's rockmelon with his fork. 'I guess you figured that we're interested in that Lombok building in Maliana, right?'

'Well, I got you a sample – the analysis says it's a vaccine program for one of those super-pneumonias.'

'Sure – it's a vaccine, and it does have a WHO registration,' said Jim.

'So?'

'We just want a closer look, okay?'

'So what's the gig?' asked Mac, pouring coffee.

'We'll have a chat about the details,' said Jim, thanking the waitress as she arrived with his cup. 'But the number-one objective of Totem is to snatch Maria Gersao, bring her to safety.'

'Thought you didn't know who she was?' said Mac.

'You know how it is – we've had eyes on your Blackbird for some time, making sure she doesn't get into trouble,' said Jim. 'Before we could bring her in, she disappeared.'

'I see,' said Mac. 'So why is Blackbird so important?'

'She photocopied a document at army HQ.'

'A document?' asked Mac. 'What was it?'

'It concerned something called Operasi Boa – you're aware of it?'

'Yes,' said Mac, 'but I don't know what it is.'

'We want any copies she made, and we'd like to talk with her,' said Jim. 'If we can get to her, we might just save her life.'

CHAPTER 36

Tommy aimed his pointer at the large black-and-white aerial photograph being projected onto the wall of the briefing room. One of the analysts with the Defense Intelligence Agency, Tommy was a swaggering, bearish operative whose job was to track the supply chains of medical and scientific research programs.

'This is the Maliana area of Bobonaro regency, taken ten days ago,' said Tommy.

Mac was sitting in the first-floor briefing room of the DIA building in Denpasar with Jim and a yuppie analyst called Simon who looked as if he would be happier in a stockbroker's office.

'Lombok is a vaccine facility,' said Tommy in his no-nonsense Brooklyn accent. 'And most matériel used in this program is DPI.'

'Which is?' asked Mac.

'Dual-Purpose Items – they can be used for purposes other than those declared,' said Tommy.

'Don't countries have to file reports on what these facilities do?' asked Mac.

'Yes, Mr McQueen,' said Tommy, his black trop shirt rustling as he turned. 'You're talking about a Confidence-Building Measure. It's a declaration of materials, weapons and processes that each state must make annually.'

'So what do the Indonesians say about Lombok?' asked Mac.

'Indonesia has never filed a CBM return,' said Tommy, as if Mac might be a bit slow.

Swapping a glance with Jim, Mac let the briefing continue.

'The Lombok site is registered with WHO and it produces a vaccine that seems to work,' said Tommy. 'But we have some questions.'

The DIA people scrolled through their surveillance pictures and explained their concerns: the incinerator was burning too often and too hot to be destroying the waste Lombok officially produced, the food supplies to the site were too great for the residential staff, the water reservoir was eight times larger than required and the Siemens gas turbine that powered the Lombok site produced enough power to drive a small car plant.

'We like this one,' said Tommy, clicking to a photo of a dock worker standing in front of an open shipping container. 'Lombok declared this as a shipment of Petri dishes from Malaysia, but when we bribed this fellow to open that container, we found something interesting.'

'Yes?' said Mac.

'There was a single wall of boxes, and behind them were four sterile drying cabinets, made in Germany.'

'That a bad thing?' asked Mac.

'It's a good thing if you're producing large amounts of meth-amphetamine – especially the crystal meth drug they're calling "ice".'

'Okay, so Lombok is much bigger than they claim because a secret part of it is a drug lab?' said Mac, swigging down his bad American coffee.

'Perhaps,' said Tommy, clicking his button until the area north and west of the Lombok buildings came back into the picture. 'Hiding an illegal program with a legitimate one is a popular business decision in this part of the world.'

Nodding, Mac thought back to his recent infiltration of a medical research facility that turned out to be a paracetamol counterfeiting ring.

'So where's all the extra capacity?' asked Mac.

'Good question,' said Tommy, aiming his pointer back at the screen. 'The Lombok AgriCorp facility is built on a campus of about one hundred acres, with only a few buildings on it, grouped in one corner.'

Clicking, Tommy changed the photo to a close-up of the empty part of the campus, on which had been drawn parallel dotted lines along the ground linking six objects in the middle of the open area.

'So what do we have here?' demanded Tommy, slapping his pointer at close-ups of six ventilation stacks in the middle of a large field, camouflaged by trees and shrubs. 'Why do we have ventilators in the middle of a field?'

'It's underground?' asked Mac.

'We think so,' said Tommy.

Bringing up a new picture, Tommy indicated a rectangular building. 'We believe this is a refrigeration plant. It runs twenty-four hours a day and gives off a heat signature associated with a meat-packing plant or an ice-cream factory.'

'I see,' said Mac.

'I hope so, sir,' smiled Tommy. 'Because whatever else you do, this unit has to keep working, or the heat sensors will trigger an alarm.'

'What do you mean, *whatever else I do*?' laughed Mac. 'What would I be doing there?'

'Didn't Jim tell you?' asked Tommy confused. 'We need someone inside.'

'Someone?' asked Mac, shifting in his chair. 'You mean this little black Aussie duck?'

'Well –' said Tommy.

'Where's the SEALs or the Delta boys?' said Mac, turning to Jim. 'And I thought this was about Blackbird? Now I'm going back into a place where I've already been made, to infiltrate an underground drug lab? How did we get *here*?'

'Sorry, buddy,' said Jim. 'You're the only person in Western intelligence to have entered Lombok – we can't get to Yarrow right now, so you're a better bet than briefing a Delta operator. Besides – it dovetails with Blackbird.'

'Dovetails?' said Mac, ears pricked. 'We're snatching Blackbird to find out about Boa. So you're saying Lombok is tied-up with Boa?'

'I'm saying we have to take a look – it's a volatile time for Indonesia and we don't like some of the personnel associated with this site. We need eyes.'

'Then it's about time we talked about this personnel,' said Mac, annoyed.

'Fair enough,' said Jim. 'Fifteen years ago, when Soeharto's New Order was going to transform Indonesia, the government decided the country had to be modernised.'

'Sure,' said Mac, holding out his mug for Simon to pour more coffee.

'There was housing, defence, education and IT,' said Jim. 'And there was science and technology and medical research . . .' He did the wind-up signal to illustrate a lot more categories. 'Government departments had to help fund projects that were going to lift Indonesia into the realms of international greatness.'

'Like Malaysia and Singapore,' said Mac.

'That's it,' said Jim. 'Except the financial fruit didn't fall far from the tree in Indonesia, and there weren't as many medical research projects as Soeharto's ministers expected. So this enterprising young officer in Kopassus, Ishy Haryono, used his family connections to promote a couple of medical research programs that attracted most of the funding.'

Jim signalled to Tommy, who found a picture of Haryono – a heavy-faced, pock-marked Javanese man with a moustache.

'He looks very Noriega,' said Mac. 'He CIA?'

'Well,' started Jim. 'You know how –'

'That's classified, Mr McQueen,' said Simon, leaning over. 'The US Department of Defense does not confirm or deny its associations with foreign nationals.'

'He's right,' said Jim, shrugging. 'We don't.'

'Did Haryono's projects work?' said Mac.

'Some of them,' said Jim. 'But besides making Haryono very wealthy, these early programs attracted our friends the North Koreans.'

'Why?' asked Mac.

'The North Korean military derives its main income from drug manufacture and distribution, which is outsourced to people like Haryono.'

'Operasi Boa has something to do with Lombok and Haryono? It's about drugs?' asked Mac.

'We want to cross it off our list,' said Jim, as Simon loudly cleared his throat.

'I'm sorry, Jim,' said Simon, flustered and standing. 'That is classified. McQueen's operation is tightly defined: recon at Lombok and render Maria Gersao. Period.'

'Let me tightly define it for you, Simon,' said Mac, standing and looking the American in the eye.

'I'm sorry, Mr McQueen,' said Simon, his New England accent a little too superior for Mac's liking. 'We can't compromise our own intelligence sources to tell you what we think *might* be happening.'

'He's right, McQueen,' said Jim, edging between them. 'We can't judge the intelligence before we even collect it. Operasi Boa is still unconfirmed – that's why we need the woman you call Blackbird.'

Addressing all of them, Jim tried to defuse the tension. 'Guys, let's do this the way Washington and Canberra want it done, okay? We collect the intelligence, and we've done our jobs.'

Looking at his hands, Mac made a noncommittal noise. Davidson had warned him about how close post-Soeharto Indonesia was to democracy and how easy it would be for the Indonesian generals to scuttle that by goading Australia or the US into direct actions. He was going to keep his mouth shut.

'Okay, priority one,' said Jim, holding his left thumb. 'Snatch Blackbird and do so with minimum heat. Priority two: get as much intel on this Lombok facility as we can. Who knows what they're making down there?'

'Okay,' said Mac.

'And let's remember that, as things stand,' said Jim, 'McQueen's sample from Lombok shows that Indonesia has a legal and WHO-registered vaccine that could inoculate millions of Asians against a SARS-like respiratory disease. How many Western politicians want to claim responsibility for destroying that?'

'So, who's the cavalry?' asked Mac.

'Aussie special forces,' said Jim. 'Technically 4RAR Commandos – if that means anything – but for our purposes, known as the Six-Three Recon, okay?'

'Where we meeting?' asked Mac.

'They're in Timor.'

'Cheeky buggers,' said Mac as he stood.

CHAPTER 37

Mac left the officers' mess of the east-bound *Madura Star* – a Malaysian-registered container ship – and made his way to the guest stateroom. Shutting the door softly and snibbing the lock, he hauled a large green canvas kitbag from the floor onto the bed.

The locks were untouched and there were no signs of tampering. Jim had packed him two sets of drill fatigues, one in black and one in tan, as well as a black field jacket. There was a large digital camera and accompanying cable in a Ziploc bag and a black sat phone with which Mac could transmit digital pics. Spare batteries for the phone and camera were provided in their own ziplocked plastic bags along with a full set of marking flares. The single item Mac had requested – a Heckler & Koch P9s automatic pistol – was nestled in an aluminium gun box with two spare mags and a box of Ruger loads. Also in the box was a large screw-on suppressor that was longer than the gun itself. The P9s was no longer the weapon of choice in Mac's circles because the fifteen-round Glocks and SIG Sauers – with their longer barrels for accuracy – were superseding the seven-round, close-range Heckler. But in Mac's opinion the Heckler was still the most robust handgun you could buy, and its slide action worked best for sound-suppression, which was why the US Navy SEALs still used a version of it. Putting the box back in the bag, Mac noticed a pair of black

Altama boots and a nylon bag containing two biohazard helmets – rubberised grey face masks with two breather cylinders sticking out of the jawpiece and a kind of hood that fell down the sides and back, making the wearer look like Darth Vader.

At the bottom of the bag was a packet of disposable rubber gloves and a small samples kit, not much bigger than a travelling first-aid kit. If he could manage to get into Lombok's underground facility, DIA wanted samples of what was there, with the correct labelling protocol. There was also an electrical engineer's work-up on the Lombok AgriCorp facility. It didn't mean much to Mac, although the notes attached indicated that while DIA had no blueprints for the actual buildings, the wiring schemata showed PIN-enabled security doors, but no motion sensors in the buildings. However, it appeared there was circuitry for a security camera system.

Jim had also included a bulk pack of Hershey chocolate bars, about thirty of them in a sealed brown plastic bag. It was a reminder that, in the end, most spooks were shameless charmers and manipulators.

Dressing in the black fatigues, Mac put his boots beside the bunk, hit the bedside lamp, lay down in the dark and let his mind drift with the soft roll of the ship.

There'd be plenty of time for the cold, single focus of the gig. For now he thought about a girl named Jessica, and wondered at how she affected him. He'd always seen women as smart or hot or funny. They either ran rings around Mac, or they had him in stitches, or they looked great in a bikini. And sometimes they were all three. But Mac actually admired Jessica – she was a UCLA law student wandering around a war zone, demanding answers about her father; she had the strength to shoot a man dead, and the compassion to feel bad about it. As he dozed off he was wondering if he only liked her so much because it could never be, or if it could never be because he liked her too much.

Some time later a rap on the door woke Mac and for a moment he didn't know where he was.

'Ready, sir?' came the first officer's voice.

'Yeah, mate,' whispered Mac, looking at his G-Shock. It was 10.02 pm. Time to go.

The Royal Australian Navy's submariners already had the flying-fox line over Madura Star's sides where it had been lashed to the poop railing. As Mac got to the edge of the decking he felt the warm sea breeze from the Indian Ocean. Slinging the kitbag over his shoulders he put on the harness, looped the pulley wheel over the rope and put his weight on it to make sure the wheel sat snugly.

Leaning forward, he swung first one leg then another over the railing, before pushing off from the side of the Madura Star. He felt the acceleration as he hurtled into the night, his feet held out in front of him like shock absorbers. Halfway across the gap, the submarine loomed out of the black, and Mac's speed was slowed by the safety ropes. His bum fell slightly until he thought he was going into the dark, oily water below, then he was being hauled to the sail of a sub with a large 62 emblazoned on its side – it was the last of Australia's Oberon-class boats, soon to be scrapped in favour of the Collins class.

'Thanks, boys,' said Mac to the crew who dragged him up to the duckboards and unfastened his harness.

Below decks, Mac was led to the officers' wardroom, where he took a seat on a sofa that curved around the main table. Accepting the offer of coffee, Mac pulled the sealed manila envelope containing Jim's work-up from the bag.

The envelope contained a plastic-covered map of the Cova Lima and Bobonaro districts – those areas immediately east of the West Timor border – and a list of the objectives that corresponded to designations on the map. By earlier agreement with Jim, the Americans had changed Blackbird's location to Mars and the Lombok AgriCorp site was labelled Saturn.

A third marking on the map, labelled Neptune, was a recon target-of-opportunity. In the DIA briefing room, Tommy had two indistinct U2 fly-over pictures of Neptune which showed what looked like a small airfield, high in a valley in East Timor, near the border. There had been some radio and cell-phone chatter from around the site in which the word Boa had been detected, and they wanted Mac to take a look.

There was also a pocket-sized GPS device with the coordinates pre-programmed, although Mac trusted that with the 4RAR Commando boys the GPS would be redundant.

A muffled knock at the wardroom hatch was followed by the appearance of a smiling XO, who introduced himself.

'Cranleigh – XO, sir,' said the trim, fortyish bloke, before grabbing a coffee and sitting at the table opposite Mac. Pushing a piece of paper across the table, Cranleigh retained the one he was carrying.

'Won't be landing you by tender tonight, sir,' he said in a cheery voice. 'Indon Navy's sweeping the south coast so we'll go to Plan B, if that's okay, sir?'

Mac read the message quickly and pushed it into his pocket as the sub eased over, as if it was freewheeling down a hill. The final orders – held back till he was on the sub – gave him an exact landing point on the shore, the E&E call sign of 'Chinchilla' and the colour blue. If the whole thing went pear-shaped, they'd go to an 'evade and escape' plan where he'd use the Commandos' radio, issue 'Chinchilla' as the call to the Royal Australian Navy, give his coordinates and then throw blue flares when the helo got close. If he got it wrong, triggered red or orange flares, the helo would abort and head back to its ship.

Mac looked up at Cranleigh as the sub gained speed in its downward trajectory. 'Sorry, mate. Did you say Plan B?'

'Yes, sir. Don't want you punting about on the Timor Sea with that lot patrolling, so we'll use the diver's lock, okay? Let's aim for twenty minutes earlier than –'

'I'm sorry,' said Mac, who'd been concentrating on his objectives. 'Diver's lock?'

'Yes, sir. My notes say you're former Royal Marines? Commandos, I gather, so diving's not a –'

'Yeah, yeah,' said Mac, trying to keep the irritation out of his voice. 'Combat diving's in there somewhere.'

One of the most annoying aspects of having a special forces CV was its capacity to create Plan Bs. Mac had completed P-company at Aldershot, the Parachute Regiment's base, and a year didn't go by without some planner turning a routine assignment into a chance to make Mac jump out of an aeroplane. It was the same with his completion of the SBS jungle survival course in Brunei, the final component of the brutal swimmer-canoeist program. On the basis of that near-death experience, his various controllers had spent almost a decade ensuring that Mac spent more time in the boonies of South-East Asia than he ever got to spend at cocktail parties.

His combat-diving history had also drawn a lot of Plan Bs, the worst being the time Mac had been 'volunteered' by Australia's reps on IAEA to join French frogmen in a search of the Badush dam north of Baghdad. They'd been looking for the underwater entrance to a nuclear breeder reactor with a highly enriched uranium capacity. That job had combined just about all of Mac's phobias in a single four-day adventure and he'd almost received an early ride home when he'd asked the IAEA head-shed why they didn't just lower the water in the dam. Mac's superior had gone red with rage, but the French thought it was hilarious: *Jerst lower ze wort tur! Mais par course!*

Now they were talking diver's locks, the submariner's version of the pilot's ejector seat. Mac had done scores of dives from locks, bells and chambers. But there was a major problem with what the XO was proposing.

'So, Cranleigh – we got a moon tonight?' smiled Mac, in hope more than expectation.

'No, sir,' said the XO, obviously thinking this was good news. 'She's darker than the deep.'

'That so?' said Mac, coffee rising in his throat.

Something not listed in Mac's military CV was that he'd done the marines' hardest frogman section after a few rums. And he wasn't alone. Like many of Britain's finest, Mac didn't like diving at night.

CHAPTER 38

Sitting in the small steel capsule in the ceiling of the torpedo room, Mac tried to stay calm as he ran through his final checks: rebreather unit strapped to his back, face mask, regulator console with compass and depth gauge, and the waterproof gear bag now attached to his belt on the side. He checked the compass, which had an orange luminous bar preset to his course heading, then he put his hand on his Heckler, holstered in a marinised pocket down his right leg.

Below him the XO peered up with curiosity. In the Oberon-class subs the diver's lock over the torpedo room was generally used in drills for emergency evacuation.

'Right, sir?' asked the seaman, sitting on the aluminium stepladder that rose to the lock.

'Good as gold,' lied Mac, giving the thumbs-up.

'When the inside hatch is sealed, the red light will come on,' said the seaman, pointing. 'Then I'll open the exterior valves, sir, and the lock will fill in about six seconds.'

'Gotcha,' gulped Mac, his dinner threatening to erupt in the face mask hanging beneath his chin.

'Then – when the pressure equalises in the lock – I'll open the exterior hatch and the green light will come on,' said the bloke, 'at which point you can push through the hatch, sir.'

'Thanks, champ,' said Mac, struggling to control nervous reflux.

'And I know you know this, sir, but I have to remind you: please breathe out all the way to the surface.'

'Can do,' said Mac, dreading the darkness that would soon envelop him like a fog, taking him back into a zone he'd sworn he'd never again enter after the Royal Marines.

The bolts in the interior hatch were slid home, leaving Mac sealed in a space about the size of a car boot, the darkness and clammy heat made worse by the dim red light above Mac's right eyebrow and the bulky old RAN Dräger rebreather weighing down on his back like a tortoise shell.

Keeping his mask off, Mac tried hopelessly to keep his breathing regular as two metallic taps sounded on the interior hatch. The sub was running at about twenty metres and because Mac had been put in the lock at the same air pressure as sea level, he'd have to exhale all the way to the surface to stop his lungs exploding. Some frogmen put their rebreather mask on at this stage, but Mac was breathing so hard that he left his off in case he breathed in by mistake. He'd put it on when he reached the surface and had oriented himself with the shore. A small grating sound filled his ears and then the outside ocean was racing into the chamber, drenching his black bodysuit and filling the lock. Keeping his eye on the red light, Mac took last breaths as the chamber flooded and then the sparkling water that effervesced around him like a large glass of mineral water suddenly switched from an eerie red glow to a bright green hue as the bolts pulled free in the exterior hatch. He checked the depth gauge on the side of the rebreather, which said nineteen metres, meaning it had immediately acknowledged the pressure equalisation of the diver's lock.

Pushing out of the lock, Mac left the glow of lights, plunging into the inky blackness, a sensation so overpowering that he almost gasped. There was nothing quite like being underwater in the ocean at night. Mac gave a flip of his fins, consciously blowing bubbles as he ascended. His ears screaming, he slowly slapped his fins against the water and concentrated on a gentle exhalation of bubbles, relieving his lungs of the pressure as he rose to the surface.

The blackness closed around him, inducing a nameless fear. The combat-diver section in the Royal Marines Commandos was a watershed for the young men who endured it. Having gone through the basics of free diving, SCUBA and rebreathers, one night the candidates were hauled out of bed to go diving in the dark.

Mac recalled hearing blokes sobbing in the barracks after those dives, and others who requested a return to unit. Diving at night made you face what you feared most and made you do it completely alone. Along with many of the other blokes, by the time they got to the three-hour nocturnal missions around harbours and up rivers, Mac was fortifying himself with grog to get through it. Nothing to be proud of, but there it was.

Making himself blow bubbles, Mac got to nine metres, humming 'Nadine, honey, is that you?' to keep him in touch with himself. Almost out of air at five metres, Mac kicked out and pursed his lips, saving the last dregs of expanding air for the final three metres. As his depth dial showed one metre, he kicked and blew the final air from his lungs and came up for air like a cork.

Gasping as he surfaced, Mac scanned the ocean. The night was dark and the sea relatively smooth. A light, warm breeze came from the west, off the Indian Ocean. Treading water, he did a three-sixty and saw no vessels, heard no aircraft. Filling his lungs with air, he acclimatised to his environment.

Lifting the dive console so he could see the compass better, he aimed himself along the course where the compass spindle lined up with the setting made by the orange bar. Besides the compass, Mac also had the GPS on his right wrist, but he would use that later for confirmation – he wouldn't swim by it.

Making a final check of the regulator settings as he trod water with his fins, Mac breathed in and out – nice and slow – the familiar closed-cycle hiss of the rebreather on his back keeping time with his breaths.

Dipping his head below the surface, Mac swam to about two metres, pulling the compass in front of his eyes. Finding his course, he balanced his kicking with his breathing, and set out for the south coast of East Timor.

Fifty metres from shore, Mac trod water, removed his mask and scanned the beach. He was searching for a rocky point overlooked by three pines, the tallest on the left, the smallest in the middle. But Mac wasn't looking at a rocky point – he was looking at a white-sand beach with no pines.

Checking on the GPS, he realised he'd come into shore too far east. Refastening his mask, he swam submerged along the shoreline for ten minutes before checking on his GPS and coming up to the surface. In front of him were three pine trees overlooking a rocky point, with a mix of beech trees and palms stretching away on either side. The tide was out revealing a tongue of sand between two lines of rocks. With any luck, he'd get out of this swim without scraping himself on the rocks and avoid the scourge of combat divers: tropical ulcers.

Getting into the shallows, Mac crouched in the lapping waves while he removed his mask and fins, keeping his shoulders under the water. Seeing no one on the point, he waded through the shallows and jogged to a hide below a rocky outcrop, his legs almost giving way beneath him. It was 1.09 am local time – nine minutes late for the RV, which wasn't bad for a bloke who'd had to swim it rather than be delivered by boat.

Unharnessing the rebreather unit, Mac dropped it on the sand, removed his neoprene head piece and pulled the Heckler from its holster. Casing the area, he moved out from the behind the rock and stealthed towards the trees, wanting the cover of foliage.

Making beyond the rocky point, he got to the tree line, panting as he crouched behind a fallen log, the warm breeze drying his wet scalp. This was one of the more heavily patrolled areas of East Timor and, with the ballot getting closer, it was now Indonesian Navy, Marines and Army patrolling the land and sea borders, not just the militias. Looking into the trees, Mac searched for a good hide while he waited for the Commando escort from 4RAR.

The stand of trees looked clear of unfriendlies and Mac was readying to move when he heard someone speak.

Throwing himself to the ground and rolling away, Mac came up with the Heckler in cup-and-saucer, his heart banging in his throat.

'Settle, Macca,' came an Aussie voice from somewhere in front of the tree line. 'You'll hurt yourself carrying on like that.'

'Identify!' rasped Mac, barely able to get enough air in his lungs.

'Robbo, from Holsworthy,' came the voice.

Next thing Mac knew, Jason Robertson, the sergeant with the 63 Recon Troop, was walking into the open, M4 assault rifle over his forearm.

'Robbo,' said Mac, relief replacing panic.

'Shit, Macca,' said the Aussie as he approached, hand outstretched. 'Like the bodysuit, mate – that lycra?'

CHAPTER 39

While Mac got out of the diving suit and into his clothes, Robbo mumbled into the field radio strapped to his head. Soon after, two other commandos sauntered from either end of the rocky point.

'This is Beast,' said Robbo, gesturing at a heavyset Anglo with thinning red hair.

'Mate,' said Mac, shaking.

'And Didge. Our night tracker.'

They shook and Didge – a large, dark Aborigine – flashed his teeth. 'Made you swim, eh bra?'

'Yeah, the cheeky buggers,' said Mac, smiling. 'Probably ask for their gear back and all.'

Tying the laces on his Altamas, Mac couldn't douse his curiosity any longer. 'So, Robbo – what's with the new dress code?'

'Orders,' shrugged Robbo, nodding at the other soldiers, who were dressed like they were on a hunting trip. 'Got a message couple of days ago, after that army supply depot was bombed – go to civvies.'

Mac chuckled, realising Bongo's enthusiastic approach to his work might have pushed Canberra into changing the orders for political damage control: it was now a covert action and if caught they'd be shot as spies, not imprisoned as soldiers. That wasn't new for Mac, but he hoped it wasn't going to distract the soldiers.

'So what do you know about the gig?' asked Mac, checking the contents of his waterproof bag and repacking what he needed in a small rucksack.

'Take this good-looking Aussie bloke up to Bobonaro without wrecking his new perm.'

'That's about it,' smiled Mac, disassembling and then reassembling the Heckler before jamming it into the hidden holster he had at the small of his back. 'No details, but basically there's three sites – two recon, one snatch.'

'Will the snatch be voluntary or involuntary?' asked Robbo, pensive.

Mac hadn't given that much thought. 'She's on our side, mate. We do the gig, and then you and I will decide the best exfil from there, okay? I'm not particular so long as I don't get any holes in me.'

'Okay, Macca,' nodded Robbo, pulling two apples from his backpack and offering one to Mac. 'Who is she?'

'It's not important. What's important is where we snatch her from – it'll be hot, mate, so I was hoping for a little more cavalry.'

'Got three more up the hill,' said Robbo, jacking his thumb over his shoulder. 'We've been in an OP for two weeks – we're working men, Macca.'

'Okay for comms?' asked Mac, standing and looking around him.

'Yep.'

'Any contact?'

'No, mate – we're clean and we're green,' said Robbo.

'Good, 'cos the recon elements are hush-hush, okay?' said Mac.

'Suits me,' said Robbo, signalling for Didge and Beast to prep for moving.

There was usually some tension between the special forces and intel guys on an escorted mission. Mac had the technical leadership in terms of determining if the mission objective had been met, but in reality he allowed all the operational decisions to be made by the Robbos of the Australian military. When Mac had worked with Rod Scott in Iraq during the aftermath of Desert Storm, he'd learned the rules fast. After one incident, in which a couple of CIA geeks had wasted an entire morning by micromanaging the US Marines Recon escort team, Scotty had taken Mac for a drink and given him the drum. 'Your job is to score the goal, not referee the match,' he'd said. 'If God had wanted you to be a soldier he'd have given you a dodgy haircut!'

'So?' asked Robbo as they assembled.

'So, get us to Maliana in one piece, and let's nail this thing without ruining my perm,' said Mac.

'Bagged and tagged,' said Robbo, as they slung their rifles.

'And the spook buys the beers,' said Beast, before Mac ducked under a branch and was plunged into the dark of the jungle.

They made fast time, moving in a close-formed duck line behind Didge. As promised, the big Cape Yorker was the night tracker, moving with constant speed and amazing silence through the pitch-black. It was clear the rest of the troop trusted him totally.

After ninety minutes they hit a river valley and Didge moved to a light jog up the centuries-old footpad that followed the waterway, past villages of three huts and cattle standing in wallows on the river bank. Hitting the head of the valley, Didge slowed to a march and they climbed over a saddle to a natural vantage point tucked under a ridge line, looking south to the Timor Sea in the distance.

Calling a rest, Robbo pulled a pair of binos from his backpack and scoured the area while Mac sat with the others, slugging down water from a bottle and eating the small local bananas.

'Here she comes,' mumbled Robbo.

Turning around, Mac realised there was a slight halo on the ridge behind them, and silvery light on the ocean. The moon was coming out. As always in the tropics, it was an amazing thing to watch.

'So why do they call you Didge?' asked Mac, trying to peel a second banana without breaking it, his hands still clumsy with exertion.

''Cos they're cheeky bastards, that's why,' said Didge, slugging at the water, a sheen of sweat on his forehead.

'Stick around,' winked Beast. 'You'll see for yourself.'

'And what does the Beast refer to?' asked Mac, though he had his suspicions. Growing up in Rockie meant knowing blokes who earned that title the hard way.

'Always up for a blue when he's pissed,' said Robbo, chuckling.

'That wasn't my fault, Sarge, and you know it,' said Beast as Didge joined in the laughter.

'Yeah, mate, but it's always not your fault when you're three sheets,' said Robbo, joining them on the ground and grabbing a banana.

Looking at his G-Shock, Mac saw they'd only been going two hours and his new boots were already giving him grief.

'How much further, Dad?' asked Mac.

'Two more legs like this and we're at the OP, mate. Then we'll get some sleep and plan the recon and snatch for tomorrow night, copy?'

'Roger that,' said Mac, wincing at his relative lack of fitness, something that didn't show up until you had to run through the jungle with special forces guys. 'How we looking, with the Indonesian Army?'

'We're in a quiet corridor – it's why we use it to get up and down to the coast,' said Robbo.

'Quiet corridor?' asked Mac. 'Thought it was pretty dangerous on the south coast, around Suai?'

'It is,' smiled Robbo. 'That's why we're in West Timor.'

Fifteen minutes later, Mac stood with Beast on a deserted mountain track, bathed in moonlight. An engine revved suddenly, followed by the sound of wheels spinning before a battered white kijang bounced onto the track twenty metres away, Didge at the wheel.

'Your coach, sir,' said Robbo from the passenger seat as the kijang pulled up, monkeys and birds kicking up a protest.

Having seen the checkpoints across the island, Mac was paranoid about doing this. 'No way, mate, I'm not driving into a Kopassus ambush.'

'This road's got no army, no militia, Macca. Trust me – this is how we move around, it's quiet up here.'

'It's not quiet anywhere on Timor,' mumbled Mac, climbing into the tray on the back of the kijang, Beast joining him.

The road was a disaster and the kijang kicked like a mule, each time landing Mac on the most tender part of his bum. Four times they had to get out and push the vehicle across washouts and landslides, the jungle so close that trees constantly washed across the tray, threatening to take Mac's face with them.

'Where you from?' he asked Beast.

'Winton, mate. Heard of it?'

'Yeah,' said Mac. 'I'm from Rockie – played some footy up there couple of times.'

'Yeah? For who?'

'Junior Capras, group reps – usual shit.'

'They let you out alive?' said Beast, referring to the intense passion rugby league aroused in Winton.

'Yeah, mate,' said Mac. 'But the ref didn't make it.'

As promised, the road was quiet, and at 4.16 am, they put the kijang in its hide and set off eastwards, aiming for the border of West and East Timor, about eight k south of Memo.

Keeping to a light jog now that there was moonlight, they covered the jungle floor quickly. Heaving for breath and fatigued, Mac came to a halt with the rest of the troop shortly after five o'clock. They were looking over the river that formed the border. Beyond were thick stands of forest that shone in the moonlight. Below them was a hairpin in the slow-moving river, an apron of river rocks on the inside of the bend and then a river flat of about five acres before the bush started.

'That's the bush market,' whispered Robbo, pointing down at the grassed river flat at the big bend. 'That's our observation. There's a hundred people down there most days,' he said, referring to the OP – or observation post – that was a hide set up to observe a piece of territory.

Murmuring into his headset to let the team across the river know they'd arrived, Robbo waited for a response then gave the nod. Didge slid down the long river bank to the water's edge, sweeping the area with his rifle.

Giving the thumbs-up, Robbo followed, taking Mac with him. The water was cold as Mac followed Robbo into the river and they waded across chest-high, covered by Didge. On reaching the other bank, Mac tucked in behind Robbo, who was now covering for Beast, and then they fanned out and covered for Didge as he waded across the river.

They followed the river downstream for five minutes and then went into the jungle and doubled around the long way before arriving in a totally concealed hide in the hills behind the bush market. Lifting a flap of branches, Robbo gestured Mac inside while Beast and Didge recce'd the approach area for unfriendlies.

Behind the flap was an area set up with sleeping bags – called 'farters' in the Australian Army – stacks of cold rations and radio equipment. Looking around, Mac was impressed with the place but caught his breath when he realised a large set of eyes were only a few centimetres from the left side of his face.

'Shit, mate!' he exclaimed. 'Give me a fright, why don't you?'

'Johnno,' came the voice. 'You must be the spook?'

Mac shook hands, his heart pounding. As his eyes adjusted he realised Johnno was a Maori bloke. 'Something like that.'

'Johnno's our comms guy,' whispered Robbo as Beast and Didge squeezed into the hide. 'Other two – Toolie and Mitch – are down at the OP. You can doss there,' he said, pointing to a space in the gloom.

Throwing his rucksack into the corner, Mac paused.

'It'll be okay, mate,' whispered Didge, seeing Mac's hesitation. 'Army rules – don't mess with another bloke's stuff. Okay?'

Didge said it like it was one of the Ten Commandments.

'Okay,' said Mac, his fatigues dripping river water as he pulled the briefing papers from his bag and followed Robbo through the exit on the other side of the hide.

CHAPTER 40

After crawling through thick undergrowth in total silence for ninety seconds, Mac and Robbo slipped under another screen made of branches and came out in a foliage-covered hide made of bamboo.

Inside the hide, two men were visible in the moonlight-dappled darkness. One was lying on his stomach, looking through a small telescope on a stand; the other sat cross-legged, a set of binos around his neck, eating an orange.

They swivelled, guns at the ready.

'Boys, this is McQueen,' said Robbo.

Both gave gruff hellos. It turned out the tall blond bloke eating the orange was called Toolie. The other, a thick-set, dark-haired man with a grumpy face, was Mitch.

'Anything?' asked Robbo.

'Another mule line, Sarge,' said Toolie, wiping his mouth.

'How many?' asked Robbo.

'Counted two. Boys, local, well fed, no uniforms. Same old.'

'No militia markings?' asked Robbo.

'No, Sarge – just those big packs on their backs.'

'Gee, I'd love to snatch one of these blokes, just to see what they're carrying,' snarled Mitch.

'Plenty of time for that, mate,' said Robbo. 'For now the orders are clear – no direct action, just eyes.'

'Well, with those two boys,' said Toolie, 'there's going to be a whole line tomorrow.'

'Really?' asked Mac.

'Yeah, mate – I mean, sir,' said Toolie. 'They send out a couple of boys and then the next day a whole mule line comes through, with these packs on their backs.'

'Okay,' said Robbo. 'Good work, boys. Get back to the bivvy and write it up. We'll take over here.'

After Mitch and Toolie had cleared out, Mac and Robbo took their places, which allowed a perfect vista of the entire bush market area and the far side of the river crossing. Mac was impressed – it must have taken several days to build and finetune the OP, and he knew from operating with Aussie special forces that these structures were virtually invisible during the day.

'So let's get this sorted now, okay, Macca?' said Robbo, squinting through the short, boxy telescope. 'Don't want the boys getting nervous.'

Although there were night-vision goggles hanging on the wall, Mac could see the OP was choosing not to use them.

'Okay,' said Mac, weighing his words as he took the map-reader from Robbo. He wanted to be very careful how he introduced the concept of a vaccine factory – he might even leave that part for later.

'I need eyes at a site about half a mile outside of Maliana – operation name Saturn,' said Mac, pulling the U2 pics from the satchel and aiming the dull red light of the map-reader on the first photo. 'It's this one here, and that's the entrance. Reckon I need half an hour in there.'

'Any intel on the security?' asked Robbo, intent on the map.

'Seems to be four or five MPs but they're flatfoots – they're not Kopassus, Marines, anything like that.'

'You have a preference?' asked Robbo, turning the photo to get a better angle.

'Trucks are going in and out of this gate, into this loading area here,' said Mac, pointing. 'There's a lot of activity. Thought we might infiltrate that way, or just do a break-in. The vents look like the weak point.'

'Can do,' muttered Robbo. 'We'll recce it today, maybe tonight, see what's doing.'

'The second recon job is an airfield halfway between Maliana and Memo,' said Mac, shuffling the next photo to the top of the pile, where it glinted in the red light. 'It's a basic look-see with a camera.'

'What are we looking for?' asked Robbo.

'General recce. Look, listen and report.'

'We going into these hangars?' asked Robbo, pointing.

'Make a plan once we're there, huh?' said Mac, both of them knowing that Mac was going into those hangars.

'Which leaves –'

'Yeah, it leaves the girl,' said Mac.

Shuffling the next photo to the top of the deck, he held back on tabling it.

'Expecting trouble?' asked Robbo. 'What exactly are we talking about here?'

Exhaling, Mac decided it wasn't smart to keep the details from Robbo for much longer. 'Mate, you know the Ginasio in Maliana?' he said, taking his hand away from the U2 pic.

'Sure do,' said Robbo, concentrating on the eight-by-five.

'The Kodim 1636 base is adjacent – operation name Mars – this collection of buildings here, right?' said Mac, gesturing to the photo.

'Yep,' said Robbo.

Kodim 1636 was the regiment covering the Bobonaro district and the command centre for most of the militia atrocities.

'We have two credible sightings of our target – Blackbird – at this base,' said Mac, avoiding Robbo's looks.

'Local girl?' asked Robbo.

'Yep,' said Mac, showing the eight-by-five of Maria Gersao.

'Where do you think she is?' asked Robbo.

'She could be in the Kodim's detention centre, here beside their main barracks,' said Mac, pointing it out.

'I know the building,' said Robbo. 'Didn't know it was the prison.'

'It's actually more likely she's in the intelligence compound,' said Mac, moving his finger across to a fenced precinct within the base.

Silence dragged out between the two men, Robbo's eyes large and white in the gloom. 'Intelligence compound?' he asked, aggressive.

'Yeah, mate,' answered Mac, stammering slightly. 'It's this area up the back of the main Kodim –'

'I know it, Macca,' said Robbo, his jaw tensing, eyeballing Mac.

'Okay, so –'

'So there's only six of us, mate.'

'Seven if you –'

'No offence, Macca.'

Staring at each other, Mac gulped first. It was never easy to sell these missions to the soldiers who bore the brunt of them. But in this case, they had less than two weeks before the ballot result was announced and Mac was under intense pressure to deliver Blackbird.

'Okay, Macca, we'll recce it and have a chat, okay? But it's far from ideal.'

'Sorry, mate, but –' started Mac, but Robbo was already leaving.

Picking up his photos and replacing them in the satchel, Mac wondered how he could have sold it any better. The problem centred on the real occupants of the so-called intelligence compound at the Kodim Maliana. Robbo's six commandos were being asked to snatch a girl from the second-largest Kopassus base in Timor.

Mac woke to the beeping of his G-Shock, his brain still craving sleep. It was 6.55 am and in five minutes he had to make his first call to Jim in Denpasar.

Sitting up in his sleeping bag, he saw Johnno scraping soap suds off his cheeks at the other side of the hide. Turning, the soldier offered him a smile, his face half-shaved.

'Some rats for you, McQueen,' he said, nodding at the water bottles and foil tins stacked beside Mac's bed. 'That top one's the meat sauce and pasta – tastes okay cold.'

Thanking him, Mac stood and stretched in his undies, then took a look through the gaps in the bamboo and foliage walls of the hide. The morning was lighting up the jungle and the birds and monkeys were at full roar.

'Where are the others?' asked Mac, grabbing a bottle of water and slugging at it.

'Scouting, observing,' shrugged Johnno. 'I was supposed to be here when you woke up, tell you not to go wandering out alone.'

'Gotcha,' said Mac.

Johnno left as Mac readied to talk with Jim. The call was as simple as a cell-phone conversation in a major city. The sat phone supplied by DIA operated via the Pentagon's own satellite network. No communication that travelled through the atmosphere was one hundred per cent secure, but the Pentagon's satellites were what they called 'five nines' – that was, 99.999 per cent secure. Virtually impossible to hack.

'In place?' asked Jim, a small sucking sound telling Mac that the American was smoking with his morning coffee.

'Yeah, sweet as,' yawned Mac. 'Could have done without the swim, though.'

'You can catch my Learjet home.'

'Tell 'em I like my beer cold and chicks hot.'

'Can do,' laughed Jim. 'Got Tony here – he'd like a word later. But first, we're both getting heat about soldiers and spooks in-country for the start of the referendum on Monday. Tony and I have tossed it around, and your DIO guys have been up here too – sorry to put the bite on you, McQueen, but we want the lot of you out of there before sunrise on Sunday, copy?'

'Fuck's sake, Jim!' spat Mac, latent fear rising in him. 'It's fucking Friday morning! *Jesus!*'

He knew if he didn't calm down he'd get a visit from Johnno, so Mac deepened his breaths and attempted to quell the overreaction.

'Sorry about that, McQueen,' said Jim into the silence. 'It'd be nice to do these things under perfect conditions, but there's too much riding on this ballot. Washington and Canberra want to be cleanskins, you know, in case it turns to shit.'

Mac didn't like doing anything to a politician's timetable, but rushing something as dangerous as the Blackbird snatch was crazy. The way Jim was talking, they'd have to grab Blackbird by Saturday evening at the latest – regardless of the risk factors.

'Here's Tony,' said the American, and Davidson came on the line.

'You okay, Macca?'

'Fine, mate,' Mac lied.

'Got back from Dili last night,' said Davidson. 'Made some progress.'

'Speak with Moerpati?' asked Mac.

'Sure did – the guy's like a rabbit in the headlights. Totally paranoid.'

'What's the story?' asked Mac.

'He and Rahmid were trying to get information on Operasi Boa, and getting nowhere. The President's office is being undermined and the Habibie loyalists are worried that the generals are pushing Wiranto for a coup.'

'Shit,' said Mac.

'The military wants a big display of power, and it looks like East Timor will be the unlucky recipient. There's a lot of fear in Jakarta right now – just knowing about Boa can get you shot, which is why Rahmid was trying to connect with us. I guess it puts the disappearance of Blackbird and the Canadian into perspective.'

'So, Tony, Jim was saying that Canberra and Washington want to be cleanskins on this, hence the new timetable.'

'Sure, Macca.'

'So what about my exfil?' asked Mac. It had occurred to him that governments might not want their helicopters and reinforcements landing in foreign territory so close to a politically sensitive event like East Timor's ballot.

'Yeah, well – Jim hasn't told you?'

'No,' snapped Mac, tired, hungry and sick of being dicked.

'Well, Macca, there's army infantry, Kopassus and Brimob flooding into Bobonaro right now and the military is massing undeclared forces just over the border.'

'And?' barked Mac, knowing what was coming.

'So, the helo exfil is in the too-hard basket for now,' said Davidson.

'Really?'

'Yeah, so it's a navy pick-up, okay?'

'Navy?'

'Yep – you got radio comms, you got the call signs?'

'Yeah, Tony – got all that,' said Mac, rubbing his temples with his fingers. 'We'll do what we can, but with any luck we'll be travelling with a nineteen-year-old girl. Understand?'

'I know, Macca,' said Davidson. 'And getting her out has never been more crucial.'

'Shit, Tony — anything else? Perhaps a double-axel with pike?'

Davidson's laugh boomed down the line. 'Like my old cricket coach used to say when I was about to bowl my first over . . .'

'What?' asked Mac.

'Don't fuck it up.'

CHAPTER 41

Sweat ran down Mac's back like a river by the time they'd trekked two hours north of the OP through the overwhelming humidity of the tropical montane forest. When Robbo called for a smoko under a rocky overhang, they all drank deeply from their water bottles. Sitting in the shade, Mac noticed the rest of the troop avoiding eye contact and sitting away from him. Though he appreciated that soldiers entered their own zone on an op, he sensed trouble and knew that none of them wanted to be fed to a compound full of Kopassus.

Digging in his rucksack, he pulled out the Hershey bars Jim had packed.

'Well, well, well,' said Mac. 'What 'ave we 'ere?'

Johnno dug Toolie in the ribs as Mac tore the bag open with his teeth. Next thing, they were all staring at Mac, and when he threw the whole bag to Johnno, the rest of the troop converged like hyenas. One of the first things you missed when you went bush in the army was sugar, and soldiers on operations always feasted on it when the opportunity arose.

Taking a bite from his bar, Robbo walked past Mac and gestured with his head. 'Let's talk.'

They found a place around the corner that looked down the savannah river valley they'd be tabbing along for the rest of the morning. Like many river valleys in Timor, you could plot the water course by the snaking stands of corypha palms contrasting with the brown grasslands. Putting his green rubber-covered field-glasses to his eyes, Robbo touched the buttons on the top of the glasses and fixed on a spot.

'The boys don't like it,' said Robbo, not taking his eyes from the glasses. 'A Kopassus depot, secured inside an infantry base? Going in hot, with only six troopers? Lads aren't happy.'

He passed the binos to Mac. 'That stand of palms and bush at the end of the valley, just to the left,' he said, pointing.

Mac picked up the airfield with the field-glasses. It was smallish and didn't look busy.

'I'm not happy with the mission either, Robbo,' said Mac, passing the field-glasses back and drinking his water. 'I'm the one going in there, remember that.'

'I remember,' said Robbo, pocketing the chocolate wrapper. 'But I should warn you, I've told the boys that if there's no exit strategy, I'm not going to make them do it.'

'Go in?'

'At Maliana,' nodded Robbo, munching on the chocolate.

'They can still cover me?' asked Mac, aware he was treading on dangerous ground.

A pause opened between them. 'Watch it, mate,' said Robbo, very slow.

'This girl – she's important, okay?' said Mac, not liking the way Robbo was looking at him. In threatening to enter the Kopassus compound alone, Mac was getting close to calling the commandos chicken.

Pouring a small handful of water, Mac removed his cap and ran the cool liquid over his face and through his hair. It felt good and calmed him before dropping the bombshell.

'Let's do our recon and see how Maliana looks when we get there, okay?' said Mac, his tone reasonable. 'If we're fast on the recon, we give ourselves more time for the snatch.'

'Agreed,' said Robbo, chewing.

'And by then we might have worked out a good alternative exfil strategy –'

'*Alternative?*' said Robbo, no longer chewing. 'Thought the exfil was helo? Right, McQueen?'

'No helo. Sorry, mate,' said Mac.

'If there's no helo then there's no QRF element,' said Robbo, referring to the Australian Quick Reaction Force – the cavalry poised to support an exfiltration should things get hairy.

Nodding ruefully, Mac kicked at a stone.

'So it's just us?!' continued Robbo. 'Six diggers and a spook? And we have to break into a Kopassus compound, snatch a girl and then escape across country to –'

'Navy pick-up – it's all they offered me.'

His expression furious, Robbo finished his chocolate bar, shaking his head. 'Can't wait for the next surprise,' he snapped, before stomping back to his troop.

Mac had wanted to talk about another surprise, but the moment was gone.

The security fence around the airfield was a single layer without sensors on it. Standing in the lee of the southernmost hangar, out of the sight line of the guard posted at the gate, Mac watched Toolie strain at the wire-cutters while Beast pulled the cyclone fencing backwards to create a door.

'Bastards in Townie switched my fucking cutters,' snarled Toolie as another strand gave way. 'Left me with the blunt ones – pricks!'

The radio crackled and Robbo sit-repped from his position on the ridge opposite the airfield gates, reporting two Indonesian soldiers leaving the two-storey admin and barracks block and walking across the main courtyard. Mac could tell he was worried but trying to remain calm.

'They're doing a perimeter check, boys,' said Robbo. 'Fix your handiwork and stand off – you've got thirty seconds.'

Straining his large forearms, Toolie swore softly as he puffed his cheeks and twisted the loose fence wires together with the reverse side of the wire-cutters. He was amazingly quick, and as Robbo fired another warning over the radio, Mac, Toolie and Beast made it into the bush line and blended with the shade.

Crouching behind a tree, catching his breath, Mac watched the soldiers do their rounds, relieved when they passed the patched-up fence without a second look.

'I'm going to give it another half-hour, Robbo,' said Mac into his mouthpiece, as they sweated in the bushes. 'Then we'll take some pics and move on.'

'Check that, Macca,' came Robbo's voice on the radio. 'We've got activity up here – helos coming in from the east.'

'Fuck,' muttered Mac, deciding they would not be going into the hangars today. 'Okay – we'll see you in five. We're pulling the pin.'

Taking the long way around the western end of the dusty old runway, the three of them stealthed through the jungle. As they rounded the end of the runway, they heard the thromp of incoming helicopters and watched the first of them land on the apron in front of the admin block. Setting on their way again, they jogged through the jungle in the thirty-seven-degree heat as Robbo gave them updates on the aircraft.

Arriving back at the observation post, Mac collapsed to his knees beside Robbo, who was lying on his stomach, field-glasses to his eyes.

'Take a look at this, Macca,' he said after a while, rolling to his side and offering the binos.

Lying down beside the soldiers, Mac rested the glasses on his elbows and looked at the site from the reverse of where he'd been trying to enter. Along the bright lime runway were scattered years' worth of broken planes, hoists, trucks and an old Euclid road grader with its cables snapped, long abandoned to the weeds. It felt like a Cold War-era facility, built with American money back when the CIA wanted Soekarno out, and Soeharto running the show.

Parked on the main apron in front of the airfield admin block, Mac counted seven Black Hawk helicopters, flight crews wandering towards the admin block in grey overalls. Mac focused the lenses of the field-glasses, looking closer.

'Robbo, what's the Indonesian Army helicopter of choice?' he asked, scanning each aircraft and verifying they were all Black Hawks.

'Hueys, made under licence,' said Robbo.

'So what do you make of this little squadron?'

'Contractors?' said Robbo, more of a question than an answer. 'UN?'

'Not UN,' said Mac.

Pulling the Nikon digital camera from his bag, Mac fired it up and checked the settings. The hangars he'd wanted to investigate were directly across from where he lay, and bringing the viewfinder to his eye, Mac increased the zoom of the camera into the gloom of the buildings. There were twenty large spray booms of the type he'd seen used in agricultural projects, lined up in rows. Refilling tanks sat behind them. It explained to Mac the presence of the non-Indonesian helicopters – spraying contractors, probably for a mosquito-eradication program. He'd seen this occur many times in Asia – a foreign organisation would put up the money for a public works project and the local military commanders would win the contract to carry out the work through their own regimental corporations. At least Haryono was using contracted helicopters, thought Mac; in the Philippines the commanders would use military helicopters but pocket the fee themselves.

Taking a few shots of the helicopters, Mac was frustrated with the angle they'd been parked at, since the sun's reflection meant he couldn't get a proper shot of their registrations. There was something familiar about them, even given their anonymity.

A new sound grew from the south and a small dark helicopter appeared on the horizon, its Indonesian Army markings evident. A cloud of lime dust flew into the still air as the helo touched down and then military people from the admin building were surrounding it.

'Wonder who the VIP is?' asked Mac.

'Dunno,' said Robbo, 'but he must be important.'

'Sorry?' said Mac as a large Javanese man in a white trop shirt and black slacks stepped out of the helo with two young men following, and shook hands with a wearer of fruit salad.

'Last week the boys followed one of those mule lines that cross the river,' whispered Robbo. 'It led here.'

'That so?' asked Mac, as the VIP in the trop shirt looked around, his hand resting on the lower back of one of the young men.

'You'd like to see what's in those packs?' said Robbo.

'It's about time,' agreed Mac, as the VIP turned and Mac released the shutter on the camera. He was looking at Ishy Haryono.

CHAPTER 42

The photographs were transmitted inside of three minutes. Mac had heard about the joys of digital imaging but he had no idea it would be so easy. All he'd done was plug the camera into the sat phone, dial the number Jim had preprogrammed into the phone, and the contents were downloading into DIA's computers.

'So, you want to have a look into this VIP?' asked Robbo, nodding at the helos in front of the airfield's admin building.

'Ideally, yes,' said Mac, annoyed with himself for having already spent so much time at this airfield. 'But we've got the Lombok recon and then we have to be out of Dodge, with the girl, by Sunday – I think we'll push on.'

Mac didn't want to become sidetracked by the sighting of Haryono. If Operasi Boa was a part of a deportation program, then it wasn't being hatched from this airfield. He had no doubt that Haryono was a potential drug lord and that he used this airfield for taking money and distributing his product – but that was a matter for the police.

'You said those boys with their packs come here?' said Mac. 'And based on the pattern, we're expecting the full mule line to be here tomorrow?' asked Mac.

'Sure are,' said Robbo.

'Let's keep that in mind,' said Mac. 'If we cross paths it'd be good to have a nosey-poke.'

As he shifted to leave, Robbo put a hand out. 'Actually, Macca, we have a situation.'

'Yeah?' asked Mac.

'We've detained a local,' Robbo said, embarrassed. 'Well, two actually.'

'Shit, Robbo!' barked Mac, too many pressures to juggle already.

'Yeah – Didge was taking a pee and someone walked into him.'

'Jesus wept!' said Mac, adrenaline rising. 'Where? Where's Didge?'

'Back there.' Robbo gestured with his thumb.

Thirty metres into the jungle, Mac and Robbo came into a copse where the 63 Recon Troop stood around two boys in their early teens. Mac and Robbo edged into the circle and listened to Johnno talking Bahasa Indonesia with them.

'Johnno?' said Robbo, and indicated for him to let Mac closer to the kids.

'Found this,' said Toolie, handing Robbo one of the boy's packs.

Robbo looked inside, pulled out a plastic bag, and threw it to Mac, who knew what it was before he even caught it. The clear plastic was filled with US greenbacks and the Cambodian stamp would translate as 'Vacation Palace'.

Mac didn't ask too many questions before the boy wearing the San Francisco 49ers T-shirt started crying.

'Rodrigo says he never wanted to do it. He says his brother talked him into carrying these packs for the Koreans,' said Johnno. 'Apparently the Koreans give the packs to the mules, then they are paid at the airfield base, one dollar US per run.'

Ruffling Rodrigo's hair, Mac switched his attention to Yohannnes, who looked cockier than his friend.

'How's your English, Yohannes?' asked Mac.

'Okay, mister,' said the boy, scared but showing more front than his companion.

'Where you come from today?' asked Mac.

'Atambua, last night,' said the boy.

'Who gave you the bag?' asked Mac, bending down for his rucksack.

'Korea,' said Yohannes. 'Always Korea.'

'What does Korea say?' said Mac, opening his rucksack and putting his hand inside.

'He say, *Take this to there,*' said Yohannes, eyes lighting up as Mac pulled the pack of Hershey bars out of his rucksack.

'And what else?' asked Mac, pointing at the radio handset that sat the bottom of Yohannes's pack.

'Call him, if problem in jungle,' said the boy, eyes like saucers as Mac handed him a chocolate bar before giving one to Rodrigo, who cheered up with the gift.

'What problem?' asked Mac.

'Soldier, thief, militia,' said Yohannes, getting the Hershey wrapper off in record time. 'If anyone try to take pack, if soldier around, we must call Korea.'

'And then?' asked Mac.

'Then, walk back and then a lot of carrier come along then,' nodded Yohannes. ''Cos safe now.'

'Who do you take the packs to?' asked Mac.

Pointing, Yohannes indicated the airfield.

'You take it down there?'

'Yes, mister,' said Yohannes.

'You know his name?'

'No, mister.'

'No?'

'No, mister – a secret.'

'I bet it is,' muttered Mac, and handed another chocolate bar to each kid.

Looking down on the airfield from the OP, Mac slugged at water and tried to get his mind clear. He hated complications, disliked civilians involving themselves in the action.

'What do you want to do with them?' came Robbo's voice from behind him.

'Can't let them go down to the base,' said Mac, eyes on the admin block. 'We'd be made and we still have two locations to cover.'

'So?' asked Robbo.

'So I don't want them with us either,' admitted Mac. 'We don't have enough food, and we don't have the numbers to run a security detail while doing the op.'

'It's better than the alternative,' said Robbo after a pause.

'The choice is between bad and worse,' said Mac. 'Bad might be one thing; worse might be six troopers and a spook getting torn to pieces by a door-gunner doing some target practice. We're sitting ducks out here once we're made.'

'Well, the obvious is out of the question, Macca,' said Robbo, uneasy, his foot kicking into the dust.

Jaw muscles clenching, Mac tried to stay calm. 'The fact that we both know the obvious sort of resolves the question, doesn't it?'

'My boys wouldn't let us do it, McQueen. And I'd side with them, so no – it doesn't resolve the question.'

Mac nodded and looked down at the ground, tried to think of a way forward. 'Okay, Robbo. The lesser evil is taking them along but we need a stop-loss.'

'Fair enough,' said Robbo. Mac knew he'd been a handy bullrider as a teenager and Robbo sometimes took his leave in Canada and the United States, taking eight-second rides for cash. There was a coiled quality to the man that wasn't always relaxing to be around.

'If they directly endanger our lives, then we vote on it,' said Robbo. 'There's seven of us, so stop-loss is four votes in favour.'

'And the proposer gets the gig,' said Mac.

'Of course,' said Robbo.

It was 12.34 when they arrived at the escarpment overlooking the river gorge. The local boys walked in the middle of the troop, rope nooses around their throats which were connected by a rope leash to Toolie's hand. The idea was that if they tried to run, a decent tug on the leash would tighten the rope around their necks.

'This your footpad?' Mac asked Yohannes.

'Yes, mister,' said the boy.

'Got an idea,' said Mac.

They stopped and Johnno and Didge jogged up a rise to assess the ground ahead.

Pulling the money bags from the boys' packs, Mac smashed the radio on a tree and threw it in pieces on the ground.

'Never liked that radio much anyhow,' mumbled Beast.

After asking Beast for his knife, Mac cut a slice into the inside of his forearm and held the wound over the first empty pack, letting the blood run over it.

'Robbo, can we get some more blood?' asked Mac.

Nodding at Beast, the big redhead took his knife back and gave Mac a questioning look.

'The other one,' said Mac, 'and some on the radio if you want.'

When there was enough blood to make it look good, Mac asked for Rodrigo's shirt, took it and wrapped it around a small log, making sure the 49ers emblem was visible. Then he tied it up by the sleeves on the reverse side, hoping it would look like a boy floating in the river at the foot of the gorge.

After swinging the log back and forth until he had some momentum, Robbo let go of it and they watched as it arced through the air and plunged into the river twenty metres below. Within seconds, the T-shirt-covered log had submerged and disappeared, ruining the desired effect of a body floating in the river.

They watched and waited, but the log didn't resurface.

'Fucked that up good and proper,' mumbled Robbo.

'Have to think of something else,' said Mac. 'Just don't want the Indonesian Army chasing us for their money.'

As they took turns on the water bottles, Robbo and Mac looked at the map and decided on the safest way into the Lombok facility.

Panting, Didge and Johnno came down from the peak.

'More helos heading for that airfield,' said Didge. 'Four of them.'

'No interest in us?' asked Robbo. 'Shooters hanging out the doors?'

'Couldn't see,' said Didge. 'Too far away and they were gone before we got the binos on them.'

'Okay,' said Robbo, nodding. 'Let's move.'

Mac pulled the rucksack over his shoulders onto his wet back, letting out the straps slightly. He was now carrying what he estimated was two hundred thousand US dollars through the Timor bush.

Didge led them out, and as he did, he looked over the escarpment. 'Shit!' he said. 'That looks like the kid.'

Looking over, Mac saw the 49ers T-shirt floating with the other logs in the river eddy. It looked like a body and, with any luck, the people looking for their money might think that the boys had been whacked.

CHAPTER 43

Pillars of smoke rose into the sky as Robbo stopped them on the outskirts of Maliana.

They had camped in a hide overnight and travelled carefully but slowly through the well-populated countryside during the day, avoiding contact with the locals or military. It was now Saturday afternoon and they'd have about ten hours of darkness in which to infiltrate Lombok and then snatch Blackbird, before heading back across the island to the Sunday RV with the Royal Australian Navy. On Monday the ballot would open and by then Mac and the 63 Recon Troop were supposed to be out of harm's way.

'Shit,' said Robbo, before passing the field-glasses to Mac. 'How many more houses can they burn?'

Making his own sweep with the binos, Mac saw thick smoke erupting from one of Maliana's satellite hamlets about eight kilometres in the distance.

'Got a pain-free route to Saturn?' asked Mac, referring to Lombok by its operational code name. 'Lot of open ground out there.'

'If we go to the west of this village, we can tab down that river valley to the target,' said Robbo, pointing.

The sound of distant assault-rifle fire drifted to their position and Mac felt nervous reflux threatening. He wanted to say something about Rodrigo, who'd been sulking since they'd picked him up and had then descended into hysterical tears once he'd seen the smoke around Maliana. But the time wasn't right.

'Can you give me eyes on this valley over here, boys?' Robbo asked Mitch and Toolie. 'We'll RV in thirty minutes at the head of the valley. Can do?'

'Can do, Sarge,' said Toolie, before the two of them moved off in a crouch.

Back with the main group, Mac drank from a water bottle and saw Didge sitting and talking with Rodrigo. The kid wiped his eyes with the back of his hand, his bottom lip puffy. For Mac, the two kids were still an unwanted complication, impairing the troop's ability to saddle up and move quickly and silently through the countryside. The militias and soldiers around Maliana had scared him shitless the first time around. Mac just wanted to do his job without ending up on his knees in the changing sheds of the Ginasio.

As Robbo signalled for the group to get moving, there was a familiar sound.

Searching for the source, Mac's eyes settled on Didge, who was puffing into his cupped hands, fingers fanning over the top, making an improvised didgeridoo. The music quacked out of Didge's hands, making the two boys smile and laugh.

'Here come the brolga,' said Didge quickly, creating a squeaking sound above the hum of the didgeridoo.

'And then along come goanna,' he smiled, adding a hiss to the orchestra of sounds as the boys started clapping with joy.

Mac slugged at his water and decided to relax and enjoy Didge's performance. Robbo took a seat beside him as Didge added the croc to his story.

'We were in Bougainville for BEL-ISI last year and Didge starts up with this stuff in the bar,' said Robbo, shaking his head. 'Ten minutes later the whole boozer's crying like a bunch of girls.'

'Homesick?' asked Mac.

'Something bad,' said Robbo.

'When I was growing up in Rockie, they didn't let the blackfellas play their didge in town,' said Mac. 'But it still sounds like home.'

'I'm from out Narrabri,' said Robbo, 'and I'll tell ya, mate, no blackfella would have dared come into my dad's pub and do the didge. Would have got bashed for that.'

'Kids seem to like it,' said Mac, lost in the sounds of Cape York.

'Yeah, and Didge isn't just an entertainer,' said Robbo. 'When the shit starts, he's the bloke you want beside you.'

It was late afternoon when Robbo signalled for them to establish base in the uplands surrounding the Lombok facility. After they'd set up, Robbo called Didge, Johnno and Mac to have a recce. From a stand of trees overlooking the Lombok AgriCorp car park, they saw about a hundred people milling in the same place where Amir Sudarto had apprehended Mac a few days earlier. The incinerator stack was not operating but the six ventilator outlets were visible in their stands of shrubs, line abreast down the middle of the otherwise empty paddock.

'Four sentries at the gate house,' mumbled Robbo as he looked through the field-glasses.

Army trucks were idling, waiting to leave the facility, their drivers handing over clipboards which were checked by the sentries. The people in the car park were lining up, suitcases in hand, and were being escorted into the back of army trucks. It wasn't what Mac had been expecting.

Mac took the field-glasses from Robbo. Looking through them, he saw a bunch of women close up: hair pulled back in tight buns, glasses, middle-class blouses and expensive rings. They were laughing as their suitcases were loaded by soldiers. If Mac had to guess, he'd say the technical staff at the facility had finished their contracts and were heading home.

Sweeping the glasses around towards the other end of the compound, Mac concentrated on the pillbox guard tower in the middle of the far fence line, where DIA suspected there was an underground facility. There were no soldiers in the tower and Mac decided that if the ventilator outlets weren't too tricky to open, they could be the best way into the hidden part of Lombok.

'Well?' asked Robbo.

'Can you see any unfriendlies in that far sentry box?' asked Mac, handing the field-glasses back to Robbo. 'I think they might be shutting down the facility, and reducing the security – that might give us our way in.'

'We talking about those ventilators?' asked Robbo, adjusting the focus ring.

'I reckon we stealth to them and break in,' said Mac. 'I can't see anything easier.'

'Roger that,' said Robbo, 'but check the K-9, your eleven.'

Mac turned slightly and clocked them immediately: two MPs, one of them with a German shepherd straining on a chain leash. 'Fuck!' muttered Mac.

As the sun set Mac knelt and pushed caps of Xanax out of the foil while Didge created slits in the chunks of cuscus flesh and pushed the capsules into the meat.

Beside them, Robbo averted his eyes and his nose.

'That's disgusting,' he mumbled.

'Nah, boss,' said Didge, chuckling as he pushed another Xanax capsule into a chunk of cuscus. 'Good eating, him,' he said, playing up the Cape York talk. 'Feed a whole mob on him, there.'

'Your mob from down Barmaga, down there?' aped Mac.

'Watch it, bra,' growled Didge, reverting to Strine. 'Don't get cheeky.'

They waited for the guards to start another loop, then Mac followed Didge down to an area by the fence where they were partially unsighted to the main entry guard house.

'You're clear, boys,' crackled Robbo's voice over the radio headsets.

Mac followed Didge to the fence, grabbed four chunks of cuscus meat and threw them onto the grass on the other side.

Moving back to Robbo, they waited for the guards to do their tour. Darkness was settling as the guards walked the near fence, smoking. The German shepherd tried to lurch at one of the chunks of meat as the guards passed it, but he couldn't reach and was wrenched back into line.

'Dammit,' snarled Didge.

The guards kept to their route and Mac prayed the dog would notice the baits that Didge threw. But then the guards stopped, lighting cigarettes, while the talkative one remonstrated.

'Are these people going to talk all night?' whispered Robbo. 'It's like a bloody sewing circle down there.'

The guards moved on and, as they settled back into their rhythm, the shepherd suddenly lurched to his right, snapped at a bait with flashing teeth, and was back in line before the handler could tug at him.

'Sleep tight,' said Robbo.

Robbo talked them through the final instructions: Mitch and Beast were covering the fence lines with supporting fire should the need arise, while Johnno was going to access the main switchboard for the facility and see if he could disable the security camera systems. Didge was going into the facility with Mac, while Toolie played babysitter.

Going through final prep for the gig, Mac listened to Robbo give the various contingencies and warnings. There was a chance that the radios wouldn't operate underground, so they agreed on a sixty-minute shutdown for the gig. If Didge and Mac weren't out of there in under an hour, the rest of 63 Recon would do the Harold.

As Didge checked and rechecked his B&E gear, Robbo's tone of voice changed.

'What the fuck's that?' he hissed.

Mac followed Robbo's gaze through his field-glasses to the main block of the compound.

'Shit!' muttered Mac when he saw what Robbo was looking at. Three people were standing in front of the main loading bay, illuminated by floodlights and all dressed in white NIOSH-10 clothing – better known as biohazard suits.

'What the fuck is this, McQueen?' snarled Robbo, still looking through the glasses. 'What is this place?'

'You know, vaccines and –'

'Vaccines?' rasped Robbo.

'Look,' said Mac, voice soothing. 'It may be nothing, we're just checking –'

'What is this fucking place?' demanded Robbo, slow and threatening.

Though he realised it didn't look good, Mac tried to hold firm. 'It's classified, Robbo.'

Robbo planted his hands on his hips, his face furious.

'Okay,' said Mac, trying to lighten it. 'It's officially vaccine research, but there's an undeclared area underground, okay? It's probably a drug lab.'

'Vaccines? Are you fucking *kidding* me?!'

'Look –'

'It's just a place where they grow diseases, McQueen!' said Robbo.

'Yeah, I know, mate,' said Mac. 'It's the underground facility we're interested in.'

'Oh, now I feel better,' said Robbo sarcastically. 'When were you going to tell me? Huh?' said Robbo, tapping Mac in the chest. 'You don't think I have the right to warn my own men about walking into a place like this?'

'I've got two masks, gloves for Didge –'

Robbo looked Mac in the eye. 'You were going to tell Didge *when*? When you got the top off the fucking *ventilator*?'

That was precisely what Mac had intended, though he decided not to say so.

'Sorry, mate,' said Mac. 'That's the gig.'

'That's the gig?' demanded Robbo. 'You mean, if the dumb soldiers knew where they were taking you, we might find a way not to get there?'

Mac just shrugged.

Sighing, Robbo gave Didge a look and then turned back to Mac. 'Why is it, McQueen, that all of you spooks are just total fuckers?'

CHAPTER 44

The army trucks continued transporting people out of the facility as Mac cased the campus from behind the middle ventilator. After the flare-up about vaccines and diseases, Mac was leaving the topic alone with Didge. Mac harboured his own fears about scientists playing with diseases, but his objective was to infiltrate the underground section of Lombok – the fact that it could be a drug lab was only very small comfort.

The paddock area had been dog-free for twenty minutes thanks to the Xanax baits and the five floodlights around the paddock were weak enough to create darkness around the ventilators.

After a concerted effort, Didge loosened the final screw on the circular vent cover and he and Mac lifted it off in silence, placing it quietly on the grass beside the vent.

'Cap off, Blue Leader. How we doing on the circuit boards?' asked Mac over the headset.

'Standing by, Albion,' said Robbo, cool but professional. 'We're in – gonna use a bio-suit to infiltrate.'

Heart thumping, Mac listened for any out-of-place sounds as the crickets started up and the birds died down. Bats flapped and monkeys chattered as the last line of orange-red glow evaporated on the horizon. And then night came like a black velvet cloak had been thrown over the day.

Checking their handguns and controlling their breathing, they concentrated on saving their energy for the real work. Johnno was supposed to be a good operator, but Mac always got nervous when someone was going into enemy territory.

'Stand by, Albion,' came Robbo over the headset.

'Standing by, Blue Leader.'

Looking at each other, Mac and Didge got the okay forty seconds later.

'Green for go, Albion. Repeat – green for go.'

'Roger that Blue Leader. Albion out.'

Tapping Didge on the shoulder, Mac held out one of the biohazard masks. When they both had the helmets in place, he handed Didge a pair of gloves.

Looking over, Didge peered down the open shaft and then brought a flashlight up and into the shaft, turning it on and cupping a gloved hand over the lens to stop it shining too brightly below.

The light reflected on a circular shaft that dropped for fifteen metres, ending in a sealed fan unit which blocked the shaft.

'Shit,' hissed Mac, his voice bouncing within the confines of the biohazard mask.

'You okay, Albion?' asked Robbo over the headset.

'Affirmative, Blue Leader,' said Mac, watching as Didge looped his rope, strained at the knot and then put a slip-knot at the base of a tree next to the vent. 'Fan unit blocking entry. It's sealed, but working on it. Out.'

Didge picked up a new set of wrenches and screwdrivers from his B&E kit, clambered over the edge of the vent shaft and rappelled into it, disappearing quickly.

From above, Mac shone the flashlight at the sides of the shiny steel, letting the light bounce around long enough for Didge to release the screws. Standing on the far corners of the fan unit, Didge undid his rappel harness and attached it to the metre-wide fan.

Climbing out of the shaft, Didge jumped down, then turned and tried to pull the fan out with the rope. Mac joined him, the two of them straining until a groaning sound came from the shaft, followed by the fan unit coming loose as Mac and Didge fell back on the grass.

Shining the flashlight down the shaft again, Mac saw that it ended in a right-angle intersection with a box-section air shaft that ran parallel to the ground. Pulling a small cloth bag from his breast pocket, Didge put his fingers in and sprinkled a substance that looked like talc. As it drifted downwards through the light, Mac guessed he was looking for motion-sensing beams. Mac had already told him that there was no wiring for such a system, but he liked that Didge was thorough.

Packing his B&E kit, Didge dropped down first. Touching on the parallel shaft, he pulled himself into it head-first and started crawling forwards. Mac stood on the bottom of the shaft, removed his rucksack, and pushed it ahead of him behind Didge as he followed into the dark hole.

Lying behind Didge's boots, with all lights killed, Mac listened to himself breathing in the biohazard mask and tried not to think about the enclosed space and his fear of being trapped. It was hot in the shaft and even hotter in his mask.

A faint clink sounded and Didge moved forward. Up ahead, Mac could make out the talc floating, then the rope they'd dragged through went taut beside Mac's head as Didge disappeared through a new hole in the shaft.

The radio headset crackled and Didge gave a sit-rep. Mac crawled forwards, pushed head-first into the hole and looked around. Didge stood on the floor of a large laboratory, machine and equipment hidden by vinyl covers, beakers, pipettes and test tubes standing upside down on racks, cleaned and sterilised.

After sliding down the rope, Mac stood beside Didge, squinting at the room. Red engineer's lights were placed at intervals in the walls and the surveillance cameras looked to be down.

'Clear,' came Didge's voice, muffled through his mask's breathers.

'Let's make this fast, mate,' said Mac, pulling the Nikon from his rucksack and setting off.

The underground component of Lombok was huge, about three times the size of the official facility. As he took pictures of the labs – largely decommissioned or mothballed by the looks of it – the camera's flash lit the area in eerie glimpses of the rooms, the strangeness intensified by the sounds of Didge and Mac breathing through the biohazard masks.

The labs led through double air-lock doors into a sterilisation area, complete with autoclave pressure cookers. Whatever they did in here, they were thorough. Walking into another long room, Mac photographed eight fermentation vats which could be used for many purposes, from making beer and MDMA, to making vaccines and bioweapons.

Pushing a stepladder up to the line of vats, Mac took wipes from three of them, before sealing the samples and moving on. Sweat rolled down his temples as he kept the Nikon's shutter going. The air-conditioning had been switched off and the combination of the stuffiness and the glow of the engineer's lights was making him queasy.

They'd just passed through another double air-lock doorway when the radio crackled to life and then crackled out again. Didge knocked at the receiver on his belt and then pressed through the helmet's material to shake the headset. Nothing. The radio crackled and then it died, possibly something to do with the negative pressure lock most of these facilities had, thought Mac, fear rising.

The next room got Mac's heart pumping. Along both walls were large cabinets made of grey painted steel and glass which Mac identified as spray driers and freeze driers – machines that could take agent from the fermentation vats, dry it, then reduce it to particles of less than ten microns. It could also reduce heroin and cocaine to desirable grains.

His hands swimming in the gloves, Mac tried to manhandle the wipes and the sample vials. Tapping on Mac's shoulder, Didge pointed to a door on their left with a large skull-and-crossbones in the middle, something written in Bahasa below. The word *Bahaya* rang a bell. Pushing through the double doors, the thick rubber seal-flaps in the middle made a grinding sound that gave both of them a start. After passing through the next air-lock door, they surveyed the scene that confronted them. There were fourteen glass panels on fourteen grey steel doors. Walking up and peering through one, Mac opened the door to a room which was the size of a small prison cell. There were four cages on each wall, their bars rising to the ceiling. Mac took a photo, knowing that DIA would want to see this. These were animal rooms – or 'inhalation chambers' – in which monkeys, dogs and cats were sealed and forced to inhale various agents to see how they reacted.

Turning, Mac saw that Didge's eyes were like saucers through the mask.

'You okay?' barked Mac through his breather cylinders.

'Yep,' came the rasped reply, unconvincing.

Mac wasn't feeling too flash either.

Mac followed Didge's gaze and saw they were standing on what looked like an internal road on the pale green lino, the car-width tyre tracks clearly marked in dull black on the pale background.

Pushing through the next doors – these ones twice as wide as the side entrance to the room – they followed the indoor 'road' down a long corridor with intermittent engineer's lights. Turning his flashlight on again, Didge led the way for fifty metres before coming to an internal loading-bay area with a truck parked in the dark. The entire far wall was a steel door with a set of electric controls at the side as well as a chain-loop manual function.

'Loading bay,' rasped Mac, looking at the twenty-tonne Hino flatbed with the Lombok AgriCorp signage on the side.

The radio crackled again, and both of them heard a couple of snippets of what sounded like Robbo yelling. Then it was dead air again. Mac decided to hurry it along, but he wanted more from this facility.

Hurriedly stowing his SIG Sauer, Didge pulled the chain loop hand-over-hand and the door started to inch up slowly.

Switching off the flashlight, Mac ducked to the side of the door as it slowly rose. When the door had gone up twelve centimetres, Mac motioned for Didge to stop it and got his head into a position where he could peer through to the other side. There was a conveyor belt four metres wide, which led upwards at a thirty-degree angle to another door at the top of the belt, the same as the one they'd just opened.

As Mac tried to get the camera in line to take a shot, a beeping sounded and the door at the top of the conveyor belt chute started to rise.

'Fuck,' said Mac, ducking back instinctively. Slowly putting his head around the corner again, the opening door revealed another set of steel doors, these ones side-opening with manually operated levers. A person in a white biohazard suit walked past at the top of the conveyor belt, and as the door opened further, Mac realised the second door also had warning signage on it.

'What's that?' asked Didge, kneeling behind him. 'That fire?'

'Sure is,' whispered Mac.

A roaring noise was followed by a thump, and the area above them shook as the roaring built to a crescendo.

'That a furnace?' asked Didge, raising his voice.

Looking down at his G-Shock, visible through the rubber gloves, Mac saw it was 6.51 pm. 'Getting ready for the evening burn,' said Mac. 'We've found the incinerator.'

CHAPTER 45

Suddenly the lights flickered and went on. Diving to the side of the conveyor-belt door, Mac scanned the tunnel and loading-bay area, both now flooded with light.

'Let's move,' said Didge, as the conveyor-belt door started moving up.

Heart thumping, Mac jogged out of the loading bay and along the tunnel, sweat running down the backs of his legs as he struggled to keep up with the soldier. His breathing was becoming ragged and hot.

Didge slowed down and waited for Mac when he reached the air-lock door they'd come through two minutes ago. Stealthing through they stopped, turned back and cased the tunnel through a gap. Four figures in white biohazard suits walked through a door into the loading bay, one yelling something up the conveyor-belt chute before scrambling into the crew-cab truck with the other three. The truck took off and then it was heading towards Mac and Didge.

Pulling back into the room, Mac raced after Didge through the next set of doors and into the space filled with inhalation chambers. Didge crept towards the door leading back into the labs, but Mac stopped him. He wanted to see where the truck was going and to check if there was an easy way to get samples from the incinerator.

'Gotta get outa here,' crackled Didge through the breather cylinders as the double air-lock doors automatically opened, allowing the truck to drive through.

'Back to the labs,' said Mac, heading for the doors that would allow them to escape through the venting system.

The air-lock doors to the lab area did not contain glass panels, and Mac held back to observe where the truck was going and what the workers were doing. The point of a recon exercise was to see or hear what was going on.

'Mate – no glass,' said Mac, pointing at the door. 'I need to take some snaps, okay?'

Reluctantly, Didge followed Mac across the internal lino road and they made for one of the inhalation chambers where the internal lights had not been activated. Pulling the grey steel door back on themselves, they stood in the shadows of the inhalation chamber, breathing hard. The throb of the truck's diesel engine sounded outside the area, and then intensified as the doors were opened. Craning his neck, Mac saw another double air-lock door at the end of the chambers which was also being opened.

Struggling for air, Mac realised they'd stumbled into the heart of the operation. Whatever was burned in that incinerator at such high heats, on a daily basis, was probably waiting on the other side of those doors. What was it, he wondered. Bad vaccines? Killer heroin? Monkeys who didn't like what they were inhaling?

'We've got to get in there, okay?' rasped Mac, pointing towards the truck as it slipped through the opened air-lock doors.

Didge nodded, though his face was grim and his breathing was laboured.

'You okay, mate?' asked Mac as the Hino moved on, bringing some quiet again to the inhalation chambers.

'Yeah, bra,' said Didge.

'Let's get our breathing right, okay?' said Mac.

Working together, they brought each other down to long deep breathing and then Mac pushed back the door to the inhalation chamber and they snuck out. Didge went in front with his SIG Sauer and they crept along the wall of inhalation chambers until they got to the door the Hino had just disappeared through. Sticking his head around the corner of the opened door, Didge checked their situation, hesitating a split second.

'Okay, mate?' asked Mac, as Didge groaned and sagged against the wall.

'Holy shit,' he hissed, staring into the mid-distance.

Mac angled himself around Didge and peeked around the corner to see for himself.

Taking it in, Mac's breathing seized. The Hino was fifty metres away at the end of a long room, with people in biohazard suits moving around like ants in a colony. Large, glass-sided inhalation chambers ran the length of the space, all of them filled with naked humans. Most looked dead, but some of them were still alive.

Pulling back, stunned, Mac thought fast – he needed to manage Didge out of the situation without both of them being made.

'Okay, we're gonna do the gig and get out, right, mate?' said Mac, who used his body to block Didge from walking into the room of inhalation chambers.

'But, there's people –' started Didge, his eyes far away.

'Don't worry about that, mate,' said Mac, feeling quite nauseous himself. 'Let's just focus on the gig, okay?'

'Robbo – let's call Robbo,' said Didge, sounding as if he might be in shock.

Things balanced on a knife's edge as Mac tried to catch the soldier's eye. Didge was bigger and stronger than him, and by the way the other 4RAR commandos treated the big Cape Yorker, Mac suspected he was their wet-work guy: the one who took out the sentries, who slit the throats and made stealth entries possible. If Didge decided on a certain course of action, it would be hard to stop him.

'C'mon, Didge – there's nothing we can really do here,' said Mac, trying to get Didge beyond his immediate desire to walk into that hall of horrors and start killing bad guys.

'Let 'em go,' said Didge, pushing at Mac.

'Go where?' asked Mac, gripping Didge's elbows. 'Out into the open? If we raise the alarm with the soldiers, the poor bastards will be shot anyway.'

Now Didge's head and body were shaking and Mac suspected he was hyperventilating.

'Or let 'em go so they can run around screaming and get us made?' Mac continued. 'We've still got a job to do in Maliana, mate.'

'We gotta get them outa here,' whispered Didge. 'Can't walk away, McQueen.'

'Not walking away, mate,' said Mac. 'Trying to keep us alive and get the gig done. Maybe we save more lives with these photos and samples than by whacking a few soldiers, okay?'

Giving Didge another shake of the elbows, Mac tried to lock eyes with him, even as he lost his own cool about this place.

'Okay, Didge?'

'Whatever you say,' said Didge, face stony.

Mac watched as the workers in biohazard suits threw body after body onto the back of the Hino. They seemed to be taking corpses from the right-hand inhalation chambers while the Timorese on the left were banging on the glass sides of their inhalation chambers.

Shouts rang out before the Hino beeped as it reversed. The next thing, the workers in the biohazard suits were walking back towards Mac and Didge.

Retreating back into their hide in the inhalation chamber, Mac and Didge waited in the dark as the truck drove past. After a few minutes the noise of the truck faded and then voices echoed from the loading bay as bodies were loaded onto the conveyor belt.

After a while the noises faded to silence and the entire area was plunged into darkness again as the lights were killed. Venturing out, Mac and Didge stealthed back to the large hall of inhalation chambers, pushed through the doors and entered the area where they'd just witnessed the horrifying scenes.

'We'll do this fast, okay, Didge?' asked Mac as they walked quietly down the dim corridor between the chambers. A rustling noise started up, followed by voices and then thumping on the glass. It was overwhelming but Mac was determined to gather the intelligence that would see the operators of this place prosecuted.

Mac raised the Nikon and took a shot of the long chamber with the people in it. The bursting flash revealed the creepy sight of at least eighty people, staring out of the glass like living ghosts – naked, skinny and distressed. Realising that Mac and Didge were not the normal workers, the prisoners – or whatever they were – swarmed to the glass.

'Fuck,' muttered Didge, his voice shocked and disbelieving.

Turning, Mac gently took Didge's arm and reminded him that they needed to keep going in order to save these folks' lives. He took several shots of the empty chamber on the other side before walking to its sealed door. As he opened it, Mac heard the sigh of air pressure as he broke the seal. Didge joined him and they stepped into the chamber, which reeked of urine and faeces. Noticing a patch of wetness near the rear of the chamber, Mac knelt and took several wipes which he put in the sample jars.

Standing again, Mac saw Didge double over and then heave, his mask filling with vomit.

'Shit,' said Mac, grabbing at Didge as his own stomach turned.

'Can't take it off, mate,' yelled Mac as Didge grabbed at the mask. 'Don't want to catch what these guys have got.'

Didge heaved again, then stood with his head down as he tried to pull himself together.

'Mate, we're out of here, okay?' said Mac, helping Didge through the chamber door and into the clear space between the lines of inhalation chambers.

Stopping, Didge put both hands on the sides of his biohazard helmet and moved his head around inside, trying to find a better way to breathe with the vomit.

Sweat dripped into Mac's shoes and, making a huge effort to block out the anguish around him, he aimed the Nikon at the chamber filled with people. Some of them still had the energy to slap their hands on the glass. Flashing off a final picture, he froze. Caught in his mind was an image that was too familiar, too recent. An image he couldn't ignore by creating professional distance.

Taking a closer look at the inhalation chamber, Mac stared at a face that served him cold beer a week earlier.

'Mickey, that you?' shouted Mac.

The man slapped at the glass, his thin old body somehow dignified in the glow of the engineer's light.

'Fuck's sake,' snarled Mac, feeling the gig going pear-shaped. 'Mickey Costa!'

CHAPTER 46

'Mr Richard?' mouthed Mickey through the thick glass, his face transforming from curiosity to amazement as he realised who was behind the biohazard mask.

Holding Mickey's desperate stare, utter rage swept over Mac, even knowing that two minutes earlier he'd been telling Didge to hold the emotions, to just do the gig.

Feeling a hand on his bicep, Mac turned to see Didge up close.

'Know this guy?' said Didge.

Nodding, Mac walked to the chamber door and reached forward to open it, but realised the latch was secured by a long-shank padlock.

The radio crackled and both Mac and Didge instinctively reached for the side of their biohazard helmets, relieved to be on the net again.

'Albion, this is Blue Leader,' came Robbo's voice, slightly breathless. 'Repeat, Albion, this is Blue Leader – confirm.'

'Blue Leader, this is Albion,' said Mac, as he touched the huge shank.

'Albion – the cameras are operational, Bad Guys massing topside, copy?'

'Roger that Blue Leader,' shouted Mac, heart racing, wondering how fast they could get back to the vent shaft. 'We okay for exfil via the vent shaft?'

'Negative,' said Robbo, the signal still not strong. 'Complications topside, Albion. Third-party involvement – stand by.'

'Roger that Blue Leader,' said Mac again, as the sound of automatic gunfire squawked into their headsets, followed by another break in the radio connection. Listening intently for the radio signal to come back, Mac heard the noise of gunfire echoing from somewhere distant. Swapping looks, Mac and Didge waited for more signals from the dead radio. Before anything came there was the distinct sound of boots slapping on concrete nearby. Holding still and focusing on the footfalls, they sourced the intrusion coming from behind the air-lock doors. They had company.

Checking his SIG Sauer, Didge moved back towards the air-lock doors, towards the source of the footfalls. Shoving his Nikon into the rucksack, Mac followed, fumbling with his Heckler to check load and safety.

Easing through the air-lock, Mac and Didge paused, listening to the shooting from topside and the slap of boots coming closer. In the confined space, with its low visibility, the cracks and staccato rumbles of assault rifles sounded as if they were on top of them. They could even hear men panting and whispered commands passing between them.

Swapping a glance, the two men realised they had to get back to the open vent shaft – it was their only escape route.

Veering back into the lab area, a shot cracked and Didge suddenly sagged in front of Mac, his gun arm swinging to a point in the darkness.

'Shit!' gasped the soldier, shifting to his good leg while keeping his gun hand level.

Mac dropped to a knee and fired two shots above where the flash had originated, then moved in behind Didge, who limped towards the open vent as he fired off five shots from the SIG.

Grabbing Didge under the shoulders, Mac rammed into the air-lock doors, crashing through them as soldiers' voices yelled in Bahasa Indonesia behind them. Concrete exploded and splinters flew around their heads as what felt like three or four magazines of 5.56mm were unloaded at them on full-auto.

Helping Didge towards the labs as one of the doors behind them was blown off its hinges, Mac stopped around the corner, turned back and fired a shot into the darkness, ducking behind the doorjamb as the incoming ripped the other door apart. Grabbing a flash-bang from his rucksack, he pulled the pin and threw it around the corner before catching up with Didge.

The concussion from the grenade almost threw Mac off his feet as he reached Didge, got a grip under his armpits and headed through the lab containing the spray driers, fermentation vats and the sterilisation equipment. Racing breathlessly into the room where the rappel rope hung from the open vent, Mac pulled his rucksack onto both shoulders, but did so too quickly. The motion threw the Nikon out of the bag and it bounced on the white linoleum floor. Retrieving it, Mac shoved it to the bottom of his rucksack and, trousering the Heckler, cupped two hands into a platform for Didge, who grabbed the rope with one hand and threw the other hand over the edge of the ventilator duct. Suddenly the lights arced up, filling the room with clinical whiteness as Didge groaned with exertion and disappeared into the duct.

Mac heaved for breath, barely able to contain his panic as he tied the rappel rope to the sealed fan section that had blocked the vent. Reaching down from the duct, Didge offered his forearm. Taking it, Mac clambered up into the duct, then turned to help Didge retrieve the fan and pull it back into place. Replacing the fan was not going to fool anyone looking for them, but in the confusion of gun battles, a ten-second advantage was better than no advantage at all.

With no time to fasten the screws, they moved back along the duct as fast as they could, the sound of gunfire growing stronger from above them. After a few seconds of crawling, Didge found the vertical venting shaft that would take them to the surface. As he pointed it out to Mac, a round of full-auto gunfire ripped through the horizontal vent shaft, punching along its steel sides just inches from Mac's Altama boots. Men shouted in Bahasa Indonesia and a rifle tapped against the fan section they'd just replaced, before the voices indicated the men were moving to another lab.

Waiting for Didge to get to the top on the rappel rope, Mac wondered whether Robbo was maintaining silence or if the commandos had become engaged in the battle above them. At the top of the rope, Mac clambered over the edge of the venting shaft and duck-walked to where Didge crouched under a bush, his mask on the ground as he slapped a fresh magazine into his SIG Sauer.

Chucking away his own mask, Mac looked across to the Lombok buildings, where fighting was carrying on sporadically but intensely around the main compound.

'What've we got, mate?' asked Mac, trying to work out who was fighting. 'Is it our guys?'

'Can't see any of ours,' murmured Didge. 'It looks like Indonesian soldiers against irregulars.'

Keying the radio, Mac asked for Blue Leader and stood by, but only dead air came back. Mac tried again. Nothing.

'How's the wound?' asked Mac, scanning the ground.

'Okay, but I'm losing blood,' said Didge. 'Got any binos, McQueen?'

Foraging in his rucksack, Mac passed the mini Leicas and then tried again on the radio. He didn't want to be running across open ground, just the two of them, while there were unfriendlies out there shooting at people.

'Fucking classic,' snarled Didge, the Leicas focused on a group of shooters crouched behind an army truck in the main courtyard.

'What?' asked Mac.

'Thought these brothers were all a myth,' chuckled Didge.

'Myth?' asked Mac.

'All that noise? That's Falintil.'

Mac and Didge took the long way back to the field base, breaking out of the fence on the north side, then trekking around behind the guard houses at the end of the compound, up into the jungle to the ridge from which Robbo was supposed to be running the op.

Mac tried to keep Didge's spirits up, assuring him he'd only sustained a flesh wound, there wasn't too much bleeding, and Toolie would be able to deal with it.

Slowing for the approach to the base, Didge crouched with a wince and gestured Mac closer.

'What –' Mac started, before realising the barrel of an assault rifle was trained on him. He raised his hands, dropping his gun.

Someone grabbed Mac's shirt, dragging him into a standing position. Their three captors were skinny locals, badly dressed in various types of jungle fatigues, suggesting they were Falintil.

'How's it going?' said Mac to the mestizo guerrilla who was obviously in charge. There was no response as gunfire rattled in the background and an explosion boomed. The lead man waited for a moment then gestured with his G3, and Mac's rucksack was taken from him.

Mac's mind spun with the possibilities as he and Didge were led through the jungle at gunpoint. Was being Australian an advantage or, given Canberra's acquiescence with the Indonesian occupation, would it get them killed? And if they were in open conflict with the Falintil guerrillas, were Robbo and his men even alive? It was a tall order to deal with Falintil on their own ground; fighting Falintil at night was virtually impossible. The might of the Indonesian military had spent a quarter of a century attempting to do it and had failed repeatedly.

They paused before dropping to the commandos' field base and as they came into the clearing, Mac was pushed in the back and stumbled into Robbo, Toolie and Mitch, who were sitting on the forest floor, hands bound behind their backs.

Hitting the dirt beside Robbo, Mac decided to try his luck.

'Got an injured guy here, mate,' said Mac to the leader, pointing at Didge. 'Can we get a medic on him?'

The leader stared, stony-faced, and Mitch leapt into the awkward pause, making the same request in Bahasa Indonesia. Nodding slowly, the Falintil leader issued a command while the guerrillas found the commandos' medic pack. The guerrillas had already checked the packs, noticed Mac, and he was happy that he'd found a hiding place for the US dollars before he'd gone on the gig. It might turn out to be the only leverage he had.

The guerrilla medic knelt beside Didge and worked on the leg injury, as another guerrilla knelt behind Mac and bound his wrists.

Turning to the leader, Mac tried to keep it friendly. 'We're Aussies, mate – we're on your side, okay? I was with you guys a few days ago –'

The leader raised his hand slightly to stop Mac from talking. It was dark in the jungle and the silence of the guerrillas against the boom and crack of a fight in the Lombok compound was a strange mix. Johnno and Beast were still out there somewhere and Mac hoped they were alive and working on a rescue.

The guerrilla finished tying Mac's wrists and stood with his rucksack. Out came the Nikon and the field-glasses, and Mac prayed they wouldn't destroy the camera or the samples.

'Easy on the camera, eh boys?' said Mac, as the guerrilla threw it to the leader. Mac's heart beat against his chest – the last thing he needed was a bunch of hungry freedom fighters finding the digital images he'd taken of the Timorese in those inhalation chambers. He thought back to the argument he'd had with Didge, as he refused to release those captives. Should he have released those people in the inhalation chamber, like Didge wanted? Would his refusal to do the right thing get both of them killed now?

Rodrigo and Yohannes were also absent – a particularly bad development if those kids told the guerrillas that Aussie soldiers were taking children hostage.

'What do they want?' Mac asked Robbo.

'Waiting for someone, I think,' said Robbo.

'What's the damage, Didge?' Robbo asked, as the soldier's wound was bandaged.

'Rifle – M16 I think. Through the thigh muscle,' grunted Didge, staunch in spite of the pain.

There was a small commotion and then a group of four men entered the camp, senior by the look of how their captors came to attention. After some muffled discussions in the darkness, Mac saw the glow of the Nikon's viewing panel light up.

Mac's adrenaline surged as the chatter around the Nikon became animated. He held his breath, waiting for one of them to take exception to what he'd been photographing.

Finally the tall figure in dark fatigues who was handling the camera came out of the darkness and crouched where Mac could see his face.

'Well, Mr Richard,' he said, holding a Browning handgun at Mac's throat. 'Decided to return to sunny Timor-Leste?'

'Well it's cheaper than Bali,' said Mac with no conviction. 'How you been, anyway, Joao?'

CHAPTER 47

A huge explosion shook the trees and they looked down at the Lombok facility, parts of which were now engulfed in flames.

'So tell me what you saw down there, Mr Richard,' said Joao.

'The buildings you can see house an official vaccine program, registered with the WHO and everything,' said Mac.

'Vaccine program?' asked Joao.

'Yeah, but there's a hidden underground facility. It's three, four times as big as the one you can see. I thought it was a drug lab, but there's a lot of people down there.'

'People?' said Joao.

'Hundreds – I think they're being used for testing,' said Mac, still trying to work it out for himself.

'Testing? What, they're guinea pigs for the vaccine?' asked Joao, even and calm.

'I don't know – that's what the pics are for,' said Mac, working towards an information swap that would set them free and perhaps create the diversion he needed for the Blackbird snatch.

'Alive?' asked Joao.

'Some,' said Mac. 'About eighty or so.'

'So people are dying from this vaccine?' asked Joao.

'Too early to tell,' nodded Mac. 'We saw a lot of bodies being loaded onto the back of a truck, taken to the incinerator.'

'A vaccine that kills people? Sounds more like a weapon,' said Joao.

Pausing at Joao's comment, Mac wondered; surely the Indonesians wouldn't have a bio-weapons program.

'I understand this vaccine covers the super-pneumonia they're calling SARS,' said Mac. 'Maybe they're using their manmade SARS on human beings to create a better vaccine? Either way, it's entirely illegal.'

Going silent for a moment, Joao grew pensive as he looked down at the burning hulk of Lombok AgriCorp. 'Is this anything to do with the camp we found behind Memo?'

'I have no idea,' said Mac, slightly taken aback.

Looking over his shoulder, Joao called forth one of his lieutenants and issued a command which saw some of his men run off into the bush.

'You're not a salesman, I take it?' said Joao, watching a posse of Falintil run from the jungle and race towards the Lombok buildings. Soon they were leading their comrades towards the ventilators in the paddock. Although annoyed at being made, Mac was elated that some survivors would get out of there.

'Look, Joao, we're friendlies, okay? We're on the same side – those were Indonesians who shot Didge down there,' said Mac, trying to work out if divulging the Blackbird gig to Joao might help him. 'And we've got business in Maliana.'

In the distance, the sound of helos boomed against the hills, signalling that the Indonesian Army's Kodim 1636 in Maliana was mobilised. That wasn't totally bad news for Mac so long as he could get himself and his escort out of the area before the soldiers came and engaged the Falintil fighters.

'Maliana's hot,' said Joao, still observing Mac with scepticism.

'I don't have a choice,' said Mac.

'Who?' asked Joao.

'No one important,' said Mac.

'I've got the gun, Mr Richard. And I have every reason to shoot you.'

'What was I going to do with eighty people, Joao?' snapped Mac, knowing he sounded guilty.

'Letting them go home would have been a start,' said Joao.

'They wouldn't have got home, Joao, and you know it,' said Mac.

'Okay,' nodded the guerrilla. 'But standing there, taking their photo – that was the best you could do?'

The helos' thromping was coming closer and Mac could see the lights of four of the aircraft heading their way.

'Could have done much better than that, Joao,' agreed Mac.

Joao was quiet, thinking, and Mac decided to try another tack. 'Well, that's me, mate – what are your guys doing here?'

Joao's face darkened. 'Some of the southcoast villages have been losing people – they've been disappearing. That camp at Memo was a dead-end, right, but then we got word that they were also being taken here.'

Mac waited, sensing he shouldn't push any further.

'You've put me in a position,' snarled Joao. 'I've got an Aussie spy and Aussie soldiers working undercover in the jungle, and by morning half of Falintil is going to be saying that you stood by and took photos of genocide – of our people!'

'Look, Joao –'

'And these same people kidnapped a couple of local boys, faked their deaths, made their families think they'd gone.'

'Okay, so –'

'And by the time that story has gone around the island, they're going to be asking one question.'

'Joao –'

'They gonna say, *Why the priest let those Aussies go? Why they not pig-food?*'

'Okay, mate,' said Mac. 'But let the soldiers go, okay? They're just an escort and they wanted to open those doors, let the prisoners go free.'

'Really?' said Joao.

'Yes, and I argued it would compromise all of us – no way the Indonesians would allow those people to tell the world what happened. They'd be caught and shot.'

Joao stood silently as the helos flared over the Lombok buildings. Mac could see he was tired and angry. Looking Mac in the eye, Joao stepped forward and held his Browning to Mac's forehead. Closing his eyes, Mac prepared for death as he decided to try one final option.

'Does Falintil need money?' asked Mac, opening one eye. 'US dollars, cash, tax-free?'

'US dollars?' asked Joao, pulling the gun's muzzle away from Mac's skin.

'One hundred thousand now – could be as much as two million later,' said Mac as he exhaled.

Joao made a face that said *Don't manipulate me you arrogant Australian prick.* Lack of funds was always a big issue for Falintil, especially if independence should win the day in the East Timor ballot. It was one thing to have an independent new nation, but without a financial base the Falintil freedom fighters would lose the subsequent political battle to the returning bankers, industrialists and powerful families – all the elites who cleared out in 1975.

'And let me guess, Mr Richard – you show me how to get this money, and you get to live, right?'

'Could be a plan,' said Mac, smiling thinly.

'Just a pity more Timorese don't have that kind of cash floating around, eh Mr Richard? Wouldn't have to sit in a cage, being fed a disease.'

'Falintil's going to need cash for East Timor's new nationhood,' said Mac, trying not to seem cocky. 'You don't win the peace – you buy it.'

'You think I needed a privileged white man to tell me that?' asked Joao, shouldering Mac out of the way as he left.

Sitting with the commandos, Mac tried to send his photos while Toolie rechecked Didge's wound. At the base of the hill, fighting still raged, most of it now underground.

'At least one transmission is working,' said Robbo, pointing at the American sat phone which Mac was trying to connect to the Nikon.

'It *was* working,' said Mac, failing to connect the data cable to the mangled jack in the camera. 'Teach me to go dropping the damn thing on a concrete floor.'

'So what did the Falintil bloke say?' asked Robbo, crouching.

'You mean after he told me he was going to execute me for not letting those people go?' said Mac, putting the data cable and camera into his rucksack.

'Yeah,' said Robbo, with an edge.

'He decided that two million US dollars into Falintil's pocket was a good exchange for our lives,' said Mac, not mentioning that he also wanted the mule line of money heisted to further break the connection between North Korea and the Indonesian military. 'Rodrigo and Yohannes are going to be helpful on that score.'

'So he's out of our hair?' said Robbo, looking suspicious.

'Don't know for certain,' said Mac truthfully. 'But he knows we have business in Maliana, and I'm pretty sure his crew will leave us alone.'

'So, we're still going in? To Maliana?' said Robbo.

'Yep,' said Mac. 'I'm thinking this mess is as good a distraction as we could have hoped for.'

'In that case, we'd better move now,' said Robbo, standing. 'By the way, about before – I know you don't dream up these operations, but I need warning –'

'Would it make the boys any happier?' asked Mac.

'Not happier, mate, but you holding back reflects badly on me.'

'Can you imagine tabbing all the way across Timor when the boys know that the target is a facility that grows a deadly disease?' said Mac, drinking water. 'Next thing you know, you have soldiers drawing straws and getting all political with each other, see who gets to suit up and who doesn't, right?'

Robbo nodded, conceding the truth of what Mac was saying. In general, soldiers did not like going into the environment that existed at Lombok, regardless of their training.

'I needed to be down there with the best, not with the guy who got the short straw or who's out of favour with Robbo,' said Mac. 'Maybe even the person who was taking a piss when the warning order was made.'

'Fair enough,' said Robbo.

'You simply gave me the best, and we did the gig, mate,' said Mac, checking his rucksack. 'I'll buy you a beer if we nail it – but you know what, Robbo?'

'What?'

'I'd do it the same way again,' said Mac.

***

Spirits lifted among the troop when Beast and Johnno reappeared, having been cut off from the base by the gunfight. As they regrouped and checked their gear, Robbo told them that the time to hit the Kopassus compound was now, while the distraction at Lombok was active.

As they walked through the darkness, tension high, Mac went over the recent events, trying to piece them together. The Americans at DIA had briefed Mac on the possibility of a secret facility underground at Lombok but, having found it, he wasn't sure that Lee Wa Dae and Ishy Haryono were making nightclub drugs for Australia and Japan. He'd never heard of a drug lord using inhalation chambers – that sort of terminology was associated with vaccine testing on animals. What had Haryono got himself into at Lombok, wondered Mac. It was either illegal vaccine testing or it was bioweapons. And the scientists packing up to leave? Had they succeeded or failed in their research?

There was one thing that niggled at Mac. The people still alive in one bank of inhalation chambers were all Portuguese and mestizo – straight-haired East Timorese. The bodies that Mac saw loaded onto that Hino truck came from the other bank of inhalation chambers, and they all seemed to have been Maubere – the native Melanesians of East Timor. It was probably nothing, thought Mac.

At a little after 9.30 they entered the farm belt that surrounded Maliana.

Didge halted at a ridge and looked down. 'That's it, boss,' he said, pointing.

Stepping up, Robbo peered through his field-glasses at a large compound with a main group of buildings next to a smaller compound of buildings – the Kopassus camp.

'Looks quiet,' whispered Robbo, handing the glasses to Mac. 'And I never trust quiet. Check the main gate – I make it three, regular infantry.'

Mac nodded.

'Behind all that, you have that secondary compound which is the Kopassus intel base,' said Robbo. 'I'm assuming that any prisoner would be kept in the interrogation centre right inside the entrance, that white building with the six windows. See it?'

'So what's the call?' asked Mac.

'Go in the fence nearest to the jungle,' said Robbo, pointing, 'and make it real fast. Lightning raid – just rush 'em.'

'Who?'

'Johnno, Beast and me,' said Robbo. 'The rest covering with rifles and grenades.'

'I'm going in,' said Mac. 'If it goes to shit, I have to be there.'

'No – we need you out here,' said Robbo. 'If we have to get out of Timor with that girl, I want you running it, not lying in a Kopassus camp with a bullet in your head.'

CHAPTER 48

Mac lay on the knoll overlooking the Kopassus intel camp, observing the action through his Leica binos. Below him, Beast and Johnno covered Robbo, who stood in the lee of the main building, examining a little screen he held in two hands. Having augered through the side of the building and pushed a fibre-optic camera through the hole, Robbo was now looking at the screen to see what was inside.

'Come on!' hissed Mac, checking his G-Shock. It was 12.11 am.

'Worth getting this part right,' whispered Didge, lying beside Mac, his M4 shouldered, ready to create supporting fire.

'I know,' said Mac. 'But I'd like to have a few hours' start on these guys before sun-up. I hate –'

'Look,' said Didge, interrupting Mac.

Robbo slowly pulled his fibre optic from the hole in the wall and gestured for Beast, who turned around so Robbo could put the screen and camera in his pack. Robbo then gave a hand command which led to suppressors being screwed onto handguns and Johnno drawing his black Ka-bar combat knife. Next thing, they were moving out of sight around the front of the building.

Raising himself from his prone position, Didge groaned slightly at the pain in his leg. Then, assuming a kneeling-marksman pose he shouldered the M4. Adrenaline rising, Mac swung his Leicas to the left as Mitch emerged from the tree line – weapon at his shoulder – and stealthed further along the security fence. Toolie remained absolutely still in the standing-marksman pose, still looking like a bloke going fishing. It was a classic supporting-fire configuration, covering the raiding party from both inside and outside aggression.

Mac forced himself to stay calm. If the snatch didn't go well, he reckoned they'd get about five hundred metres before they were taken apart by the Indonesian military. Their only advantage was that the base seemed deserted while the Kodim Maliana took care of the Falintil problem at the Lombok facility.

Didge nudged Mac and pointed at the Kopassus camp entry. Two soldiers in red berets and jungle cams walked up the slight rise into the camp.

'Blue Dog, this is Albion – two Bandits at your four o'clock; repeat Bandits at your four,' said Mac into his radio mic.

The soldier nearest the intel building suddenly swivelled, looking at the building the commandos had just entered. Suddenly, his eyes widened and Johnno appeared from the shadows, slapped a hand across the Indonesian's face and brought his knife quickly across the bloke's throat. As the soldier sagged in Johnno's arms, the second Kopassus soldier froze, then fell to the ground as three shots tore silently into his chest. Suppressors were a hassle to configure and to carry, but they were amazingly effective.

'Nice work, Blue Team,' mumbled Didge as Johnno and Beast pulled the two soldiers into the far lee of the building, where they could no longer be seen by Mac and Didge.

Abruptly, Robbo appeared around the corner of the building, suppressed handgun held in cup-and-saucer. Pausing, he nodded and crept quickly towards the gap they'd cut in the fence, followed by Beast with a body in a blanket carried in a fireman's lift. Johnno worked the sweep as they moved out of the Kopassus camp.

'Nice work, boys,' said Didge, standing and sweeping his rifle across the camp, looking for any problems.

Blackbird proved to be both cooperative and fit, and they got to the camp at the observation post shortly before 3.30 am. Leaving Mac and Blackbird in the bivvy, the rest of the 63 Recon Troop grabbed food and water and crawled through to the OP to check what they'd been missing in the past twenty-four hours.

Getting himself comfortable against the bamboo wall, Mac took a decent look at the girl for the first time since they'd cleared out of Maliana. She was tall and athletic, intelligent-looking and quite beautiful, even in a set of borrowed jeans and a sweatshirt.

'We'll have a rest, something to eat, and then we're off,' said Mac.

'Where are we going?' she said in a deep register, not betraying too much in the way of nerves.

'Out of here,' said Mac. 'To a safer place.'

'Australia? Java?' she asked, quite self-assured.

'Not up to me,' said Mac, trying to keep the annoyance out of his voice. 'All you have to do is keep walking and I'll take care of the rest, okay?'

'Okay,' she said, peeling an orange. 'Your name Mac, right?'

'That's it.'

'You Australian intelligence?'

'Let's have a bigger conversation once we're out of here, okay, Maria?'

'Sure,' she shrugged. 'Can talk now if you want.'

'I'm not going to debrief you,' said Mac, 'but I *would* like to get an idea what you've been speaking to Kopassus about.'

'Just what I told the Australians,' she said, matter-of-fact. 'I tell the *malai* all the things I was saying to Canadian.'

'Everything? You told them everything?' asked Mac. 'They torture you, Maria?'

'No,' she said, looking away.

'They threaten your family?'

'Yes,' she nodded.

Fishing in his bag, Mac came out with some bars of chocolate, which he handed to Blackbird. He tried to soften the questions.

'They ask you what you looked at in the army headquarters in Dili?'

'Yes,' she said.

'They ask you if you stole anything?'

'Yes, and I told them what I taken.'

'They ask if you'd taken copies?' said Mac with a smile.

'No, mister,' said Blackbird, shaking her head but keeping her eyes on Mac's in the dark.

Informal interrogation was best conducted with enough light to clock every reaction, every shift of the eyes and set of the mouth. But Mac had fallen into this line of conversation and he didn't want to halt the momentum, even as he detected a lie.

'Did you make any copies at army headquarters, Maria?' asked Mac.

'No,' she said, quite calm.

'Did you tell the Canadian everything you discovered?'

'Yes, mister,' she said, smiling.

'Did you see any papers in army headquarters about Operasi Ipoh?' asked Mac conversationally.

'No, mister,' she said.

'Operasi Bali?' he asked.

'No.'

'Operasi Boa?'

'No – not that one.'

'And no copies of any army papers?' said Mac, bringing his cadence down to suggest the end of a conversation.

'No, mister,' she said, her voice relieved.

'Where did you hide the copies, Maria?'

'I didn't . . . I mean, I took no copies.'

'The copies of Operasi Boa?'

Waving her hands, and then putting her face in them, Blackbird hesitated. 'Now I all confused.'

'Take your time, Maria,' said Mac, like her best friend.

'Okay,' she sighed, breathing out.

Handing her a fresh bottle of water, Mac looked at his G-Shock. 'Drink up, we'll leave in five.'

Looking out through the bamboo walls, Mac's heart was racing. Was there an ambush? Was the snatch a set-up? He did not know. What he did know was that Kopassus intel failing to ask Blackbird if she copied files during her time at army HQ was about as likely as the Ferrari F-1 pit crew turning up for a race without a single wrench. It was a spurious story, and meant that either Kopassus was after something totally different to what Mac and Tony Davidson assumed they were after, or Blackbird was walking both sides of the street.

Mac's coded radio call to the Royal Australian Navy was successful and he got a commitment for an exfil at midnight, from the same place where he'd set down after the swim from the submarine. Getting close to finishing a successful gig, Mac's excitement was counterbalanced by stress and fatigue. If someone gave him an air-bed, a shower and a proper pillow, he'd sleep for twelve hours without touching the sides. But for now he was buzzing along on adrenaline, trying to get to the finish line.

They made fast time across the river into West Timor and overland to the kijang's hide with Robbo and Beast as the escort. The soldiers flirted with Blackbird, who deflected their attentions with a cold politeness that she'd probably been practising since childhood. She was a cool cookie, this one, thought Mac, and he vowed to test her again before he handed her over.

At 7.03 am the soldiers led them to the head of the river valley that they'd run up two days ago, and Mac made his seven o'clock call to Jim at DIA.

'Saturn recon was a success,' said Mac. 'But I can't send the pics – busted the camera, so I'll have to walk them out. Got samples too.'

'That'll do,' said Jim.

'There were a bunch of people in that underground facility,' said Mac, wanting to know more about Lombok. 'Most of them were dead.'

'Okay – any alive?' asked Jim.

'Yeah, about eighty,' said Mac, wanting Jim to do more of the explaining.

'Do we have Blackbird?' said Jim, before Mac could push.

'She's here, but she's claiming no knowledge of Boa or any file copies,' said Mac.

'She lying?' asked Jim.

'I reckon,' said Mac.

'Well that's unfortunate,' said Jim.

'Yeah?'

'Yeah, because comms chatter from the Indonesian Army suggests Boa is being brought forward – looks like whatever it is will start around the ballot results.'

'That's a week away,' said Mac.

'Sure. That reminds me,' said Jim, sounding concerned, 'you didn't start that direct action at Saturn?'

'No, that was Falintil. Villagers on the south coast had been disappearing and they traced them to Saturn. The guards didn't want to open the gates.'

'Don't want to pressure you, buddy,' said Jim. 'But Blackbird is now the key to this. Got an ETA?'

'I'll get her there as fast as I can,' said Mac.

'Drive safely, McQueen – Tony wants a word.'

'Macca!' came the greeting, so loud Mac had to pull his ear from the sat phone.

'Tony, how's it going?' asked Mac.

'Good, mate – just got back from Dili, where I had a chat with our friend.'

'Yeah?'

'Yep. Still don't know who the President's Men are in Jakarta, but he said Kopassus had been running some disinformation strategies.'

'Like what?' asked Mac.

'Like the false flag Operation Extermination – which is really a cover for Boa,' said Davidson. 'Like some of the assurances that Canberra is relying on assurances that the Indonesian military is trying to bring order to Timor, rather than supporting the militias.'

'Okay,' said Mac, distracted and tired. 'Well Blackbird tells me she doesn't know about Boa and she never copied a document that covers it.'

'Does she just?'

'Yeah, but I'll bring her in, get to the bottom of it, right?'

'Sure, Macca,' said Davidson, a resigned tone in his voice. 'Let's see what this bird sings.' He hung up.

'That Jim as in DIA?' asked Robbo, surprising Mac. 'In Denpasar?'

'Ah, yeah,' said Mac, who didn't like eavesdroppers. 'Maybe.'

'Come on, McQueen,' said Robbo with a smile. 'I remember him in Jordan, after he was kicked out of UNSCOM. I heard he was in Denpasar.'

'UNSCOM?' said Mac. 'What was Jim doing with the weapons inspectors?'

'Who knows?' said Robbo, distracted by a bird flapping noisily out of a tree. 'I think he was on loan from Detrick – Saddam's people challenged him and the UN asked him to leave.'

'Really?' said Mac.

'Yeah, mate,' said Robbo, turning to go. 'All that UN political shit.'

Head pounding with the possibilities, Mac tried not to dwell on it. Detrick was the nickname for the US Army's Medical Research Institute for Infectious Disease. Fort Detrick was where you went when you wanted to know everything there was to know about biological weapons.

CHAPTER 49

The Timor Sea looked oily as the sun rose above the horizon, turning the ocean from a deep vermilion to green.

Mac's hide looked over the point on the south coast where he'd come ashore two days earlier, and as the birds started their morning song, Robbo and Beast prepared a natural crow's nest beneath the palms. Throwing a couple of field jackets on the sea grasses, they gave Blackbird a bed of sorts – somewhere to relax and lay low till the exfil at midnight.

'Okay here, Macca?' asked Robbo, M4 held across his forearm, sunnies pushed up. 'Thought we'd recce the area, see who's who.'

'Yeah, sweet, mate,' said Mac with a small yawn. 'Might get a kip myself.'

As Robbo and Beast moved out into the surrounding beachhead, Mac built a sleeping hollow for himself at Blackbird's nine o'clock, but higher in the crow's nest where he could see anyone approaching.

Making to lie down, he noticed Blackbird sitting up and looking at him.

'Have a headache,' she groaned, rubbing the heel of her left hand into her forehead. 'Shouldn't wake me and then make me walk so far.'

'I know the feeling,' said Mac. 'I haven't slept properly for more than two days.'

Mac gave her his spare bottle of water and dug into his rucksack. 'We thought you were being tortured up there.'

'They didn't hurt me,' she said, long black hair held up in a topknot. 'Just lots of questions.'

'Benni ask you the questions, Maria?'

In the slight hesitation that followed, Mac could see her constructing a lie. It was the immutable law of his profession that the true liars always believed they were going unnoticed.

'Benni?' she asked, sipping some water.

'Benni wasn't asking the questions?'

'I not know –'

'Florita said you knew him, Maria,' said Mac softly, then let the silence hang. It was Blackbird's turn to do the running.

Pulling his small first-aid pack from the rucksack, Mac found some packets of Xanax and Mogadon. Burrowing deeper into the small zippered bag, he found the Nurofens, typically used with snatchees who felt nauseous from the benzodiazepines Mac gave the uncooperative ones.

Pushing a couple of the painkillers from the foil, he passed them to Blackbird, who was looking sadly into her water.

'You know my sister?' she asked finally.

'I met her a week ago, in a hut with some soldiers.'

'Was she okay?' said Blackbird, snapping out of her sulk. 'Tell me she was okay!'

'We helped her out, Maria.'

'She okay now? She home?' she wanted to know, concern in her dark eyes.

'She was fine, but anything that happened was against her will, okay?'

'You do not have to tell me *that*!' she said, firing up. 'Florita is a good girl!'

After a quiet *sorry*, Mac mused on the pride of the Timorese even as the women accepted the risk of official rape and the boys knew that a military execution might result from a simple cheeky comment.

Wiping tears from her cheeks, Blackbird tried to regain her composure. 'What did Florita tell you?'

'She told me about Benni Sudarto,' said Mac.

'What did she say?!' she snapped.

'Why don't you tell me?' asked Mac.

Blackbird looked away, her back heaving through the sweatshirt.

'You have no right!' she cried. 'Do not come in my country and be the judge of me.'

'It was a question, Maria – not a judgment. What is your relationship with Benni Sudarto?'

Shaking her head slowly, she gave him a hard look. 'You people – the Indonesi, the Australi – you come to Timor and play with us like a chess game.'

'That's not –'

'All I wanted was to go to the university in Surabaya, okay?' she said, defiant. 'First, Indonesi army say, *Work for us for a year and we maybe sponsor you to Surabaya.* Then Australi say, *Tell us the Indonesi secrets and we'll send you and Florita to any university you want; Surabaya, Sydney, Queensland – you naming it, Maria!* Then Captain Sudarto, he take me out in his car, and he tell me, *Work for me, Maria, and your family will live. Let me down, and I kill them in front of you.*' She was really sobbing now, tears streaming down her cheeks.

'What's Operasi Boa?' asked Mac, thinking he might be able to unhinge her.

'Boa?' she said, recovering her former poise. 'I don't even know who *you* are.'

'I told –'

'You could be anyone, you could be working for anybody. I never met you.'

Shrugging, Mac conceded her point. His job was to bring her out of East Timor, and then her trusted controller – Atkins most likely – would run the debrief.

'I am sorry to waste your time and make you run around in jungle,' she said, with kind eyes. 'But I did what you asked, I took the files and did the drop box, so please do not ask me to betray my own family.'

'I thought the Timorese were proud people,' said Mac, trying for one last manipulation to turn her back.

'We are,' smiled the young woman, sniffling. 'And I am proud to keep my family alive.'

***

Looking out over the beach, Mac assessed possible problem points for the exfil. The tide was in and by midnight it would be almost back in the same place. He would have to be careful to bring the boat in between a couple of markers and, walking to the water's edge, he identified the distinctive rocks, gave them names and committed them to memory. He wanted to be able to give the navy boat crew some basic trig points to get them to shore without being snagged on the reef just below the surface.

Looking at his G-Shock, he felt a wave of fatigue and wondered if he shouldn't take a nap while the commandos were still guarding the perimeter.

Making a single round of the crow's nest, he made back to his hide and slugged at his water while Blackbird slept. It was amazing how sweet water tasted when it was all you had, he mused. As he replaced the bottle in his rucksack, he noticed the water was slightly milky. Licking at his lips, he realised it actually was sweet – his thirst had nothing to do with it.

Mind spinning, Mac reached for his rucksack, eyelids starting to droop. Pulling out the first-aid kit, he clocked that one of the benzo boxes had been torn open, the half-empty foil beside it.

'Fuck,' thought Mac, 'she's used half a packet.'

Darkness closed in from the sides of his vision and a warm, safe sleepiness engulfed him. After nine years of pushing them into people's mouths, he finally knew what Mogadon felt like.

The onshore wind felt beautiful on Mac's face as he opened his eyes, becoming aware of the crashing surf and the night sky through the swishing palms.

Leaning over him, Beast peered and waved his hand from side to side. 'Awake, Macca?' he asked, squinting.

'Think so,' croaked Mac, his voice sounding like it was coming from a thousand miles away.

Robbo appeared beside Beast and they pulled him up into a sitting position, Mac's brain swirling like a top.

'Sorry, boys . . .' he started, and then leaned to the side and vomited as Beast jumped back to keep his pants clean.

He felt foggy in the brain and hungry in the stomach, but mostly Mac was confused. 'What's up, guys?' he asked, wiping his mouth with his shirt front.

'You lost the girl,' said Robbo, pushing up Mac's eyeballs and shining his flashlight in them. 'You were out to it, mate – girl drugged you. Mogadon by the looks of it.'

Shaking some clarity into his brain, Mac recalled some of the morning's events and moaned as he realised he'd been duped.

'She gone?' he slurred.

'No, we caught her,' said Robbo. 'But we had to move, and you have to get on the net, re-call the exfil.'

'I do?' asked Mac, still waking up.

Behind Robbo, Blackbird's hair blew in the sea breeze. Locking eyes with Mac, she gave a shrug that might have been an apology.

'Our position was blown,' said Robbo. 'And you're the one with the exfil call signs – we've been waiting for you to wake up.'

'We've been made?' said Mac.

'No, mate – we moved before that,' said Robbo, offering him another banana.

'How did you know we were blown?' asked Mac, confused.

'The girl took off with your sat phone.'

'Bitch,' sighed Mac, despite some begrudging admiration.

'Something like that,' said Robbo.

CHAPTER 50

It was past midday when Mac awoke to the trilling of the Nokia on his beside table. Scrambling for the phone in the dimness of his room at the Natour Bali he listened before hanging up and rolling out of the bed with a groan. The debrief location had been changed from Atkins' offices to DIA's headquarters in Denpasar.

As the shower water pelted his head, Mac willed himself to wake up and get his thoughts together. After delaying the Blackbird exfil by a day, during which he got almost no sleep, he'd then spent another day and night on boats, ships and a helo before hitting his pillow just ten hours earlier. Putting the exhaustion to one side, he thought about what he would say at the debrief and, more importantly, what he wouldn't say. Having spent four days in East Timor on Operation Totem, he could claim that he and the 4RAR Commandos nailed two of the three objectives: Blackbird snatched and exfiltrated to a secret location for debriefing by Australian SIS and the Pentagon, and Lombok AgriCorp's secret facility infiltrated, photographed and sampled.

It was a difficult tasking, and Mac was proud of the Aussies for punching above their weight.

The secret airfield was not so successful, but Mac wasn't concerned. It looked like Haryono's administration offices for his various interests, one of which was making illegal drugs for sale to middle-class fools in Australia and Japan. The actual set-up was obviously an agricultural spraying depot, probably for mosquitos. If the Indonesians wanted to conduct secret DDT programs in contravention of the UN's ban on outdoor spraying, then it was fine with Mac – DDT being the cheapest and most powerful enhancer of quality of life for anyone who lived in malarial zones, regardless of what non-malarial greenies in London and San Francisco said about it.

There were loose ends that niggled at Mac's mind, but they weren't enough to ruin his morning. The underground facility at Lombok, for instance, didn't strike him as being a drug lab. Mac had never seen a methamphetamine factory, or a cocaine lab, but he'd heard they smelled of powerful solvents and he assumed they didn't include live testing programs. After his debrief, he would be eased out of Totem, but he might ask around – see how others interpreted that strange underground world.

Making a cup of green tea, he found himself thinking about Blackbird. She was no longer his problem – he'd been sent to find Australia's hottest spy and he'd done it. But it was an anticlimax to risk so much only to discover that she was ambivalent at best, treacherous at worst.

Seeing the time, Mac stood to go and noticed his rucksack. The American courier at the base behind Denpasar's Ngurah Rai Airport had been so insistent about getting Mac's samples as soon he stepped off the helo that she hadn't asked for the return of DIA's digital Nikon.

Lifting it from the bag, Mac inspected the camera's damaged data-jack area and had an idea.

Scanning the street outside the Natour, Mac grabbed the fourth cab, waving the first three away as soon as they stopped.

Giving an address four blocks south of Puputan Square, Mac settled in the back seat of the air-conditioned Camry and sat directly behind the driver so he could clock the bloke's face in the rear-vision mirror.

'Still the dry weather – good for you, sir,' said the driver, a well-presented man in his early thirties.

'Better than the monsoon?' asked Mac, smiling.

'No good for tourist,' said the bloke, shaking his head slowly. 'They get wet and crazy, then go home and say Bali is wet and crazy.'

'That's about right,' said Mac, chuckling as the street stalls and crowds flashed by in his window.

Flipping the driver a US fifty-dollar note as they stopped, Mac asked him to drive to the Golden Lantern and wait outside for ten minutes.

'For sure, sir,' said the driver, eyes looking at a week's profit in one fare. 'I wait an hour for you.'

'Ten minutes is fine, thanks, champ,' said Mac, alighting with his businessman's satchel and casing the street.

Walking back along the market street, he used the profusion of traders and locals to find a tail. Deciding he was clear, Mac ducked down an alley connecting the market street with a more sedate avenue, and counted seven shops before slipping into Bali Vision World, an inconspicuous camera store.

At the counter, a small Javanese man with neat features looked over his half-glasses and frowned.

'You not meant to be here, Mr Richard,' he said, whipping off his glasses and walking around the counter to meet Mac in front of the camera bag section. 'I not do any of that no more.'

'Calm down, Set,' said Mac, modulating his voice. 'I had no idea this was your shop, mate – just needed some images transferred.'

'You are bad liar, Mr Richard,' said Setawan Posi, one of the best electronic-surveillance technicians Mac had ever worked with.

'It'll take five minutes,' said Mac, rustling a US hundred-dollar note in his hand. 'Swear to God.'

Set put Mac's Nikon on his work bench behind the counter area and, with some difficulty, opened the hatch that held the memory card.

'You should not drop camera, Mr Richard,' said Set as he pulled out the card. 'They do not like it.'

Inserting the card into another identical Nikon, Set asked for the device they were going to download into.

Handing over his laptop, Mac watched as Set searched along his junk-covered workshop walls for a cable that would marry the Nikon to the laptop. Coming back with a beige connector, Set declared it a success and powered up the computer.

'We put it on the hard drive, okay?' he said, opening a file. 'What you want to call it?'

'Call it "Mickey",' said Mac.

The downloads took twenty minutes and as Mac watched the images from Operation Totem flash up while the on-screen bar showed them being downloaded, Set made tea.

'How's business?' asked Mac, sipping jasmine tea.

'Better than the other one,' said Set, lifting his mangled left hand. The smallest three fingers had been badly broken at some point and Set could no longer make a fist with them.

'What happened?' asked Mac.

'I was working for the BAKIN in Jakarta, right?' said Set. 'I put camera and bug in this Korean bank, but then I am caught, right?'

'Caught by who?' asked Mac.

'By army intelligence,' sighed Set. 'They tell me the generals own this bank with the Koreans, and they . . . well, you know, okay?'

An image on the laptop screen caught Mac's eye as it downloaded. Focusing on it, his breath caught slightly. It was one of his shots of the airfield where the spraying booms were stored, where they'd seen Haryono getting out of his helicopter. The glare that had made it impossible to see the registrations of the Black Hawk helicopters parked in front of the admin building was clear through the Nikon lens.

Peering at the screen, Mac found himself smiling. The Black Hawks' registrations all started with '9V' – the sign for Singapore.

'Can we zoom in on that one?' asked Mac, as the image downloaded and was replaced by another.

Set grabbed the laptop, found the stored image and enlarged it.

'The tail section of that helo in the front,' said Mac, watching as the registration came to life.

'That's as far it goes,' said Set, as it zoomed to the point where the image quality degraded.

'It's okay,' said Mac, slumping a little in his chair and wondering what it meant. The full registration was 9V 1124F – Pik Berger's surviving gunship.

***

The coffee machine was working overtime in DIA's front office in Denpasar as Mac was ushered through the security checks. Grabbing a mug of black coffee, he made for the briefing room and was taken aback as he found Tony Davidson and Jim sitting at a table, looking morose.

'Thought you guys would be debriefing Blackbird right now?' said Mac, sliding his satchel onto the table and taking a seat as Simon joined them.

'We were,' said Jim, sheepish.

'In Australia or Singapore – but not *here*,' said Mac.

'Tony?' said Jim, deflecting the question.

'What's the drum, guys?' said Mac.

'The debrief was in Darwin,' said Davidson. 'And that was a nice job grabbing Blackbird.'

'Thanks,' said Mac, looking to Jim and back to Davidson.

'Yeah, but we got her from Darwin air base, drove her into the city, and there was a crowd of diplomats and lawyers waiting for us down on Cavanagh Street,' said Davidson.

'But –' said Mac.

'Indonesian diplomats and lawyers,' said Davidson with a growl. 'They pulled the consular crap and they drove away with Blackbird in the back seat.'

'But can they –?'

'Yes they can,' said Simon. 'She's an Indonesian national apprehended in Indonesian territory and illegally transported across an international border.'

'Blackbird went along with this?' asked Mac.

'She didn't fight it,' said Davidson, rubbing his face.

'Bottom line,' said Jim, lighting a cigarette, 'she's gone and we have a leak.'

Mac told the truth: he didn't know where Blackbird was being rendered and he had no motive to reveal her destination even if he had known. No one on HMAS *Sydney* had asked any untoward questions and the 4RAR Commandos didn't care less.

The next part was harder. 'Perhaps I should have told you this earlier,' said Mac, feeling stupid. 'She tried to escape at the exfil point.

She drugged me with Mogadon and the Commandos rounded her up, found she'd taken the sat phone. That's why we were twenty-four hours delayed on her delivery.'

'We looked at the phone,' said Simon. 'But the only calls were to us.'

Mac took a closer look at Simon – he had steady eyes and an unmoving face. A period of silence followed, which suggested to Mac he was probably already under surveillance by DIA. He'd kicked up a fuss with Atkins, he'd proven himself a loose cannon with his Bongo partnership, and someone was bound to have made a comment about Mac's personal interest in Jessica Yarrow, possibly Gillian Baddely.

The rest of the meeting was perfunctory: Mac took the participants through his journey, the airfield, the booms, the tanks on the helos and Haryono's appearance. The underground partition of Lombok AgriCorp, the inhalation chambers filled with people, one side dead, the other looking sick but still alive. He mentioned the Falintil engagement at Lombok, the fire at the facility and the fact he'd asked the guerrillas to disrupt the mule lines of US dollars that were being walked across the border from West Timor to the airfield.

Jim responded with an analysis of the samples taken from Lombok: they were an advanced type of pneumonia, or SARS.

'Nothing new,' said Jim with a shrug, slightly too casual.

'It's the SARS vaccine?' said Mac.

'It's the same disease they're cultivating,' corrected Jim.

'Have a look at the pics,' said Mac, taking the Nikon from his satchel and handing it to Jim. 'Like to know what you think.'

'Sure,' said Jim, taking the camera. 'So let's talk about Blackbird.'

'Let's,' said Mac, grabbing at coffee.

'Snatch went okay?' asked Davidson, leaning forward.

'Yep,' said Mac. 'The 63 grabbed her from the Kopassus compound in Maliana, we took her across the island and she was cooperative and moved with the rest of us.'

'She talk?' asked Davidson, focusing.

'Sort of,' said Mac.

'What happened?'

'I overstepped with the questions, I think,' said Mac, trying to remember the point at which he'd lost her. 'I caught her in a lie – she claimed that no one at Kopassus had asked her if she'd ever copied a file at army HQ.'

'Unlikely they'd leave that off their list,' said Jim.

'What I said,' said Mac. 'She got testy so I asked her why she was seen with Benni Sudarto. She said that wasn't true and I said her sister had told me.'

'Nice,' approved Jim.

'From there she admitted to being a double agent: recruited by the Indonesian Army to work at HQ in Dili, then recruited by us on the promise of sending her to an Aussie university, and then turned by Benni Sudarto to work for Kopassus.'

'What was Benni's deal?' asked Davidson.

'Do what we ask or your family suffers – in front of you.'

'Love that Kopassus approach,' said Davidson.

'She said she'd never heard of Operasi Boa and had never copied a file on Boa,' said Mac.

'You believe her?' asked Davidson.

Thinking back to the conversation again, Mac took his time. 'No, I don't, Tony. I think she knows what Boa is.'

'Any evidence?' asked Simon.

'No,' said Mac.

'So she did copy it?' asked Jim.

'I'm not sure,' said Mac. 'But if she did, it's not worth her while to let us know about it. They got to her, mate – they got to her bad.'

CHAPTER 51

Walking in the sunshine, Mac wrestled with a few aspects of the DIA operation that were not adding up for him. He wondered why Jim had pulled that too-casual deflection of the samples from the underground rooms of Lombok. It perhaps wasn't a complete fabrication, but Jim hadn't wanted to dwell on the samples Mac and Didge had risked their lives for. Jim was also surprisingly calm about what Mac and Didge had seen down there – not a drug factory but a human-testing lab. Even given DIA's famous intelligence-exclusion policy when dealing with allies, Mac had expected more. An explanation perhaps. There was a disconnect between the drug lord, Lee Wa Dae, and the vaccine program at Lombok: the two didn't marry. Yet, the airfield where Pik Berger's helicopters visited Ishy Haryono did seem to be joined to the Koreans by the bags of money arriving there. It looked like a drug network, not something that the Pentagon would pursue with such vigour.

Moving east on Hasanudin, Mac walked a conservative hundred metres behind Jim. Mac had bought a dark jacket, was wearing sunglasses, and he hadn't been made as they moved towards the park at the river.

Mac's biggest concern was with the underground facility at Lombok. He now replayed in his mind the conversation he'd had with

Joao. The Falintil commander had told him the village clearances on the south coast had been traced to both the death camp near Memo and the Lombok facility. They were the same program, run by the same people, according to Falintil, who Mac recognised as the most authoritative intelligence source in East Timor. Testing Falintil's intel and motives, Mac couldn't see how they were deceiving or provoking Aussie intelligence. Joao had had no idea who Mac really was on the visit to the death camp and he'd seemed prepared to shoot Mac at the Lombok site.

If the people at the death camp and the people in the inhalation chambers were part of the same program of vaccine-testing, thought Mac, why didn't any of the corpses at the death camp have evidence of an inoculation? Bongo had checked a cross-section of the bodies, which were naked. He'd said they were clear of any marking or punctures – unlikely for a bunch of people being forcibly injected with a SARS vaccine.

Jim turned right off Hasanudin Street and onto the paths that snaked alongside the river through the city's parklands. Following, Mac stayed behind an entwined couple.

So if the people cleared from the villages of the south coast weren't being tested with a vaccine for SARS, what were they dying from? The conclusions chased him around in circles about as fast as the questions, and as Jim stopped at a park bench and sat down, Mac edged behind a family group and keyed his phone. The narrow point of all the information he'd seen so far – on Lombok, Sudarto, Lee Wa Dae and Haryono – was Jim himself. Jim had apparently been at Fort Detrick at some point in his career, which didn't necessarily mean anything. Detrick was certainly the American headquarters of research into bio-weapons, but intelligence people were regularly trained in specific disciplines before being sent into the field. Mac had been trained in economic and financial sabotage, he'd done a rotation at the US Army's Aberdeen testing grounds and also with Israel's domestic intelligence service. It didn't mean much.

Mac just wanted to chat with Jim, see what was really going on.

Waiting for the phone to answer, Mac sidled behind a tree and kept an eye on the American.

'Yep,' came the gruff reply after the phone had rung several times.

'Scotty,' said Mac. 'It's Albion.'

'Macca!' said Mac's first mentor in the Aussie SIS, Rod Scott. 'How's it going?'

'Good, mate,' said Mac, glad to hear Scotty's voice again, even as he sucked on his ever-present cigarettes. 'How's Canberra? Cold enough for you?'

'Fuck, mate,' said Scotty. 'Jack Ormiston took me out sailing on the lake last weekend. Never been so cold, mate – had to get the barman to liberate that bottle of Glayva, didn't I, Macca? Warm a bloke up.'

'Doctor's orders,' said Mac, laughing.

'So what can I do you for?' said Scotty.

'I needed a quick reminder on someone I'm dealing with up here.'

'Yeah?' said Scotty.

'Yeah, bloke called Jim – DIA,' said Mac, hoping that Scotty wasn't going to stonewall him, pull any cellular bullshit.

'About your size, five years older? Sandy hair, Annapolis ring?' said Scotty, who had spent most of his career with the firm in the Middle East, ensuring Canadian and Russian wheat growers never gained an advantage over Australian exporters.

'That's the one – thought you might have run into him during UNSCOM or INVO,' said Mac, referring to the weapons inspection teams in Iraq.

'I remember him from the Rasheed Hotel in Baggers,' said Scotty. 'He was a funny bugger.'

'Yeah?' asked Mac.

'Yeah, very intense – he played cat-and-mouse for months with this Asian guy who was working for Saddam. Next thing I heard, Jim was punching out a State Department luncher after being refused a place on UNSCOM Four.'

'Why?'

'State Department sided with the White House and allowed Saddam to blackball DIA's appointments. And Jim knocked out someone's teeth.'

'That's it?'

'I was never dealing with him, Macca,' said Scotty. 'But Jim's up there? Jakarta? Denpasar?'

'That surprise you?' asked Mac, none the wiser.

'It's just that – well, you know Jim's background?'

'Fort Detrick?' said Mac.

'Yeah, but I think his taskings come from the Twentieth Support Command,' said Scotty.

'Oh shit,' uttered Mac.

'Yeah, mate – that's why the Iraqis wouldn't let him onto that inspection team,' said Scotty. 'He doesn't inspect bio-weapons – he shuts them down.'

The Balinese man in the suit but no tie walked past Jim, and Mac slipped from behind his tree to approach the American. As Mac set out, the Balinese man stopped at the railing beside the river and looked at a folded newspaper. Then Jim stood and walked to him.

Leaping behind a set of shrubs that got him out of sight, Mac peeked around and saw Jim stand next to the Balinese man, and then Jim was walking towards Mac, the newspaper now under his arm.

His breathing getting faster, Mac tried to plot the best course. But then Jim came into sight and slowed as he saw Mac.

'Nice afternoon for a walk,' said Mac, as they both stopped.

'Beautiful,' said Jim, recovering from the surprise and continuing on his way.

'Mind if I join you?' asked Mac, and fell in with Jim as he strolled by.

'It's not what you think, McQueen,' said Jim as they walked through the park.

'What do I think?' said Mac.

'This isn't the time for games, pal,' said Jim, lips whitening.

'Good,' said Mac. 'So let's talk.'

'What do you want?' said Jim, casing the park and then moving to a bench facing the river. 'And can we make it quick?'

Sitting beside Jim, Mac tried to be clear. 'I guess when Aussies deal with the Americans, we can get a bit dazzled by it all.'

'Dazzled?' said Jim, smirking.

'Yeah, the confidence and the power,' said Mac. 'I'm seconded to Defense Intelligence Agency and because I trust the man who seconded me, I don't question too much the people I'm being briefed by.'

'I see,' said Jim.

'So I think I'm chasing a woman called Blackbird because she has the key to a military operation called Boa,' said Mac. 'But there's also an unrelated facility I have to infiltrate while I'm over there and the only intel I'm given by the Americans is that it's part of a vaccine program and it's connected to a drug lord.'

'Okay,' said Jim, lighting a cigarette.

'So there I am, down in this underground hell, being shot at in the darkness, and I can't really see what's in front of my eyes because I can only see it in the context of what I've been supplied. I'm looking for a vaccine program and a drug lab — and I have eyes staring back at me. Human eyes!'

'I'm sorry —'

'And then, after I'm back, and I'm more confused than when I started, I realise that the place I should have begun is you, Jim, and who exactly you are.'

'I'm sure you're going to tell me.'

'You're not a DIA generalist, sent to observe the East Timor situation for the US government,' said Mac. 'You work for the Twentieth Support Command of the US Army.'

'Look, McQueen —'

'You're a bio-weapons expert who got ejected from UNSCOM Four and you believe Lombok AgriCorp is a bio-weapons facility, don't you?'

Silence lingered for a moment as Jim focused on his cigarette.

'Things are complicated right now, McQueen,' said Jim finally. 'I'm sorry if you feel misled in any way.'

'You sound like a politician, Jim,' said Mac.

'I'm telling the truth, McQueen. Just about any vaccine program can look like a bio-weapons facility,' he said. 'From experience I've learned that you have to build a totally airtight case for it being bio-weapons, or the politicians won't act and the bad guys scuttle away under their rocks. So yes, it's complicated.'

'So uncomplicate it,' said Mac.

'What do you want from me?' asked the American. 'You going to beat me to death with your bare hands? That's your reputation, right?'

'I'm not beating anyone, Jim,' said Mac. 'I'm trying to do my job, and right now my job is to resolve the intel on the Lombok facility and try to get something cogent to my government.'

'Okay, buddy,' said the American, suddenly looking tired. 'Feel like a drink?'

'Sure,' said Mac.

'Meet you at six – Bar Barong on Gajah Mada Street. Know it?'

'See you then,' said Mac.

'And that wasn't what you thought,' said Jim, handing over the newspaper he'd taken from the Balinese man.

Taking the paper, Mac unfolded it and took out a filing card. The words were written in black ballpoint: *Boa rumor – planned Sept. 4 or 5.*

Mac handed back the newspaper and watched Jim leave. If he timed it right, he'd be able to meet with Davidson before having a drink with Jim.

'What are these?' asked Mac as he and Davidson grabbed an early meal in a Balinese restaurant on the edge of Puputan Square. On the table in front of him were three black-and-white eight-by-fives showing two headless corpses, without hands or feet.

'Just in this arvo,' said Davidson, eating a crab leg. 'Fished out of the bay at Dili early this morning.'

'Who?' asked Mac, thinking he recognised one of the bodies.

'One on the right is Adam Moerpati,' said Davidson, wiping his fingers. 'Executed.'

'Any ideas?' asked Mac.

'Could be the Koreans,' said Davidson. 'Two million of their dollars go missing, so they target a couple of people they've vaguely suspected of spying, and whack 'em to prove a point. It's a pity – Moerpati was a brave guy.'

'That's our connection to the President's office ruined,' said Mac, peering at the other man in the photo. 'Who's the other one? He looks familiar.'

'Unidentified, according to my Polri guy.'

Shuffling to the last photo, Mac's heart thumped. The final

shot was a close-up of the unidentified man's back, and a tattooed Conquistador cross with the legend *INRI* inscribed on the cross bar.

'Fuck!' he cried.

'Everything okay?' asked Davidson.

'Bongo,' said Mac, shaking his head. 'I think this is Bongo Morales.'

Davidson was quiet, knowing not to talk. It was one of the comforting aspects of Australian males that they were more relaxed with silences than any other type of human being. If there was nothing to say, don't say it.

Gulping it down, and feeling more upset with the Bongo revelation than he really wanted to feel, Mac manned up. 'So, what do I do now, Tony? Back to Canberra? Manila?'

'Nah, get some sleep, and I'll keep you posted,' said Davidson.

'Mission totally possible,' said Mac.

Davidson suddenly got serious and pointed his spoon at Mac. 'Get drunk, find a girlfriend – I don't care, right? But whatever you do, stay away from Atkins.'

'Okay, but I'm not the leak,' said Mac, still annoyed that his own firm might think he compromised the Blackbird debrief.

'Of course you're not,' said Davidson. 'But you go looking for a fight with Atkins and they'll get you on a plane to Canberra or Tokyo before the last word's out of your mouth.'

'Okay, okay,' sighed Mac.

'Stay in your box for once, mate, and leave the office shenanigans to me.'

Staring at Davidson, Mac felt some pieces come together. 'Box? Did you say *box*?'

Going back to his nasi goreng, Davidson looked puzzled. 'That's what I said, mate.'

'Okay,' said Mac, his mind buzzing.

'What's up?' asked Davidson, wiping his mouth with a napkin and looking around the room.

'There was no reason for Blackbird to know about the drop boxes at Santa Cruz cemetery, right?' asked Mac, grabbing at his beer as he looked out onto the streets of Denpasar, where the street vendors were starting to pack up.

'None that I can think of.'

'Absolutely not,' said Mac. 'So we can check with Atkins and Tobin about this, but those drop boxes at the cemetery were for the cut-out we used – that lawyer in Dili. They weren't used by Blackbird, right?'

'Of course not,' said Davidson. 'Otherwise, what's the point of a cut-out?'

'Precisely,' said Mac, leaning in. 'So I'm out in the bush with Blackbird and she's losing it at me about being caught between Aussie and Indon intelligence, and she's telling me that she's done everything asked of her, she's taken the files and done the drop box.'

'Why would she do a drop?' asked Davidson, confused. 'She's meeting direct with the Canadian.'

'What I thought,' smiled Mac.

'So she was using a drop box in Dili . . .' said Davidson.

'Maybe for emergencies, maybe for files that were too hot to carry around Dili . . .'

'Files about post-ballot contingencies . . .'

'Files like Operasi Boa . . .'

'Especially if you're under surveillance by the Indonesians, by Kopassus,' said Davidson.

'By a person who's threatened to kill your family,' said Mac.

'Maybe,' said Davidson, slugging at his beer. 'And maybe not.'

'It's worth a look, right, boss?' said Mac. 'I mean, Blackbird and this damn Boa file were important enough that we went into Bobonaro, invaded a Kopassus compound and then exfiltrated the girl to Darwin, but what if the file is sitting somewhere in Dili? There could a hundred reasons why she would try to park a dangerous document until the heat is off.'

Davidson looked out into the crowded street. 'I know what you're thinking, mate, but it's too risky. I'm not sure I want you back in Dili – I'm not sure I can go back in there either.'

'Why don't we confirm the drop box first?' asked Mac, not wanting to be left out. 'Atkins told me about two – there could be more.'

'I know where it is,' sighed Davidson, reading the label on the beer bottle. 'But that's not the point.'

'No, boss,' smiled Mac. 'The point is whether you'd rather send Atkins or Garvey.'

'Okay, Macca,' said Davidson, staring him in the eye. 'For the purposes of discussion, you're in, but –'

'I'll be okay,' winked Mac, wondering where lost sleep went to.

'Don't be cocky,' said Davidson.

'You know me,' laughed Mac. 'By the way – this drop box, which one is it if it's not at the cemetery?'

'It's the Hotel Resende,' whispered Davidson, casing the room.

'The Resende?!' squawked Mac. 'I thought that was a joke!'

'No, mate, it's real,' said Davidson. 'But just be careful, okay? This girl is with the Indonesians and she's confused. I don't want a hunch turning into a trap.'

CHAPTER 52

Cutting through the Pasar Badung markets in downtown, Mac made his way to the meeting with Jim.

He thought about his hunch that Blackbird had dumped her copy of Boa in the ASIS drop box in the Resende. It was a location known to Mac, but only as a joke. The Resende was owned by a syndicate of generals and during the occupation years had been a home-away-from-home for the Indonesian Army officers and their families. One of the distinctive features of the Resende – aside from the listening devices – was the karaoke machines in the ballroom of the hotel. One of the generals in the owners' syndicate reputedly loved singing 'Da Doo Ron Ron' and had equipped the Resende with the best karaoke technology.

Just to show that Australians had a sense of humour, the original ASIS operative in Dili – back in the late 1970s – had created a drop box in the back of the largest karaoke machine, up on the small stage that the machines occupied. If this was the box that Blackbird had been talking about, then Mac was hoping the Operasi Boa documents were in there.

The Bar Barwong was half full, rocking with locals and back-packers. Mac found Jim at one end of the bar and they ordered beers after greeting each other and checking the room for eyes. A TV screen on the wall was running a CNN bulletin featuring a coiffured woman standing in front of what looked like the Texas statehouse. Across the bottom of the screen ran the banner *George W. Bush avoids questions on whether he ever used illegal drugs*, and above it ran a small box saying, *Viewer poll: is the media too hard on George W. Bush's past personal life?*

They couldn't hear what she was saying because 'Living La Vida Loca' was blasting out over the speaker system.

'Never trust a man who can't hold his drink,' said Jim, pointing his bottle of Tiger at the footage of George W. Bush on the screen.

'Never trust a man who stands behind you at the urinal,' said Mac, and they clinked bottles.

'So,' said Jim. 'You want to know about Lombok AgriCorp?'

'It would be nice,' said Mac. 'Since on the two occasions I've been up there someone's tried to kill me.'

'Might be simpler to start with Lee Wa Dae.'

'The Korean drug guy,' said Mac, wanting Jim to get on with it.

'Not entirely,' said Jim.

'That's what the file −'

'That file came from us, McQueen,' said Jim, looking exhausted. 'We wanted him running, to be confident, so we washed his file.'

'You mean, you fabricated intelligence that was shared with your allies?'

'Okay,' nodded Jim. 'That's what we did − after the snafu in Iraq, we became a little isolated, a bit paranoid perhaps. We didn't want another situation where we were drawn into a joint operation like UNSCOM, only to have the bad guys reading our secret briefings word for word.'

'That bad?'

'Worse,' said Jim, sipping his beer. 'When I was tapped to join UNSCOM Four as the head of operations, Saddam's goons vetoed me, went around UNSCOM to the UN Secretary-General's office, which then won the support of my President. They knew everything about me and a whole lot of stuff I'd forgotten − I was deep-sixed.'

'You punched out a guy from the State Department?'

'It was a push that went too far,' said Jim. 'The jungle telegraph did the rest.'

'So, Lee Wa Dae,' said Mac.

'He *is* a drug lord of sorts, but he's also a master procurer of matériel and feedstock for chemical, biological and nuclear programs,' said Jim. 'Lee Wa Dae was always the bag man for the North Korean generals; he arranged joint-venture bio-weapons projects, which were essentially Korean R&D conducted in another country.'

'How did he get in touch with Haryono?' asked Mac.

'Haryono had always run these highly profitable but bogus medical research projects, under the auspices of the Indonesian Army. As Soeharto's power waned, and oversight was minimal, Lee Wa Dae approached him with a pay-to-play deal and Lombok AgriCorp was born. Haryono was a scammer, rather than a bio-weapons nutcase.'

'No one thought to tell the Aussies?'

'What was there to say?' asked Jim. 'There's a SARS vaccine program in the East Timor hills and it's registered with WHO. You know how warm and fuzzy that makes journalists and UN-types feel?'

'So you used an innocent Aussie to go in there?' said Mac.

'Sure beats tipping the Indonesians off by having a bunch of Yanks up there.'

'Okay,' said Mac, annoyed about being played. 'So this bio-weapon actually works?'

'Possibly,' said Jim, stubbing out his cigarette. 'Based on the samples, we think they've finalised a super-pneumonia – what the scientists are calling SARS. Of course, having the disease agent is only part of the project,' he continued. 'Then you have to weaponise it so it endures heat and concussion. Other versions have to be light enough to float on the breeze when you spray them.'

Images from CNN flashed on the screen in front of them. The sound was down but the images showed the ballot boxes in East Timor while the island was in flames. Militiamen ran along streets with assault rifles, T-shirts wrapped around their faces – many of them Kopassus operatives, no doubt, thought Mac as his anger rose. *Kijangs* filled with young thugs sped through the smoke, mothers ran with their kids, uniformed soldiers and police directing the mayhem like a movie. An Anglo man in a Banana Republic safari shirt said his piece to camera, probably before dashing to the airport – the same airport Mac was flying into the following morning.

'So the Indonesians have weaponised SARS?' asked Mac. 'That's what we were looking at underground in Lombok? Those corpses were the victims of SARS? And up at the death camp too?'

'We think so, yes,' said Jim. 'It's not confirmed.'

'The generals are hosting this for a nice fee?' asked Mac.

'Yeah,' smiled Jim. 'Heroin money from North Korea, laundered in Poi Pet, delivered in cash to the generals in East Timor.'

'The money we found on those boys in the bush?'

'Sure. About a million US couriered into Bobonaro every month – now we know the destination was Neptune. Wa Dae used to carry it himself from Dili, but he got spooked by your Canadian friend's capture, and changed to a run coming from Kupang instead. That's what you intercepted, I guess.'

'A super-pneumonia. What does it do?' asked Mac, still not clear.

'People with no immunity have twelve to eighteen hours,' said the American. 'They drown in their own phlegm.'

CHAPTER 53

The Boeing 737 descended through the early morning cloud and lined up for Comoro airport in west Dili, revealing a panorama of smoke which, if it was Queensland, would have signalled bushfire season. Looking in the reflection of his cabin window, Mac clocked his dark hair, brown contact lenses and black moustache and felt his guts drop as the plane steepened its trajectory.

He was feeling cornered, having been woken at 5 am by Tony Davidson and informed that DIA would be playing a backup role in clearing the drop box at the Resende. Mac had argued, not wanting the Yanks charging around in what was the maelstrom of Dili. But politics had won the day: Australia had intelligence-sharing arrangements with the US, UK and Canada, and the price to pay for the high-quality product was to allow the senior partner to take any chair he wanted.

He just hoped the Americans stood off and let Mac do his job. His stomach churned with a dark fear – someone, either the Koreans or Kopassus, had got to Bongo and killed him. If someone could kill Bongo Morales, then they'd make easy work of an Aussie spy if they really wanted to.

After emerging from the panicked crowds in the concourse at Comoro, Mac grabbed a minicab from the apron. Settling in the back with a crowd of journalists and cameramen, he noticed Jim waiting in a queue surrounded by Brimob officers as the van surged away.

Driving through the official military roadblocks and the unofficial ones put there by militias and pro-independence locals, a French reporter told an Englishman in a fishing vest that the Turismo was the only Euro-friendly place in town. An American camera guy with a blue do-rag pulled a can of mace from his breast pocket and shoved it in the Frenchie's face.

'Don't mess with Texas,' he laughed, getting some sniggers from the Aussies and English.

'One can of mace against one of the largest armies in the world,' snarled the Frog. 'You Yankees are so smart.'

Mac looked away, lost in thought. Certain types of journalists thought themselves a breed apart if they went someplace dangerous while hiding behind the protective shroud their profession gave them. At least half of these people would be back at the airport within two days, begging for a standby seat, he reckoned.

The Resende was still a utilitarian structure that looked more like a Stalin-era office block in Warsaw than a hotel in a tropical paradise. Checking in as Doug Crawford, Mac accepted the warnings of the manager that this was no place for outsiders right now, and went to his room. Hitting the Nokia as soon as he put his bags down, Mac made loud declamations to his Southern Cross Trading associates in Sydney about the climate for organic cosmetics and synergies with the government in East Timor. Everything in the Resende was bugged and the staff were often informers, but Mac sometimes found it easier to sleep with enemies than to evade them.

After waiting ten minutes, Mac wandered down the stairs to the lobby, stopping to look at a rack of tourist brochures while he checked for suspicious types. A few minutes later a Brimob van screamed past in the street, broadcasting orders over a loudhailer. When a woman ducked into the hotel with two children, the manager at the desk tried to shoo her out.

'Busy out there, eh?' said Mac with a smile as he moved alongside the woman and the manager.

'Dangerous, mister,' said the woman as the manager walked away, tut-tutting.

Having second thoughts about being in Dili, Mac saw Jim walking towards him with an overnight bag.

'Warren?' asked Mac, loud enough to make it play for the manager. 'Warren Johnson? Holiday Inn, Waikiki – what was it? A cosmetics expo or something?'

Straight into character, Jim responded warmly. 'Doug Crawford – you're the organic cosmetics guy.'

'That's the one.'

'And everyone's like, *Organic?! I don't want to eat it!*'

'That's the problem with a nation of people that thinks cheese comes out of a spray can,' said Mac, smiling and shaking hands.

Thirty-five minutes later, Mac sat at a sidewalk cafe on the Esplanada, waiting for Jim. He'd had a chance to do a recce of the Resende's ballroom, which had been filled with military types drinking coffee.

His stomach churning, Mac ran through the mission: he needed to be in and out quickly. And he needed to do it undercover, not with an American QRF coming to the rescue with eleven choppers.

Jim was supposed to be touching base with his Dili asset to get a driver and secure a couple of firearms, then meet Mac at the cafe. And he was late, a bad omen. As Mac checked his G-Shock, his breath caught as he glimpsed a tall bloke loping along the Esplanada. It was the cut-out.

Sliding down in his chair, wishing the big white Bintang parasol was lower, Mac made himself breathe through the nose as the man glanced to his left, but not far enough to clock Mac. Walking north and buttoning a navy blue linen sports coat, he hurried past, stress etched on his face.

Breathing returning to normal, Mac watched the local lawyer disappear towards downtown, swerving through pedestrians and looking from side to side amid the chaos on the streets. Blackbird and the Canadian were no longer around, so Mac wondered what the man was in such a panic for. His family, probably.

'Hey, Doug,' said Jim as he sat, *Jakarta Post* folded under his arm. 'Everything okay? Looks like you've seen a ghost.'

'I'm fine, what have we got?' said Mac, summoning a waiter and ordering two coffees.

'I think we're compromised,' said Jim. 'The tip-off that got Blackbird sprung may not be a one-off.'

'Don't look at me like that,' said Mac, too tired for head games. 'I infiltrated a fucking bio-weapons factory for this gig – I've earned immunity from that look.'

Sighing, Jim looked out to the choppy sea across the street. 'Sorry, buddy, force of habit.'

'So what's up?' asked Mac.

Lighting a smoke, Jim waved his hand. 'Could be nothing – the SIGINT guys picked up some chatter about Boa being retrieved today, seemed too coincidental.'

'Shit!' said Mac, clenching his fist and trying to find the cut-out again in the crowds.

'There was two calls with "Boa" in them, to this number,' he said, opening the *Jakarta Post* and showing Mac a printed page with *Da Silva, Carvalho Júdice e Associados – (Augusto Da Silva e Christian Carvalho)* printed on it, with an address.

'It's a law firm in Dili,' said Jim.

'Law firm,' muttered Mac, his head snapping up as he looked for the cut-out.

Trying to maintain a disciplined walk, Mac rounded the corner and peeled away from Jim to the other side of the street as he headed towards the Resende. Jim kept a safe distance, providing support.

Getting to the Resende, Mac paused at the glass door to regain his composure, before pushing into the cool of the lobby. His head swam with the possibilities, all of them negative: he didn't like the way Jim sprang the news of the compromised operation and he didn't like the urgency with which Da Silva had been moving towards the Resende. Mac was at his best when he was the one creating the timetable and the panic.

'Ah, Mr Crawford,' said the manager cheerily, in total contrast to how he'd treated the local woman and her kids. 'How are we today?'

'Good thanks,' smiled Mac as he passed, before stopping as if in afterthought. 'Actually, perhaps you could help me.'

'Certainly, Mr Crawford,' he smiled.

'My manager asked me to have a look at the function facilities at the Resende for our conferences or expos. It's a nice distance from Australia, China, Japan and India – if you see what I mean?'

'Certainly, Mr Crawford,' said the manager, coming around the counter and clicking his fingers for the bellboy. 'Ernesto, please show Mr Crawford the ballroom and conference facilities.'

Following Ernesto's dandruff-dusted black coat through to the rear of the Resende, Mac saw a large restaurant, a bar and a family-TV nook filled with sofas and coffee tables.

As they approached two large doors that met at the middle, Ernesto pulled out his master key, only to realise that the doors were now swinging open. After pushing through, Ernesto went to hit the lights, but they were already on.

'This is the Resende famous ballroom,' said Ernesto, sweeping his arm around a large space with parquetry floors, high chandeliered ceilings and a stage along the far wall, dominated by two enormous karaoke machines. Walking around the space, Mac marvelled at the aesthetic, somewhere between 1960s Las Vegas and 1980s Seoul.

'Thanks, mate,' said Mac with a wink, palming ten US dollars into Ernesto's hand. 'I just need to *feel* my way around this space for a few minutes, okay?'

Smiling, Ernesto headed to the doors, which Mac shut gently behind him before latching them.

There were two tall karaoke stacks on the stage, leading to two consoles, two microphones and two screens in the middle. Mac had spent enough evenings on the booze in Asia to know that many a duet had been sung on that stage, by people who had no right to do what they were doing to 'Islands in the Stream' or 'You Don't Bring Me Flowers'.

Checking the karaoke machine on the left, Mac pulled down the back flap which opened into a cable-storage compartment the size of two shoe boxes. It was empty.

Moving to the other side of the stage, Mac saw it before he got there: the flap was open, the compartment empty.

'Fuck!' said Mac, breathing fast.

Mac tried to think as he reached the doors. Had the cut-out been tipped off to Mac picking up a copy of Operasi Boa? He'd been in a panic when Mac saw him. Who – outside of Mac, Jim and Davidson – knew that they were looking for a copy of Operasi Boa at the Resende? It gnawed at Mac as he made for the lobby. Gesturing through the glass doors for Jim to join him at the front desk, Mac turned back to the manager.

'Nice facilities – might get back to you on that. But tell me, I was meant to meet Augusto here ten minutes ago,' said Mac. 'And Christian.'

'Augusto?' shrugged the manager. 'I not know any Augusto, mister.'

Mac thanked him and made for the doors.

'Have we got it?' hissed Jim as they spilled onto the street, Mac scanning the area for any sign of the cut-out.

'Everything okay, mister?' asked Ernesto, who was walking from a minivan with two suitcases.

'Mate, I was supposed to meet Augusto and Christian here ten minutes ago – they're our lawyers and it's fairly important. I was wondering if they turned up, maybe I missed them?' said Mac, looking at his watch.

'Sure,' said Ernesto. 'I saw Mr Da Silva at back of hotel, after I show you ballroom.'

'Shit,' said Mac, looking over the crowds. 'Did he say anything?'

'No, mister,' said Ernesto, eyes wide. 'He running.'

'I bet he was,' growled Mac, wishing he had a weapon.

CHAPTER 54

The offices of Da Silva, Carvalho Júdice e Associados were exactly where Ernesto had sent Mac and Jim – over the road from the government engineer's offices, upstairs in a swank professional suite, a block back from the ocean.

In an alley between buildings, they cased Da Silva's offices while shots rang out from several blocks away and diesel engines screamed.

'Kopassus intel front?' asked Jim, looking up and down the street.

'He told me he did their paperwork, gave the military's extra-judicial trials some legitimacy,' shrugged Mac, trying to get a look past the sun blinds into the law offices. 'The best lies are actually the truth, eh Jim?'

Jim ducked that one. US intelligence used a network of law firms to make things work smoothly. One of the world's largest law firms got rich from a list of clients that were CIA fronts.

'I don't think we can wait,' said Jim, opening the large courier box he'd received on arrival at the Resende, and passing Mac one of two Colt Defender handguns.

'I agree,' said Mac. 'Any ideas for a dignified entry?'

'None,' said Jim, checking the mag and the spout.

'Okay,' said Mac, feeling the nerves starting. 'I'll take Da Silva direct – you want to deal with the ancillary targets?'

'Sure,' said Jim, pulling back into the shadows as a Brimob armoured vehicle flew past. 'Let's go.'

Pushing out into the street, they jogged in their chinos and polo shirts, guns tucked into waistbands, and moved up onto the pavement, where they pushed through swinging glass doors.

Ignoring the elevators, Mac and Jim raced up the stairs two at a time, Mac coming to a standstill behind Jim as the American opened the fire door and peeked down the hall.

'One receptionist, glass walls . . . wait, wait,' he whispered. 'Shit! The entry has an electronic lock on it. We have to get the receptionist to open it from inside.'

A door slammed and the sound of feet slapping on concrete echoed up to them. Moving away from the door, Mac gave Jim a wink as a signal to get in character.

'So I'm not comfortable with that kind of dilution, champion. I need a sign-off on the tax position before we carve up the equity,' said Mac, in as self important a tone as he could muster, as a courier appeared behind them, a large package in hand.

Pretending to try to get out of the bloke's way, Mac looked down and saw the package was addressed to Carvalho and Da Silva.

'We can give you that buddy,' said Jim. 'But if my guys can't get over twelve per cent equity at your NPV, they don't even want to talk about the tax position. I told you – our deal is accretive, apples for apples.'

'Twelve per cent?!' snapped Mac as they followed the courier into the hallway. 'You gotta stop drinking before lunch, speedy.'

The courier walked down the corridor without looking at Mac and Jim, obviously accustomed to lawyers snarling at each other in stairwells.

'Okay, buddy,' said Jim, keeping it going as they got closer to the courier and neared the entry door to the law firm. 'But know this before we go in there – they got a full dance card, man.'

'Doesn't mean I don't want to be kissed before I lift my skirts,' said Mac.

'Do us all a favour, buddy,' said Jim, as the entry door opened to the courier and they walked in behind him. 'Don't be the plain girl playing hard-to-get, okay?'

Leaving Jim with the receptionist and courier, Mac walked straight down mahogany row. The first door was open and Mac smiled at a lawyer at his desk as he walked past. The second open door revealed an empty office. Mac opened the third door and leaned in. A man lay asleep on the floor – probably a first-time father, thought Mac, shutting the door silently.

Mac had about thirty seconds before the receptionist got away from Jim and came looking for him. There were two doors at the end of the hallway, both of which would open onto larger corner spaces overlooking the bay – the partners' offices.

Slipping the Colt from his waistband, Mac took a deep breath as he reached for the door handle on the left. It was then he smelled it, faintly at first. But after a deeper whiff, it was unmistakable. Someone was burning paper.

Pushing into the left-hand office, Mac kept his hand behind his back and smiled as he saw Carvalho behind his desk.

'Sorry – looking for Augusto,' said Mac.

Mac breathed out long and deep, brought the Colt up to his navel, and pushed into the next room.

The room was filling with smoke. Behind the desk, by the open window, Augusto Da Silva – the cut-out – straightened up from the wastepaper bin, a surprised look on his face.

Instinctively going for the burning document, Mac didn't notice the man to his right until he shouted out. Mac turned to him as the guy reached for his gun. It was Amir Sudarto, the towering Kopassus thug who'd interrogated Mac that night in the Ginasio.

In his brief moment of hesitation before Mac could swing his gun, Amir lashed out with a roundhouse kick to Mac's right hand, connecting with the inside wrist bone and sending the little Colt flying.

Seeing Mac was momentarily off-balance and distracted by the pain in his wrist, Amir used the chance to aim a stamp kick to the solar plexus which sent Mac flying backwards into the plasterboard.

As he hit the wall, Mac saw Da Silva bending over the bin as Amir pulled his gun. Using his momentum off the wall to bounce back at Amir, Mac grabbed his right wrist as the gun came around. Headbutting Amir in the face, Mac dropped to the ground with his assailant, slamming his forearm across Amir's nose as they landed, spraying blood across the room.

Amir's gun fired as they struggled for control of it, Mac now kneeling over the fallen man's chest, throwing a knife-hand at his throat and then waiting for a split second before dropping the mother of all headbutts into his face. At the last moment Amir moved his face and Mac's forehead glanced off the side of his attacker's skull and hit the carpet, stunning him slightly.

Amir threw Mac to the ground by the hair. As he felt fingers going into his eyes, Mac let go of the wrist-lock he'd found. His wrist free, Amir pulled the gun around to point at Mac. Seeing a chance for a clean shot at Amir's head, Mac lashed out with a straight left punch, connecting flush with Amir's left temple and dropping him like a sandbag.

Grabbing at Amir's SIG Sauer, Mac leapt to his feet as Augusto Da Silva's gun levelled at him. Tossing the SIG Sauer to Da Silva – as if giving it to him – Mac used the lawyer's momentary confusion and inexperience with a gun to launch himself across the desk at the man.

Bringing his left forearm down hard on Da Silva's wrist as he landed on the other side of the desk, Mac knocked the handgun from his grip.

Spinning expertly, as if matadoring a bull, Da Silva let the bulk of Mac's momentum go past him, taking only a minor hit from Mac's left shoulder. Picking himself off the floor, Mac took a kick in the jaw which staggered him back towards the still-smoking rubbish bin. Wanting to reach in there and pull out whatever was burning, Mac could only steal a quick peek before Da Silva lashed out with a roundhouse kick to Mac's mouth followed by a perfectly balanced one-two-three punching combination, which Mac managed to block and back away from.

Great, thought Mac as he heaved for breath: a lawyer who knows kung-fu!

'It's over, Augusto,' barked Mac through his mashed mouth. 'Just let me have the file.'

'Think you're the big man, eh?' snarled Da Silva, advancing with equal parts poise and desperation. 'Locking a man in a car trunk? Well where's that big ape to save you now, McQueen?'

Blocking Da Silva's thigh kick with a raised knee, Mac jerked to his right as a straight left sailed half a centimetre past his nose, giving him an opening to Da Silva's exposed left temple. Mac lashed at the open target with a straight right but Da Silva was quicker, simply shrugging enough to glance the punch off the point of his shoulder. Mac still had momentum on his side, and followed the failed straight right with an elbow to the teeth, which turned into a forearm to the throat. Grunting and staggering back, Da Silva didn't see Mac's stamp kick to the groin, a shot that connected with the pubic bone, bringing Da Silva down to Mac's height and allowing Mac a big uppercut off his left hand. Connecting perfectly on the point of Da Silva's chin, the tall lawyer briefly lost his balance but collected himself as Mac tried to force the advantage and get a choke-hold on the bloke.

Throwing a fast round-fend with his left hand, Da Silva whacked Mac's right hand out of the way and flat-handed him on the bridge of the nose, forcing Mac's face upwards against the set of his neck and his body. Falling to the side, Mac struggled for balance, his nose busted and eyes filling with tears as he tried to keep contact with Da Silva. The bloke liked to swing those long arms and legs, and if Mac could stay close he might just out-mongrel him.

Grabbing a handful of Da Silva's silky hair, Mac endured three fast punches in the face in order to get a second hand onto the hair and use the double-fist hold to tug the head around. Swinging punches wildly, Da Silva connected with Mac's cheekbones and chin. Suddenly, Mac jerked upwards with the hair, and then pulled downwards with a snap of both hands, driving Da Silva's face into the corner of the glass-covered desk, spraying blood across the files and blotter.

Hands writhing up, Da Silva clawed for eyeballs but Mac twisted his face away from the long hands and pulled back on his hair-hold. Then, throwing his hip into the taller man, he used the leverage of the hair to initiate a hip-throw, tipping the taller man over and slamming his head into the floor with a sickening crunch. Mac knew he'd hurt him enough to finish this if he wanted Da Silva dead.

'One of these would have been cleaner,' came Jim's voice from behind as Mac stood over Da Silva, heaving for breath and pinching his nose to stop the bleeding.

Jim had his gun on Amir Sudarto, whose fingers had stopped a centimetre short of retrieving Mac's Colt. Pushing Amir away, Jim threw Mac's gun back to him and rushed to the smouldering rubbish bin. Kneeling at the wastepaper bin, the American reached in and came out with ashes.

'Shit!' he growled.

'Watch the other guy, mate,' said Mac, pointing to Amir. 'I think Augusto wants to speak.'

'Fuck you,' mumbled Da Silva. There was a huge gash across his forehead from his collision with the desk and his voice was slurred.

Kicking him hard on the point of the chin, Mac watched a tooth fly as the lawyer's face snapped back, laying him flat on his back.

'No, Augie – fuck you.'

Moving to the desk, but keeping his eyes on Da Silva, Mac checked the drawers of the desk. There were calculators, cell phones, dictaphones and statements from the Bank of Singapore, a Darwin branch of the ANZ Bank and a weird-looking bank statement from the Phnom Penh branch of Koryo Bank – the Koryo had been established by North Korea's general staff, for what was officially called 'joint ventures with foreign countries'.

'Thing I love about you lawyers,' snarled Mac, waving the statement at Da Silva as he tried to sit up, 'you want to get paid by everyone – coming and going.'

'Fuck you, Skippy,' mumbled the lawyer through his hand.

'Am I going to find Operasi Boa in this desk?' asked Mac.

Da Silva laughed, and Mac stood over him, looking him in the eye.

'I won the fight, Augusto – without the big ape. So now I'm asking and you're telling, okay?'

'Gotta go, buddy,' said Jim.

'Okay,' said Mac, still panting. 'Let's take them with us.'

'I don't like it,' said Jim.

'These guys are all we've got – besides, I think I've worked out what was happening,' said Mac.

Amir suddenly rushed at Mac, Jim swinging his gun to take a shot. Gunfire resounded in the office and then a window was breaking. Shards of glass exploded as Jim and Mac swung their guns and fired, but Amir was horizontal through the space where the window had recently been.

Moving to the jagged hole, Mac looked down and saw Amir Sudarto climbing out of a hedgerow. Jim fired and shots hit the concrete car park as Amir sprinted out of view.

'Shit,' said Jim. 'Was that Amir Sudarto?'

'That's him,' said Mac, heaving for breath.

'Then we've got about five seconds before Kopassus arrives,' said Jim.

Mac grabbed a handful of tissues from the box on the desk and stemmed his nose. 'We can't leave him,' he said, nodding at Da Silva.

'Okay, we take him. But if he causes trouble, I'm gonna whack him, okay?' asked Jim, loud enough for Da Silva to hear. 'No one – especially not some failed lawyer – is going to hold me for one second longer than I have to be in this hellhole.'

'That's the choice, Augusto,' said Mac, 'and you have one second to decide.'

'I liked you better as a blond,' said Da Silva, spitting a chunk of flesh from his mouth as he stood. 'But you must do me favour.'

'What?' asked Mac, checking the Colt.

'Hold the gun to my head when we leave – these *malai* have no sense of humour.'

CHAPTER 55

Jim's driver pulled the Mitsubishi into the shade of some trees after a twenty-minute drive east of Dili along the coast road. Any further east and they'd start running into army and militia road-blocks.

The support staff at the law office, and Señor Carvalho, were locked in a storage room and now Mac pulled Da Silva out of the back of the car by his hair.

Moving down to the beach, they found a secluded place behind a stand of trees, and sat Da Silva down on the grass while Jim's driver stood guard by the road.

'You wrote Operasi Boa, didn't you?' said Mac, his nosebleed having finally set.

'No comment,' said Da Silva, not so brave now.

'That's a nice lawyerism, isn't it?' said Mac quietly. 'But it wasn't always Augusto the lawyer, was it?'

Looking down at the sand, arms tied behind his back, Da Silva didn't answer.

'Let me see – Augusto goes to university on a military scholar-ship, he gets a law degree, starts his five years in the army, does his officer training, and then the boys from Kopassus get hold of him, right?'

Da Silva said nothing.

'You were never really special forces material – you were always going to be head-shed with that big brain and fancy degree, right? But you complete Kopassus basic, and then suddenly you work out what they want you for. Intelligence section, right?'

'No comment,' said Da Silva.

'Oh yeah, the good old boys from Kopassus intel – trained you to be a spook, then set you up with a law firm so you could always cover their tracks. Making every torture, detention and execution legal, right, Da Silva? Maybe even some property confiscations, right?'

'What do you want, McQueen?' flashed Da Silva. 'You can't get me off the island, so you have to kill me or torture me.'

'I want to know what's in Operasi Boa,' said Mac, slow and calm. 'I want to know who's running it and what the goals are.'

'Or?' asked Da Silva, squinting up at Mac.

'Or I tell Benni Sudarto you ratted him out, turned on your Kopassus brothers. I'll tell him we pulled that ambush in Memo based on you squealing.'

'He wouldn't believe you,' croaked Da Silva.

'Perhaps. But I'm gonna have fun trying.'

'What's my guarantee?' asked Da Silva. 'What about my family?'

'That depends on the quality of the information,' said Mac, face stony.

'The first stage of Operasi Boa was to get executive orders signed by the minister for health,' said Da Silva. 'It was a military operation to immunise the East Timorese against certain strains of pneumonia which start as a virus, incubate in humans and become bacterial diseases.'

'They become contagious?' asked Jim.

'That's my understanding,' said Da Silva. 'I'm a lawyer, not a doctor. The scientists were working on a mass-vaccination project.'

'Of whom?' asked Jim.

'Well, it was originally called BOACL, so it covered the populations of Bobonaro, Oecussi, Ainaro and Cova Lima.'

'Why those places?' asked Mac.

'I don't know,' said de Silva, looking up. 'I suppose they're rural communities, native enclaves?'

'Where did Lombok come in?' asked Jim.

'Lombok is a joint venture between a Kopassus company and a North Korean consortium. It makes the vaccine.'

'Wasn't Lombok also making the Boa virus?' asked Mac.

'I don't know,' said Da Silva. 'I told you – I'm a lawyer.'

'Okay,' said Mac.

'My job was to tidy up the orders so they'd be signed off in Jakarta and Kopassus could make all this money from the fees they'd charge – apparently the World Health Organisation pays organisations to do this and the Asia Development Bank makes interest-free loans. Then, two months before Soeharto was gone, a high-powered major-general came into my offices.'

'Haryono?' asked Jim.

'Let's call him Major-General, okay?' asked Da Silva, noticeably scared. 'He was with my intel controller –'

'Amir?' asked Mac.

Nodding, Da Silva continued. 'The general wanted it shortened to Boa and incorporated in a military operation.'

'Hidden?' asked Mac, thinking back to Rahmid Ali's final words.

'Disguised is a better word for it,' said Da Silva. 'I had to rework some clauses of a battle order called Operation Extermination so they alluded to Operasi Boa without spelling it out. You'd really have to be looking for Boa in that document.'

'The purpose of this?' asked Jim.

'They wanted a signed battle order that covered them legally. They were using the power vacuum of Soeharto's fall to get away with it, I suppose.'

'So what was Operasi Boa?' asked Jim.

'It was the same vaccine program,' said Da Silva. 'But it changed the delivery slightly.'

'Yeah?' asked Mac.

'Yeah, rather than vaccinations delivered by needles, into the skin, they shifted it to what in English is called a line-source delivery system.'

'Which is?' said Mac.

'It means you spray the agent – but when it's written in Bahasa Indonesia, it looks like you'll vaccinate villagers by lining up the patients.'

'Nice,' said Jim, giving Da Silva a clip over the ear. 'Ever heard of a vaccine that can be sprayed on people?'

'What are you talking about?' said Da Silva.

'Your bosses are planning to put that disease into the villages, they're not immunising anyone,' said Jim, angry.

Looking pleadingly into Mac's eyes, Da Silva shook his head. 'I don't know what you're talking about.'

'We're talking about Extermination,' said Jim, snarling in Da Silva's ear.

'That's the operation name,' said Da Silva, confused. 'It's about deporting people across the border, isn't it?'

'We'll see,' said Mac. 'When is Boa happening?'

'Same time as Extermination – the day of the ballot result. Maybe waiting for the right weather for the spraying.'

'So you depopulate an area yet you're trying to save the villagers from this super-pneumonia?'

'It was strange, and I guess that's why Maria –'

Silence fell on them as the surf pounded.

'Tell me,' said Mac.

'Does she have to be in this?' asked Da Silva. 'She's young and idealistic.'

'Tell me,' said Mac, harsher.

'Maria was put together with me by Cedar Rail – the Australian intel. She was talking with me in my office and she must have seen Operasi Boa when I was called away. She had an attack of conscience – she copied it.'

'But we miss out?' said Mac, annoyed that Da Silva had burned the document.

'Um, no,' said Da Silva, slow. 'I burned it, remember?'

'Yeah,' said Mac. 'So Cedar Rail didn't get the document that he'd been after?'

'No,' said Da Silva, looking Mac in the eye. 'Cedar Rail didn't want the Operasi Boa document – he wanted it destroyed.'

'Destroyed?' yelled Mac, moving at Da Silva. 'Why would Aussie intelligence want to destroy it?'

'That's what he wanted me to do this morning,' said Da Silva, gulping, obviously worried he'd triggered another attack.

'But to *destroy* it?' snapped Mac. 'You must have got it wrong, mate.'

'No, McQueen,' said Da Silva softly. 'Coded message this morning – told me exactly where it was. The codes were correct.'

'At the Resende?' asked Mac.

'Sure,' said Da Silva, now enjoying seeing Mac off-balance. 'I was surprised because suddenly he knows where this document is hiding.'

'I bet he did,' said Mac, seething. 'I fucking bet he did.'

CHAPTER 56

The first shot exploded out of Da Silva's chest. The second took most of his head away before he collapsed in the sand.

Mac dived for the ground, fishing for his Colt as he joined Jim behind a small sand dune. Looking up to the small cliffs under the coast road, they scanned for the shooter.

Three shots in quick succession plopped into the sand, the final one less than a foot from Mac's boot.

'The guy in white, behind the central rock,' hissed Jim, peeping over the dune.

'I can see him now,' breathed Mac, checking for load and safety. 'What's he got?'

'Sniper rifle,' said Jim, his back heaving. 'Automatic action.'

Shots rang out from the car park, where Jim's driver was waiting, and the sniper ducked behind his rock.

'Let's go,' said Jim. Standing, they hurtled behind trees and sand dunes as a hail of bullets tore through the foliage.

'How many?' Jim asked his Timorese driver, as they joined him in the lee of the Mitsubishi.

'Two at least,' said the driver.

Opening the boot, Jim pulled out two M4 assault rifles and

a handful of mags as bullets zinged into the steel of the open lid, narrowly missing him.

'Fuck!' he spat as he hit the ground, handing M4s to Mac and the driver. While Jim keyed the sat phone, Mac ducked up and loosed a couple of bursts of three-shot at the rock.

'What the fuck are you doing?' asked Mac, crouching back behind the car and seeing Jim on the phone. 'No pizza delivery round here, mate!'

'I promised I wouldn't do the Yank thing of bringing in the cavalry, right?' said Jim.

'Yep,' said Mac as the rear windscreen erupted in a shower of glass.

'I lied,' said Jim, raising a finger as he got his connection.

A long volley of gunfire smashed into the Mitsubishi, rupturing the fuel tank, shredding three of the tyres and removing what was left of the auto glass. Looking over the sill of the door he was crouched behind, Mac watched the three shooters making their way down the cliff to the beach, and fired off a few rounds, hitting one in the leg.

Feeling a knock on his arm, Mac looked where Jim was pointing and saw a large black power boat surging into sight. The size of a twelve-metre power cruiser, it was painted drab black and had a rotating radar dish mounted over the open cockpit. Mac could see it also had a gunner's pit on the long bow decks holding a Mark 38 machine-gun system – a one-inch naval machine-gun.

'That a Mark 38?' asked Mac, feeling nauseous from the gasoline fumes spewing from the car's shredded fuel tank.

Jim didn't hear, his attention divided between the sat phone and the shooters as the US Navy power boat leapt across the swell doing about fifty knots.

'Got a bead?' asked Jim into the phone. 'Okay, yeah, we're getting down,' he replied as one of the snipers ducked from behind a rock with an RPG on his shoulder. He launched the grenade, a great trail of smoke gushing across the beach as it accelerated towards the power boat.

An unearthly screaming, like a thousand hound-dogs crying, sounded across the water, rising to a shrieking crescendo that had Mac and Jim simultaneously putting their hands to their ears. Transfixed, they watched the Mark 38 bellow fire as it churned out its one-inch bullets at almost three rounds per second.

The RPG disintegrated in a ball of fire, and a glorious silence followed as the Mark 38 was shut down while debris scattered on the beach.

The snipers ran among the rocks, clambering back to the big boulder.

As the snipers made their goal, the awesome firepower focused on the large rock and turned it to rubble as the rounds found their mark. The air shook, the sand vibrated and the sound was incredible – the concussion of such enormous fire-rate shaking Mac's body.

One of the shooters tried to run from behind the disappearing rock and got caught in the bullet hail, an arm sailing upwards and onto the road and the rest of him vanishing.

The rock now completely obliterated, Mac could see bits of clothing and body parts exploding out of the coastal cliff with the dust and stones from where the rock used to be.

Finally, there was silence again.

'Guess that's gunboat diplomacy?' said Mac, his ears ringing.

'Nice work, guys,' said Jim into the sat phone. 'Can we get a ride?'

They made the north side of Alor in under an hour, the boat coasting along at sixty knots, its turbocharged Cummins diesels singing at a constant pitch.

Sitting under a blanket in his soaked clothes, Mac accepted a coffee from a sailor who – like the officer in charge – was in civvies.

'Thanks for the help,' said Mac to the sailor.

'Thank Mark,' said the sailor with a smile, nodding at the gun in the bow.

'That, mate,' said Mac, 'is the scariest thing I've ever seen. *Ever!*'

'Yeah, my brother,' laughed the sailor. 'And just so long as the bad guys are feeling that too – know what I'm sayin'?'

***

An unmarked Black Hawk helo was waiting on the beach when they arrived. It flew them into Denpasar, dropping them at the military annexe of Ngurah Rai, where Jim's sidekicks had a Voyager van waiting on the tarmac. As Mac was making to get in the van, a white Holden Commodore screeched to a stop beside the van.

Hesitating beside the DIA van, Mac saw two hulking shapes emerge from the Commodore. As they paced towards him, Mac realised one was his old mate and colleague, Garvs. The other was Barry Bray, the leader of the Australian Commonwealth's I-team, a crew of ex-cops and soldiers who retrieved wayward Commonwealth employees from foreign service.

Garvs showing up with Bray made Mac feel vaguely insulted.

'Hey, champ,' said Garvs, big hands resting on his hips as he chewed gum. 'Time for a chat, yeah?'

Shaking hands with Garvs, Mac greeted Bray with a handshake too. 'Barry – how's it going?'

'Not bad, Macca,' he replied, grinning. 'Wouldn't be dead for quids.'

The ride into town was silent, Mac reading the order that brought his Operation Totem secondment to an end. Handing it back to Garvs in the front seat, Mac looked at the outskirts of Denpasar flashing by, dusty and heat-bleached in the warmth of early afternoon.

'So, secondment's over – guess that means Davidson's left town,' said Mac.

'Yep,' said Garvs, turning to look at Mac. 'Flew out for Auckland this morning.'

'APEC?' asked Mac, talking about the systems and agents that the firm liked to plant at the APEC summits before they began.

'Yeah – should be fun this year. Got that Integration of Women project, so we might have some of those Mexican and Chilean feminists down there.'

'Sorry?' said Mac, missing the point.

'You know, mate,' said Garvs, excited. 'Those Latin American feminists still like sex, mate. It's a proven fact.'

'But, with you?' said Mac, laughing.

'Well,' said Garvs, embarrassed as Barry Bray started laughing too, 'they could do worse.'

'Could do better, too, mate,' said Mac.

Garvs turned back to the windscreen, sulking.

Mac sat in the ASIS briefing room, his damp clothes gripping his legs. Marty Atkins sipped his coffee and leaned back, while Garvs sat at Mac's ten o'clock playing with a pen.

'So, looks like you're back in the firm's camp,' said Atkins, smiling.

'Tony leaves and you overturn his secondment, right, Marty?'

'Wasn't like that, Macca,' said Atkins. 'Just that we have some gigs to get on with.'

'Like?' asked Mac.

'Like this Banda Sea situation. Dutch are testing for gas beds and we don't like it.'

Sighing, Mac could feel himself being drawn into a meaningless gig. 'For the final time, Marty — those Dutchies are looking for another Tang Treasure, mate,' he said, referring to the Arab shipwreck discovered in the Java Sea by a German crew. 'It's got nothing to do with gas beds. The Yanks and the Poms have been all over this area and it's uneconomic.'

'Well, sometimes we have to get the product for ourselves, right, Macca?' said Atkins, going for an avuncular tone despite being barely a year older than Mac. 'Besides, that Totem business was turning into a dead-end, eh?'

'Totem isn't a dead-end, Marty,' said Mac, determined not to let it slip into the past tense.

'Really, what did you get?' asked Atkins, quite aware that a debriefing about Totem was DIA's prerogative, not Mac's. 'Besides a whole bunch of US dollars that you haven't declared yet?'

Mac teetered on the edge of telling Marty Atkins to go fuck himself, but he kept it tight. 'It's worse than what I told you in this room a few days ago.'

'Worse than what?' asked Atkins, actually enjoying this.

'Under cover of Operation Extermination, Kopassus could be trying to infect a large swathe of the East Timor population with a fatal disease.'

'A disease?' said Atkins, sitting up.

'A powerful pneumonia, SARS.'

'And I suppose you have some evidence?' said Atkins, super-cilious.

'Actually, no, Marty – thanks to you.'

'What's that mean?' asked Atkins, eyes narrowing.

'Augusto Da Silva was told by Cedar Rail where the Boa file was hidden – when we got there ourselves, the Boa file was gone.'

'Well, that's quite a story, Macca,' chuckled Atkins, encouraging Garvey to join him.

'It's the truth is what it is, Marty,' said Mac, holding back on the burning of Boa in the hope that Atkins would slip and incriminate himself.

'Oh really, Macca?' smiled Atkins. 'So let's start with basics.'

'Okay,' said Mac.

'I'm not Cedar Rail,' said Atkins. 'That would be Greg Tobin. I *act* as Cedar Rail to run assets in eastern Indonesia on Greg's behalf. All messages are coded – anyone could be Cedar Rail.'

'I –' said Mac.

'No, McQueen,' snapped Atkins. 'My turn. The second point is, why the surprise that Da Silva is looking for Boa, or that he found it? He's been under instructions to find it for weeks now, since the Canadian went missing.'

'I didn't say you were Cedar Rail, Marty,' snarled Mac. 'I'm saying that an Australian who Augusto believed to be Cedar Rail called him this morning and sent him to retrieve Boa.'

'And you believe Augusto Da Silva?' sniggered Atkins. 'That little worm?'

'Little worm?' said Mac. 'He was *our* little worm, mate – can't just write him off like that.'

'Can't I Macca?' said Atkins in a quiet voice. 'But you can just write Rahmid Ali out of the story? Pretend you never met him, that he never handed you a document?'

'That wasn't my call, Marty,' snapped Mac, blushing with embarrassment.

'Of course not, mate,' said Atkins, smiling. 'It was Davidson's good judgment to save you the humiliation.'

'Screw you, Marty,' said Mac, seeing Garvs chuckling.

'Whatever,' said Atkins, having some fun. 'So an Indonesian spy hands you secret papers from the general staff, which have been translated for your convenience, and now you're on a personal assignment to save the president?'

As Mac looked out the window over Denpasar, the laughter burned into him like a welding torch.

CHAPTER 57

Lying back, gazing at the ceiling of his bungalow, Mac listened to the television reports of East Timor being overrun my violent militias. Atkins had given him two days off before starting on the Banda Sea assignment, a rest he needed. What he hadn't needed was being banned from entering East or West Timor.

The meeting had gone well if keeping his job was the measure of success. Atkins had played him perfectly, even avoiding the issue of asking Da Silva to destroy the Boa document. Mac was certain that Atkins had made the call as Cedar Rail, and given the order to destroy the document – he and Greg Tobin were the only people who knew the call signs and coded sequences for running the ASIS assets in this part of the world.

Mac wasn't ready to let things go until he'd achieved some objectives. First, ask Davidson who he'd told about Mac's hunch that the copy of Operasi Boa was in the old drop box in the Resende. Second, find a phone log that showed Atkins made that call to Da Silva. Most important, try to stop Operasi Boa before the weather was right and they started spraying that crap on civilians.

Keying his replacement Nokia – the one in his pocket had died during the swim to the DIA boat – Mac tried Davidson. It was almost 2 am in Auckland, so Mac left a voicemail message.

Then he tapped into Canberra's secure lines and got Leena, the researcher, on the line again.

'They got you on the night shift?' asked Mac after she'd cleared his credentials.

'I've lost track,' she said.

'I've got a mission for you, Leena – I need you to tap our best contacts in TI, find the source of these calls between six and nine, this morning, to these numbers, okay?' asked Mac, before reading Da Silva's mobile phone and work lines, given to him by Jim. 'Then I need you to check the Dili home number of Augusto Da Silva – big D – and give me every phone call made to that number during the same period, okay?'

'Okay, Albion,' said Leena. 'You on this phone?'

'Yes, hear from you soon.'

Lying back on the bed, Mac tried to work it out. With Moerpati and Rahmid Ali dead, he'd lost his connection to the Indonesian President's own intel operation. The assassins had basically smashed it, and almost taken Jim and Mac along for the ride. The assassination of Augusto Da Silva removed the person who had written Operasi Boa and Mac had no doubt that Blackbird was either dead or so scared for her life that she'd never resurface.

He had ways of going forwards, but had no way to the Indonesian President's operation.

Or did he?

Rolling off the bed, he went searching through the pockets of his chinos, coming up empty. Cursing his haphazard filing system, Mac tried to remember: he'd shown Davidson a list of the names, phone numbers and addresses associated with Rahmid Ali, and Davidson had said that none rang a bell. Then he'd pocketed the list, taken it back to the hotel . . .

Rummaging though his main wheelie suitcase, which had been sitting at the Natour for a week, he pulled out the plastic pillow filled with US dollars and found his piece of paper from his first phone session with Leena. Flattening it on the writing desk, he took another look, through new eyes. The addresses he had for Andromeda IT and the entities associated with the phone calls made from Rahmid Ali's phone were still there: he had an address in KL and one in Singapore.

There was also the extension of the chief of staff's number in the presidential building. Mac had dismissed it as being too high profile, but now he might have a look at it.

But first, he took a quick shower and restored his hair colour, using an N10 blonding rinse.

After drying off, he lay down and sleep came fast.

The Nokia's singsong ring tone woke him from a nightmare of Mickey Costa scratching at the glass door.

'Yep,' he rasped into the phone, trying to sit up but so bruised he was only able to roll onto his side.

'McQueen!' came the man's voice, South-East Asian accent with a touch of American. 'That you?'

'Yeah,' whispered Mac, still half asleep but fully dressed. 'Who's this?'

'Bongo, brother,' roared the big ape cheerfully. 'Time for a beer?'

'Shit, Bongo,' laughed Mac, relieved and happy. 'Thought you'd carked it.'

'I'd *what*?'

'Dead, mate.'

A pause, then, 'You being funny?'

'No, mate,' laughed Mac. 'I'll tell you about it.'

Walking to the Bar Barong through the fragrant evening air of Denpasar, Mac felt elated. He didn't make many friends in his profession, and most of them were embassy colony types – cops, customs and diplomats. The idea that Bongo was dead had affected him more deeply than he was comfortable with, and finding that he was alive was like a gift. And not just because he liked him – but because right now he needed someone on his side. Someone who knew how to look after himself.

Standing at the end of the bar that Mac always held up, Bongo was nursing a beer and watching TV when Mac arrived.

'Hey, bro,' said the big Filipino as they gave each other an open-palm handshake. 'Been fighting again?' He nodded at Mac's facial injuries.

'Should see the other bloke.'

'I'm telling Mum,' said Bongo, ordering a Tiger for Mac. 'So you thought I was dead?'

'Saw a photo – Moerpati and a headless corpse with the Conquistador crucifix. Thought it was you, mate.'

Laughing, Bongo slapped him on the back. 'Lots of Catholics got the tattoo like that.'

Bongo listened to Mac recount the events of the past two days.

'That's bad news about Moerpati,' said Bongo. 'Very bad.'

'Why?' asked Mac.

'Because Moerpati's the Soeharto clique. He's from the right family, made the right marriage, had the right connections – he's New Order, head to toe.'

'So, he gets killed?'

'Yeah, it means there's another power base in Jakarta thinks it's strong enough to move on the New Order – and that kind of fight is no good for anyone.'

'A bio-weapon's no good for us, either,' said Mac. 'The scientists tell me it's based on SARS – gives the victims a fatal pneumonia.'

'Fucking Koreans,' said Bongo, shaking his head. 'They been chasing this shit for years. It's like an obsession.'

'What about the Indonesians?' asked Mac.

'Yeah, it's the money behind it,' said Bongo, collecting the new beers and handing one to Mac. 'Money rules everything in Asia, and the Koreans know that. We were once looking into this immunisation program in Cambodia, in my NICA days,' he said, referring to the Philippines intelligence agency. 'But it weren't no immunisation program, brother – least, not like we'd know it, right?'

'What was it?'

'It was the Cambodian army testing a disease on these mountain peasants.'

'So it's the same as East Timor?' asked Mac, casing the bar.

'All the lines worked back to North Korea, to the cash from Poi Pet and accounts at the military's banks – it's sick, brother, what some people do for the money.'

'The thing I can't work out,' said Mac, 'is where it goes from here.'

'Easy,' said Bongo. 'The Javas take the money but then they have all this bio-weapon, right?

'Yeah – but what do they do with it? That Lombok plant was a big facility, they were set up to make tons of the stuff.'

'Have a look at your Operation Extermination again,' said Bongo. 'Remember we were reading it in the car, on the way into the hills that morning?'

'Yeah,' said Mac.

'Extermination has already begun, brother, it's on the TV every night. And it's all about deporting Timorese to West Papua – what they call Irian Jaya, right?'

'Sure.'

'So, get the undesirables from Indonesia in one place, and then . . .' Bongo made a throat-slitting gesture. 'The bio-weapon developed in East Timor can now be used on the bigger problem – the Timors and Papuans, all in one place.'

'That's sick,' said Mac, discounting Bongo's opinions as exaggeration.

'That's Indonesia, brother.'

Mac told Bongo he needed him for a week, and the payment would be whatever was in the casino bag from Poi Pet. Agreed, Bongo fixed Mac with a grin.

'So, McQueen. How'd we go with Jessica?'

'Oh, you know,' said Mac, inspecting the Tiger label.

'Do I?' asked Bongo, drinking but not taking his laughing eyes off Mac.

'What can I say, mate? She's gorgeous and funny and – you know – can't ask for much more, right?'

'You gonna take it further?'

'Mate!' said Mac, not wanting to go into it.

'You know, McQueen, if you gonna come out and say who you are, brother, then you gotta do it now, right? Don't do what I did.'

'What did you do, Bongo?' asked Mac.

'This girl, when I was stationed in Hong Kong, right?'

'In the NICA days?'

'Yep – Shari was an Indian girl, father was a big businessman, and I'm – well, you know,' hurried Bongo, not wanting to talk about old identities. 'I can't tell her who I really am and she's beautiful, brother!'

'Yeah?' asked Mac.

'Oh, man! Forget it,' smiled Bongo, shaking his head and going quiet with the memory. 'We loved each other, bro.'

'Bongo Morales? In love?' laughed Mac.

Nodding and looking away, Bongo's face changed slightly. 'Worst decision of my life, McQueen.'

'How did it end?'

'Controller wanted me to work her, and I couldn't do that. So about six weeks after I met her a new gig came up and I caught a plane,' said Bongo, looking into his beer. 'That was ten years ago. I was twenty-nine, thought I was hard – and now? I think about her every day.'

They were quiet again, Mac praying Bongo wouldn't cry.

Then the Filipino bounced back. 'Hey, how did this become about me? Jessica! She liked you, brother – I know it, man.'

'Yeah, well I liked her too,' said Mac, trying to smile.

'What?' asked Bongo, his teeth flashing against his tanned skin. 'You give her your number?'

'No.'

'Your address?'

'No.'

'Make some plan?'

'Nope,' breathed Mac.

'I can't believe that,' said Bongo. 'I picked her – she really liked you, man!'

'Well, she wrote me a letter,' said Mac.

'Yeah?' laughed Bongo. 'Tell!'

'I can't, mate.'

'Come on – it's not that embarrassing.'

'No, I mean I can't . . . I didn't read it.'

Pausing, Bongo tried to get it. 'So, it was the kiss-off, huh? Nice to meet you, but . . .'

'No, mate,' chuckled Mac, his face heating up like he was a kid and his mother was telling him off. 'I didn't read it.'

'Okay – I'll read it for you, McQueen, you big cat,' he said, flicking his fingers for the letter. 'Come on.'

'Can't,' said Mac, looking out of the bar.

'Why not?'

''Cos I chucked it, mate,' admitted Mac.

'What? In the trash?' said Bongo, incredulous.

Nodding, Mac tried a nonchalant shrug.

'Oh, man!' said Bongo, slapping his palm on the table.

'What?' asked Mac, face burning.

'You Anglo men are something else, brother,' he said, shaking his head. 'One of these days your women are gonna rise up and kill the lot of you, swear to God.'

'Yeah, well . . .' said Mac, gulping at his beer.

'You *chucked* it? That's cold, brother,' laughed Bongo. 'That's *cold*.'

CHAPTER 58

Halfway across the grassed courtyard area of the hotel, Mac's Nokia trilled once.

'Just getting to my room, Leena,' said Mac, answering before it rang again. 'Gimme a second.'

Checking the area around his bungalow, Mac let himself in, hitched a chair under the door handle and, sitting at the desk, put the Nokia on speaker phone.

'The calls into those three numbers, in the time period specified, are as follows,' said Leena, then read a list of just five numbers.

Mac thought back to Da Silva hurrying past him at the cafe in Dili and asked Leena to narrow the search to calls between seven and eight in the morning.

'There's one, at 7.41, to the office number in Dili,' said Leena.

'What's the number?' asked Mac, poised with his pen.

Mac jotted down a '361' number – from Denpasar, on a landline.

'Can we get an address on that number?' asked Mac.

'Already have it, Albion,' said Leena. 'It's the Puputan Bakehouse, at –'

'Thanks,' Mac interrupted. 'I know where it is.'

The Puputan Bakehouse was a coffee shop and deli just off Puputan Square, in the heart of Denpasar. It was a favourite for Anglos working in the area because of its superior coffee – and it was the main hangout of Martin Atkins.

'Thanks, Leena,' said Mac, feeling cornered.

'There's other activity on that line, close to the time of the Denpasar call,' said Leena.

'Yeah?' he said, preoccupied.

'Yes, Albion – an incoming call that lasted seventy-three seconds, six minutes after the one from the Puputan Bakehouse.'

'Okay,' murmured Mac, doodling on his pad. 'What's the number?'

As Leena read it out, Mac noticed something immediately. 'Can you please check that prefix?' he asked.

'Yes, Albion – it's an inactive satellite designation.'

'Inactive?' asked Mac.

'It's registered with the ITU, but unused. No other information,' she said.

'Thanks, mate,' said Mac. 'Great job, much appreciated.'

Hanging up, Mac checked his G-Shock – 11.12 pm, time for some fun with Harry Song, his contact at the International Telecommunications Union in Santa Clara.

'Harry!' yelled Mac, as his call was answered. 'It's Alan McQueen – how ya been?'

After a brief pause, Harry Song's perfect diction chimed down the line. 'I am well, thank you, Mr Mac. How are you today, sir?'

'Any better and they'd have to lock me up,' said Mac.

'Glad to hear it, sir,' said Harry.

Harry Song had gone to the United States to do a master's degree at CalTech but he was still trapped in the Chinese system of manners and deportment. Mac liked to get him boozed and wind him up about what he should say into the listening devices the MSS kept planting in his house.

'I need something, Harry,' said Mac, pleasantries over.

'Such a surprise,' said Harry.

'If I'm calling an 883 115 code, what am I calling?'

'The first three numbers are a satellite phone designation, but that second series . . .' Harry trailed off.

Mac listened to him walk across a room.

'Okay, that 115 is inactive,' said Harry.

'Yeah, but it still works.'

'Sure,' said Harry.

'Sure?'

'Yeah, I've just looked it up, and that's a calling code for Delta Telecoms Group, registered in Singapore,' said Harry.

'Delta? What is it?' asked Mac.

'It's supposed to be confidential, Mr Mac,' said Harry.

'So, confide in me,' said Mac.

'Now you are taking a piss,' said Harry.

'*The* piss, Harry. *The* piss – and no, I'm not. It's serious.'

'I could lose my job, Mr Mac.'

'Hey, mate – one door closes and another opens, right?' said Mac, trying to keep him on the line. 'Just like what I told you about that mother-in-law of yours, remember?'

'What was it you said?' asked Harry.

'I said, *Don't let fear and inaction be the same thing.*'

Harry laughed. 'Yeah, and I said, *You never met my mother-in-law, or you'd know that fear and inaction are the exact same thing.*'

Mac changed tack. 'Harry, I need this, okay?'

'Okay,' he sighed. 'Delta Telecom Group is on an inactive code because it's government, military –'

'Intelligence,' said Mac.

'Precisely,' said Harry Song.

Mac ran the sat-phone number through his phone book and couldn't find any matches. Most executive government, diplomatic, military and intelligence operatives used sat phones, and in Mac's experience they were more widely used in South-East Asia than anywhere else. That number could have been Singaporean government, Korean military, Indonesian intelligence or any number of quasi-government bodies operating through corporate fronts with shady telecoms providers.

The Delta Telecoms Group did not come up with anything meaningful on Leena's radar – it was a privately held corporation, operating in Singapore with Delaware trustees and British Virgin Islands bankers. Its postal address was the Singapore office of a global law firm. What cops called a cold trail.

Looking at his watch, Mac realised he had almost enough time to walk to the Puputan Bakehouse and have a quick chat with Dewi, the owner, before she shut at midnight.

Staying forty metres back, in the shadows, Mac felt the tail as soon as he left the Natour.

Having left his room without a firearm, Mac didn't feel impregnable, but he didn't feel threatened either. There was only one of them, and if his tasking was to shoot Mac, he would have done it in the grounds of the Natour, giving the shooter multiple exit routes. He wouldn't be doing it out on the well-lit streets.

Turning left before his scheduled turn for the Bakehouse, Mac darted across the road and ducked behind a car. The tail followed around the corner without hesitation, so he obviously wasn't a pro. He also wasn't a he, judging by the female shape and gait under the loose jacket and jeans.

Watching the woman react to losing eyes on Mac, he stood slowly, not wanting to panic her.

'Nice night,' he said calmly, standing and walking between parked cars into the empty street.

The woman turned and froze, like a deer caught in the full beams.

'It's okay,' said Mac, still approaching but holding his hands open. 'But next time you want to ask me for a drink, there might be an easier way.'

Mid to late thirties, Javanese, her hair was pulled up in a chignon.

'I'm sorry,' she said, genuinely embarrassed. 'I've never done this before.'

'It's okay,' said Mac. 'It's just that I prefer to meet people face to face rather than trying to speak through the back of my head.'

Now she laughed, and Mac could see a smart, beautiful, well-educated woman.

'So, what's up?' asked Mac, looking to make sure there was no backup, no unmarked vans with mobile dental surgeries in the back.

'My name is Chloe,' she said. 'I need to speak to you.'

'Yes?' said Mac, starting slightly as an engine revved down the road.

'I work for the President, and —'

The revving engine screamed to a climax and Mac swivelled around to see a red Toyota Camry charging at forty-five degrees across the street.

As he dragged the woman to the ground behind a parked car, there was a loud screeching of metal as the car stopped twenty metres away. Mac peeked over the parked car and saw two men emerge from the Corolla with small machine-guns.

'What's happening?' screamed Chloe, as Mac dragged her away by the hand. The sound of windows shattering and car alarms going off was punctuated by the hammering of two machine pistols blasting at full auto, as they sprinted.

Feeling a sharp knock in his left bicep, Mac increased their speed along the pavement as bullets ripped into cars, lamp-posts, trees and storefronts. About forty metres in front of them, Mac could see a side alley at ninety degrees to the street.

'Let's make it to the alley, okay, Chloe?' he yelled over the gunfire.

Chloe whimpered as they turned into the alley and were plunged into the darkness of a no-nonsense Denpasar laneway. Stopping for a second, Mac tried to get his bearings. Then a bullet took a brick edge beside his shoulder and Mac raced forward, pulling the woman along through stinking puddles, slimy muck and boxes of garbage.

'Shit,' said Mac, drawing to a halt where the alley ended at a brick wall.

They ducked behind a garbage bin as a powerful torch beam reached out from the other end of the alley and filled the confined space with light. Whatever their pursuers had was not a torch in the hardware-store sense of the word, but a SWAT-team halogen system found in helicopters for search-and-rescue work.

'Over there,' whispered Chloe, squinting at the reflected light. 'There's a door.'

Following Chloe's lead, Mac found the wooden doors behind a large garbage box. The doors stood at hip-height, with a padlock in the middle of them. After backing up two paces, Mac lunged forward and kicked at the middle with all his weight.

The doors didn't budge.

CHAPTER 59

'Here,' hissed Chloe, picking up a steel bar.

Grabbing it, Mac levered it under the padlock, opening the doors in one attempt. Chloe gasped as the searchlight beam swept closer and several rounds of gunfire whacked into the wall above them.

There was a brief lull in gunfire as the male voices chattered at each other. The light was aimed over Mac and Chloe's heads as they crawled from the alley through the open doors. As Mac went to stand, he found himself falling down a chute, landing in a stinking puddle of slime at the bottom. Chloe joined him half a second later, and as they searched for an escape route in the inky darkness, a volley of machine-gun fire ricocheted into the delivery chute.

Walking along the cellar floor, hands stretched out in front of him, Mac tripped in the blackness, falling forward and hitting his head on concrete steps.

'Are you okay?' whispered Chloe, voice panicked.

'Good as gold,' said Mac, pushing himself onto his knees then leading Chloe up the steps.

They emerged in the ground floor of what looked like an old warehouse space. Moving to the most obvious exit, Mac cursed as he found it bolted. Creeping along the wall with Chloe in front of him, they slipped behind a pile of wooden crates.

Mac pulled out his Nokia as they heard their pursuers sliding down the delivery chute.

'Bongo, I need a hand, mate,' rasped Mac. Describing their location as clearly as he could, Mac asked him to hurry.

'There yesterday, brother,' said Bongo, whose apartment was two blocks away.

The rays of searchlight beams winked from the cellar entry. Mac considered ambushing the shooters as they came up the stairs, but decided against it. Clearly pros, they'd stagger the ascent of those stairs, precisely to catch an ambusher in the support fire. Besides, he couldn't leave Chloe, who was shaking like a leaf and looked as if she might collapse at any moment.

Moving further around the wall, Mac found a place where he could see the top of the cellar stairs. Torches now off, the first shooter emerged and cased the warehouse in distinct quartiles: east–west, high–low.

The second shooter joined him and they split, the taller of the two moving towards the crate they were hiding behind.

'Okay,' whispered Mac. 'We're going to move along this wall, see if we can stay one step ahead, okay?'

There was no reply and then Mac felt her slump against him.

'You okay?' asked Mac.

Looking down he saw her back was a shiny black mess of blood – she'd taken a bullet on the street.

'Fuck!' said Mac.

Looking up Mac saw a mezzanine about ten metres above the floor. Doorways and skylights led out of the area and he realised that this was their best escape route. As he plotted his course to get up to the mezzanine, he saw the short gunman racing at the stairs and charge up them three at a time. Reaching the mezzanine level, the shooter hit the power on his halogen searchlight and strobed the ground-floor area with the intense illumination.

'Hang in there,' said Mac as Chloe clung to him. 'I'm going to get us out of here.'

Up ahead was a partially unloaded crate with a panel missing. Steering Chloe into it, Mac whispered for her to stay put until he gave the okay. Though scared and injured, she looked him in the eye and nodded.

Moving back along the wall, Mac saw a pile of sacks on a filing cabinet. Picking one up, he undid his boat shoes, put them in a sack and waited for the tall shooter to come down the corridor of crates. Mac ducked back from the sweeping glare of the halogen and waited for ten seconds. The tall shooter turned right, and waved a hand over his head, his searchlight exposing a scuttling rat. Mac pulled back behind the crate as the shooter kept coming.

Taking two steps to his right, away from the corridor, Mac swung the sack into the darkness. The tall shooter swivelled around to face the sound and Mac lunged at him, kicking the shooter's groin, whipping a right elbow across his nose, and ripping the A4 counter clockwise from the shooter's right hand, breaking the fingers so that the machine pistol dropped into Mac's hand.

Getting his finger on the trigger, Mac swung the gun at the shooter who was lying in the foetal position, clutching at his wrist. Suddenly Mac was bathed in light as he squinted into the harshness of another searchlight, virtually paralysing in its intensity.

'Drop the weapon,' came the mechanical English of an Indonesian. 'You're in my sights.'

Heaving for breath and blinded, Mac felt the beam of light move off him. Then there were two shots and a weight hit Mac from the side.

Turning, he found Chloe sagged against his leg.

'Ask for George,' she whispered. 'In Singapore, okay?'

'What?' asked Mac, barely able to see.

'George – find the traitor,' said Chloe, then the air was torn with the hellish racket of gunfire. Mac fell and scrambled back to his hide between the crates.

Full-auto fire bellowed as Mac lay in his alcove, scared shitless and effectively blind.

The gunfire raged for ten seconds and Mac lay there, panting in the dark, the acrid smell of cordite and gunpowder wafting into his hide. Feeling for the breech slide and the safety of the A4, Mac pushed himself around on his elbows so he was sitting up against the crate, and looking down the narrow confines of his hide, gun pointing to where the attack would come from.

Mumbling his Hail Marys, thinking about the good things in his life, and trying to reassure himself that he'd tried his hardest with the whole Operasi Boa snafu, Mac listened to the floorboards creak with approaching footfalls.

Pulling the A4 up, Mac tried to control his breathing as the footsteps came closer, stopping short of Mac's hide.

'McQueen!' came the Filipino-English. 'It's me!'

'Bongo, in here, mate,' said Mac, fading fast.

As Bongo peered around the corner, Mac felt the warmth under his armpit from the bullet he'd taken in the arm.

'You okay, McQueen?' asked Bongo.

'No,' said Mac as his chin sagged to his chest.

CHAPTER 60

Drinking from a bottle of water, Mac was vaguely aware of the early-morning traffic noises of Denpasar as Bongo finished a conversation on the phone. Mac's throbbing arm looked worse than it really was – a graze that had been cleaned and dressed by the local hospital.

'The hospital will hold the death notification for twelve hours,' said Bongo, lighting a cigarette as he sat on the sofa. 'But if this Chloe is from the President's office, the local cops don't want the hassle of covering it up too long. We'd better find someone to take her back to Jakarta before the Sudartos find out about her, okay?'

'Okay,' said Mac. 'Twelve hours. We got that flight?'

'Locked and loaded, bro.'

'Give me an hour,' said Mac, 'and then we roll.'

Atkins picked up the whole coffee plunger and headed for his office, Mac following with two mugs and the milk. Shutting the door, Atkins gestured Mac to a seat.

'So, mate – this another telling off?' asked Atkins, pouring the coffees.

'No tellings off,' said Mac. 'A number of people have been shot and killed around me in the past week, and as my controller, I need to bring you in on it.'

'Sure, Macca – and I'm sorry about how things went the other day. It's not . . . I mean, you get to the management side and it's a juggle, okay?'

'I understand,' said Mac, sipping his coffee. 'And normally, I'd let it slide – move to the next gig, go to the Banda Sea, spy on Dutchies.'

'Sure,' laughed Atkins.

'But last night I was shot in a warehouse about three blocks from here.'

'Shot?! Holy shit, McQueen – where?' said Atkins, sitting forward, his face aghast.

Pushing his trop shirt down, Mac exposed the bandage on his upper left bicep.

'It's called a graze, but it doesn't feel like one,' said Mac.

'Jesus,' breathed Atkins, now out of his chair and peering at the wound. 'Stiches?'

'Nah, mate, but it's sore.'

Atkins' response wasn't as Mac had expected. He seemed genuinely surprised, as demonstrated by his incomplete sentences. Liars generally rehearsed their responses, which came out more fluently.

'Who did this?' asked Atkins, looking up at Mac.

'Whoever burned the copy of Operasi Boa,' said Mac, staring Atkins full in the face.

'It was burned?!' spat Atkins. 'Oh, fuck!'

'Guess who burned it, Marty?' asked Mac.

'Who?' shrugged Atkins.

'Your friend in Dili, Augusto Da Silva.'

'Augusto?!' yelled Atkins. 'Why would he burn the damn thing?'

'What I was asking him, yesterday afternoon in Dili, about a second before he was assassinated.'

'Assassinated? By who?' asked Atkins, looking shaken.

'What's important is that you told him to do it.'

'What. The. Fuck. Are. You. Talking. About?' snarled Atkins. 'What the hell drugs are you taking?'

'Davidson was the only person who knew about the Resende drop box and he briefed you on my trip to Dili before he flew out to Auckland. You called Da Silva at about ten to eight yesterday morning, you told him the copy of Operasi Boa was in one of the three Dili drop boxes, but to start with the Santa Cruz ones first before checking the Resende. Then you asked him to burn the file – clean slate.'

'Bullshit,' said Atkins.

'And to throw people like me off the trail,' continued Mac, 'you called from the Puputan Bakehouse – that phone in Dewi's office, right?'

'You know what? I did call Augusto, and I did ask him to check the boxes for a copy of this thing,' said Atkins, calming.

'Nice work, Marty – what did you think I was doing there?'

'I didn't want to tell you, mate, 'cos some of the people you've been hanging around during this whole debacle have been less than ideal.'

'Such as?' asked Mac.

'Bongo Morales, Rahmid Ali, the Falintil guerrillas and, frankly, US intelligence.'

'I was seconded to DIA by Davidson,' said Mac.

'Yeah, well Tony doesn't spend much time up here anymore and he may not understand that we have different goals to the Yanks from time to time. Cutting a long story short, I wanted the Boa file in my hands before you could share it with the Americans – guilty as charged. When it was over, I was going to buy you a beer, no hard feelings.'

'You went behind my back?' asked Mac.

'I did what I had to do – I did what you'd do. Davidson told me about the Resende drop box in front of Jim, for Christ's sake, and I decided to get there first. I'm sorry, okay?'

Mac listened, silent.

'As for telling Da Silva to burn the Boa file,' said Atkins, 'are you on crack? Why would I ask him to burn it? You need a vacation, Macca.'

'Why the Bakehouse?'

'I've been using the Bakehouse for months, ever since the Indonesians started increasing their surveillance measures. They've even worked out a way to capture email. So, for out-of-town calls, I use the Bakehouse – their spooks know I eat there, so I just visit the gents, duck into Dewi's office and make some quick calls. Come back shaking my hands.'

'Nice craft,' said Mac.

'Try to stay in practice. But honestly, mate,' said Atkins. 'What's going on here? What can I do to make you happy about this?'

'I want us to shut down their bio-weapons program,' said Mac, straight up. 'Operasi Boa is underway. It was always going to operate in the shadow of Operation Extermination, and Extermination has started – they have truckloads of Timorese going across into West Timor and boatloads going out to West Papua.'

'I don't know about the bio-weapons, but yeah, sure, the deportations seem to be starting. What do you want us to *do*?'

'I want us to put a CX to Canberra that is so clear and so unequivocal that even a politician and his most brown-nosed advisers would be unable to bury it.'

'And what would the CX say?' asked Atkins, very calm. 'Given we don't have a copy of Boa, just suppositions?'

'It would say that the Indonesians have been testing and developing bio-weapons for the North Koreans in the Bobonaro district, and intend to use them on the civilian population.'

'Are you crazy?' said Atkins.

'No,' said Mac. 'It's a SARS-related bio-weapon that they'll spray from helicopters owned by the Koreans and operated by Pik Berger's mercenaries. They've sold it to the UN as a mass-vaccination exercise. They're waiting for the wind and cloud to be right, and then it starts on, or after, the day of the ballot result. September fourth.'

'How do we know this?' asked Atkins.

'Augusto Da Silva told us before he was shot. Turns out he was working for Kopassus,' said Mac. 'Did you know he wrote Operasi Boa? For the generals?'

'No,' said Atkins, stunned.

'He had his own reasons to get the document back – Blackbird had seen it in his office and copied it.'

'Shit,' said Atkins.

'Yeah, so when he got the call yesterday morning, he ran to grab that thing, but he wasn't grabbing it for you.'

'So who for?' asked Atkins.

Shrugging, Mac looked out the window. 'Someone who he thought was you. I'd love to talk with the Canadian – bet he could . . . Marty, Da Silva left a note in the Santa Cruz drop box. It was a response from you, about Tupelo or something.'

'I remember,' said Atkins, walking to the door of his safe and passing Mac a plain folder.

'All the meaningful stuff went up to Jakarta,' said Atkins, sitting. 'That was a random piece of gibberish. No one had an answer for it, so it's just been sitting there.'

Mac read the note, which told of Bill Yarrow happening upon a group of senior Indonesian military brass at the Resende; they were talking about *Tupelo* or *Deetupelo*.

'Nothing after that?' asked Mac, already losing interest.

'No, mate.'

Shaking his head, Mac made to stand but Atkins gestured for him to stay.

'I know you don't think much of the managerial guys,' said Atkins. 'But, just so you know, I've spent fourteen months filing reports on the over-capacity of Lombok, the probable existence of Operation Extermination, the fact that the East Timor militias are funded and controlled by the army and the frequent discrepancies between what the generals are claiming and what we know for a fact. It all got re-purposed and second-guessed by the Prime Minister's guys in Canberra. It was sending Sandy Beech half-crazy – we used to go drinking down in Kuta, and he was in a bad way.'

'So I'm not alone?'

'Mate, remember that I brought you in to find Blackbird and get a copy of Boa,' said Atkins. 'We were already on this, but we work for the executive of the Commonwealth, not the people of East Timor.'

'Maybe we could further the interests of the Commonwealth by not abandoning President Habibie right now,' said Mac. 'Bloke could do with some ammunition.'

'Habibie makes all the right noises, but staying tight with the military is a basic part of good relations with Indonesia. Shit, Macca, if Canberra openly sides with a president against the generals, we can kiss goodbye to good relations with our neighbour for the next decade.'

'I'm not talking about politics, I'm talking –'

'I know you're not, Macca,' said Atkins. 'But you serve politicians, and they *are* talking about politics. If the politicians have decided that the Indonesian generals making a few million with the Koreans is not something to fight over, then that's it.'

'I want the politicians to embarrass Jakarta into shutting down this bio-weapons program,' said Mac. 'So you tell me, Marty – how am I going to do that?'

'You've got those days off, Alan,' winked Atkins, in an Aussie signal that would not be recorded by the listening posts. 'I suggest you enjoy it to the best of your ability.'

The flight arrived in Singapore at nine o'clock local time and they caught a cab straight to the Cecil Street address that Leena had dug out from Rahmid Ali's sat-phone logs. The last thing Chloe had said to Mac was for him to contact George, in Singapore. Mac was going to see where it might lead.

Atkins had basically given him a green light to do what he had to do. And after Mac had handed over the remaining bag of dollars he'd kept from Maliana, Bongo was on board. However, Mac wasn't sure what he could do – if his own organisation was determined to stay sweet with Jakarta, then his options were limited.

Stopping a block away from the eight-storey building, they paid the driver and cased the main entrances and the rear tradies' access points.

'Don't like it,' said Bongo, pointing at the entrance. 'Flush him out – ask him down to the Telok Ayer park on the corner. I'll cover.'

Mac wasn't convinced with that approach. 'Let's look at the tenant board first, okay?'

Shrugging, Bongo walked with Mac to the big glass-fronted entrance, and stood guard outside. Mac found the Penang Trading Company quickly. It was a first-floor location and, watching others get into the lifts, he saw no one swiping cards or using keys.

Mac walked Bongo back the street. 'I'm going in and I'd like you along.'

'Long as you understand that when it's time for Mr Eagle, then that's what's happening,' said Bongo, referring to the large-calibre Desert Eagle handgun he carried inside his sports jacket. 'No one comes at me without getting some back, okay?'

Mac nodded and they moved into the building and got straight into an elevator, which deposited them on the first floor in a modern space with PENANG TRADING in silver letters over the reception desk.

Mac slipped alongside a man who was talking to the receptionist and looked down at the business-card stand on the counter. The second card in the stand was in the name of George Warfield, director of marketing and communications. A classic spook front title.

As the first man took a seat next to Bongo, Mac asked for George.

'May I ask your name, sir?' asked the pretty girl at the desk.

'Alan McQueen – please tell him it's urgent.'

CHAPTER 61

'Please take a seat, Mr McQueen,' said the girl, hitting a button and holding her hand to her earpiece.

Sitting down, Bongo and Mac clocked the camera on the wall and listening devices under the coffee table. After a minute the girl stood and Mac saw she was athletic, could probably look after herself.

'Follow me, please, Mr McQueen,' she said, smiling.

They walked around the corner to a door which the girl opened with a swipe card – a copy of which was in the top right-hand drawer of her desk, hopefully.

Mac recognised the doorway as a disguised metal detector and he was happy he didn't have his Heckler. The girl gestured for Mac to pass through into an office where a middle-aged Indonesian man, dressed in an English suit and tie, sat behind a desk.

'George?' said Mac, recognising the face but under a different name.

'Mr McQueen,' said George, a nine-millimetre handgun appearing over the level of the desk. 'Where is Chloe?'

'She was shot, last night,' said Mac, gulping. 'She asked me to speak with you.'

'How did you find me?' asked George, a nervous sheen of sweat appearing on his forehead.

'Found a trail from the sat phone of a man calling himself Rahmid Ali,' said Mac.

'You're a liar,' said George. 'You're working for Haryono. You Australians are all in his pocket. I warned Chloe to go nowhere near you – and I was right.'

'I didn't shoot her,' said Mac. 'And thanks to Rahmid, I found out about Operasi Boa.'

'What is it?' asked George, shifting in his seat, a man who hadn't been getting sleep.

'I'll tell you what we know, George, but I told my companion that if I wasn't out in reception in one minute, he should feel free to shoot the place up.'

George squinted into a small video monitor he had on his desk. 'The big one? That's your friend?'

'Yep – name's Bongo Morales. Want to put down that gun, have a chat with me?'

George pressed on his intercom. 'Ask Mr Morales to join us, please.'

Putting the gun in his drawer, George Warfield suddenly looked beaten. 'This has been going on too long,' he shrugged. 'If a president doesn't control the military then he's not a real president.'

'You're trying, and I'm trying too,' said Mac. 'There are people who care, but right now my government isn't one of them. The most important thing is to stop the bio-weapons spraying.'

'We figured Boa might be bio-weapons, but spraying?' asked George, confused.

'They're going to spray East Timor with a disease that behaves like SARS,' said Mac. 'It delivers a super-pneumonia to an entire population.'

'So Operasi Boa is a pneumonia?!' he said, face screwed up. 'Oh my God!'

A beeping sounded from the metal detector and then Bongo walked into the room silently, took a seat on the sofa on the back wall.

'By the way,' said Mac, 'didn't I know you before you were George Warfield?'

'I could no longer serve my country as an officer,' said George quietly. 'Not after Ambon. When Soeharto left, I wanted to serve the new presidents, be their eyes and ears –'

'Against an organisation you know very well,' said Mac, the truth dawning. 'You're Bambang Subianto – *General* Subianto.'

'Technically, yes,' he replied flatly. 'And I want you to know, Mr McQueen, that despite what people may say, not all Javanese think that the East Timorese are non-human, okay?'

'I understand, General,' said Mac.

'We can't allow the army to depopulate an entire province,' said the general. 'The president wants a ballot for independence and that should be what happens.'

'Agreed,' said Mac. 'We can count on yourselves, a couple of Aussies and, of course, the Yanks.'

'Americans?' asked the general, suspicious.

'Yeah – DIA,' said Mac. 'They're with us on this.'

'I don't understand,' said the general, shaking his head. 'DIA are involved with Operasi Boa.'

'Involved?' Mac stammered, sitting up.

'Yes,' said the general. 'Know Lee Wa Dae?'

'Sure,' said Mac. 'He's dead now.'

'I know,' said the general. 'He was working for DIA. He was an American agent.'

Mac finally overcame his stunned surprise.

'Defense Intelligence Agency was running Lee Wa Dae? As an asset, double agent, informer? What are we talking about, General?'

'Double agent is my guess,' said the general. 'And perhaps not official. Let's say there are elements of DIA who are not to be trusted.'

'You've been surveilling them?' asked Mac.

'We uncovered Boa by following Wa Dae, and that led to DIA. The Americans tried to wash his file, to accentuate his drug dealings. But as soon as anyone from the President's office made a bio-weapons connection, the pressure to drop it was immense.'

Mac suddenly realised that Atkins was more advanced than he'd given him credit for.

'I'm going to try to stop them,' said Mac suddenly. 'Can I count you in?'

'Ha!' said the general. 'It may have gone too far. We're on the verge of a coup and the world doesn't care so long as the generals win. Just keep the shipping lanes stable, keep China and Japan happy – right, McQueen?'

'What does Habibie want to do?' asked Mac.

'When the world finds out that the Indonesian Army dropped biological weapons on its civilians, Habibie and his administration are ruined – not the generals. We have to find a copy of Operasi Boa, to have something real to put in front of the world community.'

'We still have time –' started Mac, but the general lifted his hand, not hearing it.

'It begins tomorrow morning, McQueen.'

'We could ring the papers, CNN –' said Mac.

'That would sink Habibie even faster,' the general cut in.

'Is Habibie safe?' asked Mac.

'Physically, yes,' said the general. 'But his supporters in the military can't be open about it. A small group of us run an inner circle that the President can trust, but people have been assassinated, fired, smeared, demoted – you know how it works.'

'I guess Chloe was the latest?' said Mac, mind on something else.

'Yes, she was a patriot,' said the general sadly.

'She didn't have much field experience?'

'No, of course not,' sighed the general, swinging in his chair to look out the window. 'She was my secretary. She was trying to make a difference.'

'She was a lioness,' said Mac, feeling emptied.

'Thank you, McQueen, she'd laugh to hear that,' said the general.

Deciding it was now or never, Mac pushed his luck. 'General, when the time comes, would you consider dusting off the fruit salad and pulling rank?'

'When the time comes?' said Subianto, shaking his head. 'If Boa starts when the ballot result is announced, then we're talking about less than twenty-four hours. What do you want from me?'

'It might be that only Indonesians can stop an Indonesian crime,' said Mac. 'Can we rely on you if it comes down to enforcing the army's own legal code?'

'No promises, McQueen,' said the general after a pause. 'I have nine grandchildren, and I love them all.'

CHAPTER 62

Mac and Bongo stood to board their plane at Changi, both of them transfixed by BBC World running footage of the UN scrutineers in East Timor counting the independence votes. At every shot of a helicopter, Mac's gut clenched.

They sat in silence for most of the night flight into Denpasar, Mac tired and stressed and feeling like a failure. The following morning, the ballot result would herald the start of Boa and there was nothing he could do about it. As the descent started, Mac cleared his throat.

'Mate, what am I missing?'

'You may be looking at the wrong part of the puzzle,' said Bongo.

'Tell me,' said Mac, wishing there was a large packet of Percodan hiding in one of his pockets.

'You've spent all your time collecting the information, which is your training,' mused Bongo. 'But they also trained you to educe, right?'

Mac nodded: all intelligence folks at some point had to educe information – that is, coerce it from unwilling subjects.

'Sure, mate. So who do I torture? Benni or Amir?'

'Forget the Sudartos,' said Bongo. 'Benni Sudarto is just me ten years ago, right?'

'You were that pretty?'

'Sure, and better teeth,' said Bongo. 'The key to this is Haryono, right?'

'Okay,' shrugged Mac. 'What's the deal?'

'Deal is, we use some of those US dollars, and we buy some pictures.'

'Of?'

'Of Ishy Haryono, bro.'

'Doing what?' asked Mac.

'Doing what he does when he thinks no one can see,' said Bongo.

On the first drive-past of Ishy Haryono's security compound in the lush streets where the Dutch merchants once built their mansions, Bongo threw a handful of micro listening devices in front of the guard house.

Finding a shady hide two blocks away, they parked the sedan and moved to the 'Denpasar Cabling' van, climbing into the back. Plugging his earphones into the receiver box, which he held between his legs, Bongo played with two knobs, trying to get the red LED read-outs to the numbers he wanted.

Satisfied, they changed into their tradie overalls and settled in, the heat and anxiety making both of them sweat. Nervously they slugged at their water bottles as they sweltered in their Kevlar vests, both of them exhausted having not slept much during the night.

Sitting in Bongo's door pocket was a yellow manila envelope containing fourteen eight-by-five black-and-whites of Ishy Haryono in various states of loving congress with a variety of young men. Haryono may have been an evil genius, but he was also gay, and in the Javanese military community there was no room for men loving men. The Indonesian military would dump him immediately if they found out, but Haryono's own Kopassus regiment would probably execute him for making a laughing-stock of the regiment.

'That General Subianto,' said Bongo as he found the right sound/ noise levels on his receiver. 'He was damned right about the Indonesian military.'

'Yeah?'

'Oh, yeah,' said Bongo, staring out the windscreen at a boy on a bicycle. 'They can be plain embarrassing.'

'You found this from experience?' asked Mac.

'Yeah,' said Bongo, lighting a cigarette and popping a side window. 'When I first went freelance and I took this gig up in Aceh, the job was supposed to be securing the Exxon Mobil facilities, right? They wanted me to put together a hit team and go hunting GAM scalps in the jungles and villages. It was counter-terrorism, but *we* were the terrorists.'

Shaking his head, Bongo smoked and continued. 'I remember back in '96, and one of the generals had been promised a load of cluster bombs from the Americans. Shit, brother – you'd think they'd stockpile them for a rainy day, for when the country really needs them. No way! They decide to drop them on these GAM villages, brother.'

'What happened?' asked Mac, after a long silence.

'I told the Kodim commander that I hunt terrorists, not women and children.'

'And?' asked Mac.

'He realised he'd be better off letting me walk away rather than trying any John Wayne . . . Hang on,' said Bongo, putting a hand to his right ear can.

Jotting the security details, Bongo took the cans off his head and smiled. 'Ready?'

'Ready,' said Mac.

Driving the van fast, they closed on the two soldiers at the guard house. One stood out in the sun, chatting on a mobile phone; the other could be seen through the checkpoint glass, reading a magazine.

'Only one shot at this,' said Bongo, sliding the bolt home in the suppressed Heckler & Koch A4. 'Get me close enough for two head shots, then we roll.'

As the van slowed off the tarmac and onto the dirt shoulder, Bongo raised the stockless A4 and popped one shot in the first guard's forehead, and as the van pulled to a halt in front of the guard house, Bongo had the door open before the van stopped. He walked into the small office and shot the seated guard twice in the head, before racing out – throwing his rifle in the van – and dragging the first guard into the office.

Mac's heart hammered as he watched Bongo imitate the guards into the microphone, using the security passwords he'd heard over the micro devices.

The gates swung inwards as Bongo climbed back in the van, and they accelerated up the gravel driveway towards the large colonial mansion.

Driving around the back, Mac pulled to a halt in the rear courtyard, between the house and stables.

'Let's go, said Bongo, grabbing the manila envelope. 'Straight up, brother – no toilet stops.'

Grabbing his A4 and following Bongo up the back step and straight into the storage and kitchen area of the house, they ran into a middle-aged woman rolling pastries. Bongo gave her the 'zipped lips' sign and they moved through the reception area and up the wraparound stairs.

On the first-floor landing Bongo grabbed Mac's arm and they crept down the hall, following a maid into a room. Looking around the corner they found an enormous bedroom with high ceilings and four French doors opening onto a large balcony. Bongo charmed the maid very quickly and then she was rubbing her hands down her apron and shrugging as she answered him.

Vaulting down the stairs, they turned left at the bottom and found a heavyset man standing in front of them, eyes wide. As he reached for his shoulder holster, Bongo lifted the suppressed A4 and popped him in the chest and the head.

Racing outside, they came to a large swimming pool, three white recliners along one side, two of them occupied.

Walking up to one of the sunbathers – a naked young man with a NY Yankees cap – Bongo rested the barrel of the A4 on the bloke's throat.

'Where's Haryono?' said Bongo, mouth chewing on gum.

Freezing but not letting the smile go from his face, the man raised his hands slightly as Mac pointed his own rifle at the other young sunbather, who was panicking.

'Don't know,' said NY Yankee in good English.

'Start knowing, real fast. He might like to see these before they go to Kopassus command,' said Bongo, throwing the manila envelope on the man's stomach.

'Well, well,' said NY Yankee, looking at the eight-by-fives. 'Some blackmail. Just what I expected from Bongo Morales. Still entrapping politicians at the Lar? Or was it the Marriott?

'Don't worry about the questions, brother – where's Ishy?'

'Gone,' said the young man, gaining confidence. 'You enjoy your work, Bongo? Like the faggots?'

'It's only a cock, right?' said Bongo, sliding the A4 muzzle down to the man's penis.

Gulping, NY Yankee looked up at Bongo. 'Umm . . .'

Cocking the A4, Bongo pushed down. 'I mean, there's nothing special about it, right?' Nodding, Bongo drew Mac's attention to a military jacket and pants draped on the third recliner. 'You're a Kopassus captain?' said Bongo, as the other sunbather pulled a towel up under his chin.

'Maybe.'

'Might give you a new nickname – Kapten One-Ball,' said Bongo, smiling.

'You wouldn't dare,' said the captain. 'Your life would be worth nothing.'

'Where's Haryono?'

'Go to hell,' said the captain.

After a short pause, Bongo fired the A4 and the captain leapt up, wide-eyed. The shot had gone between his legs, but he still looked to check.

'He's gone to Tim-Tim, this morning,' he said quickly.

Rubbing his chin, Bongo looked at the captain's clothes. 'So he's gone to run Boa, but he leaves you here to look after things?'

'I don't know anything,' said the captain.

'I bet you know the codes for Boa, right?' insisted Bongo, A4 lowering towards the captain's penis again.

'I don't know . . .' said the captain, as a bullet from Bongo's gun pinged off the concrete poolside area with a loud bang.

'You're his second-in-command, aren't you, captain?' said Bongo. 'I bet you could call off Boa from here if you wanted?'

Feeling himself getting closer to criminal charges and ejection from ASIS, the bile came up in Mac's throat as the stand-off continued. Bongo had a calm yet unpredictable quality to him – the situation might end in a number of ways.

'I can't do that,' shrugged the captain, now openly scared.

'Can't or won't?' asked Bongo.

'Can't,' said the captain. 'We're not running it anymore.'

'So who is?' asked Mac.

'The American,' said the captain.

'Which American?' asked Mac.

'I don't know – he call himself Champion and he from US intelligence.'

CHAPTER 63

They drove into Denpasar with a number of theories but no solid plan. Only one man could have been American intelligence's inside guy on Operasi Boa, and that was Jim. Mac had seen some things with the American spook that didn't always add up, such as his insistence that he travel with Mac to Dili, the incomplete briefing on Lombok AgriCorp and the washed file on Lee Wa Dae, which concealed his true role.

Mac now had to face the American, expose him and get him to stop Boa, turn the helos around.

'Okay, so let's run it through,' said Mac as he drove and tried to perfect their arrival at DIA. 'Give me four minutes, and then ring that number, ask for Champion and say –'

'I say, "Champion, we've found another copy of Operasi Boa – the owner is threatening to send it to the *Washington Post*,"' said Bongo, looking at the phone number Haryono's captain had given them.

'So you already had this number?' asked Bongo. 'Where from?'

'Isolated it last night,' said Mac, his mind racing. 'It was the number that called Augusto Da Silva yesterday morning, right after he got the call from Atkins.'

'So whoever called Da Silva that morning also asked him to burn the Operasi Boa file?'

'I'm sure of it,' said Mac. 'I should have seen it last night – that number is an inactive satellite number and it's linked to the classic US intelligence fronts.'

'Which are?' said Bongo.

'Delaware trustee, bank in the BVI and registered company care of the Singapore branch of an international law firm, Baxter & Menzies,' said Mac, pulling into a parking space down the street from the DIA offices.

Casing the street for eyes, they slowed their breathing as they sat in the van.

'This office is a little piece of the Pentagon,' said Mac as he pulled off his cable-guy overalls. 'I don't want you storming the ramparts, doing that Filipino macho shit, okay?'

'Okay, boss,' said Bongo, as Mac called Jim on his Nokia and was invited up.

Walking into Jim's office, Mac got a friendly welcome and the offer of coffee. CNN's footage of total anarchy in East Timor blasted on the TV in Jim's office and they watched in silence. The ballot result had been announced and the reprisals had already begun.

'I'm sorry we couldn't stop Boa,' said Jim through his teeth. 'What a dog of thing!'

'I need to talk to you about that,' said Mac.

'Yeah?' asked Jim, watching the images on TV.

'Yeah, mate,' said Mac. 'You know the Indonesian military calls you D-Dua Puluh?'

'What's that?' asked Jim.

'Translated, it's D20,' said Mac, ruing the opportunity lost when the Canadian reported the generals talking about *Deetupelo*. 'It's an intelligence joke.'

Taking a black texta, Mac wrote 'XX' on the white board. 'Latin for twenty, right?'

'I guess,' said Jim.

'The Bahasa Indonesia for twenty is *dua puluh*. To Anglo ears it sounds like *Tupelo*.'

'So?'

'So, it's two crosses – a double-cross. In the Second World War, British intelligence ran double agents in Nazi-occupied Europe, and the committee running them was called the Twenty.'

'What the fuck are you talking about, McQueen?' snapped the American.

'The generals, in Dili, called you D-Dua Puluh – D20. At first I thought it meant a double agent in Dili, but half an hour ago I realised it was Haryono's double agent in Denpasar.'

'McQueen, you need some fresh air!' said Jim, coffee mug poised an inch from his lips.

'You're the inside guy for the Koreans. I just came from Haryono's 2IC.'

'Are you drunk?' said Jim.

'You heard from ASIS that I thought the Boa file was at the Resende, so you called Augusto Da Silva as fast as you could. Next thing I know, the Operasi Boa file is being burned.'

'McQueen, slow down –'

'You had him destroy the Boa file.'

'Oh really?'

'Yeah, really, Jim. DIA has been bugging Atkins' office for months – he knew it and was worried about it. You got the control codes for Cedar Rail's agents, right?'

Jim shook his head, looked away.

'Look me in the eye, Jim, and tell me you guys don't spy on us.'

'Don't Pollyanna me, McQueen,' snapped Jim. 'Why don't you look *me* in the eye and tell me how the Aussie media knew we were siphoning data out of Larkswood?'

They both stared at images of women running down a street in Maliana. Larkswood was a huge facility in Darwin that intercepted radio, telephone and satellite communications across South-East Asia – the Americans had hacked its systems and found a way to get the feed before it went through Canberra, and the firm had found out by spying on the Yanks in Jakarta.

'So what was in Boa that linked the Pentagon to the bio-weapons program?' asked Mac.

'You *are* drunk, aren't you?' said Jim.

'You whacked the Korean, Chloe, Moerpati and then Augusto – just as he was going to spill, and then, hey presto, there's an unmarked US gunboat to take us off the beach.'

'They were shadowing us all morning, McQueen,' said Jim, eyes rolling. 'You can't take a shit at the Pentagon anymore without three HR forms – that boat was SOP.'

'How did you know about the Korean money coming across into Lombok?' asked Mac, praying for Bongo's call to come through to one of Jim's sat phones so he could nail this shut. 'Come to think of it,' taunted Mac, 'how did you guys know so much about Lombok AgriCorp?'

'We're DIA – we cut our teeth in UNSCOM and the Twentieth Support Command. This is what we do, *mate*. The Korean money? We have agents at their casinos in Poi Pet – we trace that cash from source, okay?'

'You have to trace it?' said Mac. 'I thought Lee Wa Dae was your agent?'

'Not ours, McQueen,' said Jim. 'Langley once used him as a banking front and a conduit for their black funding, especially around Korea. He created the money-laundering schemes for heroin money through those banks in Macao – remember?'

Mac nodded. A bunch of North Korean military accounts were found disguised in apparently legitimate banks in Macao.

'When the CIA realised that Wa Dae was putting the North Koreans' drug money and the Agency's corporate fronts through the same banking scams, they cut him loose,' said Jim. 'So, he *was* a US intelligence asset, but not now and never DIA.'

The sat phone trilled on a table by the door. Mac smirked, waiting for Jim to pick it up and hear someone call him 'Champion'. He wanted to see Jim's reaction, the reaction of a liar.

Standing, Jim looked at the ringing sat phone and leaned out his door. 'Simon – your phone, buddy!'

Mac watched, stunned, as Simon picked up his sat phone and turned away.

'Uh-huh,' said the DIA analyst, stress in his voice. 'Um, yeah, so I think . . . can I just . . . I'll call you . . . and, yeah, so . . .'

Looking at Jim, Mac said, 'D20.'

Turning first to Mac, then to Jim, Simon's face was a study in guilt as he hung up and folded the aerial.

'Who was that?' asked Jim, furious.

'Umm, I don't know –' started the analyst.

'So why'd you answer to *Champion?*' asked Mac.

'Look, you don't know –' stuttered Simon, the yuppieish know-it-all act crumbling like a sandcastle.

'Answer the question, buddy,' said Jim, very softly. 'Why would you answer to Champion?'

Simon kicked at the carpet, face reddening.

'Why wouldn't you express surprise when a stranger tells you that another copy of Operasi Boa has turned up?' asked Mac, feeling the anger well in him.

Lurching sideways, Simon fumbled in the coat rack and came out with a black Beretta 9mm handgun, which he waved back and forth between them while backing up for the door.

'Don't try anything,' he spluttered, nervous but quite steady with the gun.

'I don't want to try anything,' said Mac. 'I came here to get you to reverse the green light on Operasi Boa. You have to stop this madness.'

'Why?'

'Because, buddy,' said Jim. 'You can't go killing civilians just to prove a concept. Is that what you're involved in, Simon, a clinical trial that got out of hand?'

'Stop!' Simon yelled at Jim. 'You never understood, man!'

'Understood what?' asked Jim, trying to keep his voice calm.

'The importance of the science! What else?!' he yelled.

'When the science is a disease falling from a chopper, believe me, buddy, I know the importance,' said Jim.

'Shit, man,' said Simon, smiling grimly. 'The Koreans have been hounded for decades because of their Ethno-Bomb research, but you two aren't scientists, you have no spirit of curiosity, no purity of –'

'Ethno?' said Mac. 'What's –'

'Look at you, Jimbo! You're just a spook, a spy! You tear everything down to the worst human motivations, but Saddam was trying to build some –'

'Saddam?!' interrupted Jim, his hands lowering. 'You little cock-sucker – it was you! You got me barred from that team in Iraq!'

'We needed a scientist, Jimbo – UNSCOM did fine without you.'

'You little –' snarled Jim as he moved at Simon, fists clenched.

A shot fired and a lump of plasterboard leapt out of the wall behind Jim.

'Don't get confused, Jimbo,' said Simon as Jim froze. 'You might be the tough guy, but I have the gun.'

The glass of the entry door caved in with an explosion of glass, and Bongo Morales emerged in his tradesman's overalls, swinging the A4 from his hip. As Mac saw the gun aimed at Jim, he realised Bongo had been prepped to go for the wrong guy.

'No, Bongo,' yelled Mac, trying to cross in front of Jim.

In the moment of hesitation, Simon turned and shot at Bongo, the first one missing, the second one hitting him in the throat. The A4 spewed bullets as Bongo keeled over and Mac dived for cover as Jim took a bullet in the thigh from the A4 jammed on full auto. Crawling under the cordite and smoke, Mac made his way into Jim's open office, gunshots from Simon following him.

Crawling to Jim's desk, Mac stood and fumbled manically at the drawers till he found a hip rig hiding beneath a bunch of files.

Wrenching the Beretta from Jim's holster, Mac turned and found Jim standing in front of him, Simon's handgun pushed into the back of his skull.

'Drop it, McQueen,' said Simon.

The safe door swung shut, plunging the three of them into darkness. Around Mac, Jim and Bongo, shelves reached to the ceiling, packed with American files, photo satchels and state secrets.

'Reckon we've got three or four hours of oxygen in here before it gets grim,' said Jim, his teeth chattering from the shock of his bullet wound.

'Got a lighter?' asked Bongo, still holding the bleeding graze on the side of his neck. 'Left mine in the van.'

Jim pulled a lighter from his chinos and lit it. Standing, Mac looked around the tiny room, hoping for an air vent or trapdoor in the ceiling that they could use to attract attention. The ceiling of the safe was sealed but Mac noticed a red marker pen attached by string to the shelving. Grabbing a piece of paper from a file, he wrote *Help, we're in here* on it and slipped it under the door.

The lighter grew too hot for Jim's hand and they went back into darkness, Mac and Bongo tearing up Jim's chinos to put a bandage on his leg.

'So,' said Mac, as Bongo tied off the light tourniquet above Jim's wound, 'is someone going to tell me what that fruitcake was on about?'

'What part?' asked Jim.

'Did Simon say Haryono's program was an "Ethno-Bomb"? What is that?'

'Shit,' said Jim, as he moved into a better position.

'Well?' asked Mac in the darkness.

'Okay,' sighed Jim, reluctant. 'But I *was* going to tell you, okay?'

'Okay, Jim – tell.'

'The Ethno-Bomb was probably conceived by the Israelis after the Six-Day War, back in the late sixties,' said Jim. 'The IDF wanted an "Ultimate Contingency" – that is, if the Arab states finally got organised and attacked Israel simultaneously, what was the contingency for being overrun?'

'There was an answer to that?' asked Mac.

'The ultimate contingency is that you destroy yourself to beat your attackers – you burn down your town on top of them. The enemy dies but the price of victory is ashes in your own mouth.'

'So, the Ethno-Bomb?'

'Well, in those days the ultra-right wing of the Israeli military was known as the Haganah. Heard of them?'

'They were the old tough guys from the forties, weren't they?' asked Mac. 'Assassinations and bombings against the Arabs?'

'That's them. Known to each other as "the Guild". They were the hard old Russian and Polish Jews who had no time for the intellectual ideas of the German and French settlers. The Haganah was formally disbanded when the IDF was formed, in '48 or '49.'

'So the Guild was still around in the late sixties?'

'Small but influential, and they instigated a crazy project where an overrun Israel could trigger bio-weapons in its cities. This theoretical device would kill Arabs but not Jews.'

'You having a lend?' asked Mac.

'They were nervous times in Israel, paranoia was rife and the ultra-right found the means to give it a shot.'

'And?' asked Mac.

'The project went nowhere – officially at least. The government of the day wouldn't buy into it and it's rumoured the results were embarrassing. Apparently, Arabs and Jews have similar genetics – the Ethno-Bomb would have killed the lot of them.'

'Enter Lee Wa Dae,' said Mac.

'Well, enter North Korea in the late 1980s,' said Jim. 'Kim Il Sung was ailing, his son Kim Jong Il was a lunatic with an obsession about magic shows, and a bunch of shady scientists – one of them from the Guild's original project – talked Little Kim into reviving the Ethno-Bomb.'

'Who was this one aimed at?' asked Mac.

'Easy. Which race would the Kim family annihilate if you gave them a button to push?'

'The Japs, of course,' said Mac. 'So what happened to that Ethno-Bomb?'

'Clinton happened. You remember that warming period, five years ago, when Daddy Kim was dying and Jimmy Carter got the North Koreans to shut down the spent-fuel extraction and the uranium enrichment, in exchange for the United States trading with them again?'

'Yeah,' said Mac.

'Well the Commies were required to shut down their bio-weapons research at the same time.'

'But they didn't?' asked Mac.

'Technically they did. The bio-weapons projects left North Korea, but an enterprising Korean found a country willing to host the Ethno-Bomb program, keep it going, for a nice fee, paid for by heroin money.'

'You're kidding,' said Mac.

'No, McQueen – the person was Lee Wa Dae, and in Indonesia he found a man who ran spurious research projects to line his own pockets.'

'Ishy Haryono,' said Mac, painful images from Lombok AgriCorp filling his mind. 'Why Timor?' he croaked.

'It's isolated, it's poor, it's run like a medieval fiefdom,' said Jim. 'And the Western media doesn't give a shit about it. It's the way it seems to go in South-East Asia – you wouldn't believe some of the wacko shit happening in northern Burma.'

'So what's the ethnic divide in –'

Mac trailed off, suddenly recalling that the native Timorese – the Maubere – were Melanesian, unlike the Malay ethnicity of the Javanese.

'Shit,' he mumbled. 'Operasi Boa wipes out the Melanesians, but not the rest?'

'Seems to be what they're working on,' said Jim. 'Europeans and Asians get a bad cold from this weaponised SARS, but the Melanesians have no defence. They last two days, tops.'

CHAPTER 64

It was some time before the door to the safe swung back, revealing Tommy pointing a gun into the airless room.

'The fuck?' muttered the burly DIA analyst, before shoving the gun into his waistband and moving to aid Jim.

'Day off?' asked Mac, forearm shielding his eyes from the glare.

'Dentist,' said Tommy, helping Jim to his feet.

They recounted the events to Tommy as the US military doctor dressed Jim's wound. The bullet had torn a hole but the slug hadn't stayed in the flesh. Bongo's wound was more like a nick, and while the doctor strapped bandages around his thick neck, Jim hit the phones.

'You leading a charge?' asked Mac.

'This has gone on long enough,' said Jim, rustling a key chain and opening a steel gun cabinet against the wall. 'I like letting a target run as much as anyone, but DIA's involvement in this thing has become plain embarrassing.'

Joining Jim at the gun cabinet, Mac made his case. 'I want to be part of it, Jim,' he said. 'I think I've earned it.'

'You think I'd leave you behind, McQueen?' said Jim, passing a Kevlar vest. 'We can't do this with American soldiers, so you're up.'

***

The unmarked Cessna Citation jet reduced throttle as it approached the island of Alor. Inside, Mac and Jim faced one another while Bongo and Tommy were belted into the facing seats on the other side of the small cabin.

'Yes, sir, that's affirmative,' said Jim into his sat phone. 'No direct actions, sir, you have my word.'

Hanging up, Jim grimaced. 'Tommy and I are tasked for retrieval of Simon – nothing else. We can only carry firearms for self-defence.'

'That's about as useful as a bicycle pump in a hen-house,' said Mac. 'Any word on Simon?'

'The guys at Halim say an army Huey took off from Denpasar just after 1500 hours, bound for East Timor. They picked up some radio chatter – an American male talking to an Indonesian. I'm assuming we're following Simon to Neptune, although it's hard to tell – he's dumped his sat phone, which had a beacon in it.'

'Might get there at the same time if he's humping it in a Huey,' said Tommy, looking up from the laptop he'd taken from the DIA office. Every Pentagon-issued computer backed up to a central hard drive and Tommy was reviewing Simon's shadow computer via a satellite broadband link with the Department of Defense in Washington DC.

'What have we got, buddy?' asked Jim, growing more nervous the closer they got to East Timor.

'I'm searching his sent emails for clues,' said Tommy. 'Any ideas for a word search? I'm betting if there's any correspondence with Lombok or Wa Dae, he's done it in a rush, done it from a DIA email server, but embedded it in a legitimate email. There'll be a type of email that has an innocuous first paragraph, followed by the real message.'

'What have you tried?' asked Jim.

'Mum, birthday, darling, golf, fishing, skiing, shares, mortgage – all the basics . . .'

'What about you, McQueen?' said Bongo, who'd filled his own canvas bag of weapons at the DIA offices. 'You get those special forces of yours to pitch in?'

'Probably not,' said Mac, thinking of the political considerations that meant they had to rush the Blackbird snatch and then disappear from Bobonaro. 'But I can try.'

Unbuckling and moving forward in the cabin, Mac powered up the Harris radio that was built into US military aircraft. Shielding the settings from his comrades, he found a frequency on the UHF band, picked up the chunky handset and keyed the mic.

'Six-Three, 63 – this is Albion, copy?'

Waiting, Mac could envisage Robbo's crew trying to stealth up to a militia or a Kopassus troop, and getting his annoying message.

'Six-Three, 63 – this is Albion, are you copying, over?'

A faint sound of static hissed from the earpiece and Mac was about to contact the navy's Shoal Bay comms centre in Darwin when a familiar Aussie voice crackled into Mac's ear.

'Albion, Albion this is 63 – please confirm ID, over.'

The cheeky bastard, thought Mac. 'Six-Three – bullriders from Narrabri wear skirts, confirm, over.'

'ID confirmed. And you'll keep, Albion,' growled Robbo. 'You'll fucking keep.'

'Six-Three, we might need fire support at Neptune, can do?'

'Negative, Albion – currently Mars-bound and covert, over.'

'Understand, 63 – good luck, over.'

Sitting back in his seat, Mac buckled up as they swooped onto the tiny island that lay between Dili and Flores. As they depowered on the plantation runway, Mac looked out his window and saw an unmarked Black Hawk being refuelled beside a red Quonset building.

The Citation's co-pilot unlatched the door and they all unbuckled.

'What about MIT10?' said Jim suddenly.

'Shit, that's right,' said Tommy, fingers flashing on the keyboard. 'He had that golf shirt with the logo –'

'MIT10?' asked Mac.

'Yeah,' said Tommy. 'It's an MIT alumni association.'

'For people who can't get over how smart they are,' said Jim.

'Eureka! Nice work, boss,' said Tommy, turning the laptop and letting Jim see.

'Fuck me,' muttered Jim as the Citation's foldout stairs hit the tarmac. 'He was setting this up under our noses. Look at this one – sent four days ago.'

'Probably after you briefed me,' said Mac. 'Anything we can use?'

'Oh, yeah,' said Jim, swapping a look with Tommy. 'If I'm not mistaken, we have the bank numbers and the agreements here.'

Tapping through the MIT10 emails, Jim's face lightened.

'Simon is running a trust account containing forty million US dollars,' said Jim, thoughtful. 'From the wording of the emails, I'd say Haryono can see it but Simon controls it – Simon's been holding it out there as bait, as a carrot to get the project finished.'

'If we can access it, we could have some fun,' said Mac.

'We'd need somewhere to push it,' said Tommy.

'Here's the sick part, guys,' said Jim, pointing at the screen. 'Haryono is getting a bonus of ten million to spray the SARS over the populated areas of Bobonaro, Oecussi, Ainaro and Cova Lima, and then he gets a bonus of thirty million if the UN declares at least ninety per cent of the Maubere population of those regencies dead within three days of the spraying.'

'Shit,' said Bongo, disgusted.

'I've got an idea,' said Mac, trying to stay calm. 'We have to get Haryono and Kopassus to shut this down – we need the Indonesians to do this themselves, to turn on Simon and the Koreans.'

'By using the money?' asked Bongo, smiling.

'You're reading me, brother,' said Mac.

'Let's hear it,' said Jim.

'Okay,' said Mac, getting it straight in his own mind. 'But first, Bongo has to call his mate Joao and hope he has his sat phone switched on.'

Lugging the gun bags across the tarmac, the four of them clambered into the Black Hawk as the humidity and fumes swirled around them.

'Neptune's hot,' said Jim to Mac and Bongo, taking his seat and yelling over the engines. 'But it's where we'll find Haryono – we'll deplane in the adjacent valley, hike back over. Copy?'

Mac and Bongo nodded.

'Last chance for anyone to get off,' said Jim as the loadmaster slid home the side door and the revs came up. 'All I can offer is a damaged career and a lifelong feud with Kopassus. But it might be fun.'

'Never much liked Indonesia anyhow,' said Bongo, staring out of his wraparound sunnies.

Smiling and giving thumbs-up, Mac resigned himself to a course of action that owed more to the heart than the mind. He crossed himself briefly, watched Bongo do the same, and then the Hawk was climbing into the clear skies above Alor and their hands were reaching into the gun bags.

The pillars of smoke were flattened over the pale-green hills of East Timor as they chugged into the valley south of Neptune airfield. It looked as though half the province was on fire. Taking turns with Jim's field-glasses, they saw Indonesian Huey helicopters in the distance and small spotter planes, but no sign of the Singapore-registered Black Hawks carrying spray booms on their undercarriage.

'Too much breeze?' shouted Mac, handing the binos to Jim. 'It'll be sundown in a couple of hours – we may have a chance to stop this tonight.'

The sat phone rang and Jim held it to his ear, covering the other ear with his cupped hand.

'Yep?' said Jim, and then he shook a finger at Tommy, who pulled the laptop from his backpack and opened it.

'Okay,' yelled Jim into the phone. 'I'll put him on.'

Handing the sat phone to Tommy, who started typing as he hooked it under his chin, Jim smiled at Mac.

'Thank Christ for the privacy-invading capacity of the US intelligence community,' he said.

'What have we got?' yelled Mac.

'NSA code-breakers have run the account numbers and name on Simon's trust account at the Koryo Bank, and they've got us in. We now control the money.'

Bongo waited until Tommy had finished with the sat phone, then tried Joao again.

'No luck,' he said, shrugging at Mac.

'Try again,' said Mac, as the helo pushed on.

Mac wasn't entirely sure how they were going to stop Operasi Boa. There were only four of them, they would be on foot, in an army base and surrounded by Kopassus special forces. They had to have some-thing up the sleeve, and given that the entire Lombok-Korean-Simon consortium seemed to be about money, he wanted to lever the situation with the moolah.

'We got company!' said Jim, eyes now glued to the field-glasses. 'F-16s, at our nine o'clock.'

Squinting out the window in the port-side door, Mac saw two blue-grey jet fighters streaking low across the sky, about fifteen kilometres north.

'They interested?' asked Mac.

Crouching forward, Jim leaned into the cockpit and had a shouted conversation with the pilot before pushing back to sit beside Mac.

'We just got a "friend or foe" challenge,' said Jim, bringing the glasses back to his face and peering out the window. 'Might be time to touch down.'

The co-pilot's visored face appeared and Jim gave thumbs-up.

'Shit,' said Jim, as the helo descended.

'Better down there than up here,' shouted Bongo, zipping his gun bag and checking his M4 for load and safety.

The Black Hawk dropped to the tree line as the F-16s banked and turned like a couple of blue sharks.

As the Hawk eased to a clearing in the jungle, the four of them leapt to the forest floor and ran for cover. As fast as it had descended the helo was back in the air, climbing and banking away.

'Let's get out of here,' said Jim, and Bongo moved to point, leading the group down to a small river.

A moment later the whooshing scream of two fighter jets roared over them, driving the birds and monkeys crazy.

Mac clung to a rock face, now sweating in the jungle humidity, and looked skywards as the roar faded.

'The rules of travelling with me in the jungle,' said Bongo, addressing the group but scanning the environment. 'Don't speak, don't smoke, obey instructions, okay? It might be the difference between living and dying.'

Without waiting for the reply, Bongo hefted his gun bag's hand-grips over both shoulders and swung the M4's strap over his neck.

'I'll walk point, then comes Jim and then Tommy,' said Bongo. 'McQueen, you can sweep, okay?'

'Okay,' said Jim, who Mac had noticed was limping. 'But let's get it straight, for when we get to Neptune.'

'Sure,' said Bongo, looking around.

'The priority is Simon – we have to snatch him, and I'd rather have him alive.'

'This is no time for Pentagon politics,' said Bongo, chewing gum.

'Not politics, buddy,' said Jim, lowering his voice. 'If we can root out Simon, debrief him somewhere, maybe we shut down an entire network.'

'Mate, the priority has to be Boa,' said Mac. 'Let's stop the spraying, then worry about the network – I agree with Bongo, this isn't the time for damage control at the Pentagon.'

'I have to insist,' said Jim. 'Sorry guys, but this operation is DIA.'

'Actually,' said Bongo, his voice a monotone, 'when I take a bunch of white boys through the jungle, it's a Bongo operation.'

'Okay,' said Jim. 'But I –'

'And by the way, I'm employed by McQueen. And this dude, Simon, he shot me, right? So he comes into the open, he'll probably have to drop.'

'Okay, Bongo,' said Jim, carefully. 'It's just that Simon seems to be running Operasi Boa, and if we shoot him, and the money strategy doesn't work, how do we call it off?'

'Let's hope the Simon dude doesn't want to shoot it out,' said Bongo, as he turned to go. ''Cos that won't work for anyone, right?'

It was 7.12 pm, just after dusk, when they reached the ridge that looked over the airfield renamed Neptune. Floodlights illuminated the admin section at the east end of the dusty lime runway, and an armada of unmarked helos with large spray booms underneath were lined up in front of the hangars. Some of the soldiers moving towards a long wooden building wore the red beret of Kopassus – Indonesian special forces. But most did not.

'Two men on the gate,' said Bongo. 'And there's a regiment stationed here and judging by their flag . . .' Taking Jim's field-glasses, Bongo took another look at the dark flags on the parade-ground pole. 'Two regiments in the barracks,' said Bongo, a smile on his face. 'Kopassus and the 1635.'

'Does that work for us?' asked Jim, wanting his binos back.

'Well, from what McQueen tells me, Kopassus is running Operasi Boa, which is a bad thing.'

'And the 1635?' asked Jim.

'That could be good,' said Bongo, handing back the field-glasses. 'They're the local regiment.'

'Where does Haryono stay?' asked Jim.

'See that main administration building?' asked Mac. 'The officers' quarters sit right behind it, with their own guard. Simon will be there, and so will Amir Sudarto – maybe Benni too.'

The sat phone trilled and Jim picked up. 'For you, Bongo,' he said, handing it over.

'Yep?' said Bongo, and then clicked his fingers at Tommy, who opened the laptop and started typing as Bongo mumbled in his ear.

'You thought there'd be some mercenaries?' said Jim to Mac.

'Those helos belong to a mob called Shareholder Services, Pik Berger's crew,' said Mac. 'They're very pro – Saffas and Aussies, mostly. But they're also contractors, so with any luck they won't fight.'

Mac and Jim swapped a look and then hammered out a plan: infiltrate the Neptune camp, hold Simon and Haryono, and coerce them to shut down the operation.

Signing off on the phone call, Bongo picked up the conversation. 'We'll need Haryono as a hostage. No offence, but an American won't count for Kopassus.'

'And once we have him, we need to make him angry with Simon,' said Mac.

'Understood,' said Jim.

'I think we should go now,' said Bongo, rifling in his gun bag.

'Why?' asked Jim.

'Smell that?' said Bongo. 'Chow time – we know exactly where they are for the next thirty minutes.'

'Still only four of us,' said Jim, unsure.

'Sure,' said Bongo, screwing a suppressor onto the Beretta 9mm. 'Grab a snake by the head, and you control the snake.'

'Grab the head wrong, and you die,' said Tommy.

'So let's grab it right,' said Bongo, slamming a magazine into the grip of the Beretta.

Mac gasped for breath as he dived into the long grass abutting the security fence behind the officers' quarters and mess. Jim followed with a thump, his injured leg starting to weaken.

'What was that shit about a snake?' breathed Jim, as they looked through the grass at a glowing set of windows along the side of the quarters.

'Just that if we grab Haryono then we control the Kopassus element,' said Mac, seeing a guard at the foot of the main stairs to the officers' building. 'The Kopassus guys will stand off if their major-general is in our hands. Then we have a chance to turn Haryono against the treacherous Anglo.'

'So what about this 1635 Regiment?' said Jim, not convinced.

'Bongo was probably thinking that a regiment comprised of young East Timorese men might rebel if they know what's in those spray tanks.'

'You agree?' asked Jim.

'They have a history of mutiny and desertion,' said Mac, getting the wire-cutters onto the first ring of the fence and snipping. 'East Timor and Java might as well be different planets . . . Time?' he asked, as he peeled back the small door he'd made in the cyclone fencing.

'Nineteen fifty,' whispered Jim, tensing.

'Let's go,' said Mac.

Slipping through the hole, Mac grabbed his suppressed Beretta and ran with Jim for the side of the officers' building, both of them lying flat against it while the guard lit a cigarette.

'How's the leg?' asked Mac.

'I'll live,' said the American.

'Through the wooden walls they heard the sound of chairs being scraped back too fast, and raised voices of panic – Bongo and Tommy were in the officers' mess, via the side entrance. Running fast but silently along the side of the building, Mac came around the corner to the main entrance, his handgun in a cup-and-saucer grip.

The soldier reacted quickly and went for his rifle but Mac shot him in the temple, the slide-action of the Beretta making more noise than the small spitting sound of the bullet.

Joining Mac, Jim helped drag the young man's body around the side of the building.

The chow time was dragging on, and although Mac could see the guards at the front gate through the buildings, the alarm had not gone up.

Pushing into the building's entrance, they closed the doors silently behind them and moved down a dimly lit corridor. They looked for the portico and pushed through the mahogany swinging doors into a large and well-appointed mess. In front of them about fifteen men sat at dining tables, hands above their heads, looking at Bongo and Tommy.

Bongo stood beside Ishy Haryono, the suppressed Beretta against the major-general's ear.

'Okay, okay,' said Haryono. 'What you want, Morales? Money? Drug?'

'Where's the American?' said Bongo.

Spreading out to cover the officers with Jim, Mac looked into Amir Sudarto's face, a white strap of plaster across his broken nose. The big Indonesian made a throat-slitting gesture as Mac levelled his gun.

'Just bring the American,' said Bongo.

Shrugging, Haryono tried to stall, and Bongo aimed his gun past the major-general's head, shooting the next officer in the shoulder. Groaning, the officer fell to the floor.

'The American, Ishy,' said Bongo, very calm. 'Pretty young white boy – can't miss him.'

'He around,' said Haryono, trying to look at Bongo without turning his head.

Looking at Mac, Bongo lifted his eyebrows. Darting out of the mess, Mac headed back down the corridor, found the stairwell he'd passed and ascended the worn steps as quietly as he could.

The wood creaked as he carefully came around the first landing, and he continued to the next floor.

There were three doors off the large landing and Mac moved

for the first. As he did, he noticed light creeping from under the middle one.

Stealthing to the door, his heart banging in his temples, he slowly pushed it open, hoping the hinges were oiled. The door swung back as Mac brought up his Beretta, trying to stay behind the doorjamb as he did. There was a desk at the other end of the room and a white man sitting behind it, a phone to his ear.

The man looked up and Mac looked into Simon's wide eyes as he tried to make the ground to the desk. Simon's hand went for a handgun on the blotter, and as Mac brought the unwieldy suppressed handgun up, Simon shot at him twice. Diving to his right, Mac crashed into a chair and sent a hat rack flying. Aiming for the desk, Mac waited for Simon to emerge and finish him off but suddenly his assailant was running across the room and through a side door.

Picking himself up, Mac moved carefully to the side door, panting and scared but uninjured from the fire-fight.

'Simon!' said Mac at the doorway, from his hide around the corner. 'Time to end this, okay?'

'It ends when I say so, McQueen,' screamed Simon, his superior accent in no way diminished by his anger. 'Those choppers are taking off tomorrow morning and there's not a damn thing you can do about it.'

'I'm not going to let you do it, Simon,' said Mac, trying to control his ragged breathing. He just wanted Simon sitting in front of Haryono.

'What do you care?' taunted the American. 'I mean, really?!'

'Care?' asked Mac.

'I mean, come on – a bunch of jungle-bunnies? Why would you care if a few thousand of them died from a bad pneumonia? Every year millions die in the Third World from malaria and yellow fever.'

'Come out and I'll explain it,' said Mac, getting his breath back.

'Oh, I'm coming out, my friend,' came Simon's voice, getting closer to the door. 'But you can't shoot, okay?'

'I'm not going to shoot, Simon,' said Mac, meaning it. 'You were the only one shooting, mate.'

'Okay, McQueen, I'm coming out, so go easy, okay?'

Pulse pounding in his temple, Mac stood back from the doorjamb and aimed his gun.

Simon moved out of the doorway, holding a woman by a choker chain.

'Shit!' said Mac, immediately lowering his gun.

'My sentiments exactly,' said Simon, as Jessica Yarrow tried to move her lips beneath the grey duct tape.

———

CHAPTER 65

Mac stumbled forward into the officers' mess as Simon shoved him in the back. Faces turned as Mac stood still in front of the dining tables, embarrassed to be disarmed and to be dragging Jessica into this situation.

Bongo quickly grabbed Haryono by the hair and shoved his gun into the major-general's neck, but Simon kept his nerve.

'I don't think so, Morales,' said the American. 'Pretty white girl versus an ugly old Javanese – do the math.'

Looking first to Jim and getting no backup, Bongo stared at Mac, who averted his eyes and stared at the carpet.

'Fuck,' muttered Bongo, allowing the Kopassus officers to rush him and take the weapon from his hands as Tommy and Jim were roughly disarmed. Amir Sudarto stood and issued orders to his men, who raced out of the mess. Through the windows, Mac could see the soldiers being roused from chow to search the base for more interlopers.

'Don't harm them,' said Simon, waving his gun towards a group of chairs. 'I have an idea.'

As the officers searched the captives and pushed them towards the chairs, Amir Sudarto walked back to Mac and eye-balled him.

'G'day, Amir,' said Mac. 'Nasty scratch you got there.'

Sudarto's nostrils flared and his dark eyes bore into Mac's. 'You and me, McQueen – we got the unfinished business, yeah?'

'Sure, Amy,' said Mac as Sudarto leaned in. 'Guess we're up for round three, right?'

'So you can count?' said Sudarto.

'Sure,' said Mac, poised for an attack. 'But don't let fear hold you back.'

His eyes turning to saucers, Sudarto threw a fast left elbow at Mac's jaw, dropping him on the floor. Slightly dazed, Mac pushed himself onto his elbows, waiting for his vision to clear.

'That's enough, lieutenant,' said Simon. 'Let's think about how we can use them?'

Sitting with Bongo, Jim and Tommy in the middle of the mess, surrounded by armed Kopassus officers, Mac watched Haryono and Sudarto storm out of the mess and he tried to think of options. Across the room, Jessica's big blue eyes stared at Mac, pleading. She looked scared but not injured.

'This what Mom and Dad thought you'd be doing when you got accepted for a master's at MIT?' said Jim, his cold rage aimed at Simon.

'They wouldn't understand,' said Simon, his tone slightly dream-like. 'There are things I never knew about the world until I knew them.'

'Think that makes you smart?' snarled Jim, who had a dribble of blood running down his lip from an altercation with a Kopassus officer.

'Not smart, Jimbo – just a greater understanding.'

'Of what?' asked Mac. 'You make an Ethno-Bomb to prove you can?'

'Oppenheimer did it,' snapped Simon, jerking the choker chain around Jessica's throat. 'Apollo was the same thing – we went to the Moon, McQueen! What the fuck was that about?'

'It wasn't about weaponising a disease that kills one race,' said Mac. 'There's already enough diseases that kill poor brown people – we don't need to create weapons out of them.'

Mac could sense Bongo bristling beside him. Bongo Morales was a shoot-out guy and he'd be annoyed that Jim and Mac didn't want to go with him.

'Forget the weapons side of it,' said Simon. 'Think of the research, think of the applications!'

'Applications?' said Jim.

'Can you imagine how fast we could evolve ourselves if we exploited the secrets of which races were the strongest, which ones had the genes to become super-beings?' said Simon, his face flushed with excitement.

'No offence, Simon,' said Mac, 'but why is it always dudes like you who have the super-race fantasies?'

The bullet sailed past his face and Mac ducked instinctively.

'Don't do it, Simon,' Mac begged. 'Just get on the phone and call it off, okay?'

'Jesus,' said Simon, rueful. 'It was all going fine, we were going to launch this program and the UN were going to pay us for it.'

'Clever guy,' said Mac.

'But you,' said Simon, pointing at Mac, 'the boy scout from Australia – you found that camp up in Memo, and you had no idea what you'd stumbled on, did you?'

'Looked like a refugee camp that had got out of hand,' shrugged Mac. 'Turned into a death camp.'

'Yeah, but they thought they knew,' he said, indicating Jim and Tommy. 'And suddenly, these idiots who were supposed to be monitoring Lombok are now sending an Aussie in there to take photos and have a look? I was thinking, "Holy shit! A bunch of morons from intel are going to unravel this whole thing?"'

The room buzzed as Haryono and Sudarto returned.

'Base is secure – it's just them,' said the major-general.

'So we're clear for Boa?' asked Simon.

'Clear,' said Haryono.

'Just a pity you're not getting the bonus, eh Ishy?' said Bongo, an island of calm in an adrenaline-charged room. 'Would have been nice – buy that private jet, get you to Surfers Paradise faster, yeah?'

Simon threw Jessica to the floor and moved at Bongo, threatening him with the gun. 'Shut up, moron.'

'Wait,' said Haryono, advancing on Bongo. 'Last thing I heard about you, Morales, you were flying a Mirage jet from Manila to Colombo.'

'A 737, actually,' said Bongo.

'Still a cheeky little monkey, I see,' said Haryono, pulling up a chair to face Bongo. 'What you know about a bonus?'

'He's lying –' said Simon, but stopping at Haryono's raised hand.

'I want to hear this from the legendary Bongo Morales – might be the last lie he ever tells,' said Haryono, prompting laughter from the Kopassus officers.

'Simple, Ishy,' said Bongo. 'Simon's spent your bonus.'

Staring at Bongo, Haryono's eyes went through several emotional seasons before arriving back at the indulgent uncle.

'Spent it?' said Haryono, very slow.

'The whole forty mill,' said Bongo, like ice ran in his veins.

Mac gulped at his dry throat, wondering where Bongo got the balls. Swapping a look with Jim, he saw the American beside himself with fear; if there was one thing guaranteed to incite unpredictable acts of violence, it was stealing money from a Javanese soldier.

'He's messing with us –' Simon started again, but this time a burly Kopassus second lieutenant moved in closer from the American's three o'clock, silencing him immediately.

'Tell me,' said Haryono, smiling at Bongo with big white teeth.

'Got a laptop?' asked Bongo.

'I think so,' said Haryono, looking at Amir Sudarto and getting a nod.

'See that bag over there,' nodded Bongo at the backpack Jim had hauled through the jungle. 'There's a sat phone in there, it lets you connect with the internet, lets you see the trust account at the Koryo.'

'Trust account? How he know that?' said Haryono, turning on Simon like a shark. 'How he know it Koryo?!'

'He's lying – we have bigger things –' stammered Simon, stopping now as he realised the second lieutenant had a gun trained on him.

Snapping a command in Bahasa Indonesia, Haryono looked Bongo in the eye as the bag was brought to him and an officer retrieved a laptop.

Opening the laptop and connecting the data cable to the sat phone, Bongo remained calm while Mac's heart did backflips – Haryono was waiting to confirm that Bongo was making a fool of him, at which point it was likely he'd personally execute the Filipino.

'The Koryo website,' said Bongo, turning the laptop for Haryono. 'Put in your numbers and let's see.'

Tapping at the keyboard, Haryono looked up momentarily with an expression which suggested Bongo was already dead. Then the laptop buzzed, there was a change of light reflected on Haryono's face, and his eyes refocused.

Jessica writhed on the floor, hands busy behind her back, looking Mac in the eye. Mac wanted to tell her to stay down, stay tied up, but he didn't dare speak.

Suddenly, Haryono's hands flew away from the computer as if it was a leper and he erupted in a blast of Bahasa Indonesia. The second lieutenant pushed his gun into Simon's ear, and confiscated the American's handgun as Haryono stood in front of him.

'We agreed, Mr Simon,' said Haryono, putting out his hand for a SIG Sauer 9mm. 'We bring Operasi Boa to a successful conclusion, and there is a bonus of forty million dollars US.'

'It's a trick,' said Simon, wide-eyed. 'Bongo's a con man, you know who he –'

'Do not tell me what I know,' said Haryono. 'Tell me what I don't know, like where is my forty million dollars?'

'It's there!' screamed Simon, pointing at the laptop. 'It was there this morning – I checked because the first bonus was going to be paid tomorrow.'

'Look for yourself,' gestured Haryono.

Taking the laptop from Bongo, Simon sat and scrolled up and down frenetically, his face dropping as his eyes confirmed Haryono's anger.

'I can't . . . it's not possible,' he said, then looked at Bongo. 'What did you do with it?' he yelled, going for Bongo's throat.

Slapping Simon to the floor, Bongo looked at Haryono and shrugged.

Waving the handgun, Haryono fixed Bongo with a homicidal stare. 'So, Morales – what do you know about this problem?'

'Not much, Ishy,' said Bongo, smoother than honey pouring out of a jar. 'Just got a call from Joao about an hour ago.'

'Joao?' said Haryono, his face darkening.

'Yeah, he'd just been told about a very large, very recent deposit in the bank,' said Bongo. 'He thought I might see the funny side of it.'

'Joao?!' yelled Simon. 'Who the fuck is *Joao*?!'

'Silence!' barked Amir Sudarto, training his gun on the American scientist.

The room fell quiet, except for the sounds of Simon whimpering on the carpet. Haryono stood over him and looked at his SIG. 'It's one thing for a man to get greedy, steal something for himself, for his family,' said Haryono.

'You can't –' said Simon.

'But when a man steals from me and then adds the insult, then it is time for the hard hand, right?' said Haryono, almost whispering.

'He did it!' cried Simon, pointing at Bongo.

'How would Bongo get bank codes for the North Korean Department of Defense bank?' asked Haryono, pointing the SIG at Simon. 'Unless you gave them to him? Bongo pretends to be homosexual at the Lar, he drug passenger in first class and then search their bags. Bongo not the computer thief, Mr Simon. That you.'

'It's them,' spluttered Simon, sweeping his arm at Mac, Tommy and Jim. 'They're spies, they set this up!'

'Really?' asked Haryono.

'Yes – they traced Lee Wa Dae through the Koryo Bank.'

'You know how I know you the liar?' asked Haryono, his face impassive.

'No, I –'

'Look at where the money gone!'

'To the Sentosa Pacific Bank in Singapore,' said Simon, having seen the transfer. 'It's one of McQueen's accounts!'

'Really?' asked Haryono. 'So the spies steal forty million dollars from me, and then they travel all the way here, into army compound in East Timor – four against two hundred – to say hello to me?'

'Well . . .' said Simon.

'But it the insult,' said Haryono, doing a big Javanese shrug. 'You had to send my money to these people?'

'What people?' asked Simon, confused.

'Look at the account,' instructed Haryono, grabbing Simon by the hair and forcing his face at the screen.

'It's . . . I . . . I don't know any Santa Cruz Trust,' said Simon, looking at the details on the screen, tears streaming down his face. 'What is –'

'Santa Cruz Trust Number Three,' snarled Haryono, cocking the SIG with his thumb. 'Think – what communist organisation in Tim-Tim would name their bank accounts after the Santa Cruz cemetery?'

Simon wiped his tears and looked up at Haryono. 'Look, Ish, I –'

'Which organisation?!' screamed Haryono.

'Falinitil?' asked Simon quietly.

'Correct,' said Haryono, shooting the American in the face. 'And do not call me Ish.'

CHAPTER 66

The pre-dawn birdsong started and Mac felt Jessica snoring on his chest. The first grey light snuck in through the barred window at the top of the cell wall, illuminating Bongo, who was pacing beside the door, mumbling.

'What's up?' whispered Mac, as Bongo raised his hand for silence.

Bongo's mumbled conversations had started up each time they'd heard footfalls in the stockade outside their cell door. The base stockade was staffed by soldiers of the 1635 Regiment, and Bongo was conversing with them in Tetum, the native dialect of East Timor.

'He says one of the white people will be found in a helicopter, after the spraying,' said Bongo. 'The others will be found in the rubble of the base – they're dynamiting the whole place.'

Their first plan had been to turn Haryono against Simon, which had worked too well. Simon was dead, and the rest of them – with Jessica along for the ride – now looked like being the fall guys for Operasi Boa. The Indonesian Army would find their bodies, connect them with the SARS deaths and the helicopters, and the story would hit the newspapers. Mac already knew what part he'd play – he was connected with Shareholder Services under his Don Jeffries alias, and he had no doubt he'd be 'found' in a downed helo belonging to Pik Berger's company, filled with the SARS bio-weapon. He'd be just another greedy Aussie mercenary, and the papers would love it.

'These local soldiers don't care what's being sprayed on their own families?' asked Jim, annoyed.

'I didn't say that,' said Bongo, sliding down the concrete wall to take a seat on the floor. 'They don't understand what I'm talking about. Spraying a disease onto a village is something they don't comprehend – they think it's a joke.'

Stirring, Jessica pushed herself off Mac's chest and yawned. She was filthy, her face drawn, eyes puffy from fatigue and from crying; she'd been overwhelmed by Simon's shooting.

'Where are we?' she asked.

'Jail,' said Mac. 'But I have to ask – where were you?'

'Would you believe Kota Baru barracks?' she said sheepishly.

'Kota Baru?!' said Mac. 'That's in East Timor. Are you crazy? I thought you were heading back to California?'

'I was, but a very nice woman at Larrakeyah Army Base told me that Dad was seen at Kota Baru,' said Jessica, looking pointedly at Mac and then Bongo.

'Really?' asked Mac, thinking that Gillian Baddely should keep her scheming female mind to herself.

'Yeah, so I decided to go up there and see if I could make a deal and they arrested me,' she said, shrugging. 'Next thing I know, I'm taken to an airfield and this crazy American is telling me what a genius he is.'

'Jesus,' said Mac. 'You drove up to the Kota Baru barracks to cut a deal with Kopassus?'

'Don't mess with me, buster!' said Jessica, sitting up. 'What was that finely tuned operation in the mess? And by the way, I guess I'm now calling you McQueen? And Manny – you're Bongo, right?'

'Sure,' said Bongo. 'You okay?'

'Yeah, I'll live,' she said. 'This happened before, in Guatemala.'

'Guatemala?' asked Mac, surprised.

'I was doing charity work through BruinCorps, building schools and stuff, and I got caught by the local Marxists,' said Jessica, matter-of-fact.

'And?' asked Mac.

'We talked about their grievances and they let me go,' she said.

'But – hang on,' said Mac. '*Guatemala?* What were you doing down there?'

'Remember I told you Dad paid my college fees?' said Jessica.

'Yep,' said Mac.

'He said I had to do a week of community service each year – he didn't want me to become a spoiled brat.'

'A brat?' said Mac, chuckling.

'It was a drag at first,' said Jessica. 'But in my second year at UCLA, I started spending most of the summer vacation down there.'

'You hear that?' asked Bongo, laughing and kicking at Mac's foot.

'Yeah, I heard it,' said Mac, avoiding Jessica's gaze.

'So, you guys soldiers, spies – something like that?' asked Jessica, sitting cross-legged.

'Nothing like that,' said Mac.

'And you two?' asked Jessica, turning to Jim and Tommy, who just smiled noncommittally.

'So what is this place?' asked Jessica.

'See the helicopters?' asked Mac. 'And those tanks, and the booms that attach to the underside of the helos?'

'Yes, I did,' said Jessica.

'They spray a bio-weapon,' said Mac, so tired he could barely keep his eyelids from dropping.

'Bio-weapon?' asked Jessica. 'You mean like anthrax or something?'

'Like that,' said Jim. 'But this one won't kill most people.'

'So –'

'It gives most people a bad cold,' said Jim, sounding resigned. 'But Melanesian – and perhaps Polynesian – people contract a powerful pneumonia and die within forty-eight hours.'

'Oh my God,' said Jessica, looking from Mac to Bongo to make sure no one was pulling her leg. 'It's racially selective?'

'No,' said Jim. 'It affects everyone, but it will kill the local Maubere people that it's dropped on today. They have no immunity. It's called an "Ethno-Bomb".'

'It even has a name?!' said Jessica, amazed. 'That's *disgusting!* Why pick on people who already have so little?'

The four men sighed and looked away – nothing left to say. They'd done what they could and been caught in an historical no-man's-land, unable to move militarily on Lombok AgriCorp for fear of disrupting the democratic process, yet unable to act within democratic norms because the Indonesian military still ran East Timor. They held a terrible secret yet were unable to do anything about it. Even the US Defense Department, when faced with a rogue from DIA, wanted the embarrassment minimised rather than Operasi Boa shut down. Mac wondered what the East Timorese had done to deserve their lot.

Grimacing in pain, Jessica fished in her pocket, pulled out a pocket knife and threw it to Bongo.

'I forgot to give it back in Suai,' said Jessica. 'Although I guess you have no use for it now.'

Eyes glowing as he picked it up, Bongo opened the blade and then a series of long steel picks.

'Farrier's pocket knife,' said Bongo, standing. 'The most useless tool known to man – unless he owns a horse . . .'

'Or is locked in a cell,' said Mac, joining Bongo at the door.

Bongo removed the back-plate from the door and tumbled the last barrel in the old lock in less than five minutes.

'I think the best we can do is disable the choppers and get out of here,' whispered Jim. 'I don't know how to destroy that bio-weapon safely.'

Bongo spoke Tetum through the door and there was no reply, so he pulled back on the cell door and moved into the stockade corridor.

'Okay,' he mouthed, and the rest followed him through.

At the end of the hallway a fire axe was mounted on the wall, above a red pail. Grabbing the axe, Mac moved in behind Bongo, holding Jessica by the hand.

Pausing at the vestibule that led into the provost's office, Bongo peeked through the door and indicated two guards to Mac. Unclasping the long blade of the farrier's pocket knife, Bongo showed that he'd go right, leaving the left guard for Mac.

The bile rising in his throat, Mac watched Bongo count down from three and then they were through the door, the pale light before dawn gently caressing the sleepy young guard's face as Mac brought the axe to his throat and held it there.

Waking with a start in his chair, the youngster from the 1635 Regiment tried to yell but Mac had a hand over his mouth. Grabbing the guards' keys, Mac picked up their M16s and led them to a cell, threw them in and locked the door.

Joining the other four back at the guard's station, Mac listened to Bongo spell it out: there were no other officers in this part of the building, and the other two guards were down the end of the building.

'Look at this, McQueen,' whispered Jim.

Following the American's finger, Mac saw for the first time how close they were to the unmarked helicopters that would be doing the spraying. They were not thirty metres away, the large tanks obvious in their load space and the big spray booms attached to the undercarriage making them look like giant insects.

'That true about your ability with aircraft?' said Jim to Bongo. 'That extend to Black Hawks?'

'Not specifically,' said Bongo, eyes scanning the ground in front of him.

'Helicopters generally?' asked Jim.

'Not lately,' said Bongo. 'I say we aim for the hangars, get behind them so we're shielded from the sentry posts at the gate, run around the length of the hangars, come out at the end. Take that last helo, okay?'

'Sounds good,' said Mac.

'Can you fly us out of here?' asked Jim, annoyed.

'I have the ability, yes,' said Bongo. 'But we need some explosives.'

Searching the stockade, they found a locked room and opened it with the confiscated keys. It was a small armoury and, hitting the lights, Mac and Bongo found a box of phosphorous grenades – perfect for sabotage – and loaded them into a small canvas carry bag.

Flagging them through like a traffic warden, Bongo brought up the rear as they ran silently behind the first hangar.

Pausing for breath in the lee of the steel-clad building, Mac looked back at the camp. No one had stirred. They ran the length of the hangars, jumping over piles of airfield junk, and arrived at the far end as the sun touched the horizon. Jessica stayed close to Mac – she was scared but composed, noticed Mac.

'Now or never,' said Bongo. 'Guard changes soon.'

Panting for breath, they scanned for unfriendlies.

'Want to check the helo?' asked Mac, wondering if Bongo needed a key or something.

'We're all in the helo,' snarled Bongo. 'Or none of us are. No one gets left behind. I need Jim in the front with me. McQueen, you're in the back, with Tommy and Jessica. You guys are the shooters, okay?'

Tommy nodded as Bongo handed over his M16 and, falling in behind the Filipino, they stealthed to the last Black Hawk.

The side door creaked slightly as Mac pulled it back and realised the rear load space was almost entirely filled with a tank of the bio-weapon. Moving forward, he slid back the jump-seat door that sat between the pilot's hatch and the main door. Helping Jessica up into the jump-seat, he shut the small door and squeezed into the small area in front of the tank, and then pulled Tommy up alongside.

Mac and Tommy checked their weapons as Bongo and Jim clambered into their places in the cockpit.

Tension rising, Mac looked Tommy in the eye. 'Done this before?'

'No,' said Tommy, gulping down the stress. 'But I was a baseball player in Brooklyn – I'm prepped for anything.'

'Just wait for the action, make sure you get a good shoulder behind your rifle, and don't get out of the aircraft, okay?' asked Mac.

'Sure,' said Tommy.

The sounds of Bongo powering up the avionics and muttering his instrument checks to Jim were muted but audible as Mac crouched in the back of the helo, watching through the glass of the side door to clock when the camp was alerted to their escape.

Unlatching the door, Mac made a small gap to make it faster to remount the helo after his sabotage run was over. The situation seemed more hopeless the longer they waited. The sun was lighting the camp and Mac doubted that he'd have the time to grenade nine helicopters and leap into the one on the end of the line before being shot. It was long odds.

'Okay,' said Bongo, raising his voice from the cockpit. 'When you throw the first grenade, I'll spark the engine – then we see what we're made of, right?'

Slinging the canvas bag over one shoulder and the M16 over the other, Mac made to leap out of the Black Hawk when a hand grabbed him.

Looking in Jessica's eye, Mac felt almost breathless, as if he could float above the ground.

'My note,' said Jessica. 'The love note?'

'Yeah,' said Mac, aware of Tommy being able to hear.

You did read it, didn't you? I left it on your bag.'

'Um, well,' said Mac, his mind elsewhere.

'You didn't read it,' said Jessica, her face dropping. 'Oh my God.'

'I didn't, I couldn't,' said Mac, trailing off as whining sounds started in the Black Hawk's electrical systems.

'It said that I think your parents did a really good job with you, McQueen, and if I ever have kids, I'd love to know their secret.'

'Thank you,' said Mac, but no sound came out. She kissed him and Mac leapt off the rear load space onto the lime dust of the runway, and ran through the spooky light of early morning to the helo closest to the camp.

Opening the pilot's door as he caught his breath, he fished out a grenade, pulled the pin, dumped it on the pilot's seat and ran for the next helo, forty metres away, where he repeated the action. As he ran for the third helo, the first grenade detonated and ripped apart the flight deck of the helo. Trying to keep his composure as the grenades flashed and sent concussion waves and debris along the runway, Mac dumped his sixth grenade, just as the first shots were fired from a military police jeep that accelerated away from the sentry post at the gate. Turning, Mac watched the last helo's rotors spinning faster and faster and heard the telltale whining of the turbine spinning to its peak RPM. Running around the back of the seventh helo, he dumped a grenade into the rear load space beside the bio-weapon tank. As he ran the bullets hailed into the helo and the hangar as the belt-fed machine-gun on the jeep opened up.

Mac crossed the open ground to the eighth helo, bringing the M16 up to his shoulder and waiting for the jeep to come parallel before popping the driver with a three-shot burst and then the machine-gunner. Careening out of control, the vehicle swerved out into the runway as the third soldier tried to grab the wheel.

Grabbing his eighth grenade, Mac threw it into the cockpit as the grenade in the seventh helo tore the front section apart in a shuddering burst of white heat. Falling to the ground as he escaped the blast, Mac struggled to crawl around the corner of the ninth and final helo as the previous helo now blew up. Gasping for breath, he realised his left leg was bleeding – he'd been hit by a piece of flying debris. Needing the last helo for cover, Mac limped to its nose, looked out to the camp, saw a silver LandCruiser approaching him at high speed, and pulled back to the load space. Behind him, he could hear Tommy and Jim screaming at him from the powered-up Black Hawk.

Sliding back the large door of the ninth helo, Mac fished for the grenade, primed it and threw it in front of the tank.

His left calf muscle now feeling like it was on fire, Mac turned and tried to run but resigned himself to not making Bongo's helicopter. He couldn't fend off the approaching shooters in the LandCruiser and also run for his ride. He'd have to make a choice. Feeling hopeless, yet also strangely powerful, Mac ran in a limp towards the hangar rather than Bongo's helo. Stopping behind a wall, Mac looked around and fired two bursts of three-shot at the Cruiser, which veered into another hangar as its windscreen shattered.

Turning to look at Jim, who gestured for Mac to get in the helo, Mac waved them away and turned back to face the shooters who now stealthed towards Mac – not Indonesian Kopassus, but Saffas and Aussies from Berger's crew.

The window smashed above Jim's head and he ducked, and Bongo pulled the Black Hawk into the air as the steel cladding on the wall Mac was hiding behind was torn apart by bullets. Putting out more rounds at a soldier who ran around the flames from a helo, Mac dived behind a stack of oil drums as the final grenade made the Black Hawk rupture from the inside out.

Mac tried to move back along the burning helo to where he now thought the shooters would be coming from. Ducking down, he looked under the burning aircraft and saw three sets of ankles about forty metres away, and one set of pale blue eyes below a head bandage that wrapped across the forehead.

Shit, thought Mac, locking eyes with Pik Berger.

The South African's Steyr spewed rounds at Mac as he dived to the side. Landing, Mac aimed up and shot at one set of ankles which was quickly followed by a soldier falling to the ground and clutching his leg in agony. Then he aimed at Berger's ankles as he ran into the hangar. Mac got off one round and the rifle clicked – out of rounds.

Cursing, Mac looked back and waved away Bongo's helo which was now hovering a metre above the runway, throwing lime dust and fine gravel for a hundred metres.

Pulling his last grenade from his bag, Mac pulled the pin and threw it towards the hangar Berger had disappeared into. As the grenade exploded, Mac, losing blood, was vaguely aware of another helo coming in to land. And then Bongo's helo was gone and, through the smoke and dust, Mac heard the soldiers approaching, their panicked commands clearly audible over the roar of fire, and Mac was running, but as in a dream, unable to reach top speed. He ran along the runway until he collapsed into the lime dust.

Pushing himself onto his elbows and then his knees, Mac turned and saw Berger, Sudarto and a posse of the mercenaries – mostly in underwear and T-shirts – approaching out of the smoke and the dust. As Mac put his weight on his right leg and slowly stood, Pik Berger fixed him with a glare and screamed at the men not to shoot.

'He's mine,' said the South African, handing his Steyr to a subordinate and approaching Mac like a big cat.

In the periphery of his vision, Mac was aware of Bongo's helo pulling away into the sky, but another helicopter alighting on the airfield.

'So, it's Mr Jeffries – our kaffir-lover,' said Berger, bare-chested and half of his face smeared with shave soap.

'Actually, I'm a fighter not a lover,' said Mac, as Berger kicked him in the solar plexus and followed with an elbow to the jaw.

Teetering on his good, right leg, Mac stayed upright as Berger kneed him in the balls. Doubling over, Mac thought 'what the heck?' and launched a flying head-butt at the Saffa's face.

Turning slightly, Berger took a glancing blow on the cheek-bone and Mac lurched forward, hopelessly off balance.

Swinging a fast right hook, Berger connected with Mac's left jaw bone, instantly dropping him to his knees. Instinctively, Mac raised his arm in defence but Berger's boot came through with such force that it connected with Mac's chin. Feeling his teeth move in their gums, Mac's head snapped back and he hit the ground face-first.

Lying back, Mac tried to breathe as he felt unconsciousness beckoning. And then Pik Berger was kicking him in the ribs from one side and Amir Sudarto looked down from the other.

'Next time you come at me, kaffir-lover, you'd better put me in the grave,' said Berger, chest heaving.

'Consider it done,' said Mac, pushing himself into a sitting position.

'Still the smart lip – our *Kakatua*,' said Sudarto, using the Bahasa Indonesia term for the cockatoo.

'That bandage suits you, Amy,' said Mac, nodding at the Indonesian's broken nose. 'Might be more where that came from, you play it right.'

Sudarto lashed out with a kick and turning his head slightly, Mac took it on the ear and fell sideways.

Waiting for death, Mac thought about a good life, a loving family and a lot of luck. He thought about the chances he'd had to show courage and how many times he'd failed, but also the times he'd prevailed – like the time he'd rescued a junior boy from the dorm bullies, the Lenihan brothers, at Nudgee College; how he'd been expected to back down to their threats like everyone else, but for some reason he'd found himself in the middle of a fight with both of them. He'd lost, busting his nose in the process, but that episode had seen him capped in the 1st XV as a fifteen-year-old. Not bad for a leaguey from Rockie, said his dad, Frank.

'I'd do it all again, boys,' said Mac, as Sudarto's SIG levelled at Mac's eyes. 'Fuck youse all.'

The SIG cocked but then Haryono's voice was shouting. 'Leave him, leave him,' said the major-general, as the other helo depowered behind them.

Suddenly, as Mac retched, they were surrounded by a mob of soldiers in darker greens – the 1635. Then, in his delirium, Mac thought Sudarto, Haryono and Berger were lifting their hands and dropping their weapons.

Sitting up while reeling for balance, Mac saw the mess of his left calf and the burning trail of destruction leading back to the camp. A familiar-looking man with captain rank in the 1635, stepped forward and ordered the men arrested.

'Under whose authority?' demanded Haryono, who Mac noticed had not dropped his SIG.

'By mine,' came a voice from behind Haryono.

Spinning, the major-general's face dropped and he allowed a 1635 soldier to take his handgun.

'Well, sir, this is a surprise,' said Haryono. 'But this is out of your jurisdiction – this is a Kopassus command.'

Mac turned his head to see who was pulling rank.

'Actually, Major-General,' said General Bambang Subianto, fully dressed in his As and fruit salad, 'this is an army base and I'm an army general. You'll get a fair trial by court martial, but for now I order you to stand down your men and allow yourself to be taken into detention; Lieutenant Sudarto, too, and whoever these mercenaries are.'

As the soldiers from the 1635 Regiment moved in to make the arrests, Mac took the hand offered by the 1635 captain.

'Thanks, General,' said Mac, standing up but not sure he'd be able to keep his balance.

'Don't thank me,' said Subianto. 'Thank Captain Setbal, here.'

'Call me Mattias,' said the captain, who shook Mac's hand.

'What's up?' said Mac, trying to shake out the wooziness.

'The captain contacted me last night,' said Subianto. 'Seems your friend Mr Morales made quite an impression on the local soldiers while in the stockade. When Captain Setbal told me he wanted to lead an officers' mutiny but needed the legal support, I decided I couldn't sit in Singapore forever, doing nothing.'

'Shit,' said Mac, massaging his temples. 'Glad you made it when you did.'

Laughing, Subianto slapped Mac on the shoulder. 'No – I'm glad you found me when you did. You reminded me who I am.'

'And you,' said Mac to Mattias. 'Don't I know you?'

'Perhaps my brother,' said Mattias, his facial features now clearer to Mac. 'He sends his regards – just don't ask where you going, or say where you been.'

Joao! Mattias was Joao's brother.

'Wise words,' said Mac, tears escaping as he tried to smile, 'from a wise man.'

EPILOGUE

The Royal Australian Navy Seahawk landed on the rear decks of HMAS *Sydney* in light seas, and Mac took the arm of the loadmaster, who was lit up by the aft-deck floodlights.

'Welcome back, sir,' said the loadmaster, as Mac landed beside him with some pain in his left calf muscle, the soldiers disembarking around him and heading for the hatchway.

Standing back, Mac allowed the ship's medic team to remove his quarry from the hold of the helo, strap him in a rescue sled and carry him down to the medical centre.

Going below himself, Mac let himself in to his private cabin, grabbed a cold VB that he'd saved from a buy-up at the ship's canteen, and swigged on it as he slowly disrobed. Going over the snatch in his mind, he broke it down into pieces: the approach into Kota Baru barracks, the lack of serious security for the prison, the fast work that Robbo's 4RAR Commandos made of grabbing the Canadian and getting him out without anyone getting hurt.

Snatches were so dangerous that whenever he did a smooth one, Mac said a little prayer.

Down the companionway, he could hear Robbo's lads pulling the lids of a few beers and settling in for a drink. After ten minutes, the sounds of an improvised didge echoed, along with soldiers giggling. It made Mac feel good to be an Australian.

Looking at the clock, he saw it was 2.48 am, and lay on the bed. He was asleep almost before his head hit the pillow.

As they finished lunch at the Victoria Hotel in central Darwin, Davidson ran through the afternoon with Mac.

'Technically, the Commonwealth offered Yarrow a resident visa and a fine-only penalty for the excise crimes,' said Davidson, sipping at a beer. 'But I'm thinking that we should throw in a deal with the Canadians, eh? I mean, the files I've seen suggest Ottawa wants Yarrow in the can for at least ten years.'

'I saw that too,' said Mac. 'But let's be fair, Tony. Yarrow was pulling some major frauds through Vancouver – it wasn't a dodgy bottle of whisky at the bottom of the suitcase.'

'Okay – point taken,' said Davidson, standing. 'Let's see how the debrief goes and we'll go from there. No promises yet, but I'd just like your support if we decide to throw him a line – not a good reputation to go around, that your intelligence assets are left to burn.'

'By the way,' said Mac, as Davidson turned to leave. 'Just want to say thanks for making this whole operation happen. It means a lot to me.'

'No worries, Macca,' said Davidson. 'In the end it worked the way it had to work – Indonesians holding other Indonesians accountable. Making the Indon Army move on its own corrupt elements was genius.'

'You can thank a Filipino hit man for that,' said Mac, smiling. 'He's hell when he's well.'

'We'll debrief with Yarrow, find some of these supply networks,' said Davidson. 'It was a good call, mate – and the most important thing was stopping that Operation Boa before it started.'

The Larrakeyah Army Base hospital was bathed in light and Bill Yarrow's bed caught most of it. Unfortunately, his injuries were so severe that he was still sedated while he was transferred to and from

Darwin Hospital for facial reconstructions and chest surgery, and he was in no shape to speak when Mac and Davidson arrived.

After two days, and still no chat with Yarrow, Davidson left for Tokyo, asking Mac to conduct the debrief.

Using the balmy days to get fit in the pool and the gym, Mac recovered quickly and linked up with a regular rugby game between the army and navy. He ended up substituting for both – at fullback and centre, mainly, but also a glory stint at first five-eighth which featured a field goal from forty-six metres while some of the navy girls were watching.

One morning a nurse found Mac lying beside the Larrakeyah swimming pool.

'Mr Davis? Patient Yarrow is conscious, sir.'

Standing, Mac detoured through his room to get dressed and grab his tape recorders and notebooks. Walking into Yarrow's enclosure Mac was immediately aware that something was different. Sniffing, he realised it was the smell. Where did he know that from?

Standing at the end of Yarrow's bed, the bandages taken from his face but the bandages and splints still in place for his broken fingers, Mac could tell that this had been a good-looking man, accustomed to being smiled at.

'Bill Yarrow?' said Mac. 'Richard Davis, Foreign Affairs – wondering if we can have a chat?'

'Sure, Mr Davis,' Yarrow mumbled, sucking something off the inside of his mouth. 'But I have a guest – can we make it fast?'

'Yes, it'll be quick – or I can wait till we have a good piece of time.'

Looking away and seeming confused, Yarrow looked back. 'You got me, didn't you?'

'Well, I –' started Mac.

'You came for me,' whispered Bill Yarrow, and then he was crying; big heaving child-like sobs, his bottom lip quivering and tears bouncing off it.

'Look, it was more the army boys . . .'

'I thought I was in hell,' he whimpered, dabbing his eyes with his cotton blanket. 'Thank you, sir. Thank you so much.'

'Look,' said Mac, not expecting this. He'd spent so much time thinking about this chap as The Canadian, as the criminal, the informer and the procurer of bio-weapons feedstock, that to suddenly accept him as fully human was difficult. 'I was just doing my job.'

'No,' said Yarrow, shaking his head. 'You didn't need to come for me – I'm a pariah who procures supplies to make the weapons of evil. I'm a leper.'

'Look . . .' said Mac, unable to go on with it. Yarrow was telling the truth: he was all those things, plus a customs-and-excise cheat who had cost the Australian taxpayer millions of dollars, quite aside from making the Ethno-Bomb possible. Mac had fought ASIS and DFAT and the Commonwealth for the right to retrieve this man, he'd gone into a Kopassus base to do it, and he'd done it for reasons that he hadn't properly articulated. The value of a bio-weapons procurement expert to Western intelligence was how Mac had sold it to Davidson. But those weren't Mac's personal motivations.

'You have to tell me, Mr Davis – why did you come for me?' asked Yarrow.

'Yes, Mr Davis,' came a voice behind him. 'Why come back for my dad?'

Turning, Mac took her in. Still cheeky and beautiful, Jessica was looking better in a white T-shirt and jeans than most women looked in a five-thousand-dollar ballgown.

Hugging Mac and giving him a kiss, she dragged him closer to Bill Yarrow. 'Why do it?' she asked with a big smile. 'Why risk your life for an embarrassment?'

'Maybe I had to square it up with Bongo?' said Mac, not entirely sure of his reasoning.

'Bongo?' smiled Jessica fondly.

'He woke me up to myself,' said Mac. 'Reminded me of a few things.'

'What?' asked Jessica, moving to him and holding her father's hand.

'Remember what Bongo said in the jungle?' asked Mac.

'Which one?' she asked.

'When I didn't want to help the women, and he did?'

'I remember,' she said, putting her arms around his neck, the tears welling again. 'You're a wonderful man, you know that?'

'What did this Bongo say?' asked Yarrow, confused.

'Either we all matter,' said Jessica.

'Or none of us do,' said Mac.

COUNTER ATTACK

Also by Mark Abernethy

With this action-packed and gripping addition to the Alan McQueen series, Mark Abernethy confirms his status as a master thriller writer. Read the first two chapters here.

When Aussie spy Alan McQueen – aka Mac – agrees to return to ASIS, he's immediately dispatched to preside over a covert mission in Singapore during which two Australians are executed.

Not long after, Mac is sent to Saigon for supposedly routine surveillance on a consulate high-flier. When his target is also murdered, Mac is thrown into a chase to search out the killers, staying one step ahead of rogue agents along the way.

As Mac closes in on his targets, he makes some shocking discoveries about their plans to try and throw North Asia into war and fatally destabilise the Chinese government. Battling turf wars in Aussie intelligence and the shifting loyalties of American government and intelligence, Mac finds a strange ally in one of Asia's most powerful crime lords.

But can he stop the ambition of one man to overthrow the Chinese government and reduce Asia to cinders?

ISBN 978 1 74175 939 6

CHAPTER 1

There were three of them in the fifteenth-floor suite of the Hotel Pan Pacific, waiting for the radio to confirm the quarry was on its way. Alan McQueen stood at the large windows of the suite, looking over the oily waters of Singapore's Marina Bay.

Draining his coffee, Mac thought about the plan. His job was to trap a Chinese spy and persuade him to work for the Australian Secret Intelligence Service. If Mac was successful, the doubled spy would be reporting to the Firm while pretending to take orders from Beijing.

Looking into his empty cup, Mac pondered the eternal question of why hotel coffee crockery was so small.

'Any real mugs back there, Matty?' he asked Matt Johnson, his comms man.

'That's the biggest I could find,' said Johnson, an operative in his early thirties who sat at a laptop computer beneath a street map of Singapore. Mac saw his younger self in Matt, an athletic field guy who was probably starting to wonder if being good at tails and infiltrations was a clever career move in Aussie intel.

'Might have to use one of those tumblers,' said Mac, seeing the rows of glasses in the kitchenette.

'Bring out the inner-city tosser in you, eh Macca?' said Johnson, smirking behind the mic in front of his mouth.

A raw snort came from the sofa on the other side of the room, where Ray Hu's face had set in the serious rictus of sleep.

'Ray!' said Mac, raising his voice at the native of Yangzhou. 'Wake up, sunshine!'

Hu's lips vibrated in a rattling snore.

Johnson threw a peanut. 'Ray.'

The first nut missed but a second landed on the sleeping man's left eyelid.

'Wah?' said Hu, sitting up.

'It's four o'clock, old boy,' said Mac. 'Ready for your close-up?'

Groaning, Hu pushed himself off the sofa and walked stiff-legged to the bathroom.

'Fricking Sing'pore,' said Hu, his thick Chinese accent echoing out of the bathroom as he relieved himself. 'What point in a free world if I can't have a smoke?'

Dressed in his four-thousand-dollar suit and Spanish shoes, Hu slipped out to attend the five o'clock meet-and-greet function of the Asia-Pacific Naval Contractors Convention. Hu could blend into a cocktail party and be gathering information before anyone had even noticed that he'd joined the conversation. The plan hinged on the grumpy financier and Mac trusted him to perform.

The radio speakers crackled to life on Johnson's desk as the door shut behind Hu. It was the voice of Cam Bailey, an Aussie SIS operator who had started his career at naval intelligence.

Mac listened as Bailey and his Changi Airport-based team got visual identification of the target – code-named Kava – and followed him from the T2 taxi rank. One of Mac's agents was in a cab behind Kava's while Bailey and a driver brought up the rear in another cab, ensuring there was no Chinese counter-surveillance.

Mac raised the field-glasses on the windowsill to his eyes and idly checked Raffles Boulevard. He was looking for tradie vans with no tradies, men on park benches reading upside-down newspapers and 'tourists' walking about aimlessly pretending to look at maps. Singapore was a modern republic but it was in South-East Asia, which meant it was crawling with Chinese spies.

'We're on,' said Johnson, fiddling with the laptop that showed him the location of the agents' cell phones.

'We're on when Kava is sitting in a puddle of his own piss, begging me to make him a double agent,' murmured Mac, eyeing two SingTel workers on the street who didn't seem to be working.

Kava was a Brisbane-based scientist, Dr Xiang Lao, who worked for the defence contractors Raytheon Australia. His main responsibility was making sure the electronic networks in the Royal Australian Navy's SEA 4000 Air Warfare Destroyer program would issue the commands it was supposed to, even when under attack. SEA 4000 AWD was Australia's new destroyer-based defence against anti-shipping missiles, the most likely of which were China's old but reliable Silkworms and their recently upgraded ballistic series, the Dong Fengs.

Sitting back on the sofa, Mac picked up the file: Lao had come to Australia as a sixteen-year-old prodigy to study avionics engineering at the University of New South Wales; he completed his doctorate at RMIT and then landed a plum job at Raytheon in Brisbane. Several weeks later, Raytheon won the contract to supply the Navy's SEA 4000 upgrades.

A photograph of Lao had surfaced ten months later, taken by a police narcotics squad watching the Colmslie Beach Reserve on the Brisbane River. Queensland Police supplied the surveillance file to the Australian Federal Police, who claimed no interest in Dr Lao. But the biggest bounce from Lao's photo had come from the Defence Security Authority, the internal vetting and security office under the Defence Intelligence Organisation. The DSA had issued Lao a 'Top Secret' clearance to work at Raytheon but had flagged him because he applied for clearance only a few weeks after his first ten years' residency in Australia had elapsed. To receive any of the higher security clearances in government or at defence contractors, applicants had to have lived in Australia for at least a decade, and DSA had him flagged as a 'watch'. Now he was hanging around in Brisbane parks being photographed by the police.

By the time Mac had been pulled into a taskforce of ASIO, AFP, ASIS and DIO, a team of operatives had been watching Lao walk every Monday lunchtime to a park bench at Colmslie Reserve, eat his lunch, and then carefully put his garbage in the bin. It was Lao's drop box and it was traced back to a person who cleared it, and then back to Lao's controller, a mortgage broker in Logan City named Donny Koh.

Mac was supposed to be sitting in on the taskforce, as passive eyes and ears for Aussie SIS. Almost forty, he was semi-retired from the Firm and was sent up to Brisbane because he lived on the Gold Coast and sending him was easier than taking a staffer from a desk.

As the drops were intercepted, it became apparent Dr Lao was an enthusiastic seller of Australian naval secrets. There was pressure from Canberra to pounce and put on a show trial – a return to glory for Aussie intelligence after the apparently bungled Dr Haneef case.

Mac had suggested another way; let the traitor run, see what advantage Australia might gain from it. Dr Lao seemed to be a good fit as a double agent – he was selling naval secrets direct to Chinese military intelligence, he had a young family and Aussie intel had identified his controller.

Someone high up in the bureausphere – perhaps even in the Department of Prime Minister & Cabinet – had read the minutes of that taskforce meeting and Mac had felt the tap on his shoulder.

So Mac was back: back in South-East Asia, back in SIS and back in a world of gut-churning worry.

'They're five minutes away,' said Johnson, breaking into Mac's thoughts. 'You want Yellow team alerted?'

Nodding, Mac reached for the room's phone and dialled reception. He'd sent in Hu without a radio or mobile phone in case the Chinese had any of their fancy electronic eavesdropping devices at the convention.

'Could you page Mr Chan – Johnny Chan – please?' he said into the phone. 'I think he's in the bar.'

Walking to the big windows with the phone in one hand and the handset in the other, Mac looked down on what had been 'turn six' at the F1 Grand Prix two weeks earlier. The traffic seemed normal on Raffles Boulevard and it was late enough that the cops were starting to clear parked traffic – surveillance cars would either be moved on or would stand out to a trained observer. Nothing looked amiss, which didn't mean it wasn't.

'Ray,' said Mac as his agent came on the line. 'Kava's two minutes away – blue cab, white roof.'

'Okay,' said Hu.

'The place clean?' said Mac, adrenaline surging.

'It a naval contractor convention,' said Hu. 'It all spook.'

'You've got backup, Ray,' said Mac. 'Let's get Kava tucked away asap, okay? No dancing with this bloke.'

'Okay. See you when I see you.'

Putting the phone down, Mac pondered the 'ifs' of the operation: if Dr Lao had worked out that Aussie intelligence was running the drops at the rubbish bin in Brisbane; if Raymond Hu had not been accepted in his masquerade as Lao's controller; if the mortgage broker had made an unscheduled and unexpected phone call or email to Dr Lao, and discovered he was in Singapore, not Brisbane.

Mac's ruse relied on inexperienced Lao being manipulated into bringing naval secrets to his fake controller in Singapore. All of which had to happen between Monday drops and without the Chinese getting wind of it. The idea was to bring Lao out of his comfort zone in Brisbane, to elevate his importance and to have him physically more involved in espionage; to get him alone in a room and thinking he's speaking to his man from Beijing. Then record the whole thing and close the trap: *We got you on tape selling Australian Navy secrets to the Chinese, Dr Lao. The Chinese don't want you going through an Australian court system, spilling everything to the newspapers, and you don't want to worry about your family, so why not just keep business as usual with Beijing but have a little chat with us a couple of times a week? How would that be for you?*

It was blackmail but it usually worked. If Mac's team got it wrong, and they were being followed themselves, it would be a painful lesson in the interrogation techniques of the MSS – China's CIA.

'Will this work?' said Johnson.

'Like a dream, squire,' said Mac, raising the field-glasses and checking out the telecom van parked on Raffles. 'Like a fucking dream.'

CHAPTER 2

Three short knocks sounded on the suite's door and Isla Dunford moved into the room. She'd just left her post at the hotel's entry as Bailey had followed Kava into the lobby and assumed the surveillance.

'Looking good,' she said, pulling up a chair beside Johnson and peering at the laptop screen. 'Kava's in the hubcap.'

The hubcap was a lounge in the Pan Pac's lobby that had a huge round mezzanine ceiling floating above it. Among Aussie intel types, a meeting at the hubcap meant the Pan Pac's lobby lounge.

'We okay?' said Mac. 'You followed?'

'We're sweet,' said Dunford, grimacing slightly as she pulled her Colt handgun from the holster at the small of her back and placed it on Johnson's desk.

Isla Dunford was just starting her career with SIS and the fact she was actively in the field owed a lot to Mac championing her over the policy that women didn't work on gigs involving firearms. Mac had noticed her at a field-craft module he'd given in Canberra two years earlier. Dunford was a smart, calm, good-looking woman and he'd fought for her not only because she spoke Cantonese, but because female officers broke up the male pattern and made it harder for counter-surveillance.

The chaps in Canberra had a sense of humour, and the first operation Mac had scored after his return from retirement featured Isla Dunford on the surveillance team. Now, seeing the bright-eyed youngster place her gun on the desk, the responsibility of his position came into focus. Mac could no longer just do the gig and go victory-drinking with the troops. When you ran the operation, the most important part was bringing everyone home with their fingernails intact.

All of Mac's team in the lobby of the hotel were now stripped of radio gear, except for Ray Hu whose unused cell phone was being tracked by Johnson. It wasn't an ideal situation and it made Mac nervous to be off the air, but the Chinese comms-intercepts were so good that even the Americans and Israelis couldn't rely on encryptions and scrambles when they knew the MSS was about. The next-door suite they'd wired for sound had no radio transmissions – it was wired directly into their own suite.

'How's the set-up in fifteen-oh-two?' said Mac.

'Good,' said Johnson.

'Check it again,' said Mac, grabbing the field-glasses and having another look at the SingTel van on Raffles. It hadn't been moved by the cops and the tradesmen were standing at a junction box, the door flapping open.

The suite's door shut behind Dunford as Mac focused on one of the SingTel guys: their red overalls looked clean.

A voice crackled out of the speakers on the desk – Dunford speaking in Cantonese from next door, in 1502.

'What's she saying?' said Mac.

'Here I am in the lounge, here I am in the bedroom, that loo needs a clean, and . . .'

'Well?'

'She's saying, *When this is over, Macca shouts the beers.*'

'Cheeky bugger,' said Mac, lifting the field-glasses back to his eyes.

Once Lao was in room 1502 with Ray Hu, the meeting proceeded as expected, every word being downloaded onto the laptop's hard drive. Johnson adjusted the speaker volume and translated as Ray Hu coaxed the Raytheon documents from Dr Lao's attaché case and then kept the traitor talking about progress on the SEA 4000 upgrades: the key scientists, the names of the managers, the main difficulties and the testing that had taken place.

As the talk got more technical, Mac asked Dunford to grab the glasses and keep an eye on the SingTel van, tell him if there was any change.

Lao opened up about the AESA-defeat project at Raytheon which was going to form a major plank of SEA 4000. Lao explained that he was trying to get assigned to AESA-defeat but security was being run by the US Defense Intelligence Agency and the project was above his clearance.

Mac pricked up his ears at the mention of AESA, which was a hi-tech radar that could take millions of snap shots around the plane it was mounted on, in such short bursts that it was almost impossible for detectors on the ground to pick up the radar emissions – one of the main ways that defence systems detected enemy aircraft.

An AESA-type system was probably the only hope the Chinese had to make their ballistic anti-ship missile – the DF 21 – operate properly. The DF 21 was being developed to fly between one and half and two thousand kilometres from China's coast as a deterrent against US Navy carrier strike groups. A ballistic missile was a rocket that flew out of the atmosphere and on its downward trajectory took its warhead at great speeds onto the target below. To be accurate against a moving target such as a ship, it needed an AESA system onboard to steer it as it re-entered the atmosphere at speeds approaching Mach 10. An onboard AESA system was about the only way that ballistic missiles could be controlled by terminal guidance – that is, the missile could be made to fly into its target rather than simply being aimed accurately at take-off or tweaked in its mid-course trajectory.

Raytheon was the AESA pioneer for the American military and it stood to reason that the same company would be working on a weapon that defeated AESA. So Mac wasn't surprised that the Pentagon's spooks were overseeing who did and did not work on the project.

Ray Hu's interest was aroused too. 'You got your name down to work for Raytheon in the United States on AESA-defeat?'

Mac listened as Dr Lao stumbled. 'What's he saying?'

'He's saying, "No, you got it wrong – I don't have to go the US. I've been waiting to tell someone this,"' said Matt, concentrating. 'He's giggling, proud of himself. Says he's got good stuff.'

'Yeah?' said Mac.

'Yeah, wait,' said Matt, holding his hand up as the Cantonese bubbled out of the speakers. 'He's saying that he found out two days ago that an AESA-defeat prototype system is being brought to Queensland for beta testing – Raytheon and US Department of Defense are going to test it in the Aussie desert. Totally top secret: USEO.'

'Shit!' said Mac. When a project was stamped US Eyes Only, the problem became political.

'It gets better,' said Johnson.

'Tell me,' said Mac, his dream of doubling Dr Lao all but gone. There was no way they could put a Chinese spy with that sort of information back into circulation in the hope that he wouldn't blab to his Beijing masters. It wasn't worth the risk – not to Australian military security and certainly not to the US-Australian alliance.

'Ray's asked him how come the Australian outback? Why not Alaska, New Mexico?'

'And?' said Mac as the sounds of laughter roared out of the speakers.

'He says, "Nah – America full of Chinese spies."'

'Funny guy,' said Mac, grabbing his handgun from under the sofa cushion.

Matt held up his hand. 'He's saying, "Aussie intel is only interested in beer and girls – we can be using the beta telemetry even before the Pentagon sees it."'

'Yeah, yeah,' said Mac, checking his Heckler & Koch P9s for load and safety. 'I'll let ASIO know they have a fan club. Matt, get on the phone. Tell Doug at the embassy to fast-track an extradition order for Xiang Lao. Make sure he gets the address and date of birth correct, okay?'

Johnson reached for the phone.

'Isla, we need an AFP agent here now.'

'We going to arrest him?' said Dunford.

'We need to formally arrest Lao for terrorism financing and conspiracy, and then we'll trigger the transnational crime MOU with Singers,' said Mac, trying to stay one step ahead of the game. 'Don't use Doug for that one – go straight to Tommy in legal. The MOU needs to be sighted and acknowledged by Singapore Police within twelve hours of the arrest, so shake a leg.'

'Sure, boss,' said Isla, standing and holstering her handgun.

'This is now about containment,' said Mac, moving towards the door as he shoved the Heckler into his waistband. 'I don't want that little weasel telling his secrets to some Chinese consular lawyer. If we do our job, the tests go ahead in the desert without any Chinese nosey-pokes.'

Looking back as he opened the suite's door, Mac saw Dunford looking down through the window. 'Everything okay?'

'The SingTel van's gone. One less thing, huh?'

Mac stepped into the corridor of the fifteenth floor, approached 1502 and slowed, readying to go through that door and shut down Kava.

As he paused, he sensed movement from his right and then someone grabbed him by the hair. Knocked off balance by the surprise, Mac tried to turn but his head was smashed hard against the hotel wall. Bouncing off the wallpaper, stunned, he was kicked hard in the solar plexus – so hard he doubled over. The hand grabbed his hair again and pushed him upright into the Hessian-covered wall and a suppressed handgun was jammed into the back of his mouth.

Unblinking eyes stared out of a black ski mask as a second man disarmed him and took the door card from his hand. Lifting his knee reflexively, Mac thought about lashing out but his captor cocked the action on the 9mm handgun and pushed harder.

Mac watched in mute horror as the second shooter pushed the door card into 1502 and entered with the elongated handgun held down his thigh. Half a second later there were four popping sounds that Mac recognised as suppressed small-arms fire. Then the shooter was back in the corridor, walking up to Mac as he shoved a handful of casings into his left pocket.

Thinking he was about to be executed, Mac started his prayers as he panted for breath. But the second shooter didn't level his gun – he raised it quickly and brought it down hard above Mac's left ear.

Mac's last thought before he blacked out was: *Red overalls – red Sing Tel overalls.*

ALSO FROM ALLEN & UNWIN

Golden Serpent
Mark Abernethy

Brilliantly written and action-packed, Mark Abernethy's first Alan McQueen thriller, Golden Serpent, will enthral fans of Andy McNab, Tom Clancy, Lee Child and Robert Ludlum. Guaranteed to satisfy even the most seasoned spy-thriller aficionado.

Alan McQueen, aka Mac, was once a star of the global intelligence community, renowned for being the Aussie spook who shot and killed Abu Sabaya, the world's most dangerous terrorist.

But that was 2002.

Now, during a routine assignment in Indonesia, McQueen discovers that Sabaya is not in fact dead. Instead he's teamed up with rogue CIA veteran Peter Garrison and is armed with a cache of stolen VX nerve agent he's threatening to deploy in a dramatic and deadly manner.

Battling to stay one step ahead of Sabaya's hit-men, CIA double-agents and deep corruption within Australian intelligence, Mac must find the stolen VX before it's too late. His mission will take him on a chase through South-East Asia and test all of his considerable courage and ingenuity.

'Golden Serpent is the most accomplished commercial spy thriller we've seen locally, a discerning read, full of action and a kind of knowing wit.'
The Australian

ISBN 978 1 74175 506 0